ANDROMEDA

ANDROMEDA

IVAN EFREMOV

All material contained herein is
Copyright © Ivan Efremov 2019 All rights reserved.
***
Originally published in Russian in 1957 as
Туманность Андромеды
***
Translated and published in English with permission.
***
Paperback ISBN: 978-1-947228-85-6
ePub ISBN: 978-1-947228-84-9
***
Written by Ivan Efremov
Published by Royal Hawaiian Press
Cover art by Tyrone Roshantha
Translated by Rafal Stachowsky
Forward by Maria Cowen
***
For more works by this author, please visit:
www.royalhawaiianpress.com
***
Version Number 1.00

LIST OF CONTENTS

Chapter 1. The Iron Star 1

Chapter 2. Epsilon Tucanae 31

Chapter 3. Captives Of The Dark 60

Chapter 4. The River Of Time...95

Chapter 5. The Horse On The Sea Bed 115

Chapter 6. The Legend Of The Blue Suns...136

Chapter 7. Symphony In F-Minor, Colour Tone 4.75, U 159

Chapter 8. Red Waves 185

Chapter 9. A Third Cycle School..205

Chapter 10. Tibetan Experiment...218

Chapter 11. The Island Of Oblivion...241

Chapter 12. The Astronautical Council...264

Chapter 13. Angels Of Heaven 287

Chapter 14. The Steel Door 314

Chapter 15. The Andromeda Nebula...328

Glossary 344

CHARACTERS IN THE STORY

Men: Erg Noor, Commander of the Expedition

Pour Hyss, astronomer

Eon Thai, biologist

Pel Lynn, astronavigator

Taron, mechanical engineer

Kay Bear, electronic engineer

Women: Nisa Greet, astronavigator

Louma Lasvy, ship's physician

Ingrid Dietra, astronomer

Beena Ledd, geologist

Ione Marr, teacher of gymnastics, storekeeper

CHARACTERS ON EARTH:

Men: Grom Orme, President of the Astronautical Council

Diss Ken, his son

Thor Ann, son of Zieg Zohr, Ken's friend

Mir Ohm, Secretary of the Astronautical Council

Darr Veter, retiring Director of the Outer Stations

Mven Mass, successor to Darr Veter

Junius Antus, Director of the Electronic Memory Machines

Kam Amat, Indian scientist (In a former age)

Liao Lang, palaeontologist

Renn Bose, physicist

Cart Sann, painter

Frith Don, Director of the Maritime Archaeological Expedition

Sherliss, mechanic to the expedition

Ahf Noot, prominent surgeon

Grimm Schar, biologist of the Institute of Nerve Currents

Zann Senn, poet-historian

Heb Uhr, soil scientist

Beth Lohn, mathematician, criminal in exile

Embe Ong, candidate for Director of the Outer Stations

Cadd Lite, engineer on Satellite 57

Women : Evda Nahl, psychiatrist Rhea, her daughter Veda Kong, historian

Miyiko Eigoro, historian, Veda's assistant

Chara Nandi, biologist, dancer, artist's model

Onar, girl of the Island of Oblivion

Eva Djann, astronomer

Liuda Pheer, psychologist (in a former age)

EXTRATERRESTRIAL CHARACTERS:

Goor Hahn, observer on the diurnal satellite

Zaph Phthet, Director of External Relations of the planet of 61 Cygni

FORWARD BY MARIA COWEN

Andromeda, A Russian Science Fiction Classic, (Russian: *Туманность Андромеды*), is a novel by the Soviet writer and paleontologist, Ivan Efremov, written and published in 1957. The novel was made into a film in 1967,

Critics have accused the heroes of the novel is more of philosophical ideas than live people. In today's world, many readers will probably shrink before the word Communist. If we eliminated this word all together, the book would be more palatable to the Western audience. We can't do it and remain true to the author's goals and ideals. We also decided to publish Andromeda in an older form of English to stress its historic meaning.

Nevertheless, the novel was a major milestone in Soviet science-fiction literature, which, in Stalin's era, had been much more short-sighted (never venturing more than a few decades into the future) and primarily focusing on technical inventions rather than social issues (the so-called "short aim" science fiction).

Boris Strugatsky wrote:
Efremov was an icebreaker of a man. He has broken the seemingly unbreakable ice of the "short aim theory". He has shown how one can and should write modern SF, and thus has ushered a new era of Soviet SF. Of course, those times were already different, the Stalin Ice Age was nearing its end, and I think that even without Andromeda, Soviet SF would soon start a new course. But the publication of Andromeda has become a symbol of the new era, its banner, in some sense. Without it, the new growth would have been an order of magnitude more difficult, and a thaw in our SF wouldn't have come until later.

CHAPTER ONE

THE IRON STAR

In the faint light emitted by the helical tube on the ceiling the rows of dials on the instrument panels had the appearance of a portrait gallery-the round dials had jovial faces, the recumbent oval physiognomies were impudently self-satisfied and the square mugs were immobile in their stupid complacency. The light- and dark-blue, orange and green lights flickering inside the instruments served to intensify the impression.

A big dial, glowing dull red, gazed out from the middle of the convex control desk. The girl in front of it had forgotten her chair and stood with her head bowed, her brow almost touching the glass, in the attitude of one in prayer. The red glow made her youthful face older and sterner, cast clear-cut shadows round her full lips and even made her slightly snub nose look pointed. Her thick eyebrows, knitted in a frown, looked jet black in that light and gave her eyes the expression of despair seen in the eyes of the doomed.

The faint hum of the meters was interrupted by a soft metallic click. The girl started and raised her head, straightening her tired back.

The door opened behind her, a big shadow appeared and turned into a man with abrupt and precise movements. A flood of golden light sprang up, making the girl's thick, dark-auburn hair sparkle like gold. She turned to the newcomer with a look that told both of her love for him and of her anxiety.

"Why aren't you sleeping? A hundred sleepless hours!" "A bad example, eh?" There was a note of gaiety in his voice but he did not smile; it was a voice marked by high metallic notes that seemed to rivet his words together. "The others are all asleep," the girl began timidly. "and … don't know anything …" she added, whispering instinctively.

"Don't be afraid to speak. Everybody else is asleep, we're the only two awake in the Cosmos and it's fifty billion[1] kilometres to Earth-a mere parsec and a half!"

"And we've got fuel for just one acceleration!" There was fascinated horror in the girl's exclamation.

In two rapid strides Erg Noor, Commander of Cosmic Expedition No. 37, reached the glowing dial.

"The fifth circle!"

"Yes, we've entered the fifth … and … still nothing." The girl cast an eloquent glance at the loudspeaker of the automatic receiver.

"And so I have no right to sleep, as you see. I have to think over all the variants and all the possibilities. We must find a solution by the end of the fifth circle."

"But that's another hundred and ten hours."

"All right, I'll go to sleep in the armchair here as soon as the effect of the sporamin wears off. I took it twenty-four hours ago."

The girl stood deep in thought for a time but at last decided to speak. "Perhaps we should decrease the radius of the circle? Suppose something's gone wrong with their transmitter?"

"Certainly not! If you reduce the radius without reducing speed you'll break up the ship. If you reduce speed you'll be left without anameson[4]… with a parsec and a half to go at the speed of the ancient lunar rockets! At that rate we'd get somewhere near our solar system in about a hundred thousand years."

"I know that. But couldn't they …"

"No, they couldn't. Aeons ago people could be careless or could deceive each other and themselves. But not today!"

"That's not what I wanted to say." The sharpness of her retort showed that the girl was offended. "I was going to say that *Algrab* may have deviated from its course looking for us."

"It couldn't have deviated so much. It *must* have left at the time computed and agreed on. If the improbable had happened and both transmitters had been put out of action it would have had to cross the circle diametrically and we should have heard it on the planetary receiver.

There's no possibility of a mistake there it is, the rendezvous planet."

Erg Noor pointed to the mirror screens in deep niches on all four sides of the control tower. Countless stars burned in the profound blackness. A tiny grey disc, barely illuminated by a sun very far away from them, from the outer edge of the system B-7336-S+87-A, was crossing the forward port screen.

"Our bomb beacons [5] are working well although we put them up four independent years " ago." Erg Noor pointed to a clear-cut line of light running along a glass panel that stretched the whole length of the left-hand wall. *"Algrab* should have been here three months ago. That means,"

Erg Noor hesitated as though he did not wish to finish the sentence, *"Algrab* is lost!"

"But suppose it isn't, suppose it has only been damaged by a meteoroid and cannot regain its speed?" objected the auburn-haired girl.

"Can't regain its speed!" repeated Erg Noor. "Isn't that the same thing? If there is a journey thousands of years long between the ship and its goal, so much the worse-instead of instantaneous death there will be years of hopelessness for the doomed. Perhaps they will call. If they do, we'll know ... on Earth ... in about six years' time."

With one of his impetuous movements Erg Noor pulled a folding armchair from under the table of the electronic computer, a little MNU-11; on account of its great weight, size and fragility, the ITU electronic brain that could make any computation was not fitted in spaceships to pilot them unaided. A navigator had always to be on duty in the control tower, especially as it was impossible to plot an exact course over such terrific distances.

The commander's hands flashed over the levers and knobs with the rapidity of a pianist's. The sharply defined features of his pale face were as immobile as those of a statue and his lofty brow, inclined stubbornly over the control desk, seemed to be challenging the elemental forces that menaced that tiny world of living beings who bad dared penetrate into the forbidden depths of space.

Nisa Greet, a young astronavigator on her first Cosmic expedition, held her breath as she watched Erg Noor in silence, and the commander himself seemed oblivious of everything but his work. How cool and collected, how clever and full of energy was the man she loved. And she had loved him for a long time, for the whole of the five years. There was no sense in hiding it from him, lie knew it already, Nisa could feel that. Now that this great misfortune had happened she had the tremendous joy of serving a watch with him, three months alone with him while the other members of the crew lay in deep hypnotic sleep. Another thirteen days and they, too, would be able to sleep for six months while the other two watches-the navigators, astronomers and mechanics-served their turns. The other members of the expedition, the biologists and geologists who would only have work to do when they arrived at their destination, could sleep longer, but the astronomers-oh! theirs was the greatest strain of all.

Erg Noor got up from his seat and Nisa's train of thought was broken.

"I'm going to the charthouse. You'll be able to sleep in-" he looked at the clock showing dependent or ship's time, "nine hours. I'll have time for some sleep before I relieve you."

"I'm not tired, I can stay here as long as is necessary -you must get some rest!"

Erg Noor frowned and wanted to object but was captivated by the tenderness of her words and by the golden hazel eyes that appealed to him so trustingly; he smiled and went out without another word.

Nisa sat down in the chair, cast an accustomed glance over the instruments and was soon lost in deep meditation.

The reflector screens through which those in the control tower could see what was happening in the space surrounding the ship gleamed black overhead. The lights of differently coloured stars pierced the eyes like needles of fire.

The spaceship was overtaking a planet and its pull made the ship vacillate in a gravitation field of changing intensity. The magnificent but malignant stars also made wild leaps in the reflector screens. The outlines of the constellations changed with a rapidity that the memory could not register.

Planet K2-2N 88, cold, lifeless, far from its sun, was known as a convenient rendezvous for spaceships ... for the meeting that had not taken place. The fifth circle- Nisa could picture her ship travelling with reduced speed around a monster circle with a radius of a thousand million kilometres and constantly gaining on a planet that crawled at tortoise speed. In a hundred and ten hours the ship would complete the fifth circle-and what then? Erg Noor's tremendous brain was now strained to the utmost to find the best solution. As commander both of the expedition and the ship he could not make mistakes for if he did First Class Spaceship *Tantra* with its crew of the world's most eminent scientists would never return from outer space! But Erg Noor would make no mistakes.

Nisa Greet was suddenly overcome by a feeling of nausea which meant that the spaceship had deviated from its course by a tiny fraction of a degree, something possible only at the reduced speed at which they were travelling: at full speed not one of the ship's fragile human load would have remained alive. The grey mist before the girl's eyes had not had time to disperse before the nausea swept over her again as the ship returned to its course. Delicately sensitive feelers had located a meteoroid, the greatest enemy of the spaceships, in the black emptiness ahead of them and had automatically made the deviation. The electronic machines guiding the ship (only they could carry out all manipulations with the necessary rapidity, since human nerves arc unsuited to Cosmic speeds) had taken her off her course in a millionth of a second and, the danger past, had returned her with equal speed.

"What could have prevented machines like these from saving *Algraby* wondered Nisa when she had recovered. That ship had most certainly been damaged by a meteoroid. Erg Noor had told her that up to then one spaceship in ten had been wrecked by meteoroids, despite the invention of such delicate locators as Voll Head's and the power screens that repelled smaller particles. After everything had been so well planned and provided for, the loss of *Algrab* had placed them in a dangerous position. Mentally Nisa went over everything that had happened since they had taken off.

Cosmic Expedition No. 37 had been sent to the planetary system of the nearest star in the Ophiuchus Constellation whose only inhabited planet, Zirda, had long been in communication with Earth and other worlds through the great Circle. Suddenly the planet had gone silent, and for over seventy years nothing more had been heard from there. It was the duty of Earth, as the nearest of the Circle planets to Zirda, to find out what had happened. With this aim in view the expedition's ship had taken on board a large number of instruments and several prominent scientists, those whose nerves, after lengthy testing, had proved capable of standing up to confinement in a spaceship for several years. The ship was fuelled with anameson; only the barely necessary amount had been taken, not because of its weight but because of the tremendous size of the containers in which it was stored. It was expected that supplies could be renewed on Zirda. In case something serious had happened to Zirda, Second Class Spaceship *Algrab* was to have met *Tantra* with fuel supplies on the orbit of planet K2-2N 88.

Nisa's attuned ear caught the changed tone in the hum of the artificial gravitational field. The discs of three instruments on the right began to wink irregularly as the starboard electron feeler came into action. An angular mass flashed on to the screen, brightening it up. It flew straight at *Tantra* like a shell which meant that it was a long way away-a huge fragment of material such as is seldom met with in cosmic space, and Nisa hurried to determine its volume, mass, velocity and direction. She did not return to her meditations until the spool of the automatic log gave a click to show that the entries were finished.

Her most vivid memory was that of a blood-red sun that had been steadily growing in their field of vision during the last months of their fourth space-borne year. It had been the fourth year for the inhabitants of the spaceship as it travelled with a speed of 5/6ths of the absolute unit, the speed of light, but on Earth seven of the years known as independent years had passed.

The filters on the screens were kind to human eyes; they reduced the composition of the rays of any celestial body to what they would have been had they been seen through the thick terrestrial atmosphere with its protective screens of ozone and water vapours. The indescribable ghostly violet light of the high temperature bodies was toned down to blue or white and the gloomy greyish-pink stars took on jolly golden-yellow hues, like our Sun. A celestial body that burned triumphantly with bright crimson fire took on a deep, blood-red colour, the tone that a terrestrial observer sees in stars of the spectral class $M^{5.7}$ The planet was much nearer to its star than Earth is to the Sun and as the ship drew nearer to Zirda the star grew into a tremendous crimson disc that irradiated a mass of heat rays.

For two months before approaching Zirda *Tantra* had begun attempts to get in touch with the planet's outer space station. There was only one such station-on a small natural satellite with no atmosphere that was much nearer to Zirda than the Moon is to Earth.

The spaceship continued calling when the planet was no more than thirty million kilometres away and the terrific speed of *Tantra* had been reduced to three thousand kilometres a second. It was Nisa's watch but all the crew were awake, sitting in anticipation in front of the control-tower screens.

Nisa kept on calling, increasing the power of the transmissions and sending rays out fanwise ahead of the ship.

At last they saw the tiny shining dot of the satellite.

The spaceship came into orbit around the planet, approaching it in a spiral and gradually adjusting its speed to that of the satellite. Soon *Tantra's* speed was the same as that of the fast-moving little satellite and it seemed as though an invisible hawser held them fast. The ship's electronic stereotelescope searched the surface of the satellite until the crew of *Tantra* were suddenly confronted with an unforgettable sight.

A huge, flat-topped glass building seemed to be on fire in the rays of the blood-red sun. Directly under the roof was something in the nature of an assembly hall. There a number of beings-unlike terrestrial humans but unmistakably people-were frozen into immobility. Excitedly, Pour Hyss, the astronomer of the expedition, continued to adjust the focus. The vague rows of people visible under the glass roof were absolutely motionless. Pour Hyss increased the instrument's magnification. Out of the vagueness a dais surrounded by instrument panels appeared, and on it a long table on which a man sat cross-legged facing the audience, his crazy, terrifying eyes staring into the distance.

"They're dead, frozen!" exclaimed Erg Noor. The spaceship continued to hover over Zirda's satellite and fourteen pairs of eyes remained fixed on that glass tomb, for such, indeed, it was. How long had the dead been sitting there in their glass house? The planet had broken off communication seventy years before and if we add to that six years for the rays to reach Earth it meant three quarters of a century.

All eyes were turned on the commander. Erg Noor, his face pale, was staring into the yellow, smoky atmosphere of the planet through which the lines of the mountain ranges and the glint of the sea were faintly discernible. But there was nothing to provide the answer they had come there for.

"The station perished seventy-five years ago and has not been re-established! That can only mean a catastrophe on the planet. We must go down into the atmosphere, perhaps even land. Everybody is present now so I'll ask your opinion."

The only objection was raised by Pour Hyss, a man on his first Cosmic trip; he had been substituted for an experienced worker who had fallen ill just before the start. Nisa looked with indignation at his big, hawk-like nose and his ugly ears set low down on his head.

"If there has been a catastrophe on the planet there is no possibility of our getting anameson there. If we circle the planet at low level we shall reduce our supply of planetary fuel, if we land, we reduce it to a still greater extent. Apart from that we don't know what's happened, there may be some powerful radiations that will kill us."

The other members of the expedition supported their commander.

"There is no planetary radiation that can be dangerous to a ship with Cosmic shielding. Weren't we sent here to find out what has happened? What are we going to tell the Great Circle? It isn't enough to establish a fact, we have to explain it-excuse me if this sounds like a lecture to schoolboys!" said Erg Noor and the usual metallic tones in his voice now had a note of ridicule in them. "I don't imagine we can evade doing what is our plain duty."

"The upper layers of the atmosphere have a normal temperature!" exclaimed Nisa, happily, on completion of her rapidly performed measurements.

Erg Noor smiled and began to put the ship down in a spiral each turn of which was slower than the last as they neared the surface of the planet. Zirda was somewhat smaller than Earth and no great speed was needed to circumnavigate it at low level. The astronomers and the geologist checked the maps of the planet with what was observed by *Tantra's* optical instruments. There had been no noticeable change in the outlines of the continents and the seas gleamed calmly in the red sun. Nor had the chains of mountains changed the shapes that were known from former photographs-but the planet was silent.

The crew spent thirty-five hours at their instruments, relieving each other occasionally.

The composition of the atmosphere, the radiation of the red sun, everything agreed with formerly recorded Zirda data. Erg Noor looked for the Zirda stratosphere tables in his reference book. Ionization was higher than they showed. A vague and alarming concept was taking form in Noor's mind.

On the sixth turn of the descending spiral the outlines of big cities became clearly visible. And still not a sound was recorded by the spaceship's receivers.

Nisa Greet was relieved from her post for a meal and seemed to have dozed off for a while. She thought, however, that she had not slept for more than a few minutes. The spaceship was crossing Zirda's night disc at a speed no greater than that of a terrestrial helicopter. Below them there should have been cities, factories and ports, but not a single light showed in the pitch blackness no matter how thoroughly the powerful stereotelescopes searched the ground. The thunder of the spaceship cutting through the atmosphere should have been audible for dozens of miles. Another hour passed and still no light was seen. The anxious waiting was becoming unbearable. Noor switched on the warning sirens hoping that their awe-inspiring howl, added to the roar of the spaceship, would be heard by the mysteriously silent inhabitants of Zirda.

A wave of fiery light swept away the evil darkness as *Tantra* reached the daylight side of the planet. Below them everything was still black. Rapidly developed and enlarged photographs showed that the earth was covered with a solid carpet of flowers something like the velvety-black poppies that grow on Earth. The masses of black poppies stretched for thousands of miles to the exclusion of all other vegetation-trees and bushes, reeds and grass. The streets of the cities looked like the ribs of giant skeletons lying on a black carpet; metal structures formed gaping rusty wounds. Not a living being, not a tree anywhere, nothing but the black poppies!

Tantra dropped an observation bomb beacon and again plunged into the night. Six hours later the robot reported the content of the air, temperature, pressure and other conditions obtaining on the surface of the planet. Everything was normal for Zirda with the exception of increased radioactivity.

"What an awful tragedy!" muttered Eon Thai, the expedition's biologist, in a dull voice as he recorded the data supplied by the station. "They have killed themselves and everything on their planet!"

"How could they?" asked Nisa, hiding the tears that were ready to flow. "Is it as bad as that? The ionisation isn't so very high."

"A long time has passed since then," answered the biologist, glumly. His manly Circassian face with its aquiline nose assumed an expression of sternness, despite his youth. "Radioactive disintegration is dangerous just because it accumulates unnoticed. For hundreds of years the total radiation could increase *corns* by *corus*, the unit of radiation; then suddenly there comes a qualitative change, heredity collapses, the reproduction of the species ceases and added to that there are epidemics of radiation diseases. This has happened more than once before, the Circle knows of similar catastrophes."

"Such as the so-called 'planet of the lilac sun,'" came Erg Noor's voice from behind them.

"Whose sun of spectral class A", with a light intensity equal to 78 of our suns, provided its inhabitants with very high energy," added the morose Pour Hyss.

"Where is that planet?" asked Eon Thai, the biologist. "Isn't that the one the Council intends to colonize?"

"That's the one, the lost *Algrab* was named after its star."

"The star Algrab, that's Delta Corvi," exclaimed the biologist. "But it's such a long way off!"

"Forty-six parsecs. But we're constantly increasing the power of our spaceship"

The biologist nodded his head and muttered that it was hardly right to call a spaceship after a star that had perished.

"The star didn't perish and the planet is still safe and sound. Before another century has passed we shall plant vegetation there and settle the planet," said Erg Noor with confidence.

He had decided to perform a difficult manoeuvre-to change the ship's orbit from latitudinal to meridional, sending the ship along a north-south line parallel to the planet's axis of rotation. How could they leave the planet until they were sure that there were no survivors? It might be that survivors were unable to communicate with the spaceship because power installations had been wrecked and instruments damaged.

This was not the first time Nisa had seen her commander at the control desk in a moment of great responsibility. With his impenetrably expressionless face and his abrupt but always precise movements he seemed like a hero of legendary times to the auburn-haired astronavigator.

Again *Tantra* continued her hopeless journey round Zirda, this time from pole to pole. In some places, especially in the temperate latitudes, there were wide belts of bare earth, a yellow haze hung over them and through it, from time to time, appeared the lines of gigantic red dunes from which the wind sent up clouds of sand.

Then again came the funereal pall of black velvet poppies, the only plant that had withstood radioactivity or had produced a mutation of its species viable under irradiation.

The whole picture was clear. It was not only useless, it was even dangerous to search for supplies of anameson that had, on the recommendation of the Great Circle, been laid in for visitors from other worlds (Zirda had no spaceships of her own, only planetships). *Tantra* began slowly unwinding the spiral away from the planet. She gained a velocity of 17 kilometres a second using her ion trigger motors, the planetary motors that gave her speed enough for trips between adjacent planets and for taking off and landing, and drew away from the dead planet. *Tantra* turned her nose towards an uninhabited system known only by its code name where bomb beacons had been thrown out and where *Algrab* should have awaited her. The anameson motors were switched on and in fifty-two hours they accelerated the spaceship to her normal speed of 900,000,000 kilometres an hour. Fifteen months' journey would take them to the meeting place-eleven months of the dependent time of the ship-and the whole crew, with the exception of those on watch, could spend that time in sleep. A month, however, passed in discussion, in calculations and in the preparation of a report for the Council. From reference books it was discovered that risky experiments had been made on Zirda with partially disintegrating atomic fuels. They found references to statements by leading scientists who warned the people that there were symptoms of the adverse biological effect of the experiments and demanded that they be stopped.

A hundred and eighteen years before a brief warning had been sent through the Great Circle; it would have been sufficient for people of the higher intellectual categories but apparently it had not been treated seriously by the government of Zirda.

There could be no doubt that Zirda had perished from an accumulation of harmful radiations following numerous careless experiments and the reckless use of dangerous forms of nuclear energy instead of wisely continuing the search for other, less harmful sources.

The mystery had long since been solved, twice the spaceship's crew had changed their three months' period of sleep for normal periods of activity of the same length.

Tantra had been circling round the grey planet for many days and with each passing hour the possibility of meeting *Algrab* grew less and less. Something terrible loomed ahead.

Erg Noor stood in the doorway with his eyes on Nisa as she sat there in meditation-her inclined head with its cap of thick hair like a luxuriant golden flower, the mischievous, boyish profile, the slightly slanting eyes that were often screwed up by restrained laughter and were now wide open, apprehensively but courageously probing the unknown.... The girl did not realize what a tremendous moral support her selfless love had become for him. Despite the long years of trial that had steeled his willpower and his senses, he sometimes grew tired of being commander, of having to be ready at any moment to shoulder any responsibility for the crew, for the ship and for the success of the expedition. Back there on Earth such single-handed responsibility had long since been abandoned-decisions there were taken collectively by the group of people who had to carry them out. If anything unusual occurred on Earth you could always get advice, and consultations on the most intricate problems could be arranged. Here there was nobody to turn to and spaceship commanders were granted special rights. It would have been easier if such responsibility had been for two or three years instead of the ten to fifteen years that were normal for space expeditions! Erg Noor entered the control tower.

Nisa jumped up to meet him. "I've got all the necessary material and the charts," he said, "we'll start the machine working!"

The commander stretched himself in his armchair and slowly turned over the thin metal sheets he had brought, calling out the numbers of coordinates, the strength of magnetic, electric and gravitational fields, the power of Cosmic dust streams and the velocity and density of me-teoroid streams. Nisa, all her muscles tensed with excitement, pressed the buttons and turned the knobs of the computing machine. Erg Noor listened to a series of answers, frowned and lapsed into deep thought.

"There's a strong gravitational field in our way, the area in the Scorpion where there is an accumulation of dark matter near star 6555 CR+11 PKU," began Noor. "We can save fuel by deviating this way, towards the Serpent. In the old days they flew without motors, using the gravitational fields as accelerators, along their edges." "Can we do the same?" asked Nisa.

"No, our spaceships are too fast. At a speed of 5/6ths of the absolute unit or 250,000 kilometres a second our weight would be 12,000 times greater in a field of gravitation and that would turn the whole expedition into dust. We can only fly like this in the Cosmos, far from large accumulations of matter. As soon as the spaceship enters a gravitational field we have to reduce speed, the stronger the field the more we must reduce."

"So there's a contradiction here," said Nisa, resting her head on her hand in a childish manner, "the stronger the gravitational field the slower we have to fly!"

"That's only true where velocities close to the speed of light are concerned, when the spaceship is something like a ray of light and can only move in a straight line or along the so-called curve of equal tension."

"If I've understood you correctly we have to aim our *Tantra* light ray straight at the solar system."

"That's where the great difficulty of space travel comes in. It's practically impossible to aim directly at any star although we make all the corrective calculations imaginable. Throughout the entire journey we have to compute the accumulating error and constantly change the course of the ship so that no automatic piloting is possible. Our position now is a dangerous one. We have nothing left to start another acceleration going so that a halt or even a considerable reduction in speed after this acceleration would be certain death. Look, the danger is here-in area 344 4- 2U that has never been explored. Here there are no stars, no inhabited planets, nothing is known except the gravitational field-there is its edge. We'll wait for the astronomers before we make the final decision -after the fifth circle we'll wake up everybody but in the meantime…." The commander rubbed his temples and yawned.

"The effect of the sporamin is wearing off," exclaimed Nisa, "you can go to sleep!"

"Good, I'll be all right here, in this chair. Suppose a miracle happens … just one sound from them!"

There was something in Erg Noor's voice that sent Nisa's heart palpitating with her love for him. She wanted to take that stubborn head of his, press it to her breast and stroke the dark hair with its prematurely grey threads.

Nisa got up, placed the reference sheets carefully together and turned out the light, leaving only a dull green glow that illuminated the instrument panels and the clocks. The spaceship was travelling quite quietly in a complete vacuum as it described its gigantic curve. The auburn-haired navigator silently took her place at the "brain" of the giant ship. The instruments, tuned to a particular note, hummed softly; the slightest disorder made them sing false. Today, however, the quiet humming kept on the right note. On rare occasions she heard soft blows, like the sounds of a gong-that was the auxiliary planet motor switching in to keep the ship truly on her curve. The powerful anameson motors were silent. The peace of a long night hung over the sleepy ship as though no serious danger threatened her and her inhabitants. At any moment the long-awaited call signal would be heard in the loudspeaker and the two ships would begin to check their unbelievably rapid flight, would draw closer on parallel courses and would at last so equalize their speeds that they would be as good as lying still beside each other. A wide tubular gallery would connect the two ships and *Tantra* would regain her tremendous strength.

Deep down in her heart Nisa was calm, she had faith in her commander. Five years of travel had not seemed either long or tiring. Especially since Nisa had begun to love…. But even before that the absorbingly interesting observations, the electronic recordings of books, music and films gave her every opportunity to increase her fund of knowledge and not feel the loss of beautiful Earth, that tiny speck of dust lost in the depths of the infinity of darkness. Her fellow-travellers were people of great erudition and then, when her nerves were exhausted by a surfeit of impressions or lengthy, strenuous work, there was continued sleep. Sleep was maintained by attuning the patient to hypnotic oscillations and, after certain preliminary medical treatment, big stretches of time were lost in forgetfulness and passed without leaving a trace. Nisa was happy because she was near the man she loved. The only thing that troubled her was the thought that others were having a harder time, especially Erg Noor. If only she could ... no, what could a young and still very green astronavigator do, compared with such a man! Perhaps her tenderness, her constant fund of good will, her ardent desire to give up everything in order to make easier that tremendous labour would help.

The commander of the expedition woke up and raised his sleep-heavy head. The instruments were humming evenly as before, there were still the occasional thuds of the planetary motors. Nisa Greet was at the instruments, bending slightly over them, the shadows of fatigue on her young face. Erg Noor cast a glance at the clock showing spaceship time and in a single athletic bound leaped out of the deep chair.

"I've been asleep fourteen hours! And you didn't wake me, Nisa! That's...." Meeting her radiant glance he cut himself short. "Off to bed at once!"

"May I sleep here, like you did?" asked the girl. She took a hurried meal, washed herself and dropped into the deep armchair. Her flashing hazel eyes, framed in dark rings, were stealthily following Erg Noor as he took his place at the instrument panels after a refreshing wave bath and a good meal. He checked up the indicators on the electronics communications protector and then began to walk up and down with rapid strides.

"Why aren't you sleeping?" he asked the navigator. She shook her red curls that were by then in need of clipping-women on extra-terrestrial expeditions did not wear long hair.

"I was thinking ..." she began hesitantly, "and now, when we are faced with great danger I bow my head before the might and majesty of man who has penetrated to the stars, far, far into the depths of space! Much of this is customary for you, but I'm in the Cosmos for the first time. Just think of it, I'm taking part in a magnificent journey through the stars to new worlds!"

Erg Noor smiled wanly and rubbed his forehead. "I shall have to disappoint you, or rather, I must show you the real measure of our might. Look ..." he stopped beside a projector and on the back wall of the control tower the glittering spiral of the Galaxy appeared.

Erg Noor pointed to a ragged outer branch of the spiral composed of sparse stars looking like dull dust and scarcely perceptible in the surrounding darkness.

"This is a desert area in the Galaxy, an outer fringe poor in light and life, and it is there that our solar system is situated and where we are at present. That branch of the Galaxy stretches, as you can see, from Cygnus to Carina and, in addition to being far removed from the central zone, it contains a dark cloud, here…. Just to travel along that one branch of the Galaxy would take our *Tantra* 40,000 independent years. To cross the empty space that separates our branch from our neighbours would take 4,000 years.

So you see that our flights into the depths of space are still nothing more than just marking time on our own ground, a ground with a diameter of no more than fifty light years! How little we should know of the Universe if it were not for the might of the Great Circle. Reports, images and ideas transmitted through space that is unconquerable in man's brief span of life reach us sooner or later, and we get to know still more distant worlds. Knowledge is constantly piling up and the work goes on all the time!"

Nisa listened in silence.

"The first interstellar flights …" continued Erg Noor, still lost in thought. "Little ships of low speed with no powerful protective installations … and people in those days lived only half as long as we do-that was the period of man's real greatness!"

Nisa jerked up her head as she usually did when she disagreed.

"'And when new ways of overcoming space have been discovered and people don't just force their way through it like we do, they'll say the same about you-those were the heroes who conquered space with their primitive methods!"

The commander smiled happily and held out his hand to the girl. "They'll say it about you, too, Nisa!"

"I'm proud to be here with you!" she answered, blushing. "And I'm prepared to give up everything if I can only travel into the Cosmos again and again!"

"I know that," said Erg Noor, thoughtfully, "but that's not the way everybody thinks!"

Feminine intuition gave her an insight into the thoughts of her commander. In his cabin there were two stereopor-traits, splendidly done in violet-gold tones. Both were of her, Veda Kong, a woman of great beauty, a specialist in ancient history; eyes of that same transparent blue as the skies above Earth looked out from under long eyebrows. Tanned by the sun, smiling radiantly, she had raised her hands to her ash-blonde hair. In the other picture she was seated, laughing heartily, on a ship's bronze gun, a relic of ancient days....

Erg Noor lost some of his impetuosity-he sat down slowly in front of the astronavigator.

"If you only knew, Nisa, how brutally fate dealt with my dreams, there on Zirda!" he said suddenly, in a dull voice, placing his fingers cautiously on the lever controlling the anameson motors as though he intended accelerating the spaceship to the limit.

"If Zirda had not perished and we had got our supplies of fuel," he continued, in reply to her mute question, "I would have led the expedition farther. That is what I had arranged with the Council. Zirda would have made the necessary report to Earth and *Tantra* would have continued its journey with those who wanted to go. The others would have waited for *Algrab,* it could have gone on to Zirda after its tour of duty here."

"Who would have wanted to stay on Zirda?" exclaimed the girl, indignantly. "Unless Pour Hyss would. He's a great scientist though, wouldn't he be interested in gaining further knowledge?"

"And you, Nisa?" "I'd go, of course."

"Where to?" asked Erg Noor suddenly, fixing his eyes on the girl. "Anywhere you like, even..." and she pointed to a patch of abysmal blackness between two arms of the starry spiral of the Galaxy; she returned Noor's fixed stare with one equally determined, her lips slightly parted.

"Oh, no, not as far as that! You know, Nisa, my dear little astronavigator, about eighty-five years ago. Cosmic Expedition No. 34, the so-called 'Three-Stage Expedition' left Earth. It consisted of three spaceships carrying fuel for each other and left Earth for the Lyra Constellation. The two ships that were not carrying scientists passed their anameson on to the third and then came back to Earth.

Andromeda

(handwritten note: More based on actual Astronomy than other books)

That is the way mountain-climbers reached the tops of the highest peaks. Then the third ship, *Parus*..."

"That's the ship that never returned!" whispered Nisa excitedly. "That's right, *Parus* didn't return. It reached its objective and was lost on the return journey after sending a message. The goal was the big planetary system of Vega, or Alpha Lyrae, a bright blue star that countless generations of human eyes have admired in the northern sky. The distance to Vega *is* eight parsecs and people had never been so far away from our Sun.

Anyway, *Parus* got there. We do not know the cause of its loss, whether it was a meteoroid or an irreparable break-down. It is even possible that the ship is still moving through space and the heroes whom we regard as dead are still alive."

"That would be terrible!"

"Such is the fate of any spaceship that cannot maintain a speed close to that of light. It is immediately separated from the home planet by thousands of years." "What message did *Parus* send?" asked the girl. "There wasn't much of it. It was interrupted several times and then broke off altogether. I remember every word of it: 'I am *Parus*. I am *Parus*, travelling twenty-six years from Vega ... enough ... shall wait... Vega's four planets ... nothing more beautiful... what happiness "

"But they were calling for help, they wanted to wait somewhere!"

"Of course they were calling for help, otherwise the spaceship wouldn't have used up the tremendous energy needed for the transmission. But nothing could be done, not another word was received from Parus."

"They were twenty-six independent years on their way back and the journey from Vega to the Sun is thirty-one years. They must have been somewhere near us, or even nearer to Earth."

"Hardly, unless, of course, they exceeded the normal speed and got close to the quantum limit.[8] That would have been very dangerous!"

Briefly Erg Noor explained the mathematical basis for the destructive change that takes place in matter when it approaches the speed of light, but he noticed that the girl was not paying any great attention to him.

"I understand all that!" she exclaimed the moment the commander had finished his explanation. "I would have realized it at once if your story of the loss of the spaceship hadn't taken my mind off it. Such losses are always terrible and one cannot become reconciled to them!"

"Now you realize the chief thing in the communication," said Erg Noor gloomily. "They discovered some particularly beautiful worlds. I have long been dreaming of following the route taken by *Parus;* with modern improvements we can do it with one ship now: I've been living with a dream of Vega, the blue sun with the beautiful planets, ever since early youth."

"To see such worlds ..." breathed Nisa with a breaking voice, "but to see them and return would take sixty terrestrial or forty dependent years… and that's … half a lifetime."

"Great achievements demand great sacrifices. For me, though, it would not be a sacrifice. My life on Earth has only been a few short intervals between journeys through space. I was born on a spaceship, you know!"

"How could that have happened?" asked the girl in amazement.

"Cosmic Expedition No. 35 consisted of four ships. My mother was astronomer on one of them. I was born halfway to the binary star MN19026 +, 7AL and managed to Contravene the law twice over. Twice-firstly by being born on a spaceship and secondly because I grew up and was educated by my parents and not in a children's school. What else could they have done? When the expedition returned to Earth I was eighteen years old. I had learnt the art of piloting a spaceship and had acted as astronavigator in place of one who was taken ill. I could also work as a mechanic at the planetary or the anameson motors and all this was accepted as the Labours of Hercules I had to perform on reaching maturity." "Still I don't understand ..." began Nisa. "About my mother? You'll understand when you get a bit older! Although the doctors didn't know it then, the Anti-T serum wouldn't keep…. Well, never mind what the reason was I was brought to a control tower like this one to look at the screens with my uncomprehending baby eyes and watch the stars dancing up and down on them. We were flying towards the Lupus

Constellation where there was a binary star close to the Sun. The two dwarfs, one blue and the other orange, were hidden by a dark cloud. The first tiling that impinged on my infant consciousness was the sky over a lifeless planet that I observed from under the glass dome of a temporary station. The planets of double stars are usually lifeless on account of the irregularity of their orbits. The expedition made a landing and for seven months engaged in mineral prospecting. As far as I remember there were enormous quantities of platinum; osmium and iridium there. My first toys were unbelievably heavy building blocks made of iridium. And that sky, my first sky, was black and dotted with the pure lights of unwinking stars, and there were two suns of indescribable beauty, one a deep blue and the other a bright orange. I remember how their rays sometimes crossed and at those times our planet was inundated with so much jolly green light that I shouted and sang for joy!" Erg Noor stopped. "That's enough, I got carried away by my reminiscences and you have to sleep."

"Go on, please do, I've never heard anything so interesting," Nisa begged him, but the commander was implacable. He brought a pulsating hypnotizer and, either because of his impelling eyes or the sleep-producing apparatus, the girl was soon fast asleep and did not wake up until the day before they were to enter the sixth circle. By the cold look on the commander's face Nisa Greet realized that *Algrab* had not shown up.

"You woke up just at the right time!" he said as soon as Nisa had taken her electric and wave baths and returned ready for work. "Switch on the animation music and light.

For everybody!"

Swiftly Nisa pressed a row of buttons sending intermittent bursts of light accompanied by a specific music of low, vibrant chords that gradually increased in intensity, to all the cabins where members of the Cosmic expedition were sleeping. This initiated the gradual awakening of the inhibited nervous system to bring it back to its normal active state. Five hours later all the members of the expedition gathered in the control tower; they had by then fully recovered from their sleep and had taken food and nerve stimulants.

News of the loss of the auxiliary spaceship was received in different ways by different people. As Erg Noor expected, the expedition was equal to the occasion. Not a word of despair, not a glance of fear. Pour Hyss, who had not shown himself particularly brave on Zirda heard the news without a tremor. Louma Lasvy, the expedition's young physician, went slightly pale and secretly licked her dry lips.

"To the memory of our lost comrades!" said the commander as he switched on the screen of a projector showing *Algrab,* a photograph that had been taken before *Tantra* took off. All rose to their feet. On the screen one after another came the photographs of the seven members of *Algrab's* crew, some serious, some smiling. Erg Noor named each of them in turn and the travellers gave him the farewell salute. Such was the custom of the astronauts. Spaceships that set off together always carried photographs of all the people of the expedition. When a ship disappeared it might keep travelling in Cosmic space for a long time with its crew still alive. But this made no difference, the ship would never return. There was no real possibility of searching for the ship and rendering it aid. Minor faults never, or seldom, occurred and were easily repaired, but a serious break-down in the machinery had never been successfully repaired in the Cosmos. Sometimes ships, like *Parus,* managed to send a last message, but in the majority of cases such messages did not reach their destination on account of the great difficulty of directing them. The Great Circle had, for thousands of years, been investigating exact routes for its transmissions and could vary them by directing them from planet to planet. The spaceships were usually in unexplored areas where the direction for a message could only be guessed.

There was a conviction amongst astronauts that there existed in the Cosmos certain neutral fields or zero areas in which all radiation and all communications sank like stones in water. Astrophysicists, however, regarded the zero areas to be nothing more than the idle invention of Cosmic travellers who were, in general, inclined to monstrous fantasies.

After that sad ceremony and a very short conference, Erg Noor turned *Tantra in* the direction of Earth and switched on the anameson motors. Forty-eight hours later they were switched off again and the spaceship began to approach its own planet at the rate of 21,000 million kilometres in every twenty-four hours. The journey back to the Sun would take about six terrestrial, or independent, years. Everybody was busy in the control tower and in the ship's combined library and laboratory where a new course was being computed and plotted on the charts.

The task was to fly the whole six years and use anameson only for purposes of correcting the ship's course. In other words the spaceship had to be flown with as little loss of acceleration as possible. Everybody was worried about the unexplored area 344 +2U that lay between the Sun and *Tantra*. There was no way of avoiding it: on both sides of it, as far as the Sun, lay belts of free meteoroids and, apart from that, they would lose velocity in turning the ship.

Two months later the computation of the line of flight had been completed. *Tantra* began to describe a long, flat curve. The wonderful ship was in excellent condition and her speed was kept within the computed limits. Now nothing but time, about four dependent years, separated the ship from its home.

Erg Noor and Nisa Creet finished their watch and, dead tired, started their period of long sleep. Together with them two astronomers, the geologist, biologist, physician and four engineers departed into temporary forgetful-ness.

The watch was taken over by an experienced astronavigator, Pel Lynn, who was on his second expedition, assisted by astronomer Ingrid Dietra and electronic engineer Kay Bear who had volunteered to join them. Ingrid, with Pel Lynn's consent, often went away to the library adjoining the control tower. She and her old friend, Kay Bear, were writing a monumental symphony. *Death of a Planet,* inspired by the tragedy of Zirda. Pel Lynn, whenever he grew tired of the hum of the instruments and his contemplation of the black void of the Cosmos, left Ingrid at the control desk and plunged into the thrilling task of deciphering puzzling inscriptions brought from a planet in the system of the nearest stars of the Centaur whose inhabitants had mysteriously quit it. He believed in the success of his impossible undertaking....

Twice again watches were changed, the spaceship had drawn ten billion kilometres nearer Earth and still the anameson motors had only been run for a few hours.

One of Pel Lynn's watches, the fourth since *Tantra* had left the place where she was to have met *Algrab,* was coming to an end.

Ingrid Dietra, the astronomer, had finished a calculation and turned to Pel Lynn who was watching, with melancholy mien, the constant flickering of the red arrows on the graded blue scales of the gravitation meters. The usual sluggishness of psychic reaction that not even the strongest people could avoid made itself felt during the second half of the watch. For months and years the spaceship had been automatically piloted along a given course. If anything untoward had happened, something that the electronic machines were incapable of dealing with, it would have meant the loss of the ship, for human intervention could not have saved it since the human brain, no matter how well trained it may be, cannot react with the necessary alacrity. "In my opinion we are already deep in the unknown area 344 - 2U. The commander wanted to take over the watch himself when we reached it," said Ingrid to the astronavigator. Pel Lynn glanced up at the counter that marked off the days.

"Another two days and we change watches. So far there doesn't seem to be anything to worry about. Shall we see the watch through?"

Ingrid nodded assent. Kay Bear came into the control tower from the stern of the ship and took his usual seat beside the equilibrium mechanism. Pel Lynn yawned and stood up.

"I'll get some sleep for a couple of hours," he said to Ingrid. She got up obediently and went forward to the control desk.

Tantra was travelling smoothly in an absolute vacuum.

Not a single meteoroid, not even at a great distance, had been registered by the super-sensitive Voll Hoad detectors. The spaceship's course now lay somewhat to one side of the Sun, about one and a half flying years. The screens of the forward observation instruments were of an astounding blackness, it seemed as though the spaceship was diving into the very heart of universal darkness. The side telescopes still showed needles of light from countless stars.

Ingrid's nerves tingled with a strange sensation of alarm.

She returned to her machines and telescopes, again and again checked their readings as she mapped the unknown area. Everything was quiet but still Ingrid could not take her eyes off the malignant blackness ahead of the ship. Kay Bear noticed her anxiety and for a long time studied and listened to the instruments.

"I don't see anything," he said at last, "aren't you imagining things?"

"I don't know why, but that unusual blackness ahead of us bothers me.

It seems to me that our ship is diving straight into a dark nebula."

"There should be a dark cloud here," Kay Bear agreed, "but we shall only scratch the edge of it. That's what was calculated! The strength of the gravitational field is increasing slowly and regularly. On our way through this area we should pass close to some centre of gravity. What does it matter whether it's light or dark?"

"That's true enough," admitted Ingrid, *more* calmly.

"We've got the finest commander and officers there are. We're proceeding along a set course even faster than was computed. If there are no changes we'll be out of our trouble and we'll get safely to Triton despite our short supply of anameson."

Even at the thought of the spaceship's station on Triton, Neptune's satellite on the fringe of the solar system, Ingrid felt much happier. To reach Triton would mean that they were home.

"I was hoping we'd be able to work on the symphony together but Lynn's asleep. He'll sleep six or seven hours so I'll think over the orchestration of the coda of the second movement-you know, the place where we couldn't find a means of expressing the integrated accession of the menace. This piece...." Kay sang a few notes.

"Tee-ee-e, tee-ee-e, ta-rara-ra," came the immediate response from the very walls of the control tower. Ingrid started and looked round, but a moment later realized what it was. There had been an increase in the force of gravity and the instruments had responded by changing the melody of the artificial gravitation apparatus.

"What an amusing coincidence," laughed Ingrid, with an air of guilt. "There is stronger gravitation, as there should be in a black cloud. Now you can calm yourself altogether and let Lynn sleep."

Kay Bear left the control tower and entered the brightly-lit library where he sat down at a tiny electronic violin-piano. He was soon deeply immersed in his work and, no doubt, several hours must have passed before the hermetically sealed door of the library flew open and Ingrid appeared.

"Kay, please wake up Lynn." "What's wrong?"

"The strength of the gravitation field is much more than was computed." "What is ahead of us?"

"The same blackness!" Ingrid went out.

Kay Bear woke the astronavigator, who jumped up and ran to the instruments in the control tower.

"There's nothing especially dangerous. Only where does such a gravitational field come from in this area? It's too strong for a black cloud and there are no stars here." Lynn thought for a time and then pressed the knob to awaken the commander of the expedition and after another moment's thought pressed the knob of Nisa Creel's cabin as well.

"If nothing extraordinary happens they can simply take over their watch," Lynn explained to the anxious Ingrid.

"And if something does happen? Erg Noor won't return to normal for another five hours. What shall we do?"

"Wait quietly," answered the astronavigator. "What can happen here in five hours when we are so far from all stellar systems?"

The tone of the measuring instruments grew lower and lower telling of the constantly changing conditions of the flight. The tense waiting dragged out endlessly. Two hours dragged by so slowly that they seemed like a whole watch. Outwardly Pel Lynn was still calm but Ingrid's anxiety had already infected Kay Bear. He kept looking at the control-tower door expecting Erg Noor to appear with his usual rapid movements although he knew that the awakening from prolonged sleep is a lengthy process.

The long ringing of a bell caused them all to start. Ingrid grasped hold of Kay Bear.

Tantra was in danger! The gravitation was double the computed figure!

The astronavigator turned pale. The unexpected bad happened and an immediate decision was essential. The fate of the spaceship was in his hands. The steadily increasing gravitational pull made a reduction in speed necessary, both because of increasing weight in the ship and an apparent accumulation of solid matter in the ship's path. But after reducing speed what would they use for further acceleration? Pel Lynn clenched his teeth and turned the lever that started the ion trigger motors used for braking. Gong-like sounds disturbed the melody of the measuring instruments and drowned the alarming ring of those recording the ratio of gravitational pull to velocity. The ringing ceased and the indicators showed that speed had been reduced to a safe level and was normal for the growing gravitation. But no sooner had Pel Lynn switched off the brake motors than the bells began ringing again. Obviously the spaceship was flying directly into a powerful gravitation centre which was slowing it down.

The astronavigator did not dare change the course that had been plotted with such great difficulty and absolute precision. He used the planetary motors to brake the ship again although it was already clear that there had been an error in plotting the course and that it lay through an unknown mass of matter.

"The gravitational field is very great," said Ingrid softly, "perhaps"

"We must slow down still more so as to be able h turn," exclaimed the navigator, "but what can we accelerate with after that?..." There was a note of fatal hesitancy in his words.

"We have already passed the zone of outer vortices," Ingrid told him, "gravitation is increasing rapidly all the time."

The frequent clatter of the planet motors resounded through the ship; the electronic ship's pilot switched them on automatically as it felt a huge accumulation of solid matter in front of them. *Tantra* began to pitch and toss. No matter how much the ship's speed was reduced the people in the control tower began to lose consciousness. Ingrid fell to her knees. Pel Lynn, sitting in his chair, tried to raise a head as heavy as lead. Kay Bear experienced a mixture of unreasoning brute fear and puerile hopelessness.

The thuds of the motors increased in frequency until they merged into a continual roar-the electronic brain had taken up the struggle in place of its semi-conscious masters; it was a powerful brain but it had its limits, it could not foretell all possible complications and find a way out of unusual situations.

The tossing abated. The indicators showed that the supply of ion charges for the motors was dropping with catastrophic rapidity. As Pel Lynn came to he realized that the strange increase of gravity was taking place so fast that urgent measures had to be taken to stop the ship and then make a complete change of course away from the black void.

Pel Lynn turned the handle switching on the anameson motors. Four tall cylinders of boron nitride that could be seen through a slit in the control desk were lit up from inside. A bright green flame beat inside them with lightning speed, it flowed and whirled in four tight spirals. Up forward, in the nose of the spaceship, a strong magnetic field enveloped the motor jets, saving them from instantaneous destruction.

The astronavigator moved the handle farther-through the whirling green wall of light a directing ray appeared, a greyish stream of K-particles." Another movement and the grey stream was cut by a blinding flash of violet lightning, a signal that the anameson had begun its tempestuous emission. The huge bulk of the spaceship responded with an almost inaudible, unbearable, high-frequency vibration….

Erg Noor had eaten the necessary amount of food and was lying half asleep enjoying the indescribably pleasurable sensation of an electric nerve massage. The veil of forgetfulness that still covered mind and body left him very slowly. The music of animation changed to a major key and to a rhythm that increased in rapidity….

Suddenly something evil coming from without interrupted the joy of awakening from a ninety-day sleep. Erg Noor realized that he was commander of the expedition and struggled desperately to get back to normal consciousness. At last he recognized the fact that the spaceship was being braked and that the anameson motors were switched on, all of which meant that something serious had occurred. He tried to get up. His body still would not obey his will, his legs doubled under him and he collapsed like a sack on the floor of his cabin. After some time he managed to crawl to the door and open it. Consciousness was breaking through the mist of sleep-in the corridor he rose on all fours and made his way into the control tower.

The people staring at the screens and instrument dials looked round in alarm and then ran to their commander. He was not yet able to stand but he muttered:

"The screens ... the forward screen ... switch over to infrared ... stop the motors!"

The borason cylinders were extinguished at the same time as the vibration of the ship's hull ceased. A gigantic star, burning with a dull reddish-brown light, appeared on the forward starboard screen. For a moment they were all flabbergasted and could not take their eyes off the enormous disc that emerged from the darkness directly ahead of the spaceship.

"Oh, what a fool!" exclaimed Pel Lynn bitterly, "I was sure we were in a dark nebula! And that's "

"An iron star!" exclaimed Ingrid Dietra in horror.

Erg Noor, holding on to the back of a chair, stood up. His usually pale face had a bluish tinge to it but his eyes gleamed brightly with their usual fire.

"Yes, that's an iron star," he said slowly and the eyes of all those in the room turned to him in fear and hope, "the terror of astronauts! Nobody suspected that there would be one in this area."

"I only thought about a nebula," Pel Lyn said softly and guiltily.

"A dark nebula with such a gravitational field would contain comparatively large solid particles and *Tantra* would have been destroyed already. It would be impossible to avoid a collision in such a swarm," said the commander in a calm firm voice.

"But these sharp gravitational changes and these vortex things-aren't they a direct indication of a cloud?"

"Or that the star has a planet, perhaps more than one "

The astronavigator bit his lip so badly that it began to bleed. The commander nodded his head encouragingly and himself pressed the buttons to awaken the others.

"A report of observations as quickly as possible! We'll work out the gravitation contours."

The spaceship began to rock again. Something flashed across the screen with colossal speed, something of terrific size that passed behind them and disappeared.

"There's the answer, we've overtaken the planet. Hurry up, hurry up, get the work done!" The commander's glance fell on the fuel supply indicator. His hands gripped the back of the chair more tightly, he was going to say something but refrained.

CHAPTER TWO

EPSILON TUCANAE

The faint tinkle of glass that came from the table was accompanied by orange and blue lights. Varicoloured lights sparkled up and down the transparent partition. Darr Veter, Director of the Outer Stations of the Great Circle, was observing the lights on the Spiral Way. Its huge arc curved into the heights and scored a dull yellow line along the sea-coast. Keeping his eyes on the Way, Darr Veter stretched out his hand and turned a lever to point M, ensuring himself solitude for meditation. A great change had on that day come into his life. His successor Mven Mass, chosen by the Astronautical Council, had arrived that morning from the southern residential belt. They would carry out his last transmission round the Circle together and then ... it was precisely this "then" that had not yet been decided upon. For six years he had been doing a job that required superhuman effort, work for which the Council selected special people, those who were outstanding for their splendid memories and encyclopaedic knowledge. When attacks of complete indifference to work and to life began recurring with ominous frequency-and this is one of the most serious ailments in man-he had been examined by Evda Nahl, a noted psychiatrist. A tried remedy-sad strains of minor music in a room of blue dreams saturated with pacifying waves-did not help. The only thing left was to change his work and take a course of physical labour, any sort of work that required daily, hourly muscular effort. His best friend, Veda Kong, the historian, had offered him an opportunity to do archaeological work with her. Machines could not do all the excavation work, the last stages required human hands. There was no lack of volunteers but still Veda had promised him a long trip to the region of the ancient steppes where he would be close to nature.

If only Veda Kong ... but of course, he knew the whole story. Veda was in love with Erg Noor, Member of the Astronautical Council and Commander of Cosmic Expedition No. 37. There should have been a message from Erg Noor-from the planet Zirda he should have reported and said whether he was going farther. But if no message had come -and all space nights were computed with the greatest precision-then ... but no, he must not think of winning

Veda's love! The Vector of Friendship, that was all, that was the greatest tie that there could be between them. I Nevertheless he would go and work for her.

Darr Veter moved a lever, pressed a button and the room was flooded with light. A crystal glass window formed I one of the walls of a room situated high above land and sea, giving a view over a great distance. With a turn of another lever Darr Veter caused the window to drop inwards leaving the room open to the starry sky; the metal frame of the window shut out from his view the lights of the Spiral Way and the buildings and lighthouses on the sea-coast.

Veter's eyes were fixed on the hands of the galactic clock with three concentric rings marked in subdivisions. The transmission of information round the Great Circle followed galactic time, once in every hundred-thousandth of a galactic second, or once in eight days, 45 times a year according to terrestrial time. One revolution of the Galaxy around its axis was one day of galactic time.

The next and, for him, the last transmission would be at 9 a.m. Tibetan Mean Time or at 2 a.m. at the Mediterranean Observatory of the Council. A little more than two hours still remained.

The instrument on the table tinkled and flashed again. A man in light-coloured clothing made of some material with a silk-like sheen appeared from behind the partition.

"We are ready to transmit and receive," he said briefly, showing no outward signs of respect although in his eyes one could read admiration for his Director. Darr Veter did not say a word, nor did his assistant who stood there in a proud, unrestrained pose.

"In the Cubic Hall?" asked Veter, at last, and, getting an answer in the affirmative, asked where Mven Mass was.

"He is in the Morning Freshness Room, getting tuned up after his journey and, apart from that, I think he's a bit excited."

"I'd be excited myself if I were in his place!" said Darr Veter, thoughtfully. "That's how I felt six years ago."

The assistant was flushed from his effort to preserve his outward calm. With all the fire of youth he was sorry for his chief, perhaps he even realized that some day he, too, would live through the joys and sorrows of great work and great responsibility. The Director of the Outer Stations did not in any way show his feelings for to do so at his age was not considered decent. "When Mven Mass appears, bring him straight to me." The assistant left the room. Darr Veter walked over to one corner where the transparent partition was blackened from floor to ceiling and with an easy movement opened two shutters in a panel of polished wood. A light appeared, coming from somewhere in the depths of a mirror-like screen. It did not, however, possess the gloss of a mirror -it gave the impression of a long corridor leading into the far distance.

Using selected switches the Director of the Outer Stations switched on the Vector of Friendship, a system of direct communication between people linked by the ties of profound friendship that enabled them to contact each other at any moment. The Vector of Friendship was connected with a number of places where the person concerned was likely to be-his house, his place of work, his favourite recreation centre.

The screen grew light and in the depths there appeared familiar panels with columns of coded titles of electronic films that had succeeded the ancient photocopies of books.

When all mankind adopted a single alphabet-it was called the linear alphabet because there were no complicated signs in it-it became easy to film even the old books, so that eventually the process was fully mechanized. The blue, green and red stripes were the symbols of the central film libraries where scientific research works were stored, works that had for centuries been published only in a dozen copies. It was merely necessary to select the a code number and symbols and the film library would transmit, automatically, the full text of the book. This machine was Veda's private library. A snap of switches and the picture faded, it was followed by another room which was also empty. Another switch connected the screen with a hall in which stood a number of dimly lighted desks. The woman seated at the nearest desk raised her head and Darr Veter recognized the thick, widely separated eyebrows and the sweet, narrow face with its grey eyes. As she smiled, white teeth flashed in a big mouth with bold lines and her cheeks were chubbily rounded on either side of a slightly snub nose with a childish, round tip to it that made the face gentle and kindly.

"Veda, there are two hours left. You have to change and I would like you to come to the observatory a little before time."

The woman on the screen raised her hands to her thick, ash-blonde hair.

"I obey, my Veter," she smiled. "I'm going home." Veter's ear was not deceived by the gayness of her tones.

"Brave Veda, calm yourself. Everybody who speaks to the Great Circle had to make a first appearance."

"Don't waste words consoling me," said Veda Kong, raising her head with a stubborn gesture. "I'll be there soon.

The screen went dark. Darr Veter closed the shutters and turned to meet his successor. Mven Mass entered the room with long strides. The cast of his features and his smooth, dark-brown skin showed that he was descended from African ancestors. A white mantle fell from his powerful shoulders in heavy folds. Mven Mass took both Darr Veter's hands in his strong, thin ones. The two Directors of the Outer Stations, the new and the old, were both very tall. Veter, whose genealogy led back to the Russian people, seemed broader and more massive than the graceful African.

"It seems to me that something important ought to happen today," began Mven Mass, with that trusting sincerity that was typical of the people who lived in the Era of the Great Circle. Darr Veter shrugged his shoulders.

"Important things will happen for three people. I am handing over my work, you are taking it from me and Veda Kong will speak to the Universe for the first time."

"She is beautiful?" responded Mven Mass, half questioning, half affirming.

"You'll see her. By the way, there's nothing special about today's transmission. Veda will give a lecture on our history for planet KRZ 664456 + BS 3252."

Mven Mass made an astonishingly rapid mental calculation.

"Constellation of the Unicorn, star Ross 614, its planetary system has been known from time immemorial but has never in any way distinguished itself. I love the old names and old words," he added with a scarcely detectable note of apology.

"The Council knows how to select people," Darr Veter thought to himself. Aloud he said:

"Then you'll get on well with Junius Antus, the Director of the Electronic Memory Machines. He calls himself the Director of the Memory Lamps. He is not thinking of the lamps they used for light in ancient days but of those first electronic devices in clumsy glass envelopes with the air pumped out of them; they looked just like the electric lamps of those days."

Mven Mass laughed so heartily and frankly that Darr Veter could feel his liking for the man growing fast.

"Memory lamps! Our memory network consists of kilometres of corridors furnished with billions of cell elements." He suddenly checked himself. "I'm letting my feeling run away with me and haven't yet found out essential things. When did Ross 614 first speak?"

"Fifty-two years ago. Since then they have mastered the language of the Great Circle. They are only four par-sees away from us. They will get Veda's lecture in thirteen years' time."

"And then?"

"After the lecture we shall go over to reception. We shall get some news from the Great Circle through our old friends."

"Through 61 Cygni?"

"Of course. Sometimes we get contact through 107 Ophiuchi, to use the old terminology."

A man in the same silvery uniform of the Astronautical Council as that worn by Veter's assistant entered the room. He was of medium height, sprightly and aquiline-nosed; people liked him for the keenly attentive glance of his jet-black eyes. The newcomer stroked his hairless head.

"I'm Junius Antus," he said, apparently to Mven Mass. The African greeted him respectfully. The Directors of the Memory Machines exceeded everybody else in erudition. They decided what had to be perpetuated by the machines and what would be sent out as general information or used by the Palaces of Creative Effort.

"Another *brevus*," muttered Junius Antus, shaking hands with his new acquaintance.

"What's that?" inquired Mven Mass. "A Latin appellation I have thought up. I give that name to all those who do not live long-*vita breva*, you know-workers on the Outer Stations, pilots of the Interstellar Space Fleet, technicians at the spaceship engine plants.... And ... er ... you and I. We do not live more than half the allotted span, either. What can one do, it's more interesting. Where's Veda?"

"She intended coming earlier," began Darr Veter. His words were drowned by disturbing chords of music that followed a loud click on the dial of the galactic clock.

"Warning for all Earth. All power stations, all factories, transport and radiostations! In half an hour from now cease the output of all energy and accumulate it in high-capacity condensers till there is enough for a radiation channel to penetrate the atmosphere. The transmission will take 43 per cent of Earth's power resources. The reception will need only 8 per cent for the maintenance of the channel," explained Darr Veter.

"That's just as I imagined it would be," said Mven Mass, nodding his head. Suddenly his glance became fixed and his face glowed with admiration. Darr Veter looked round. Unobserved by them Veda Kong had arrived and was standing beside a luminescent column. For her lecture she had donned the costume that adds mostly to the beauty of women, a costume invented thousands of years before at the time of the Cretan Civilization. The heavy knot of ash-blonde hair piled high on the back of her head did not detract from her strong and graceful neck. Her smooth shoulders were bare and the bosom was open and supported by a corsage of cloth of gold. A wide, short silver skirt embroidered with blue flowers, exposed bare, suntanned legs in slippers of cherry-coloured silk. Big cherry-coloured stones brought from Venus, set with careful crudeness in a gold chain, were like balls of fire on her soft skin and matched cheeks and tiny ears that were flaming with excitement.

Mven Mass met the learned historian for the first time and he gazed at her in frank admiration. Veda lifted her troubled eyes to Darr Veter. "Very nice," he said in answer to his friend's unspoken question.

"I've spoken to many audiences, but not like this," she said.

"The Council is following a custom. Communications for the different planets are always read by beautiful women. This gives them an impression of the sense of the beautiful as perceived by the inhabitants of our world, and in general it tells them a lot," continued Darr Veter. "The Council *is* not mistaken in its choice!" exclaimed Mven Mass.

Veda gave the African a penetrating look. "Are you a bachelor?" she asked softly and, acknowledging Mven Mass's nod of affirmation, smiled.

"You wanted to talk to me?" she asked, turning to Darr Veter. The friends went out on to the circular verandah and Veda welcomed the touch of the fresh sea breeze on her face.

The Director of the Outer Stations told her of his decision to go to the dig; he told her of the way he had wavered between the 38th Cosmic Expedition, the Antarctic submarine mines and archaeology.

"Anything, but not the Cosmic Expedition!" exclaimed Veda and Darr Veter felt that he had been rather tactless.

Carried away by his own feelings he had accidentally touched the sore spot in Veda's heart.

He was helped out by the melody of disturbing chords that reached the verandah.

"It's time to go. In half an hour the Great Circle will be switched on!"

Darr Veter took Veda Kong carefully by the arm. Accompanied by the others they went down an escalator to a deep underground chamber, the Cubic Hall, carved out of living rock.

There was little in the hall but instruments. The dull black walls had the appearance of velvet divided into panels by clean lines of crystal. Gold, green, blue and orange lights lit up the dials, signs and figures. The emerald green points of needles trembled on black semi-circles, giving the broad walls an appearance of strained, quivering expectation.

The furniture consisted of a few chairs and a big black-wood table, one end of which was pushed into a huge hemispherical screen the colour of mother-of-pearl set in a massive gold frame.

Veda Kong and Mven Mass examined everything with rapt attention for this was their first visit to the observatory of the Outer Stations.

Darr Veter beckoned to Mven Mass and pointed to high black armchairs for the others. The African came towards him, walking on the balls of his feet, just as his ancestors had once walked in the sun-baked savannas on the trail of huge, savage animals. Mven Mass held his breath. Out of this deeply-hidden stone vault a window would soon be opened into the endless spaces of the Cosmos and people would join their thoughts and their knowledge to that of their brothers in other worlds. This tiny group of five represented terrestrial mankind before the whole Universe.

And from the next day on, he, Mven Mass, would be in charge of these communications. He was to be entrusted with the control of that tremendous power. A slight shiver ran down his back. He had probably only at that moment realized what a burden of responsibility he had undertaken when he had accepted the Council's proposal. As he watched Darr Veter manipulating the control switches something of the admiration that burned in the eyes of Darr Veter's young assistant could be seen in his.

A deep, ominous rumble sounded, as though a huge gong had been struck. Darr Veter turned round swiftly and threw over a long lever. The gong ceased and Veda Kong noticed that a narrow panel on the right-hand wall laid lit up from floor to ceiling. The wall seemed to have disappeared into the unfathomable distance. The phantom-like outlines of a pyramidal mountain surmounted by a gigantic stone ring appeared. Below the cap of molten stone, patches of pure white mountain snow lay here and there.

Mven Mass recognized the second highest mountain in Africa, Mount Kenya.

Again the strokes of the gong resounded through the underground chamber making all present alert and compelling them to concentrate their thoughts.

Darr Veter took Mven's hand and placed it on a handle in which a ruby eye glowed. Mven obediently turned the handle as far as it would go. All the power produced on Earth by 1,760 gigantic power stations was being concentrated on the equator, on a mountain 5,000 metres high. A multicoloured luminescence appeared over the peak, formed a sphere and then surged upwards in a spearheaded column that pierced the very depths of the sky. Like the narrow column of a whirlwind it remained poised over the glassy sphere, and over its surface, climbing upwards, ran a spiral of dazzlingly brilliant blue smoke.

The directed rays cut a regular channel through Earth's atmosphere that acted as a line of communication between Earth and the Outer Stations. At a height of 36,000 kilometres above Earth hung the diurnal satellite, a giant station that revolved around Earth's axis once in twenty-four hours and kept in the plane of the equator so that to all intents and purposes it stood motionless over Mount Kenya in East Africa, the point that had been selected for permanent communications with the Outer Stations. There was another satellite, Number 57, revolving around the 90th meridian at a height of 57,000 kilometres and communicating with the Tibetan Receiving and Transmitting Observatory. The conditions for the formation of a transmission channel were better at the Tibetan station but communication was not constant. These two giant satellites also maintained contact with a number of automatic stations situated at various points round Earth.

The narrow panel on the right went dark, a signal that the transmission channel had connected with the receiving station of the satellite. Then the gold-framed, pearl screen lit up. In its centre appeared a monstrously enlarged figure that grew clearer and then smiled with a big mouth. This was Goor Hahn, one of the observers on the diurnal satellite, whose picture on the screen grew rapidly to fantastic proportions. He nodded and stretched out a ten-foot arm to switch on all the Outer Stations around our planet. They were linked up in one circuit by the power transmitted from Earth. The sensitive eyes of receivers turned in all directions into the Universe. The planet of a dull red star in the Unicorn Constellation that had shortly before sent out a call, had a better contact with Satellite 57 and Goor Hahn switched over to it. This invisible contact between Earth and the planet of another star would last for three-quarters of an hour and not a moment of that valuable time could be lost.

Veda Kong, at a sign from Darr Veter, stood before the screen on a gleaming round metal dais. Invisible rays poured down from above and noticeably deepened the sun-tan of her skin. Electron machines worked soundlessly as they translated her words into the language of the Great Circle. In thirteen years' time the receivers on the planet of the dull-red star would write down the incoming oscillations in universal symbols and, if they had them, electron machines would translate the symbols into the living speech of the planet's inhabitants.

"All the same, it is a pity that those distant beings will not hear the soft melodious voice of a woman of Earth and will not understand its expressiveness," thought Darr Veter. "Who knows how their ears may be constructed, they may possess quite a different type of hearing. But vision, which uses that part of the electromagnetic oscillations capable of penetrating the atmosphere, is almost the same throughout the Universe and they will behold the charming Veda in her flush of excitement "

Darr Veter did not take his eyes off Veda's tiny ear, partly covered by a lock of hair, while he listened to her lecture.

Briefly but clearly Veda Kong spoke of the chief stages in the history of mankind. She spoke of the early epochs of man's existence, when there were numerous large and small nations that were in constant conflict owing to the economic and ideological hostility that divided their countries. She spoke very briefly and gave the era the name of the Era of Disunity. People living in the Era of the Great Circle were not interested in lists of destructive wars and horrible sufferings or the so-called great rulers that filled the ancient history books. More important to them was the development of productive forces and the forming of ideas, the history of art and knowledge and the struggle to create a real man, the way in which the creative urge had been developed, and people had arrived at new conceptions of the world, of social relations and of the duty, rights and happiness of man, conceptions that had nurtured the mighty tree of communist society that flourished throughout the planet.

During the last century of the Era of Disunity, known as the Fission Age, people had at last begun to understand that their misfortunes were due to a social structure that had originated in times of savagery; they realized that all their strength, all the future of mankind, lay in labour, in the correlated efforts of millions of free people, in science and in a way of life reorganized on scientific lines. Men came to understand the basic laws of social development, the dialectically contradictory course of history and the necessity to train people in the spirit of strict social discipline, something that became of greater importance as the population of the planet increased.

In the Fission Age the struggle between old and new ideas had become more acute and had led to the division of the world into two camps-the old and the new states with differing economic systems. The first kinds of atomic energy had been discovered by that time but the stubbornness of those who championed the old order bad almost led mankind into a colossal catastrophe.

The new social system was bound to win although victory was delayed on account of the difficulty of training people in the new spirit. The rebuilding of the world on communist lines entailed a radical economic change accompanied by the disappearance of poverty, hunger and heavy, exhausting toil. The changes brought about in economy made necessary an intricate system to direct production and distribution and could only be put into effect by the inculcation of social consciousness in every person.

Communist society had not been established in all countries and amongst all nations simultaneously. A tremendous effort had been required to eliminate the hostility and, especially, the lies that had remained from the propaganda prevalent during the ideological struggle of the Fission Age. Many mistakes had been made in this period when new human relations were developing. Here and there insurrections had been raised by backward people who worshipped the past and who, in their ignorance, saw a way out of man's difficulties in a return to that past.

With inevitable persistence the new way of life had spread over the entire Earth and the many races and nations were united into a single friendly and wise family.

Thus began the next era, the Era of World Unity, consisting of four ages-the Age of Alliance, the Age of Lingual Disunity, the Age of Power Development and the Age of the Common Tongue.

Society developed more rapidly and each new age passed more speedily than the preceding one as man's power over nature progressed with giant steps.

In the ancient Utopian dreams of a happy future great importance was attached to man's gradual liberation from the necessity to work. The Utopians promised man an abundance of all he needed for a short working day of two or three hours and the rest of his time lie could devote to doing nothing, to the *doice far niente* of the novelists. This fantasy, naturally, arose out of man's abhorrence of the arduous, exhausting toil of ancient days.

People soon realized that happiness can derive from labour, from a never-ceasing struggle against nature, the overcoming of difficulties and the solution of ever new problems arising out of the development of science and economy. Man needed to work to the full measure of his strength but his labour had to be creative and in accordance with his natural talents and inclinations, and it had to be varied and changed from time to time. The development of cybernetics, the technique of automatic control, a comprehensive education and the development of intellectual abilities coupled with the finest physical training of each individual, made it possible for a person to change his profession frequently, learn another easily and bring endless variety into his work so that it became more and more satisfying. Progressively expanding science embraced all aspects of life and a growing number of people came to know the joy of the creator, the discoverer of new secrets of nature. Art played a great part in social education and in forming the new way of life. Then came the most magnificent era in man's history, the Era of Common Labour consisting of four ages, the Age of Simplification, the Age of Realignment, the Age of the First Abundance and the Age of the Cosmos.

A technical revolution of the new period was the invention of concentrated electricity with its high-capacity accumulators and tiny electric motors. Before this, man had learned to use semi-conductors in intricate weak-current circuits for his automated cybernetic machines. The work of the mechanic became as delicate as that of the jeweller but at the same time it served to subordinate energy on a Cosmic scale.

The demand that everybody should have everything required the simplification of articles of everyday use. Man ceased to be the slave of his possessions, and the elaboration of standard components enabled articles and machines to be produced in great variety from a comparatively small number of elements in the same way as the great variety of living organisms is made up of a small number of different cells: the cells consist of albumins, the albumins come from proteins and so on. Feeding in former ages had been so wasteful that its rationalization made it easy to feed, without detriment, a population that had increased by thousands of millions.

All the forces of society that had formerly been expended on the creation of war machines, on the maintenance of huge armies that did no useful labour and on propaganda and its trumpery, were channelled into improving man's way of life and promoting scientific knowledge.

At a sign from Veda Kong, Darr Veter pressed a button and a huge globe rose up beside her.

"We began," continued the beautiful historian, "with the complete redistribution of Earth's surface into dewelling and industrial zones.

"The brown stripes running between thirty and forty degrees of North and South latitude represent an unbroken chain of urban settlements built on the shores of warm seas with a mild climate and no winters. Mankind no longer spends huge quantities of energy warming houses in winter and making himself clumsy clothing. The greatest concentration of people is around the cradle of human civilization, the Mediterranean Sea. The subtropical belt was doubled in breadth after the ice on the polar caps had been melted. To the north of the zone of habitation lie prairies and meadows where countless herds of domestic animals graze. The production of foodstuffs and trees for timber is confined to the tropical belt where it is a thousand times more profitable than in the colder climatic zones. Ever since the discovery was made that carbohydrates, the sugars, could be obtained artificially from sunlight and carbonic acid, agriculture has no longer had to produce all man's food. Practically speaking, there is no limit to the quantities of sugars, fats and vitamins that we can produce. For the production of albumins alone we have huge land areas and huge fields of seaweed at our disposal. Mankind has been freed from the fear of hunger that had been hanging over it for tens of thousands of years.

"One of man's greatest pleasures is travel, an urge to move from place to place that we have inherited from our distant forefathers, the wandering hunters and gatherers of scanty food. Today the entire planet is encircled by the Spiral Way whose gigantic bridges link all the continents." Veda ran her finger along a silver thread and turned the globe round. "Electric trains move along the Spiral Way all the time and hundreds of thousands of people can leave the inhabited zone very speedily for the prairies, open fields, mountains or forests.

"At last the planned organization of life put an end to the murderous race for higher speeds, the construction of faster and faster vehicles. Trains on the Spiral Way proceed at 200 kilometres an hour. Only on rare occasions do we use aircraft with a speed of thousands of kilometres an hour.

"A few centuries ago we made extensive improvements to the surface of our planet. The energy of the atomic nucleus had been discovered long before, in the Fission Age, when man learned to liberate a tiny part of its energy to produce a burst of heat but with the harmful radiation of the fall-out. It was soon realized that this meant danger to life on the planet and nuclear power possibilities were greatly curtailed. Almost at the same time astronomers studying the physics of distant stars discovered two new ways of obtaining nuclear energy, Q and F, that were more effective than the old methods and involved no harmful radiation.

"These two methods are now in use on Earth although our spaceships use another form of nuclear energy, the anameson fuel, that became known to us from our observations of the great stars of the Galaxy through the Great Circle.

"It was decided to destroy all the stocks of thermo-'nuclear materials that had been accumulating a long time-radioactive isotopes of uranium, thorium, hydrogen, cobalt and lithium-as soon as a method of ejecting them beyond Earth's atmosphere had been devised.

"In the Age of Realignment artificial suns were made and 'hung' over the north and south polar regions. These greatly reduced the size of the polar ice-caps that had been formed during the ice ages of the Quaternary Period and brought about extensive climatic changes. The level of the oceans was raised by seven metres, the cold fronts receded sharply and the ring of trade winds that had dried up the deserts on the outskirts of the tropic zone became much weaker. Hurricanes and, in general, stormy weather manifestations ceased almost completely.

"The warm steppelands spread almost as far as the sixtieth parallels north and south and beyond them the grasslands and forests of the temperate zone passed the seventieth parallels.

"Three-quarters of the Antarctic Continent was freed from ice and proved a treasure-house of minerals that were invaluable because resources on the other continents had been almost completely exhausted by the reckless destruction of metals in the universal wars of the past. The Spiral Way was completed by carrying it across the Antarctic.

"Before this radical change in climate had been achieved canals had been dug and mountain chains had had passages cut through them to balance out the circulation of air and water on the planet. Even the high mountain deserts of Asia had been irrigated by constantly operating dielectric pumps.

"The potential output of foodstuffs had grown very considerably and new lands had become habitable.

"The frail and dangerous old planetships, poor as they were, enabled us to reach the other planets of our system. Earth was encircled by a belt of artificial satellites from which scientists were able to make a close study of the Cosmos. And then, eight hundred and eight years ago, there occurred an event of such great importance that it marked a new era in the history of mankind-the Era of the Great Circle.

"For a long time the human intellect had laboured over the transmission of images, sounds and energy over great distances. Hundreds of thousands of the most talented scientists worked in a special organization that still bears the name of the Academy of Direct Radiation. They evolved methods for the directed transmission of energy over great distances without any form of conductor. This became possible when ways were found to concentrate the stream of energy in non-divergent rays. The clusters of parallel rays then transmitted provided constant communication with the artificial satellites, and, therefore, with the Cosmos. Long, long ago, towards the end of the Era of Disunity, our scientists established the fact that powerful radiation streams were pouring on to Earth from the Cosmos. Calls from the Cosmos and the transmission round the Great Circle of the Universe were reaching us together with radiation from the other constellations and galaxies. At that time we did not understand them although we had learned to receive the mysterious signals which we, at that time, thought to be natural radiation.

"Kam Amat, an Indian scientist, got the idea of conducting experiments from the satellites with television receivers and with infinite patience tried all possible wavelength combinations over a period of dozens of years.

"Kam Amat caught a transmission from the planetary system of the binary star that had long been known *as* 61 Cygni. There appeared on the screen a man, who was not like us but was undoubtedly a man, and he pointed to an inscription made in the symbols of the Great Circle. Another ninety years passed before the inscription was read and today it is inscribed in our language, the language of Earth, on a monument to Kam Amat: 'Greetings to you, our brothers, who are joining our family. Separated by space and time we are united by intellect in the Circle of Great Power.'[1]

"The language of symbols, drawings and maps used by the Great Circle proved easy to assimilate at the level of development then reached by man. In two hundred years we were able to use translation machines to converse with the planetary systems of the nearest stars and to receive and transmit whole pictures of the varied life of different worlds. We recently received an answer from the fourteen planets of Deneb, a first magnitude star and tremendous centre of life in the Cygnus; it is 122 parsecs distant from us and radiates as much light as 4,800 of our suns. Intellectual development there has proceeded on different lines but has reached a very high level.

"Strange pictures and symbols come from immeasurable distances, from the ancient worlds, from the globular clusters of our Galaxy and from the huge inhabited area around the Galactic Centre, but we do not understand them, and have not yet deciphered them. They have been recorded by the memory machines and passed on to the Academy of the Bounds of Knowledge, an institution that works on problems that our science can as yet only hint at. We are trying to understand ideas that are far from us, millions of years ahead of us, ideas that differ very greatly from ours due to life there having followed different paths of development."

Veda Kong turned away from the screen into which she had been staring as though hypnotized and cast an inquiring glance at Darr Veter. He smiled and nodded his head in approval. Veda proudly raised her head, stretched out her arms to those invisible and unknown beings who would receive her words and her image thirteen years later.

"Such *is* our history, such is the difficult, devious and lengthy ascent we have made to the heights of knowledge. We appeal to you-join us in the Great Circle to carry to the ends of the tremendous Universe the gigantic power of the intellect!"

Veda's voice had a triumphant sound to it, as though it were filled with the strength of all the generations of the people of Earth who had reached such heights that they now aspired to send their thoughts beyond the bounds of their own Galaxy to other stellar islands in the Universe....

The bronze gong sounded as Darr Veter turned over the lever that switched off the stream of transmitted energy. The screen went dark. The luminescent column of the conductor channel remained on the transparent panel on the right.

Veda, tired and subdued, curled up in the depths of her armchair. Darr Veter turned the control desk over to Mven Mass and leaned over his shoulder to watch him at work. The absolute silence was broken only by the faint clicks of switches opening and closing.

Suddenly the screen in the gold frame disappeared and its place was taken by unbelievable depths of space. It was the first time that Veda Kong had seen this marvel and she gasped loudly. Even those well acquainted with the method of the complex interference of light waves by means of which this exceptional expanse and depth of vision was achieved, found the spectacle amazing.

The dark surface of another planet was advancing from the distance, growing in size with every second. It belonged to an extraordinarily rare system of binary stars in which two suns so balanced each other that their planet had a regular orbit and life was able to emerge on it. The two suns, orange and crimson, were smaller than ours, and they lit up the ice of a frozen sea that appeared crimson in colour. A huge, squat building standing on the edge of a chain of flat-topped black hills, was visible through a mysterious violet haze. The centre of vision was focussed on a platform on the roof and then seemed to penetrate the building until the watchers saw a grey-skinned man with round eyes like those of an owl surrounded by a fringe of silvery down. He was very tall and exceedingly thin with tentacle-like limbs. The man jerked his head ridiculously as though he were making a hurried bow; turned listless, lens-like eyes to the screen and opened a lipless mouth that was covered, by a flap of soft flesh that looked like a nose.

"Zaph Phthet, Director of External Relations of 61 Cygni. Today we are transmitting for yellow star STL 3388 + 04 JF.... We are transmitting for ..."-' came the gentle, melodious voice of the translation machine.

Darr Veter and Junius Antus exchanged glances and Mven Mass squeezed Darr Veter's wrist for a second. That was the galactic call sign of Earth, or rather, of the entire solar system, that observers in other worlds had formerly regarded as one big planet rotating round the Sun once in 59 terrestrial years. Once in that period Jupiter and Saturn are in opposition which displaces the Sun in the visible sky of other systems sufficiently for astronomers on the nearer stars to observe. Our astronomers made the same mistake in respect of many planetary systems that a number of stars had long been known to possess.

Junius Antus checked up on the tuning of his memory machine with greater celerity than he had shown at the beginning of the transmission and also checked the watchful accuracy indicators.

The unchanging voice of the electron translator continued:

"We have received a transmission from star..." again a long string of figures and staccato sounds, "by chance and not during the Great Circle transmission times. They have not deciphered the language of the Circle and are wasting energy transmitting during the hours of silence. We answered them during their transmission period and the result will be known in three-tenths of a second ...." The voice broke off. The signal lamps continued to burn with the exception of the green electric eye that had gone out.

"We get these unexplained interruptions in transmission, perhaps due to the passage of the astronauts' legendary neutral fields between us," Junius Antus explained to Veda.

"Three-tenths of a galactic second-that means waiting six hundred years," muttered Darr Veter, morosely. "A lot of good that will do us!"

"As far as I can understand they are in communication with Epsilon Tucanae in the southern sky that is ninety parsecs away from us and close to the limit of our regular communications. So far we haven't established contact. with anything farther away than Deneb," Mven Mass remarked.

"But we receive the Galactic Centre and the globular clusters, don't we?" asked Veda Kong.

"Irregularly, quite by chance, or through the memory machines of other members of the Great Circle that form a circuit stretching through the Galaxy," answered Mven Mass.

"Communications sent out thousands and even tens of thousands of years ago do not get lost in space but eventually reach us," said Junius Antus.

"So that means we get a picture of the life and knowledge of the peoples of other, distant worlds, with great delay, for the Central Zone of the Galaxy, for example, a delay of about twenty thousand years?"

"Yes, it doesn't matter whether they are the records of the memory machines of other, nearer worlds, or whether they are received by our stations, we see the distant worlds as they were a very long time ago. We see people that have long been dead and forgotten in their own worlds."

"How is it that we are helpless in this field when we have achieved such great power over nature?" Veda Kong asked, petulantly. "Why can't we find some other means of contacting distant worlds, something not connected with waves or photon ray equipment?"

"How well I understand you, Veda!" exclaimed Mven Mass.

"The Academy of the Bounds of Knowledge is engaged on projects to overcome space, time and gravity," Darr Veter put in. "They are working on the fundamentals of the Cosmos, but they have not yet got even as far as the experimental stage and cannot "

The green eye suddenly flashed on again and Veda once more felt giddy as the screen opened out into endless space.

The sharply outlined edges of the image showed that it was the record of a memory machine and not a transmission received directly.

At first the onlookers saw the surface of a planet, obviously as seen from an outer station, a satellite. The huge, pale violet sun, spectral in the terrific heat it generated, deluged the cloud envelope of the planet's atmosphere with its penetrating rays.

"Yes, that's it, the luminary of the planet is Epsilon Tucanae, a high temperature star, class B", 78 times as bright as our Sun," whispered Mven Mass. Darr Veter and Junius Antus nodded in agreement.

The spectacle changed, the scene grew narrower and seemed to be descending to the very soil of the unknown world.

The rounded domes of hills that looked as though they had been cast from bronze rose high above the surrounding country. An unknown stone or metal glowed like fire in the amazingly white light of the blue sun. Even in the imperfect apparatus used for transmission the unknown world gleamed triumphantly, with a sort of victorious magnificence.

The reflected rays produced a silver pink corona around the contours of the copper-coloured hills and lay in a wide path on the slowly moving waves of a violet sea. The water, of a deep amethyst colour, seemed heavy and glowed from within with red lights that looked like an accumulation of living eyes. The waves washed the massive pedestal of a gigantic statue that stood in splendid isolation far from the coast. It was a female figure carved from dark-red stone, the head thrown back and the arms extended in ecstasy towards the naming depths of the sky. She could easily have been a daughter of Earth, the resemblance she bore to our people was no less astounding than the amazing beauty of the carving. Her body was the fulfilment of an earthly sculptor's dream; it combined great strength with inspiration in every line. The polished red stone of the statue emitted the flames of an unknown and, consequently, mysterious and attractive life.

The five people of Earth gazed in silence at that astounding new world. The only sound was a prolonged sigh that escaped the lips of Mven Mass whose every nerve had been strained in joyful anticipation from his first glance at the statue.

On the sea-coast opposite the statue, carved silver towers marked the beginning of a wide, white staircase that swept boldly over a thicket of stately trees with turquoise leaves.

"They ought to ring!" Darr Veter whispered in Veda's ear, pointing to the towers and she nodded her head in agreement.

The camera of the new planet continued its consistent and soundless journey into the country.

For a second the five people saw white walls with wide cornices through which led a portal of blue stone; the screen carried them into a high room filled with strong light. The dull, pearl-coloured, grooved walls lent unusual clarity to everything in the hall. The attention of the Earth-dwellers was attracted to a group of people standing before a polished emerald panel.

The flame-red colour of their skin was similar to that of the statue in the sea. It was not an unusual colour for Earth-coloured photographs that had been preserved from ancient days recorded some tribes of Indians in Central America whose skin was almost the same colour, perhaps just a little lighter.

There were two men and two women in the hall. They stood in pairs wearing different clothing. The pair standing closer to the emerald panel wore short golden clothes, something like elegant overalls, fastened with a number of clips. The other pair wore cloaks that covered them from head to foot and were of the same pearl tone as the walls.

Those standing before the panel made some graceful movements, touching some strings stretching diagonally from the left-hand edge of the panel. The wall of polished emerald or glass became transparent and in time with the movements of the man and woman, clearly defined pictures appeared in the crystal. They appeared and disappeared so quickly that even such trained observers as Junius Antus and Darr Veter had difficulty in following the meaning of them.

In the procession of copper-coloured mountains, violet seas and amethyst trees the history of the planet emerged. A chain of animal and plant forms, sometimes monstrously incomprehensible, sometimes beautiful, appeared as ghosts of the past. Many of the animals and plants seemed to be similar to those that have been preserved in the record of the rocks on Earth. It was a long ladder of ascending forms of life, the ladder of developing living matter. The endlessly long path of development seemed even longer, more difficult and more tortuous than the path of evolution known to every Earth-dweller.

New pictures flashed through the phantom gleam of the apparatus: the flames of huge fires, piled-up rocks on the plains, fights with savage beasts, the solemn rites of funerals and religious services. The figure of a man covered by a motley cloak of coloured skins filled the whole panel. Leaning on a spear with one band and raising the other towards the stars in an all-embracing gesture, be stood with his foot on the neck of a conquered monster with a ridge of stiff hair down its back and long, bared fangs. In the background a line of men and women had joined hands in pairs and seemed to be singing something.

The picture faded away and the place of the tableaux was taken by a dark surface of polished stone.

At this moment the pair in golden clothing moved away to the right and their place was taken by the second pair. With a movement so rapid that the eye could not follow it the cloaks were thrown aside and two dark-red bodies gleamed like living fire against the pearl of the walls. The man held out his two hands to the woman and she answered him with such a proud and dazzling smile of joy that the Earth-dwellers responded with involuntary smiles. And there, in the pearl hall of that immeasurably distant world, the two people began a slow dance. It was probably not danced for the sake of dancing, but was something more in the nature of eurhythmics, in which the dancers strove to show their perfection, the beauty of the lines and the flexibility of their bodies. A majestic and at the same time sorrowful music could be felt in the rhythmic change of movement, as though recalling the great ladder of countless unnamed victims sacrificed to the development of life that had produced man, that beautiful and intelligent being.

Mven Mass fancied he could hear a melody, a movement in pure high tones played against a background of the resonant and measured rhythm of low notes. Veda Kong squeezed Darr Veter's hand but the latter did not pay her any attention. Junius Antus stood motionless watching the scene, without even breathing, and beads of perspiration stood out on his broad forehead.

The people of the Tucana planet were so like the people of Earth that the impression of another world was gradually lost. The red people, however, possessed bodies of refined beauty such as had not by that time been universally achieved on Earth, but which lived in the dreams and the creations of artists and was to be seen only in a small number of unusually beautiful people.

"The more difficult and the longer the path of blind animal evolution up to the thinking being, the more purposeful and perfected are the higher forms of life and, therefore, the more beautiful," thought Darr Veter. "The people of Earth realized a long time ago that beauty is an instinctively comprehended purposefulness of structure that is adapted to definite objectives. The more varied the objectives, the more beautiful the form-these red people must be more versatile and agile than we are....Perhaps their civilization has progressed mainly through the development of man himself, the development of his spiritual and physical might, rather than through technical development. Even with the coming of communist society our civilization has remained rudimentally technical and only in the Era of Common Labour did we turn to the perfection of man himself and not only his machines, houses, food and amusements."

The dance was over. The young red-skinned woman came into the centre of the hall and the camera of the transmitter focussed on her alone. Her outstretched arms and her face were turned to the ceiling of the hall.

The eyes of the Earth-dwellers involuntarily followed her glance. There was no ceiling, or, perhaps, some clever optical illusion created the impression of a night sky with very large and bright stars. The strange combinations of constellations did not arouse any association. The girl waved her hand and a blue ball appeared on the index finger of her left hand. A silvery ray streamed out of the ball and served her as a gigantic pointer. A round patch of light at the end of the pointer halted first on one then on another star in the ceiling. In each case the emerald panel showed a motionless picture extremely wide in scale. As the pointer ray moved from star to star the panel demonstrated a series of inhabited and uninhabited planets. Joyless and sorrowful were the stone or sand deserts that burned in the rays of red, blue, violet and yellow suns. Sometimes the rays of a strange leaden-grey star would bring to life on its planets flattened domes or spirals, permeated with electricity, that swam like jelly-fish in a dense orange atmosphere or ocean. In the world of the red sun there grew trees of incredible height with slimy black bark, trees that stretched their millions of crooked branches heavenwards as though in despair. Other planets were completely covered with dark water. Huge living islands, either animal or vegetable, were floating everywhere, their countless hairy feelers waving over the smooth surface of the water.

"They have no planets near them that possess the higher forms of life," said Junius Antus, suddenly, without once taking his eyes off the star map of the unknown sky.

"Yes they have," said Darr Veter, "although the flattened stellar system to one side of them is one of the newest formations in the Galaxy, we know that flattened and globular systems, the old and the new, not infrequently alternate. In the direction of Eridanus there is a system with living intelligences that belongs to the Circle."

"VVR 4955 + MO 3529 ... etc.," added Mven Mass, "but why don't they know of it?"

"The system entered the Great Circle 275 years ago and this communication was made before that," answered Darr Veter.

The red-skinned girl from the distant world shook the blue ball from her finger and turned to face her audience, her arms spread out widely as though to embrace some invisible person standing before her. She threw back her head and shoulders as a woman of Earth would in a burst of passion. Her mouth was half open and her lips moved as she repeated inaudible words. So she stood, immobile, appealing, sending forth into the cold darkness of interstellar space fiery human words of an entreaty for friendship with people of other worlds.

Again her enthralling beauty held the Earth-dwellers spellbound. She had nothing of the bronze severity of the red-skinned people of Earth. Her round face, small nose and big, widely-placed blue eyes bore more resemblance to the northern peoples of Earth. Her thick, wavy black hair was not stiff. Every line of her face and body expressed a light and joyful confidence that came from a subconscious feeling of great strength.

"Is it possible that they know nothing of the Great Circle?" Veda Kong almost groaned as though in obeisance before her beautiful sister from the Cosmos.

"By now they probably know," answered Darr Veter, the scenes we have witnessed date three hundred years back."

"Eighty-eight parsecs," rumbled Mven Mass's low voice. "Eighty-eight.... All those people we have just seen have long been dead."

As though in confirmation of his words the scene from the wonderful world disappeared and the green indicator went out. The transmission around the Great Circle was over.

For another minute they were all in a trance. The first to recover was Darr Veter. Biting his lip in chagrin he hurriedly turned the granulated lever. The column of directed energy switched off with the sound of a gong that warned power station engineers to re-direct the gigantic stream of energy into its usual channels. The Director of the Outer Stations turned back to his companions only when all the necessary manipulations had been completed.

Junius Antus, with a frown on his face, was looking through pages of written notes.

"Some of the memory records taken down from the pBtellar map on the ceiling must be sent to the Southern Sky Institute!" he said, turning to Darr Veter's young assistant. The latter looked at Junius Antus in amazement as though he had just awakened from an unusual dream.

The grim scientist looked at him, a smile lurking in his eyes-what they had seen was indeed a dream of a wonderful world sent out into space three hundred years before ... a dream that thousands of millions of people on Earth and in the colonies on the Moon, Mars and Venus would now see so clearly that it would be almost tangible.

"You were right, Mven Mass," smiled Darr Veter, "when you said before the transmission began that something unusual was going to happen today. For the first time in the eight hundred years since we joined the Great Circle a planet has appeared in the Universe inhabited by beings who are our brothers not only in intellect but in body as well. You can well imagine my joy at this discovery. Your tour of duty as Director has begun auspiciously! In the old days people would have said that it was a lucky sign and our present-day psychologists would say that coincidental events have occurred that favour confidence and give you encouragement in your further work."

Darr Veter stopped suddenly: nervous reaction had made him more verbose than usual. In the Era of the Great Circle verbosity was considered one of the most disgraceful failings possible in a man-the Director of the Outer Stations stopped without finishing his sentence.

"Yes, yes ..." responded Mven Mass, absent-mindedly. Junius Antus noticed the sluggishness in his voice and in his movements; he was immediately on the alert. Veda Kong quietly ran her finger along Darr Veter's hand and nodded towards the African.

"Perhaps he is too impressionable?" wondered Darr Veter staring fixedly at his successor. Mven Mass sensed the concealed surprise of his companions; he straightened up and became his usual self, an attentive and skilled performer of the task in hand. An escalator took them to the upper storeys of the building where there were extensive windows looking out at the starry sky that was again as far away as it had always been during the whole thirty thousand years of man's existence-or rather the existence of that species of hominids known as *Homo sapiens*. Mven Mass and Darr Veter had to remain behind.

Veda Kong whispered to Darr Veter that she would never forget that night.

"It made me feel so insignificant!" she said, in conclusion, her face beaming despite her sorrowful words. Darr Veter knew what she meant and shook his head.

"I am sure that if the red woman had seen you she would have been proud of her sister, Veda. Surely our Earth isn't a bit worse than their planet!" Darr Veter's face was glowing with the light of love.

"That's seen through your eyes, my friend," smiled Veda, "but ask Mven Mass what he thinks!" Jokingly she covered his eyes with her hand and then disappeared round a corner of the wall.

When Mven Mass was, at last, left alone it was already morning. A greyish light was breaking through the cool, still air and the sky and the sea were alike in their crystal transparency, the sea silver and the sky pinkish.

For a long time the African stood on the balcony of the observatory gazing at the still unfamiliar outlines of the buildings.

On a low plateau in the distance rose a huge aluminium arch crossed by nine parallel aluminium bars, the spaces between them filled in with yellowish-cream and silvery plastic glass; this was the building of the Astronautical Council. Before the building stood a monument to the first people to enter outer space; the steep slope of a mountain reaching into clouds and whirlwinds was surmounted by an old-type spaceship, a fish-shaped rocket that pointed its sharp nose into still unattainable heights. Cast-metal figures, supporting each other in a chain, were making a superhuman effort to climb upwards, spiralling their way around the base of the monument-these were the pilots of the rocket ships, the physicists, astronomers, biologists and writers with bold imaginations…. The hull of the old spaceship and the light lattice-work of the Council building were painted red by the dawn, but still Mven Mass continued pacing up and down the balcony. Never before had he met with such a shock. He had been brought up according to the general educational rules of the Great Circle Era, had had a hard physical training and had successfully performed his Labours of Hercules- the difficult tasks performed by every young person at the end of his schooling that had been given this name in honour of ancient Greece. If a youngster performed these tasks successfully he was considered worthy to storm the heights of higher education.

Mven Mass had worked on the construction of the water-supply system of a mine in Western Tibet, on the restoration of the Araucaria pine forests on the Nahebt Plateau in South America and had taken part in the annihilation of the sharks that had again appeared off the coasts of Australia. His training, his heredity and his outstanding abilities enabled him to undertake many years of persistent study to prepare himself for difficult and responsible activities. On that day, during the first hour of his new work, there had been a meeting with a world that was related to our Earth and that had brought something new to his heart. With alarm Mven Mass felt that some great depths had opened up within him, something whose existence he had never even suspected. How he craved for another meeting with the planet of star Epsilon in the Tucan Constellation! … That was a world that seemed to have come into being by power of the best legends known to the Earth-dwellers. He would never forget the red-skinned girl, her outstretched alluring arms, her tender, half-open lips!

The fact that two hundred and ninety light years dividing him from that marvellous world was a distance that could not be covered by any means known to the technicians of Earth served to strengthen rather than weaken his dream.

Something new had grown up in Mven's heart, something that lived its own life and did not submit to the control of the will and cold intellect. The African had never been in love, he had been absorbed in his work almost as a hermit would be and had never experienced anything like the alarm and incomparable joy that had entered his heart during that meeting across the tremendous barrier of space and time.

CHAPTER THREE

CAPTIVES OF THE DARK

The fat black arrows on the orange-coloured anameson fuel indicators stood at zero. The spaceship had not escaped the iron star, its speed was still great and it was being drawn towards that horrible star that human eyes could not see.

The astronavigator helped Erg Noor, who was trembling from weakness and from the effort he had made, to sit down at the computing machine. The planetary motors, disconnected from the robot helmsman, faded out.

"Ingrid, what's an iron star?" asked Kay Bear, softly; all that time he had been standing motionless behind her back.

"An invisible star, spectral class T, that has become extinguished and is either in the process of cooling off or of reheating. It emanates the long infrared waves of the heat end of the spectrum whose rays are black to us and can only be seen through the electronic inverter. An owl can see the infrared rays and, therefore, could see the star."

"Why is it called iron?"

"There is a lot of iron in the spectrum of those that have been studied and it seems there's a lot of it in the star's composition. If the star is a big one its mass and gravity are enormous. And I'm afraid we're going to meet one of the big ones." "What comes next?"

"I don't know. You know yourself that we've got no fuel. We're flying straight towards the star. We must brake *Tantra* down to a speed one-thousandth of the absolute, at which speed sufficient angular deviation will be possible. If the planetary fuel gives out too, the spaceship will slowly approach the star until it falls on it."

Ingrid jerked her head nervously and Kay gently stroked her bare arm, all covered with goose-flesh.

The commander of the expedition went over to the control desk and concentrated on the instruments. Everybody kept silent, almost afraid to breathe, even Nisa Greet, who, although she had only just woke up, realized instinctively the danger of their situation. The fuel might be sufficient to brake the ship; but with loss of velocity it would be more difficult to get out of the tremendous gravitational field of the iron star without the ship's motors. If *Tantra* had not approached so close and if Lynn had realized in time ... but what consolation was there in those empty "ifs"?

Three hours passed before Erg Noor had made his decision. *Tantra* vibrated from the powerful thrust of the trigger motors. Her speed was reduced. An hour, a second, a third and a fourth, an elusive movement of the commander's hand, horrible nausea for everybody in the ship and the terrifying brown star disappeared from the forward screen and reappeared on the second. Invisible bonds of gravity continued to hold the ship and were recorded in the measuring instruments. Two red eyes burned over Erg Noor's head. He pulled a lever towards himself and the motors stopped working.

"We're out!" breathed Pel Lynn in relief. The commander slowly turned his glance towards him.

"We're not. We have only the iron ration of fuel left, sufficient for orbital revolution and landing."

"What can we do?"

"Wait! I have diverted the ship a little, but we are passing too close. A battle is now going on between the star's force of gravity and the reduced speed of *Tantra*. It's flying like a lunar rocket at the moment and if it can get away we shall fly towards the Sun and will be able to call Earth. The time required for the journey, of course, will he much greater. In about thirty years we'll send out our call for help and another eight years later it will come."

"Thirty-eight years!" Bear whispered in scarcely audible tones in Ingrid's ear. She pulled him sharply by the sleeve and turned away.

Erg Noor leaned back in his chair and dropped his hands on his knees. Nobody spoke and the instruments continued softly humming. Another melody, out of tune and, therefore, ominous, was added to the tuned melody of the navigation instruments. The call of the iron star, the great strength of its iron mass pulling for the weakened spaceship, was almost physically tangible.

Nisa Creet's cheeks were burning, her heart was beating wildly. This inactive waiting had become unbearable.

The hours passed slowly. One after another the awakened members of the expedition appeared in the control tower. The number of silent people increased until all fourteen were assembled.

The speed of the ship had been progressively reduced until it reached a point that was lower than the velocity of escape so that *Tantra* could not get away from the iron star. Her crew forgot all about food and sleep and did not leave the control tower for many miserable hours during which the ship's course changed more and more to a curve until she was in the fatal elliptical orbit. *Tantra's* fate was obvious to the entire crew.

A sudden howl made them all start. Astronomer Pour Hyss jumped up and waved his hands. His distorted face was unrecognizable, he bore no resemblance to a man of the Great Circle Era. Fear, self-pity and a craving for revenge had swept all signs of intellectuality from the face of the scientist.

"Him, it was him," howled Pour Hyss, pointing to Pel Lynn, "that clot, that fool, that brainless worm …." The astronomer choked as he tried to recall the swear-words of his ancestors that had long before gone out of use. Nisa, who was standing near him, moved away contemptuously. Erg Noor stood up.

"The condemnation of a colleague will not help us. The time is past when such an action could have been intentional. In this case," Noor spun the handles on the computing machine carelessly, "as you see there was a thirty per cent probability of error. If we add to that the inevitable depression that comes at the end of a tour of duty and the disturbance due to the pitching of the ship I don't doubt that you. Pour Hyss, would have made the same mistake!"

"And you?" shouted the astronomer, but with less fury than before.

"I should not. I saw a monster like this at close quarters during the 36th Space Expedition. It is mostly my fault-I hoped to pilot the ship through the unknown region myself, but I did not foresee everything, I confined myself to giving simple instructions!"

"How could you have known that they would enter this region without you?" exclaimed Nisa.

"I should have known it," answered Erg Noor, firmly, in this way refusing the friendly aid of the astronavigator, "but there's no sense in talking about it until we get bade to Earth."

"To Earth!" whined Pour Hyss and even Pel Lynn frowned in perplexity, "to say that, when all is lost and only death lies ahead of us!"

"Not death but a gigantic struggle lies ahead of us," answered Erg Noor, confidently, sitting down in a chair that stood before the table. "Sit down. There's no need to hurry until *Tantra* has made one and a half revolutions."

Those present obeyed him in silence and Nisa gave the biologist a smile, triumphant, despite the hopelessness of the moment.

"This star undoubtedly has a planet, even two, I imagine, judging by the curves of the isograve.[10] The planets, as you see," the commander made a rapid but accurate sketch, "should be big ones and, therefore, should have an atmosphere. We don't need to land, though, we have enough atomized solid oxygen." " Erg Noor stopped to gather his thoughts. "We shall become the satellite of the planet and travel in orbit around it. If the atmosphere of the planet is suitable and we use up our air, we have sufficient planetary fuel to land and call for help. In six months we can calculate the direction," he continued, "transmit to Earth the results obtained from Zirda and send for a rescue ship and save our ship."

"If we do save it…" Pour Hyss pulled a wry face as he tried to hide the joy that kindled anew in his heart.

"Yes, if we do," agreed Erg Noor. "That, however, is clearly our goal. We must muster all our forces to achieve it. You, Pour Hyss and Ingrid Dietra, make your observations and calculate the size of the planets, Bear and Nisa. compute the velocity from the mass of the planets and when you know that compute the orbital velocity of the spaceship and the optimal radiant[12] for its revolutions."

The explorers began to make preparations for a landing should it prove to be necessary. The biologist, the geologist and the physician prepared a reconnaissance robot, the mechanics adjusted the landing locators and searchlights and got ready a rocket satellite that would transmit a message to Earth.

The work went particularly well after the horror and hopelessness they had experienced and was only interrupted by the pitching of the ship in gravitational vortices. *Tantra,* however, had so reduced her speed that the pitching no longer caused the people great discomfort.

Pour Hyss and Ingrid established the presence of two planets. They had to reject the idea of approaching the outer planet--it was huge in size, cold, encircled by a thick layer of atmosphere that was probably poisonous and threatened them with death. If they had to make a choice of deaths it would probably have been better to burn up on the surface of the iron star than drown in the gloom of an ammonia atmosphere by plunging the ship into a thousand-kilometre thick layer of ammonia ice. There were similar terrible, gigantic planets in the solar system- Jupiter, Saturn, Uranus and Neptune.

Tantra continued to approach the star. In nineteen days they determined the size of the inner planet and it proved to be bigger than Earth. The planet was quite close to its sun, the iron star, and was carried round its orbit at frantic speed, its year being no more than two or three terrestrial months. The invisible star T no doubt made it quite warm with its black rays and, if there was an atmosphere, life could have emerged there. In the latter case landing would be particularly dangerous.

Alien forms of life that had developed under conditions of other planets and by other evolutionary paths and had the albumin cells common to the whole Cosmos were extremely dangerous to Earth-dwellers. The adaptation of the organism to protect itself against harmful refuse and disease bacteria that had been going on for millions of centuries on our planet was powerless against alien forms of life. To the same degree life from other planets was in similar danger on Earth.

The basic activity of animal life-in killing to devour and in devouring to kill-made its appearance with de-pressingly brutal cruelty when the animal life of different worlds clashed. Fantastic diseases, instantaneous epidemics, the terrible spreading of pests and horrible injuries beset the first explorations of habitable hut uninhabited planets. Worlds that were inhabited by intelligent beings made numerous experiments and preparations before establishing direct spaceship communications. On our Earth, far removed from the central parts of the Galaxy where life abounds, there had been no visitors from the planets of other stars, no representatives of other civilizations. The Astronautical Council had shortly before completed preparations for the reception of visitors from the planets of not too distant stars in the Ophiuchus, Cygnus, Ursa Major and Apus constellations.

Erg Noor, worried by the possibility of meeting with unknown forms of life, ordered the biological means of defence, that he had taken a big supply of in the hope of visiting Vega, to be brought out of the distant store-rooms.

At last *Tantra* equalized her orbital velocity with that of the planet and then began to revolve around it. The indefinite, dark-brown surface of the planet, or rather, of its atmosphere, with reflections of the bloody-brown sun, could only be seen through the electronic inverter. All members of the expedition were busy at the instruments.

"The temperature of the upper layers of the daylight side is 320° on the Kelvin scale." "

"Rotation about the axis approximately 20 days." "The locators show the presence of water and land." "The thickness of the atmosphere is 1,700 kilometres." "The exact mass is 43.2 times Earth's mass." The reports followed one another continuously and the nature of the planet was becoming clear.

Erg Noor summarized the figures as they came in and was making preparations to compute the orbit. The planet was a big one, 43.2 times the mass of Earth, and its force of gravity would hold the ship pressed down to the ground. The people would be as helpless as flies on a fly-paper.

The commander recalled the terrible stories he had heard, half legend, half history, of the old spaceships that had, for various reasons, come into contact with the huge planets. In those days the slow ships with low-powered fuel often perished. The end came with a roar of motors and the spasmodic shuddering of a ship that could not get away but remained stuck to the surface of the planet. The ship remained intact but the bones of the people trying to crawl about the ship were broken. The indescribable horror of great weight had been communicated in the fragmentary cries of last reports, in the farewell transmissions.

The crew of *Tantra* were not menaced by that danger as long as they revolved about the planet. If they had to land on its surface, however, only the strongest people would be able to drag the weight of their own bodies in this, the future haven that was to be theirs for many long years Could they keep alive under such conditions- crushed by the great weight, in the eternal darkness of the infrared rays of the black sun, in a dense atmosphere?

Whatever the conditions were, it was a hope of salvation, it did not mean death and, anyway, there was no choice!

Tantra's orbit drew closer to the outer fringe of the atmosphere. The expedition could not miss the opportunity of investigating a hitherto unknown planet that was comparatively close to Earth. The lighted, or rather, heated side of the planet differed from the night side not only by its much greater temperature but also by the huge agglomerations of electricity that so interfered with the powerful locators that their indications were distorted beyond recognition. Erg Noor decided to study the planet with the help of bomb stations. They sent out a physical research robot and the automatic recorder reported on an astonishing quantity of free oxygen in an atmosphere of neon and nitrogen, the presence of water vapour and a temperature of 12° C. These were conditions that, in general, were similar to those on Earth. But the pressure of the thick atmosphere was 1.4 times that of normal pressure on Earth and the force of gravity was 2.5 times greater.

"We can live here," said the biologist, smiling feebly as lie reported the station's findings to the commander.

"If we can live on that gloomy, heavy planet, then something is probably living there already, something small and harmful."

For the spaceship's fifteenth revolution a bomb beacon with a powerful transmitter was prepared. This second physical research station, dropped on the night side when the planet had rotated through 120°, disappeared without sending out any signals.

"It has fallen into the ocean," said geologist Beena Ledd, biting her lips in annoyance.

"We must feel our way with the main locator before we put out a TV robot. We've only got two of them."

Tantra emitted a bunch of directed radio waves as she revolved round the planet, feeling for the contours of seas and continents that owing to distortion were unclear. They found the outlines of a huge plain that thrust out into the ocean, or divided two oceans, almost on the planet's equator. The spaceship's ray zigzagged across a strip of land two hundred kilometres wide. Suddenly a bright point flared up on the locator screen. A whistle that lashed their strained nerves told them that it was no hallucination.

"Metal!" exclaimed the geologist, "an open deposit." Erg Noor shook his head.

"Although the flash did not last long I managed to note its regular outline. That was a huge piece of metal, a meteorite or "

"A ship!" exclaimed Nisa and the biologist together. "Fantasy!" snapped Pour Hyss.

"It may be fact," objected Erg Noor. "What does it matter, it's no use arguing," said Pour Hyss, unwilling to give in. "There's no way of proving it, we're not going to laud, are we?"

"We'll check up on it in three hours' time when we reach that plain again. Notice that the metal object is on the plain that I, too, would have chosen to land on. We'll throw out the TV robot at that very spot. Tune the locator ray to a six-second warning!"

The commander's plan was successful and *Tantra* made another three-hour flight round the dark planet. The next time the ship approached the continental plain it was met by TV broadcasts from the robot. The people peered into the light screen. With a click the visible ray was switched on and peered like a human eye, noting the outlines of things far down below, in that thousand-kilometre-deep black abyss. Kay Bear could well imagine the head of the robot station sticking out of the armour plate and revolving like a lighthouse. The zone that was swept by the instrument's eye appeared on the screen and was there and then photographed: the view consisted of low cliffs, hills and the winding black lines of watercourses. Suddenly the vision of a gleaming, fish-shaped object crossed the screen and again melted into the darkness as it was abandoned by the light ray to the darkness and the ledges of the plateau.

"A spaceship!" gasped several voices in unison. Nisa looked at Pour Hyss with undisguised triumph. The screen went dark as *Tantra* left the area of the TV robot's activity and Eon Thai immediately set about developing the film of the electronic photographs. With fingers that trembled with impatience he placed the film in the projector of the hemispherical screen that would give them stereoscopic pictures of what had been photographed. The inner walls of the hollow hemisphere gave them an enlarged picture.

The familiar cigar-shaped outlines of the ship's hows, the bulge of the stern, the high ridge of the equilibrium receiver .... No matter how unbelievable it all was, no matter how utterly impossible they might regard a meeting here, on the dark planet, the robot could not invent anything, a terrestrial spaceship lay there! It lay horizontally, in the normal landing position, supported by its powerful landing struts, undamaged, as though it had only just alighted on to the planet of the iron star.

Tantra, revolving in a shorter orbit closer to the planet, sent out signals that were not answered. A few more hours passed. The fourteen members of the expedition again gathered in the control tower. Erg Noor, who had been sitting in deep contemplation, stood up.

"I propose to land *Tantra*. Perhaps our brothers are in need of help, perhaps their ship is damaged and cannot return to Earth. If so we can take them, transfer their anameson and save ourselves. There is no sense in sending out a rescue rocket. It cannot do anything to give us fuel and will use up so much energy that there will not be enough left to send a signal to Earth."

"Suppose the ship is here because of a shortage of anameson?" asked Pel Lynn, cautiously.

"Then it should have ion planetary charges, they could not have used up everything. As you see the spaceship is in its proper position which means they landed with the planetary motors. We'll transfer the ion fuel, take off again and go into orbit; then we can call Earth for help and in case of success that won't take more than eight years. And if we can get anameson, then we shall have won out." "Maybe they have photon and not ion charges for their planetary motors," said one of the engineers.

"We can make use of them in the big motors if we fit them with auxiliary bowl reflectors."

"I see you've thought of everything.," said the engineer, giving in.

"There is still the risk of landing on a heavy planet and the risk of living there," muttered Pour Hyss. "It's awful just to think of that world of darkness!"

"The risk, of course, remains. But there is risk in our very situation and we shall hardly increase it by landing. The planet on which our spaceship will land is not a bad one as long as we do not damage the ship."

Erg Noor cast a glance at the dial of the speed regulator and walked swiftly to the control desk. For a whole minute he stood in front of the levers and vernier scales of the controls. The fingers of his big hands moved as though they were selecting chords on some musical instrument, his back was bent and his face turned to stone.

Nisa Greet went up to him, boldly took his right hand and pressed the palm to her smooth cheek, hot from excitement. Erg Noor nodded in gratitude, stroked the girl's mass of hair and straightened himself up.

"We are entering the lower layers of the atmosphere to land," he said loudly, switching on the warning siren. The howl carried throughout the ship and the crew hurried to strap themselves into hydraulic floating seats.

Erg Noor dropped into the soft embrace of the landing chair that rose up from the floor before the control desk. Then came the heavy strokes of the planetary engines and the spaceship rushed down, howling, towards the cliffs and oceans of the unknown planet.

The locators and the infrared reflectors felt their way through the primordial darkness below, red lights glowed on the altimeter scales at 15,000 metres. It was not anticipated that there would be mountains much over 10,000 metres high on the planet where water and the heat of the black sun had been working to level out the surface as was the case on Earth.

The first revolution round the planet revealed no mountains, only insignificant heights, little bigger than those of Mars. It looked as though the activity of the internal forces that gave rise to mountains had ceased or had been checked.

Erg Noor placed the altitude governor at 2,000 metres and switched on the powerful searchlights. A huge ocean stretched below the spaceship, an ocean of horror, an unbroken mass of black waves that rose and fell over unfathomable depths.

The biologist wiped away the perspiration caused by his strenuous efforts; he was trying to catch in his instrument the faint variations in reflection from the black water to determine its salt and mineral content.

The gleaming black of the water gave way to the dull black of land. The crossed rays of the searchlights cut a narrow lane between walls of darkness. Unexpectedly there were patches of colour in this lane, yellow sands and the greyish-green surface of a flat rocky ridge.

Tantra swept across the continent, obedient to the skilled hand of the commander.

At last Erg Noor found the plain he was looking for; it proved to be low-lying country that could not possibly be termed a plateau although it was obvious that the tides and storms of the black sea would not reach it, lying, as it did, some hundred metres above the surrounding country.

The locator on the spaceship's port bow whistled. *Tantra's* searchlights followed the locator beam and the clear outlines of a first class spaceship came into view.

The bow armour, made of an isotope of iridium having a reorganized crystalline structure, shone like new in the rays of the searchlight. There were no temporary structures anywhere near the ship, there were no lights on board-it stood dark and lifeless and did not in any way react to the approach of a sister ship. The searchlight rays moved past the ship and were reflected from a huge disc with spiral projections as they would have been from a blue mirror. The disc was standing on edge, leaning slightly to one side and was partly buried in the black soil. For a moment the observers got the impression that there were cliffs behind the disc and that beyond them the darkness was blacker and thicker, probably it was a precipice or a slope leading down to the lowlands ....

The deafening roar of *Tantra's* sirens shook the hull of the ship. Erg Noor intended to land close to the newly-discovered ship and was giving warning to any people who might be within the danger zone, that is, within a radius of some thousand metres from the landing place. The terrific roar of the planetary motors could be heard even inside the ship and a cloud of red-hot dust appeared in the screens. The ship's floor began to rise up and then slip backwards. The hydraulic hinges of the landing seats turned them smoothly and soundlessly, keeping them perpendicular to the now vertical floors.

The huge jointed landing struts slid out of the ship's hull, straightened out and took the first shock of the landing on an alien world. A shock, a recoil and another shock and *Tantra,* her bows still swaying, came to a standstill at the same time as the engines cut out. Erg Noor raised his hand to a lever on the control desk that was now directly over his head and released the jointed struts. Slowly, with a number of short jerks, the spaceship's bows sank towards the ground until the hull had assumed its normal, horizontal position. The landing had been accomplished. As usual, the landing had shaken the human organism BO strongly that the astronauts required some time to recover and remained semi-recumbent in their landing seats.

They were all held down by an awful weight and were scarcely able to rise to their feet, like patients recovering slowly from a serious illness. The irrepressible biologist, however, had managed to take a sample of the, air.

"It's fit to breathe," he said. "I'll take a look at it through the microscope."

"Don't bother," said Erg Noor, unfastening the cushions of his landing chair, "we can't go out without a spacesuit. There may be very dangerous spores and viruses on this planet."

In the air-lock at the exit to the ship biologically shielded spacesuits and "jumping skeletons" had been prepared in readiness for an exploring party; the "skeletons" were steel, leather-covered frames that were worn over the spacesuits and were fitted with electric motors, springs and shock absorbers to enable the explorers to move about under conditions of excessive weiglit.

After six years' travelling through interstellar space every one of them wanted to feel soil, even alien soil, under his feet. Kay Bear, Pour Hyss, Ingrid, Doctor Louma Lasvy and two engineers had to remain on board the vessel to man the radio, searchlights and various measuring and recording instruments.

Nisa stood aside from the party with her space helmet in her hands.

"Why do you hesitate, Nisa?" the commander called to her as he tested the radio set in the top of his helmet. "Come along to the spaceship!"

"I ... I ..." the girl stammered, "I believe it's dead, it's been standing here a long time .... Another catastrophe, another victim claimed by the merciless Cosmos. I know it's inevitable but still it's hard to bear, especially after Zirda and *Algrab* "

"Perhaps the death of this spaceship will mean life for us," said Pour Hyss who was busy training a short-focus telescope on the other ship which still remained unlighted.

Eight members of the expedition climbed into the air-lock and waited. "Turn on the air!" ordered Erg Noor addressing those who were remaining on the ship and from whom they were now divided by an air-tight wall.

When the pressure in the air-lock had risen to ten atmospheres and was higher than that outside, hydraulic jacks opened the hermetically sealed doors. The air pressure in the lock was so great that it almost hurled the people out of the chamber and at the same time prevented anything harmful in the alien atmosphere from entering the chamber. The door clanged to behind them. The rays of a searchlight lit up a clear road along which the explorers hobbled on their spring legs, scarcely able to drag their own heavy weight along. The gigantic spaceship stood at the other end of the beam of light, about a mile away, a distance that seemed interminable to them in their impatience. They were badly shaken up by their clumsy jumps over uneven ground covered with small boulders and greatly heated by the black sun.

The stars made pale, diffused patches when seen through the dense, highly humid atmosphere. Instead of the brilliant magnificence of the Cosmos the planet's sky showed only a faint suggestion of the constellations, the pale, reddish lanterns of their stars unable to penetrate the darkness on the planet.

The spaceship stood out in clear relief in the profound darkness of its surroundings. The thick borated zirconium lacquer on the hull plates had been rubbed off in places. The ship must have been wandering about the Cosmos for a long time.

An exclamation, repeated in all the radio telephones, came from Eon Thai. With his hand he pointed to the ship's smaller lift that had been lowered to the ground and stood with its door wide open. What were undoubtedly plants grew around the lift and under the ship's hull. Thick stems raised black bowls of parabolic shape nearly three feet above the ground; they had serrated edges something like the teeth of a cog-wheel and it was difficult to say whether they were leaves or flowers. A mass of these motionless cog-wheels growing together had an evil look about them. Still more disturbing was the silent, open door of the lift. Untouched plants and an open door could only mean that nobody had used that way for a long time, that the people were not guarding their tiny terrestrial world from that which was alien to them.

Erg Noor, Eon Thai and Nisa Greet entered the lift and the commander pressed the button. With a slight squeak the machinery was set in motion and the lift carried the explorers to the wide-open airlock. They were followed by the others. Erg Noor transmitted an order to switch off the searchlight on *Tantra*. An instant later the tiny group of Earth-dwellers was lost in utter darkness. The world of the iron sun enveloped them as though trying to absorb that feeble spark of terrestrial life pressed down to the soil of the huge black planet.

They switched on the revolving electric lanterns in their helmets. The inner door of the air-lock, leading into the ship, was closed but not locked and opened at a push. The explorers entered the central corridor and easily found their way through the dark alleyways. The spaceship differed but little from *Tantra* in its design.

"This ship was built less than a hundred years ago," said Erg Noor, drawing closer to Nisa. The girl looked round. Through the silicolloid " helmet the commander's half-lighted face looked mysterious.

"An impossible idea," he continued, "but suppose this is "

"Parus," exclaimed Nisa. She had forgotten the microphone and saw everybody turn towards her.

The explorers made their way to the chief room of the spaceship, the combined library and laboratory, and from there continued towards the ship's control tower in the bows. Staggering along in his "skeleton," swaying from side to side and banging against the walls as he went, the commander reached the main switchboard. The ship's lights were switched on but there was no current to keep them going. The phosphorescent signs and indicators still glowed in the darkness. Erg Noor found the emergency switch, pressed it and, to their surprise, the lamps glowed dimly, but to the explorers they seemed blindingly bright. The light in the lift must have gone on, too, for they heard the voice of Pour Hyss in their telephones asking about the results of the examination. Geologist Beena Ledd answered him as the commander had suddenly stopped in the doorway of the control tower. Following his glance Nisa looked up and saw, between the fore screens, a double inscription, in the letters of Earth and the symbols of the Great Circle-*Parus*. A line drawn under the word separated it from Earth's galactic call sign and the coordinates of the Solar System.

The spaceship that had disappeared eighty years before had been found in the system of the black sun, a system that had formerly been unknown and had been regarded as a dark cloud.

An examination of the interior of the spaceship did not tell them what had happened to the ship's crew. The oxygen reservoirs were not empty, there were supplies of food and water sufficient for several years but nowhere was there any trace or any remains of *Parus'* crew.

Here and there in the corridors, in the control tower and in the library there were strange dark stains on the walls. On the library floor there was another stain that looked as though something that had been spilled there had dried in a warped film of several layers. Before the open door in the after bulkhead of the stern engine room, wires had been torn apart and were hanging down, the massive uprights of the cooling system, made of phosphor-bronze, had been badly bent. Everything else in the ship was in perfect condition so that this damage, caused by a blow of tremendous force, could not be explained. The explorers were becoming exhausted by their efforts but were unable to find anything that would explain the disappearance and undoubted loss of *Parus'* crew.

They did, however, make another discovery, one of the greatest importance-the supplies of anameson fuel and ion charges for the planetary motors were sufficient for the take-off of *Tantra* and for the journey back to Earth.

This information was immediately transmitted to *Tantra* and relieved all members of the expedition of that feeling of doom that had possessed them since their spaceship had been captured by the iron star. Nor would they have to carry out the lengthy work necessary to transmit a message to Earth. There would be, however, the tremendous task of transferring the anameson containers to *Tantra*. This would not have been an easy task anywhere, but there, on a planet where everything weighed three times as much as on Earth, it would require all the skill and ingenuity of the engineers. People of the Great Circle Era, however, were not afraid of difficult mental problems; on the contrary, they enjoyed them.

From the tape recorder in the central control tower the biologist removed the unfinished spool of the ship's log-book. Erg

Noor and the biologist opened the door of the hermetically sealed main safe where the results of the *Parus* expedition were kept. The members of the expedition were burdened down with a heavy weight of numerous spools of photo-magnetic films, log-books, astronomical observations and computations. They were explorers themselves and could not dream of leaving such a valuable find even for a moment.

Dead tired the explorers were met in *Tantra's* library by their excited and impatient comrades. In surroundings to which they were accustomed, seated around a comfortable table under bright lights, the tomb-like gloom of the black world outside and the dead, abandoned spaceship seemed like a gruesome nightmare. Nevertheless the force of gravity of that awful planet continued to crush every one of them and from time to time one or another of the explorers would grimace with pain on making some movement. It had been very difficult, without considerable practice, to coordinate the movements of the body with those of the "steel skeleton" so that an ordinary walk became a series of jerks and severe shakings. The short journey to *Parus* and back had completely exhausted them. Geologist Beena Ledd was apparently suffering from a slight concussion of the brain, but she refused to go away before she had heard the last spool of the ship's log-book and remained leaning on the table with her hands pressed to her temples. Nisa expected something extraordinary from the records that had lain for eighty years in a dead ship on that horrid planet. She imagined hoarse appeals for help, howls of a suffering, tragic words of farewell. The girl shuddered when a cold, melodious voice came from the reproducer. Even Erg Noor, a man who possessed great knowledge of everything connected with interstellar flights, knew nothing of the crew of *Parus*. The crew had been made up exclusively of young people and had set out on their fantastically courageous journey to Vega without giving the Astronautical Council the usual film about the members of the crew.

The unknown voice reported events that occurred seven months after the last message had been sent to Earth. Twenty-five years before that, in crossing a Cosmic ice zone on the fringe of the Vega system, *Parus* had been damaged. The crew managed to patch the hole in the ship's stern and continue their journey but it nevertheless upset the delicate regulation of the protective field of the motors. After a struggle that lasted twenty years they had had to stop the engines. *Parus* continued going five years by inertia until she was pulled aside by a natural inaccuracy in the ship's course. That was when the first message had been sent. The spaceship was about to send another message when she was caught in the field of the iron star. Then the same thing happened to *Parus* as had happened to *Tantra* with the difference that *Parus* was without motors and had been unable to resist. Nor could *Parus* become a satellite of the black planet since the planetary motors, housed in the vessel's stern, had been wrecked at the same time as the anameson motors. *Parus* landed safely on a low plateau near the sea. The crew set about carrying out three tasks of importance: the repair of the motors, the transmission of a message to Earth and the study of the unknown planet. Before they had time to erect a rocket tower people began to disappear mysteriously.

Those sent out to look for them did not return. The exploration of the planet ceased, the remainder of the crew went out to the rocket tower only in a group and for the long periods between spells of work that the strong force of gravity made extremely exhausting, they remained in the tightly sealed spaceship. In their hurry to send off the rocket they had not even studied the strange spaceship in the vicinity of *Parus* that had, apparently, been there a long time.

"That disc!" flashed through Nisa's mind. She met the commander's glance and he, understanding her thoughts, nodded in affirmation. Six out of the fourteen of *Parus'* crew had disappeared but after the necessary measures had been taken the disappearances stopped. There then followed a break of about three days in the logbook and the story was taken up by a young woman's high-pitched voice.

"Today is the twelfth day of the seventh month, year 723 of the Great Circle, and we who have remained alive have completed the construction of the rocket transmitter. Tomorrow at this time "

Kay Bear glanced instinctively at the time gradations along the tape-5 a. m. *Parus* time, and who could know what time that would be on this planet! "We are sending a reliably computed ..." the voice broke off and then began again, this time weaker and suppressed, as though the speaker had turned away from the microphone, "... I am switching on! More!" The tape-recorder was silent although the tape continued to unwind.

"Something must have happened!" began Ingrid Dietra.

Hurried, choking words came from the tape-recorder. "... two got away ... Laik is gone, she didn't jump far enough ... the lift... they couldn't shut the outside door, only the inside one! Mechanic Sach Kthon has crawled to the engines ... we'll start the planetary motors going ... there is nothing to them but fury and horror, they are nothing! Yes, nothing ..." for some time the tape unwound in silence, then the same voice began again.

"I don't think Kthon managed it. I'm alone, but I've thought of what to do. Before I begin," the voice grew stronger and then sounded with amazing strength, "Brothers, if you find *Parus,* take heed of my warning, never leave the ship at all." The woman who was speaking heaved a deep sigh and said, as though talking to herself, "I must find out about Kthon, I'll come back and explain in detail." Then came a click and the tape continued to unwind for about twenty minutes before it reached the end. The eager listeners waited in vain, the unknown woman had been unable to give any further details just as she had probably been unable to return.

Erg Noor switched off the apparatus and turned to his companions.

"Our brothers and sisters who died in *Parus* will save us! Can't you feel the strong arm of the man of Earth! There's a supply of anameson on the ship and we've been given a warning of the mortal danger that threatens us. I have no idea what it is but it's undoubtedly some alien form of life. If it had been elemental. Cosmic forces, they'd have damaged the ship and not merely killed the people, It would be a disgrace if we could not save ourselves now that we have been given so much help; we must take our discoveries and those of *Parus* back to Earth. The great work of those who perished at their posts, their half-century's struggle against the Cosmos, must not have been in vain."

"How do you propose to get the fuel on board without leaving the ship?" asked Kay Bear.

"Why without leaving the ship? You know that's impossible and that we have to go "out and work outside. We've been warned and we'll take the necessary steps."

"I suppose you mean a barrage around the place where we're going to work," said biologist Eon Thai.

"Not only that, a barrage along the whole way between the two ships," added Pour Hyss.

"Naturally! We don't know what to expect so we'll make the barrage a double one, a radiation and an electric wall. We'll put out cables and have a path of light all the way. There's an unused rocket standing behind *Parus* that contains sufficient energy for all the time we'll have to work."

Beena Ledd's head dropped on to the table with a thud. The doctor and the second astronomer moved their heavy bodies with difficulty towards her.

"It's nothing," explained Louma Lasvy, "concussion and overstrain. Help me get Beena to bed."

Even that simple task would not have been performed very quickly if mechanic Taron had not thought of adapting an automatic robot car. With the help of the car all the eight explorers were taken to their beds-if they did not rest in time, organisms that had not yet adapted themselves to new conditions would break down. At this difficult moment every member of the expedition was essential and irreplaceable.

Soon two universal automatic cars for transport purposes and road building were linked together and used to level the road between the two spaceships. Heavy cables were hung on both sides. Watch towers with a protective hood of thick silicoborum [15] were erected at each of the spaceships. In each tower an observer from time to time would send a fan-shaped bunch of death-dealing rays along the road from an impulse chamber. During the hours of work the powerful searchlights were kept going all the time. The main hatch in *Parus'* keel was opened, some of the bulkheads were removed and four containers of anameson and thirty cylinders with ion charges were made ready to load on to the cars. It would be more difficult to load them on to *Tantra*. They could not open the spaceship the way *Parus* was opened and so allow whatever was engendered by the alien life of the planet, and which was probably lethal, to enter the ship. For this reason they only made the necessary preparations inside the ship but did not open the hatch; interior bulkheads were removed and containers of compressed air were brought from *Parus*. The plan was to blow a strong blast of air under high pressure down the shaft from the time the manhole was opened until the containers were loaded into *Tantra*. At the same time the hull of the vessel would be screened by a radiation cascade.

The expedition gradually grew accustomed to working in their "steel skeletons" and began to bear the triple weight somewhat more easily. The unbearable pain in all their bones that had begun as soon as they landed was also beginning to ease up.

Several terrestrial days passed and the mysterious "nothing" did not appear. The temperature of the surrounding atmosphere began to fall rapidly. A hurricane arose that increased in fury hour by hour. This was the setting of the black sun-the planet rotated and the continent on which the spaceship stood plunged into night. The convection currents, the heat given off by the ocean and the thick atmosphere prevented a sudden drop in temperature but towards the middle of the planetary "night" a sharp frost set in. The work continued with the heating systems in the spacesuits switched on. They had managed to get the first container out of *Parus* and transport it to *Tantra* when at "sunrise" there came a hurricane much fiercer than had been the one at "sunset." The temperature rose rapidly above freezing point, a current of dense air brought with it excessive humidity and the sky was rent by endless lightnings. The hurricane became so fierce that the spaceship began to tremble under pressure of the terrific wind. The crew concentrated all their efforts on safely anchoring the container under *Tantra's* keel. The fearful roar of the wind increased and there were dangerous whirling vortices on the plateau that closely resembled a terrestrial tornado. In the searchlight beam there appeared a huge whirlwind, a rotating column of water, snow and dust whose funnel rested on the low dark sky. The whirlwind broke the high-voltage cables and there were blue flashes caused by short circuits as the ends coiled up. The yellow light of *Parus'* searchlight disappeared as though the wind had blown it out.

Erg Noor gave the order to stop work and take cover in the ship.

"But there is an observer there!" exclaimed geologist Beena Ledd, pointing to the faintly visible light of the silicoborum turret.

"I know, Nisa's there and I'm going over there myself," answered the commander.

"The current is cut off and 'nothing' has come into his own," said Beena in serious tones.

"If the hurricane affects us it will no doubt also affect 'nothing.' I'm sure there's no danger until the storm dies down. I'm so heavy in this world that I won't be blown away if I crawl along the ground. I've been wanting to watch that 'nothing' from an observation turret for a long time." "May I come with you?" asked the biologist, jumping towards the commander.

"Come along, only remember, I won't take anybody else! You need that "

The two men crawled for a long time, hanging on to irregularities and cracks in the stones and keeping as far as possible out of the way of the whirlwinds. The hurricane did its best to tear them from the ground, turn them over and roll them along. Once it succeeded but Erg Noor managed to catch hold of Eon Thai as he rolled past, dropped flat on his stomach and caught hold of a big boulder with his hooked gloves.

Nisa opened the hatch of her turret and the two men crawled into the narrow space. It was quiet and warm inside, the turret stood firm, securely anchored against the storms their wisdom had foreseen. The auburn-headed astronavigator frowned but was glad to have companions. She frankly admitted that she was not looking forward to spending twenty-four hours alone in a storm on a strange planet.

Erg Noor informed *Tantra* of their safe arrival and the searchlight was turned off. The tiny lamp in the turret was now the only light in that kingdom of darkness. The ground trembled under the gusts of wind, the lightning and the passing whirlwinds. Nisa sat in a revolving chair with her back against the rheostat. The commander and the biologist sat at her feet on the round ledge formed by the base of the turret. In their spacesuits they occupied almost all the space inside the turret.

"I suggest we sleep," came Erg Noor's soft voice in the telephones. "It's a good twelve hours to the black sunrise when the storm will die down and it will be warmer."

His companions readily agreed. And so the three of them slept, held down by triple weight, enclosed in their spacesuits, hampered by the stiff "skeleton" in the narrow confines of a turret that was shaken by the storm. Great is the adaptability of the human organism and great its powers of resistance!

From time to time Nisa woke up, transmitted a reassuring message to the watcher on *Tantra* and dozed off again. The hurricane was blowing itself out and the earth tremors had ceased. The "nothing," or, more correctly, the "something" might appear now. The observers on the turrets took VP, vigilance pills, to liven up a tired nervous system.

"That other spaceship bothers me," confessed Nisa, "I should so much like to know who they are, where they came from and how they got here."

"So would I," answered Erg Noor, "only it's obvious how they got here. Stories of the iron stars and their planet traps have long been circulating round the Great Circle. In the more densely inhabited parts of the Galaxy, where ships have been making frequent trips for a long time already, there are planet graveyards of lost spaceships. Many ships, especially the earlier types, got stuck to those planets and many hair-raising stories are told about them, stories that are almost legend today, the legends of the arduous conquest of the Cosmos. Perhaps there are older spaceships on this planet that belong to more ancient days, although the meeting of three ships in our sparsely populated part of the Galaxy is an extraordinary event. So far not a single iron star was known to exist in the vicinity of the Sun, we have discovered the first."

"Do you intend to investigate the disc ship?" asked the biologist.

"Most certainly! Could a scientist ever forgive himself if he let such an opportunity go? We don't know of any disc spaceships in regions neighbouring on our solar system. This must be a ship from a great distance that has, perhaps, been wandering about the Galaxy for several thousand years after the death of the crew or after some irreparable damage. Many transmissions round the Great Circle may become comprehensible to us when we get whatever material there is in the disc ship. It has a very queer form,

it's a disc-shaped spiral, the ribs on its exterior are very convex. As soon as we have transferred the cargo from *Parus* we'll start on that ship but at present we cannot take a single person away from work."

"It took us only a few hours to investigate *Parus*." "I have examined the disc ship through a stereotele-scope. It is sealed tight, not a single opening is to be seen anywhere. It is very difficult to penetrate into any Cosmic ship that is reliably protected against forces that are many times stronger than our terrestrial elements. Just try and get into *Tantra,* through her armour of metal with a reorganized internal crystal structure, through the borason plating-it would be a task equal to the siege of a fortress. It's still more difficult to deal with an alien ship, the principles of whose structure are unknown to us. But we'll make an attempt to find out what it is!"

"When are we going to examine what we've found in *Parus?*" asked Nisa. "There should be some staggeringly interesting observations made in those marvellous worlds mentioned in the message."

The telephone transmitted the commander's good-natured laugh.

"I've been dreaming of Vega since childhood and am more impatient than any of you. But we'll have plenty of time for that on the way home. The first thing we have to do is get out of this darkness, out of this inferno, as they used to say in the old days. The *Parus* explorers did not make any landings otherwise we should have found the things they brought from those worlds in the collection rooms of the ship. You remember that despite the thorough search we made we found only films, measurements, lists of surveys, air tests and containers of explosive dust."

Erg Noor stopped talking and listened. Even the sensitive microphones did not register the slightest breath of wind-the storm was over. A scraping, rustling sound came through the ground from outside and was echoed by the walls of the turret.

The commander raised his hand and Nisa, who understood him without words, extinguished the light. The darkness seemed as dense inside the turret, warmed up with infrared rays, as if it were standing in black liquid on the bed of an ocean. Flashes of brown light showed through the transparent hood of silicoborum. The watchers clearly saw the lights burn up and for a second form tiny stars with dark-red or dark-green rays; they would go out and then appear again. These little stars stretched out in lines that wavered and bent into circles and figures of eight, and slid soundlessly over the smooth diamond-hard surface of the hood. The people in the turret felt a strange, acute pain in their eyes and a sharp pain along the bigger nerves of the body as though the short rays of the brown stars were stabbing the nerve stems like needles.

"Nisa," whispered Erg Noor, "turn the regulator on to 'full' and switch on the light suddenly."

The turret was lit up with a bright, bluish terrestrial light. The people were blinded by it and could see nothing, or practically nothing. Eon and Nisa managed to see- or did they imagine it?-that the darkness on the right-hand side of the turret did not disappear immediately but remained for a moment as a flattened condensation of gloom with tentacles attached. The "something" instantaneously withdrew its tentacles and sprang back into the wall of darkness that the light had pushed farther from the turret.

"Perhaps those are phantoms?" suggested Nisa, "phantom condensations of darkness around a charge of some sort of energy, like our fire balls, and not a form of life at all. If everything here is black why shouldn't the lightning be black, too?"

"That's all very poetical, Nisa," objected Erg Noor, "but hardly likely. In the first place the 'something' was obviously attacking, was after our living flesh. It or its brethren annihilated the people from *Parus*. If it's organized and stable, if it can move in the desired direction, if it can accumulate and discharge some form of energy, then, of course, there can be no question of an atmospheric phantom. It's something created from living matter and it's trying to devour us!"

The biologist supported the commander's conclusion.

"It seems to me that here, on this planet of darkness, it's dark for us alone because our eyes arc not sensitive to the infrared rays of the heat end of the spectrum; but the other end of the spectrum, the yellow and blue rays, should affect these creatures very strongly. Its reaction is so swift that the crew of *Parus* could not see anything when they illuminated the site of the attack and if they did see anything it was already too late and they were unable to tell anybody."

"Let's repeat the experiment, even if the approach of that thing is unpleasant."

Nisa switched off the light and again the three observers sat in profound darkness awaiting the approach of the denizens of the world of darkness.

"What is it armed with? Why is its approach felt through the hood and the spacesuit?" asked the biologist aloud. "Is it some new form of energy?"

"There are few forms of energy and this is most likely electromagnetic. There is no doubt that countless modifications of this form of energy exist. This being has a weapon that affects our nervous system. You can imagine what it would be like if those feelers were to touch the unprotected body!"

Erg Noor flinched and Nisa Greet shuddered inwardly as they noticed the line of brown lights rapidly approaching from three sides.

"There isn't just one being!" exclaimed Eon, softly. "Perhaps we ought not let them touch the hood."

"You're right. Let each of us turn his back on the light and look in one direction only. Nisa, switch on!"

On this occasion each of the observers noted some details that could be combined to give a general impression of creatures like huge flat jelly-fish, floating low over the ground with a dense fringe waving in the air below them. Some of the feelers were short when compared with the dimensions of the creature and could not have been more than a yard long. The acute-angled corners of the rhomboid body each had two feelers of much greater length. At the base of the feelers the biologist noticed huge bladders that glowed inside and seemed to be transmitting the star-like flashes along them.

"Hullo, observers, why are you switching the light on and off?" came Ingrid's clear voice in the helmet telephones. "Are you in need of help? The storm's over and we're going to begin work. We're coming to you now."

"Stay where you are," ordered the commander. "There is great danger abroad. Call everybody!"

Erg Noor told them about the terrible jelly-fish. After a consultation the explorers decided to move part of a planetary motor forward on an automatic car. An exhaust flame three hundred metres long swept across the stony plane removing everything visible and invisible from its path. Before half an hour had passed the crew had repaired the broken cable and protection was restored. They realized that the anameson fuel must be loaded before the planet's night came again; at the cost of superhuman effort it was done and the exhausted travellers retired behind the armour of their tightly sealed spaceship and listened calmly as it trembled in the storm. Microphones brought the roar and rumble of the hurricane to them but it only served to make more cosy the little world of light impregnable to the powers of darkness.

Ingrid and Louma opened the stereoscreen. The film had been well chosen. The blue waters of the Indian Ocean splashed at the feet of those sitting in the ship's library. The film showed the Neptune Games, the world-wide competition in all types of aquatic sports. In the Great Circle Era the entire world's population had grown accustomed to water in a way that had only been possible for the maritime peoples in earlier days. Swimming; diving and plunging, surf-board riding and the sailing of rafts had become universal sports. Thousands of beautiful young bodies, tanned by the sun, ringing songs, laughter, the festive music of the finals....

Nisa leaned towards the biologist, who sat beside her deep in thought, carried away in his mind to the far distant planet that was his, to that dear planet where nature had been harnessed by man.

"Did you ever take part in these competitions. Eon?" The biologist looked at her somewhat puzzled. "What? Oh, these? No, never. I was thinking and didn't understand you at first."

"Weren't you thinking about that?" asked the girl, pointing to the screen. "Don't you find your appreciation of the beauty of our world comes so much fresher to you after all this darkness, after the storms and the jellyfish?"

"Of course I do, but that only makes me all the more anxious to get hold of one of those jelly-fish. I was racking my brains over that, trying to think of a way to capture one."

Nisa Greet turned away from the smiling biologist and met Erg Noor's smile.

"Have you, too, been thinking about how to catch that black horror?" she asked, mockingly.

"No, but I was thinking of how to explore the disc-shaped spaceship," he said and the sly glint in the commander's eyes almost annoyed Nisa.

"Now I understand why it is that men engaged in wars in the old days! I used to think it was only the boastful-ness of your sex, the so-called strong sex of that unorganized society."

"You're not quite right although you are pretty near to understanding our old-time psychology. My ideas are simple-the more beautiful I find my planet, the more I get to love it, the more I want to serve it, to plant gardens, extract metals, produce power and food, create music, so that when I have passed on my way I shall leave behind me a little piece of something real made by my hands and my head. The only thing I know is the Cosmos, astronautics, and that is the only way I can serve mankind. The goal is not the flight itself but the acquisition of fresh knowledge, the discovery of new worlds which we shall, in time, turn into planets as beautiful as our Earth. And what aim have you in view, Nisa? Why are you so interested in the disc spaceship? Is it mere curiosity?"

With a great effort the girl overcame the weight of her tired arms and stretched them out to the commander. He took her little hands in his and stroked them gently. Nisa's cheeks flushed till they matched the tight auburn curls on her head, new strength flowed through her tired body. She pressed her cheek to Erg Noor's hand as she had done in the moment of the dangerous landing and she forgave the biologist his seeming treachery to Earth. To show that she was in agreement with both of them she told them of an idea that had just entered her head. They could furnish one of the water-tanks with a self-closing lid, place a piece of fresh preserved meat (a rare luxury that they sometimes enjoyed in addition to their canned food) as bait and, should the "black something" crawl inside and the lid close, they could fill the tank with inert terrestrial gas through a previously arranged tap and seal the edges of the lid.

Eon was very enthusiastic over the resourcefulness of the auburn-headed girl. He was almost the same age as Nisa and permitted himself the gentle familiarity that is born of school years spent together. By the end of the nine days of the planetary night the trap, perfected by the engineers, was ready.

Erg Noor was busy with the adjustment of a manlike robot and he also got ready a powerful hydraulic cutting tool with which he hoped to make his way into the spiral disc from some distant star.

The storm died down in the now familiar darkness, the frost gave way to warmth and the day that was nine terrestrial days long began. They had work for four terrestrial days to load the ion charges, some other supplies and valuable instruments. In addition to these things Erg Noor considered it necessary to take some of the personal belongings of the lost crew so that, after a thorough disinfection, they could be taken to Earth for the relatives of the dead people to keep in their memory. In the Great Circle Era people did not burden themselves with many possessions so that their transfer to *Tantra* offered no difficulties.

On the fifth day they switched off the current and the biologist and two volunteers, Kay Bear and Ingrid Dietra, shut themselves up in the observation turret at *Parus*. The black creatures appeared almost immediately. The biologist had adapted an infrared screen and could follow the movements of the jelly-fish. One of them soon approached the tank trap; it folded up its tentacles, rolled itself up into a ball and started creeping inside. Suddenly another black rhombus appeared at the open lid of the tank. The one that had first arrived unfolded its tentacles and star-like flashes came with such rapidity that they turned into a strip of vibrant dark-red light which the screen reproduced as flashes of green lightning. The first jelly-fish moved back and the second immediately rolled up into a ball and fell on to the bottom of the tank. The biologist held his hand out towards the switch but Kay Bear held it back. The first monster had also rolled up and followed the second, so that there were two of the terrible brutes in the tank. It was amazing that they could reduce their apparent proportions to such an extent. The biologist pressed the switch, the lid closed and immediately five or six of the black monsters fastened on to the zirconium covered tank. The biologist turned on the light and asked *Tantra* to switch on the protection of the road. The black phantoms, as usual, dissolved immediately except for the two that remained imprisoned in the hermetically sealed tank.

The biologist went out to the tank, touched the lid and got such a severe shock that he could not restrain himself and shouted out aloud. His left arm hung limp, paralysed.

Mechanic Taron put on a high-temperature protective spacesuit and was then able to fill the tank with pure terrestrial nitrogen and weld the lid down. The taps were also welded and then the tank was wrapped in a spare piece of ship's insulation and placed in the collection room.

Success had been achieved at a high price, for the biologist's arm remained paralysed despite the efforts of the physician. Eon Thai was in great pain hut he did not dream of refusing to take part in the expedition to the disc ship. Erg Noor, compelled to submit to his insatiable thirst for exploration, could not leave him on *Tantra*.

The spiral-disc, a visitor from distant worlds, turned out to be farther from *Parus* than they had expected. In the diffused light of the projectors they had not judged the size of the spaceship correctly. It was a truly gigantic structure nearly three hundred and fifty metres in diameter. They had to take the cables from *Parus* in order to Stretch their protective system as far as the disc. The mysterious spaceship hung over the travellers like a vertical wall, stretching high over their heads and disappearing in the speckled sky. Jet-black clouds massed around the upper edge of the giant disc. The hull of the vessel was covered in some green substance the colour of malachite; it was badly cracked in places and proved to be about a metre thick. Through the cracks gleamed some bright, light-blue metal that had turned to a dark blue in places where the malachite covering had been rubbed off. The side of the disc facing *Parus* was furnished with a protuberance that curved in a spiral fifteen metres in diameter and some ten metres thick. The other side of the disc, the side that was lost in the pitch darkness, was more convex, like a section of a sphere attached to a disc twenty metres thick. On that side also there was a spiral protuberance that looked like the end of the spiral pipe emerging from the ship.

The edge of the gigantic disc was sunk deep into the ground. At the foot of this metal wall the explorers saw that stones had melted and flowed away in all directions like thick pitch.

They spent many hours looking for some sort of entrance or hatch. Either it was hidden under the malachite paint or dross or the ship's hatches closed so neatly that no trace of them was left outside. They could not find any orifices for optical instruments or stopcocks for any sort of blast. The metal disc seemed to be solid. Erg Noor had foreseen such a possibility and had decided to open up the ship with an electro-hydraulic tool capable of cutting through the hardest and most viscous covering of the terrestrial spaceships. After a short discussion they all agreed that the robot should open the tip of the spiral. There should be a hollow space there, a pipe or a circular gangway leading round the ship, through which they hoped to get into the ship without the risk of running into a number of bulkheads that would bar their way.

The study of the spiral-disc would be of great interest. Inside this visitor from distant worlds there might be instruments and records, all the furniture and utensils of those who had brought the ship through such expanses that, in comparison, the journeys made by terrestrial astronauts were nothing but timid sallies into outer space.

On the far side of the disc the spiral came right down to the ground. A floodlight and high-voltage cable were taken there and the bluish light that was reflected from the disc was dispersed in a dull haze spreading across the plateau as far as some high objects of indefinite shape, probably cliffs, in which there was a gap of impenetrable blackness. Neither the pale reflected light of the hazy stars nor the floodlights gave any feeling of ground in that black gap; it was probably a steep slope leading down to the lowland plain that had been seen when *Tantra* was landing.

With a low, dull growl, the automatic car, loaded with the only universal robot on the ship, crawled towards the disc. The unusual weight did not make any difference to the robot and it moved quickly to its place beside the metal wall: it resembled a fat man on short legs, with a long body and a huge head that leaned forward menacingly.

The robot was controlled by Erg Noor; in its four front limbs it raised the heavy cutter and stood with its legs placed firmly apart ready to begin its dangerous undertaking.

"Only Kay Bear and I will direct the robot since we are wearing high-protection suits," said the commander in the intercommunication 'phone. "All those in light biological spacesuits will go farther away."

The commander hesitated. Something penetrated into his mind causing inexplicable anguish and made his knees weaken under him. The proud will of man had wilted away and given place to the dumb obedience of an animal. Sticky with perspiration from head to foot, Erg Noor, with no will of his own, strode towards the black gap in the darkness. A cry from Nisa that he heard in the telephone, brought him back to his senses. He stood still, but the power of darkness that had taken control of his psyche again drove him forward.

Following the commander, halting and obviously struggling with themselves, went Kay Bear and Eon Thai, who had been standing on the fringe of the circle of light, Away out there, in the gates of darkness, in the clouds of mist, there was a movement of weird forms beyond the comprehension of man and, therefore, the more awe-inspiring. This was not the now familiar jellyfish-like creature-in the grey half-light there moved a black cross with widely outstretched arms and a convex ellipse in the middle. Three points of the cross had lenses on them reflecting the light of the flood lamp that scarcely penetrated the misty, humid atmosphere. The base of the cross was invisible in the darkness of an unilluminated depression in the ground.

Erg Noor, who was walking faster than the others, drew near the unknown object and fell to the ground about a hundred paces away from it. Before the stupefied onlookers could realize that it was a life and death matter for their commander, the black cross had risen above the ring of cables. It bent forward like the stem of a plant and clearly intended leaning over the protective field to get Erg Noor.

Nisa, in a frenzy that lent her the strength of an athlete, ran to the robot and started turning the control levers at the back of its head. Slowly and somewhat uncertainly, the robot lifted the cutter. Then the girl, afraid that she would be unable to work the intricate machine, jumped forward and with her body covered the commander. Serpentine streams of light or lightning came from the three points of the cross. The girl fell on Erg Noor with her arms spread out on either side. Fortunately the robot had by this time turned the funnel of the cutter, with its sharp instrument inside, towards the centre of the black cross. The thing bent convulsively backwards, seemed to fall flat on the ground and then disappeared in the impenetrable darkness under the cliffs. Erg Noor and his two companions immediately recovered, lifted up the girl and retired back behind the disc. The others had by this time recovered from the shock and were wheeling out the cannon improvised from a planetary motor. With a savage ferocity such as he had never before experienced. Erg Noor directed the destructive radiation beam to the cliffs with their gate-like gap, taking special care to sweep the plain without missing a single inch. Eon Thai knelt on the ground in front of the motionless Nisa, calling her softly in the telephone and trying to get a glimpse of her face through the silicolloid helmet. The girl lay dead still with her eyes closed. No sound of breathing could be heard in the telephone nor could the biologist detect it through the spacesuit.

"The monster has killed Nisa!" cried Eon Thai bitterly, as soon as Erg

Noor approached them. It was impossible to see the commander's eyes through the narrow slit in the high-protection helmet.

"Take her to Louma on *Tantra* immediately." The metallic note resounded more strongly than ever in Erg Noor's voice. "You, too, help her find out the nature of the injury. The six of us will remain here and continue the investigation. The geologist can go back with you and collect specimens of all the rocks between here and *Tantra,* we cannot remain on this planet any longer. Any exploration here must be carried out in high-protection tanks but if we go on like this we'll only ruin the whole expedition! Take the third car and hurry!"

Erg Noor turned round and without looking back made his way to the disc spaceship. The "cannon" was pushed forward. The engineer-mechanic who stood behind it swept the plain with it every ten minutes, covering a semicircle, with the disc at its centre. The robot raised his cutter to the second outer loop of the spiral which, on the side where the edge of the disc was deeply sunk in the ground, was level with the robot's breast.

The loud roar that followed could be heard even through the high-protection space helmets. Thin cracks appeared on the section of the malachite coating that had been chosen. Pieces of that hard material flew off and struck resoundingly against the metal body of the robot. Lateral motions of the cutter removed a big slab of the outer layer revealing a bright light-blue granular surface that was pleasant to the eyes even in the glare of the floodlamp. Kay Bear marked out a square big enough to allow a man in a spacesuit to pass and set the robot to making a deep channel in the blue metal without cutting right through it. The robot cut a second line at an angle to the first and then began moving the sharp end of the cutter back and forth, increasing the pressure as it did so. When the mechanical servant cut the third side of the square the lines he had made began to move outwards.

"Look out! Get back, everybody- lie down!" howled Erg Noor in the microphone as he switched off the robot and staggered back. The thick slab of metal suddenly bent outwards like the lid of a tin can. A stream of extraordinarily bright, rainbow-coloured fire burst out of the hole, and flew off at a tangent from the spiral protuberance. This, and the fact that the blue metal melted and immediately closed the hold that had been cut, saved the unfortunate explorers. Nothing remained of the mighty robot but a mass of molten metal with two short metal legs sticking pitifully out of it. Erg Noor and Kay Bear escaped because of the special protection suits they were wearing. The explosion threw them far back from the peculiar spaceship; it hurled the others back, too, overturned the "cannon" and broke the high-voltage cables.

When the people recovered from the shock they realized that they were defenceless. Fortunately for them they were lying in the rays of the undamaged floodlight. Although nobody had been hurt Erg Noor decided that they had had enough. They abandoned unnecessary tools, cables and the floodlamp, piled on to the undamaged car and beat a hurried retreat to their spaceship.

This fortunate outcome of an incautious attempt to open an alien spaceship was by no means due to the foresight of the commander. A second attempt would have ended with some serious accident... and Nisa, the pretty astronavigator, what of her?,... Erg Noor hoped that the spacesuit would have weakened the lethal power of the black cross. After all the biologist had not been killed by contact with the black medusa. But out in the Cosmos, so far from the mighty terrestrial medical institutions, would they be able to counteract the effects of an unknown weapon?

In the air-lock Kay Bear drew near to the commander and pointed to the rear side of his left shoulder armour. Erg Noor turned towards the mirrors that were always provided in the locks for those who returned from an alien planet to examine themselves. The thin sheet of zircono-titanium of which the shoulder armour was made had been torn. A piece of sky-blue metal stuck out of the furrow it had cut in the insulation lining although it had not reached the inner layer of the suit. They had difficulty in removing the metal splinter. At the cost of great risk and, in the final analysis, by sheer chance, they had obtained a specimen of the mysterious metal of which the spiral-disc spaceship was made and which would now be taken back to Earth.

At last Erg Noor, divested of his heavy spacesuit, was able to enter his ship or rather to crawl in under the influence of the gravity of the fearful planet.

The entire expedition was relieved when he arrived. They had watched the catastrophe at the disc through their stereovisophones and had no need to ask what the result had been.

CHAPTER FOUR

THE RIVER OF TIME

Veda Kong and Darr Veter were standing on the little round flying platform as it swept slowly over the endless steppes. The thick, flowering grasses rolled in waves under the gentle breeze. In the distance they could see a herd of black and white cattle, the descendants of animals bred by crossing yaks, domestic cows and buffaloes.

This unchanging lowland with its low hills and quiet rivers in wide valleys, a part of Earth's crust once known as the Hanty-Mansy Territory, breathed the peace of great open spaces.

Darr Veter was gazing contemplatively at the land that had formerly been covered with the dismal swamps and sparse, stunted woods of Yamal. It brought to mind a picture by an old master that had impressed itself on his memory when he was still a child.

Where the river curved round a high promontory, there stood a church, timber-built and grey with time, its lonely gaze turned towards the wide fields and grasslands across the river. The tiny cross on the dome was black under masses of low, black clouds. In the little graveyard behind the church a cluster of birches and willows bowed their tousled heads to the wind. Their low-hanging boughs almost brushed the rotting crosses, thrown down by time and storm and overgrown with fresh damp grass. Across the river gigantic violet-grey masses of cloud were piling up until they became tangibly dense. The wide river gave off a cruel, steel-coloured gleam, a cold gleam that lay on everything round about. The whole countryside, far and near, was wet in the miserable autumn drizzle, so cold and uninviting in those northern latitudes. The whole palette of blue-grey-green tones used in the picture told of stretches of barren land, where it was hard for man to live, where man was cold and hungry, where he felt so strongly the loneliness that was typical of the long-forgotten days of human folly.

This picture, seen in a museum, had seemed to Darr Veter to be a window looking into the past; it was kept under a plexiglass shield, its colours ever fresh in the illumination of invisible rays.

Without a word Darr Veter looked at Veda. The young woman put her hand on the rail around the platform. With her head bent she stood there, deep in thought. watching the stems of the tall grass as they bent to the wind. Wave after wave swept slowly across the feathergrass and equally slowly the round platform floated over the steppe. Tiny hot whirlwinds rushed suddenly on the travellers, ruffled Veda's hair and dress and breathed heat mischievously into Darr Veter's eyes. The automatic stabilizer, however, worked more rapidly than thoughts and the flying platform merely heaved or swayed slightly.

Darr Veter bent over the chart frame: the strip of map was moving quickly, showing their movement-hadn't they flown too far north? They had crossed the sixtieth parallel some time before, had passed the junction of the Irtish and the Ob and were approaching the plateau known as the North Siberian Uval or Highlands.

The two travellers had become accustomed to the open country during their four months at the excavation of ancient grave mounds in the hot steppes of the Altai lowlands. It was as though the explorercs of the past had travelled hack to times when only occasional small parties of armed horsemen crossed the southern steppes....

Veda turned and pointed ahead without a word. A dark island, seemingly torn off from the earth, was floating in streams of heated air. A few minutes later the platform approached a small hill, probably the slag-heap of what had once been a mine. There was nothing left of the buildings and the pit-just that slag-heap overgrown with wild cherry. The round flying platform suddenly listed.

Darr Veter, acting like an automaton, seized Veda by the waist and jumped to the opposite, rising side of the platform. It straightened out for a fraction of a second only to crash down flat at the foot of the hill. The shock absorbers took the shock and the recoil threw Veda Kong and Darr Veter out on to the hill-side where they landed in a clump of stiff bushes. After a minute's silence the stillness of the steppe was broken by Veda's low, contralto laugh. Darr Veter tried to picture the look of astonishment on his own scratched face. The moment of surprised stupefaction passed and he joined in Veda's merriment, glad that she was unharmed and that there were no ill results from the accident.

"There's a good reason for forbidding these platforms to fly higher than eight metres," she said with a slight gasp, "now I understand."

"If anything goes wrong the machine drops down in a second and you have to rely entirely on the shock absorbers. What else can you expect, it's the price you have to pay for little weight and compactness. I'm afraid we'll have to pay a still higher price for all the safe flights we've had," said Darr Veter with an indifference that was slightly exaggerated.

"In what way:"" asked Veda, seriously. "The faultless functioning of the stabilizing instruments presupposes very intricate mechanisms. I'm afraid I should need a long time to find out how they work. We'll have to get away from here in the way the poorest of our ancestors did."

Veda, with a sly glint in her eyes, held her hand out to Darr Veter and lie lifted her out of the Lushes with an easy movement. They went down to the wrecked platform, put some healing salve on their scratches and glued up the tears in their clothes. Veda lay down in the shade of a bush and Darr Veter began to study the causes of the mishap. As lie had suspected, something had gone wrong with the stabilizer, and it, had cut out the engine. No sooner had Darr Veter opened the lid of the apparatus than he realized that there could be no question of repairing it-it would take him too long to delve into the nature of the intricate electronics before he could even start on it. With a sigh of annoyance he straightened his aching back and glanced at the bush where Veda Kong had curled herself up trustfully. The hot silent steppe, as far as the eye could see, was devoid of people. Two big birds of prey circled over the waving blue mirage of the grass.

The obedient machine had become nothing more than a dead disc that lay helpless on the dry earth. Darr Veter experienced a strange feeling of loneliness, of being cut off from the whole world, something that came from inside him where it had existed apart from his mind in the dull memory of his body's cells.

Al the same time lie was not afraid of anything. Let night come, the naked eye would see over greater distances and they would certainly see a light somewhere that they could make for. They had been flying without luggage and had not even taken a radiotelephone, torches or food with them.

"There was a time when we could have died in the steppes if we had not had a sufficient supply of food with us … and water!" thought Veter, shielding his eyes from the bright sunlight. He noted a patch of shade under a cherry bush near Veda and stretched himself, carefree, on the ground, the dry grass stalks pricking his body through his light clothing. The soft rustling of the wind and the heat brought forgetfulness, thoughts flowed drowsily, and pictures of long-forgotten days passed slowly, one after another, through his memory, a long procession of ancient peoples, tribes and individuals…. It was as though a gigantic river of time were flowing out of the past, with the events, people and clothes changing every second.

"Veter!" Through his sleepiness he heard the voice of his beloved calling him; awakening he sat up. The red ball of the sun was already touching the darkening horizon and not the slightest breath of wind was to be felt in the still air.

"My Lord Veter," said Veda playfully bowing before him in imitation of the women of ancient Asia, "would you deem it unworthy to awaken and remember my existence?"

Darr Veter did a few physical jerks to drive away sleep. Veda agreed with his plan to await darkness. Nightfall found them engaged in a lively discussion of their past work. Suddenly Darr Veter noticed that Veda was shivering. Her hands were cold and he realized that her light clothing was not much protection against the cold nights of those high latitudes.

The summer night on the sixtieth parallel was quite light and they were able to gather a fairly large pile of twigs.

An electric spark discharged by the machine's big accumulator gave Darr Veter fire and the bright flames of burning brushwood soon made the surrounding darkness blacker as it showered its life-giving warmth on the travellers.

Shivering Veda soon opened out again like a flower in the sunlight and the two of them fell into a sort of almost hypnotic reverie. Somewhere deep down in man's spirit, left over from that hundred thousand years during which fire had been his chief asylum and his salvation, there remained an eradicable sense of comfort and calm that came over man sitting by a fire surrounded by cold and darkness.

"What's worrying you, Veda?" said Darr Veter, disturbing the silence; there were signs of sorrow in the lines of his companion's mouth.

"I was thinking of that woman, the one in the kerchief ..." answered Veda, quietly, her eyes fixed on the burning embers that were collapsing in a shower of gold.

Darr Veter understood her immediately. The day before their trip on the flying platform they had completed the opening of a big Scythian *hiirgan* or grave mound. Inside the well-preserved log vault lay the skeleton of an old man, a chieftain; the vault was surrounded by the bones of horses and slaves lying round the fringe of the mound. The old chieftain lay with his sword, shield and armour beside him, and at his feet was the skeleton of a quite young woman in a crouching position. Over the skull lay a silk kerchief that had at some time been tightly wound about her face. Despite all their efforts they had not managed to preserve the kerchief although, before it had fallen to dust, they had succeeded in copying the outlines of the beautiful face impressed on it thousands of years before. The kerchief preserved another awful detail-the imprint of eyes starting out of their sockets; the young woman had undoubtedly been strangled and then thrown into her husband's tomb to accompany him on his journey into the unknown world beyond the grave. She could not have been more than nineteen, her husband no less than seventy, a ripe old age for those days.

Darr Veter recalled the heated discussion that had taken place between the younger members of Veda's expedition. Had the woman married him willingly or had she been forced to it? Why? For the sake of what? If she married him for a great and devoted love, why had she been killed instead of being treasured as the best memorial to him in the world he was leaving?

Then Veda Kong spoke. For a long time she had been looking at the grave mound, tier eyes shining, trying to penetrate mentally into the depths of the past.

"Try to understand those people. The great expanse of the steppe was to them really boundless, with horses, camels and oxen as the only means of transport at their disposal. These great spaces were inhabited by little groups of nomad herdsmen that not only had nothing to unite them but who were on the contrary, living in constant enmity with one another. Insults and animosity accumulated from generation to generation, every stranger was an enemy, every other tribe was legitimate prey that promised herds and slaves, that is, people who were forced to work under the whip, like cattle.... Such a system of society brought about, on the one liand, greater liberty for the individual in his petty passions and desires than we know and, dialectically, on the other, excessive limitation in relations between people, a terrible narrow-mindedness. If a nation or tribe consisted of a small number of people capable of feeding themselves by hunting and the gathering of fruits, even as free nomads they lived in constant fear of enslavement or anniliilation by their militant neighbours. In cases when the country was isolated and had a big population capable of setting up a powerful military force the people paid for their safety from warlike raids by the loss of their liberty, since despotism and tyranny always developed in such powerful states. This was the case with ancient Egypt, Assyria and Babylon.

"Women, especially if they were beautiful, were the prey and the playthings of the strong. They could not exist without the protection of a man and were completely in his power. If the man who owned them died, nothing was left to them but an unknown and ruthless life at the cruel and greedy hands of another man. Her own will and endeavours meant so little for a woman ... so terribly little, that when she was faced with such a life ... who knows, perhaps death may have seemed the easier way." Veda's ideas created a great impression on the young people. The finds in the Scythian grave mound were some-tiling that Darr Veter, too, would never forget. As though reading his thoughts Veda moved closer and slowly stirred the burning twigs, following with her eyes the blue tongues of flame that ran across the coals.

"What a tremendous amount of courage and fortitude was needed to he oneself in those days, not to become degraded but to make one's way in life," Veda Kong said softly.

"It seems to me that we exaggerate the difficulties of life in ancient days," said Darr Veter. "Quite apart from the fact that people were used to it, the chaotic nature of society was the cause of a variety of incidental happenings. Man's strength and will-power struck flashes of romantic joy out of that life in the same way as steel strikes sparks from grey stone. I shudder more at the last stages of development of capitalist society, towards the end of the Era of Disunity, when the people, shut up in towns, cut off from nature, exhausted by monotonous labour, grew weaker and more indifferent as they succumbed to widespread diseases."

"I am also at a loss to understand why it took our ancestors so long to understand the simple fact that the fate of society depended on them alone, that a community is what the moral and ideological development of all its members makes it, that it depends wholly on the economy "

"The perfect form of scientifically organized society is not merely a quantitative accumulation of productive forces but a qualitative stage in development. It's all really very simple," answered

Darr Veter. "Furthermore, there is the understanding of dialectical interdependence, that new social relations are as improbable without new people as are the new people without the new economy. When this was realized it led to the greatest attention being paid to education, to the physical and mental development of man. When was this finally realized?"

"In the Era of Disunity, at the end of the Fission Age, soon after the Second Great Revolution."

"It's a good thing it didn't come later! The destructive means of war "

Darr Veter stopped suddenly and turned towards the open space between the fire and the hill. The thunder of heavy hoofs and panting breath came from somewhere nearby, making the two travellers jump to their feet.

A gigantic black bull appeared before the fire. The flames were reflected in blood-red lights in his wicked rolling eyes. He was snorting and pawing up the dry ground, obviously contemplating an attack. In the feeble light he seemed of gigantic size, his lowered head was like a granite boulder, his mighty withers rose behind it like a mountain of solid muscle. Never before had either Veda Kong or Darr Veter been close to an animal that possessed malicious, death-dealing strength and whose unthinking brain was deaf to the voice of reason.

Veda pressed her hands tightly to her bosom and stood stock still, as though hypnotized by the vision that appeared suddenly out of the darkness. Darr Veter, obeying some powerful instinct, stood in front of the bull to protect Veda as his ancestors had done thousands and thousands of times before him. The hands of the man of the New Era, however, were empty.

"Veda, jump to the right," lie just managed to say as the bull plunged at them. In their rapidity of action the well-trained bodies of the two travellers were equal to the primeval agility of the bull. The giant flashed past them and crashed into the thicket of bushes and Veda and Darr found themselves in darkness a few paces from the platform. Away from the fire the night did not seem so dark and Veda's dress could no doubt be seen from some distance. The bull extracted itself from the wild cherry bushes and Darr Veter heaved his companion towards the machine: with well-performed vault she landed on the little platform. While the animal was turning, tearing up the ground with its lioofs, Darr Veter got on to the platform beside Veda. They exchanged hurried glances and in the eyes of his companion Darr saw nothing but frank admiration. He had removed the cover from the motor during the day when he had tried to find out how it worked. Mustering every ounce of strength, he tore the cable of the balancing field from the rail of the platform, put one end under the spring of the accumulator terminal and pushed Veda protectively to one side. In the meantime the bull had its horn under the rail and the machine was swaying dangerously. With a happy grin Darr Veter pushed the end of the cable into the animal's muzzle. There was a flash of lightning, a dull thud, and the savage beast collapsed in a heap.

"Oh! You've killed it!" exclaimed Veda disapprovingly. "I don't think so, the ground's dry!" exclaimed the ingenious hero with a smirk of satisfaction. As though in confirmation of his words the bull grunted feebly, got to its feet and, without looking round, staggered off at a trot from the scene of its disgrace. The travellers returned to their fire and another armful of twigs gave new life to the dying embers.

"I don't feel the cold any more," said Veda, "let's climb the hill."

The top of the hill hid the light of the fire from them and the pale stars of the northern summer formed balls of *mist* on the horizon.

There was nothing to be seen in the west; in the north, rows of lights, faintly discernible, flickered on the slopes of some hills; in the south burned the bright star of a herdsmen's watch tower, also a long way off.

"Too bad, we'll have to walk all night," muttered Darr Veter.

"No, look over there!" Veda pointed to the east where four lights placed in the form of a square, had flashed on suddenly. They were only a couple of miles away. Taking note of the direction by the stars they returned to the fire. Veda Kong stopped for a while before the dying embers as though trying to remember something.

"Farewell to our home," she said contemplatively. "The nomads probably had such homes as this all the time, uncertain and short-lived. Today I have become a woman of that epoch."

She turned to Darr Veter and put her arm trustingly round his neck.

"I felt the need for protection so strongly! I was not afraid, it wasn't that. but there was some sort of tempting submission to fate … or so it seems."

Veda placed her hands behind her head and stretched herself gracefully before the fire. A second later her dimming eyes had again acquired their roguish sparkle.

"All right, lead the way … hero!" and the tone of her deep voice became gentle and filled with unfathomable mystery.

The bright night was full of the perfumes of grasses, the rustling of small animals and the cries of night birds. Veda and Darr walked cautiously, afraid of falling into some unseen hole or crack in the dry earth. The brush-headed grass stalks stealthily grazed their ankles. Darr Veter looked around vigilantly whenever they came in sight of dark clusters of bushes. Veda laughed softly.

"Perhaps we should have taken the accumulator and I cable with us?"

"You're thoughtless, Veda," said Darr Veter good-, humouredly, "more so than I thought!"

The young woman suddenly became serious. " I felt your protection too strongly "

And Veda began to speak, or rather, to think aloud, about further plans for the work of her expedition. The first stage of the work at the grave mounds in the steppes was finished ^ and her workers had returned to their old employments or were seeking something new. Darr Veter, however, had not chosen another job and was free to follow the woman ' he loved. Judging by reports that reached them Mven Mass' work was going well. Even if he had done badly the Council would not have appointed Darr Veter again so soon. In the Great Circle Era it was not thought advisable to keep people too long at any one job. The most valuable possession of man, his creative inspiration, grew weaker and he could only return to an old job after a long break.

"Doesn't our work seem petty and monotonous to you after six years communion with the Cosmos?"

Veda's clear and attentive glance was fixed on him. "This isn't petty or monotonous work," he objected, "but it certainly doesn't provide me with that tension to which I am accustomed. I need the strain, otherwise I'll become too calm and good-natured, as though I were being treated with blue sleep!"

"Blue sleep ..." began Veda and the catch in her breath told Darr Veter more than the burning cheeks that he could not see in the dark.

"I'm going to continue my exploration farther to the south," she said, interrupting herself, "but not until I have gathered a new group of volunteer diggers. Until then I am going to take part in the maritime excavations, I have been asked to help there."

Darr Veter understood her and his heart beat faster with joy. A second later, however, he had hidden his feelings in a distant corner of his heart and hurried to Veda's help.

"Do you mean the excavation of the submarine city to the south of Sicily?" he asked. "I saw some wonderful things from there in the Atlantis Palace."

"No, not there, we're working on the coasts of the Eastern Mediterranean, the Red Sea and India now. We are looking for cultural treasures under the water, beginning from the Creto-Indian period and ending with the Dark Ages."

"You mean what was hidden or, more often, simply thrown into the sea when the islands of civilization were destroyed under the impact of new forces, fresh, barbaric, ignorant and reckless-that is something I can understand," said Darr Veter thoughtfully, his eyes carefully Studying the whitish plain. "I can also understand the great destruction of ancient civilizations, when the states of antiquity, strong in their bonds with nature, were unable to make changes in their world, to cope with the growing horror of slavery and the parasitic upper strata of society."

"And people exchanged the primitive materialism that had led them into a blind alley for the religious darkness of the Middle Ages," added Veda, "but what is there that you cannot understand?"

"It's just that I have a very poor idea of the Creto-Indian civilization."

"You don't know the latest researches. Traces of that civilization are now being found over a huge area from Africa, through Crete, the southern part of Central Asia, Northern India to Western China."

"I did not suspect that in those ancient days there could have been secret treasure-houses for works of art like tliose of Carthage, Greece and Rome."

"Come with me and you'll sec," said Veda, softly. Darr Veter walked beside her in silence. They were ascending a long, gentle slope and had reached the ridge when Darr Veter suddenly stopped.

"Thanks for your offer, I'll come."

Veda turned her head towards him somewhat mistrustfully but in the half-light of the northern night her companion's eyes were dark and impenetrable.

Once past the ridge the lights turned out to be quite close. Lamps in polarizing hoods did not disperse the light rays and that made them seem farther away than they really were. Such concentrated light was a sign of night work and this was confirmed by a low roar that increased in volume as they neared it. Huge latticed trusses shone like silver under blue lamps high up in the air; a warning howl of sirens brought them to a standstill as the protective robots began working.

"Danger, keep to the left, don't approach the line of posts!" shouted the loudspeaker of an invisible amplifier. They turned obediently towards a group of white portable houses.

"Don't look in the direction of the field!" the robot continued warning them.

The doors of two houses opened simultaneously and two beams of light crossed on the dark road. A group of men and women gave the travellers a hearty welcome but were surprised at the imperfect means of transport that had brought them there, especially at night.

The cupboard-like cabin of the shower-bath with its streams of aromatic water saturated with gas and electricity, with the merry play of tiny electric charges on the skin, was a place that gave gentle pleasure. Refreshed, the travellers met at table. "Veter, my dear, we've come across some of our colleagues!" exclaimed Veda, freshly bathed and extremely young, as she poured out a golden liquid.

"The ten tonics, right now!" he exclaimed, reaching for his glass.

"Bullfighter, you're growing savage in the steppes," protested Veda. "I'm telling you interesting news and you only think of eating!"

"Are there excavations here?" said Darr Veter, doubtingly.

"There are, only they're palaeontological, not archaeological. They're studying the fossilized animals of the Permian period, two hundred million years old. That puts us in the shade with our petty thousands."

"Are they studying them in the ground, without digging them up? How's that?"

"Yes, in the ground, although as yet I don't know how."

One of those sitting at the table, a thin, yellow-faced man, joined in the conversation.

"Our group is now relieving another. We have just finished preparations and are about to start work on depth photography."

"Hard irradiation," hazarded Darr Veter.

"If you are not too tired I would advise you to watch it. Tomorrow we shall be moving the whole apparatus to another site and that will not be interesting."

Veda and Darr gladly consented. Their hospitable hosts rose from the table and led them into a neighbouring house, where protective clothing hung in niches with a clock-face indicator over each of them.

"There is very great ionization from our powerful electron tubes," said a tall, slightly round-shouldered woman with a faint suggestion of apology as she helped Veda into a suit of closely-woven fabric and a transparent helmet, and fastened a container with batteries on her back. In the polarized light every hillock in the steppes stood out with unnatural clarity. A dull groan came from a square space marked off by thin rails. The earth heaved, cracked and opened up in a crater in the centre of which appeared a sharp-nosed silver cylinder. Its polished walls were encircled by a spiral ridge and the sharp end was fitted with an intricate electric milling head of blue metal rotating as the machine appeared. The cylinder rolled over the edge of the crater, turned over, showed blades that moved quickly at the rear end and began digging in again a few metres away from the crater, diving almost vertically with its polished nose into the ground. Darr Veter noticed a double cable that the cylinder pulled behind it,

one of the cables was insulated, the other made of some highly-polished metal. Veda jerked his sleeve and pointed in front of them, beyond the fence of magnesium rails. A second cylinder, similar to the first, had come out of the earth and with just the same movements had rolled over to the left and disappeared as though it had dived into water.

The yellow-faced man made a sign to his visitors to hurry.

"I remember now who lie is," whispered Veda, *as* they hastened to overtake the group ahead of them, "he is Liao Lang, the palaeontologist who discovered the secret of the settlement of the Asian continent in the Palaeozoic."

"Is he of Chinese origin?'" asked Darr Veter, recalling the sombre glance of the scientist's slightly slant eyes. "I'm ashamed to admit it, hut I don't know anything about his work."

"I see you don't know much about our terrestrial palaeontology," Veda remarked, "you probably know more about that of other stellar worlds."

Before Darr's mind's eye there passed the countless forms of life, millions of strange skeletons in the rocks of various planets- monuments to the past hidden in the different strata of all inhabited worlds. This was nature's memory, recorded by her until such times as a reasoning being appeared, a being not only capable of remembering but also of restoring that which had been forgotten.

They went on to a small platform fixed to the end of a half-arch of lattice-work. In the centre of the floor there was a big, unlighted screen with low benches around it on which the visitors sat and waited.

"The 'moles' will finish soon," said Liao Lang. "As you have probably guessed they are carrying the hare wire through the rocks and weaving a metallic net. The skeletons of extinct animals lie in friable sandstone at a depth of fourteen metres below the surface. Lower, at seventeen metres, the whole field is covered by the metallic net which is connected to powerful inductors. A field of reflection is thus created which throws X-rays on to the. screen giving us the image of the fossilized bones."

Two big metal globes turned on massive pedestals. Floodlights were switched on and the howl of sirens warned everybody of danger. Direct current at a tension of a million volts filled the air with the fresh smell of ozone and made the terminals and insulators glow blue in the dark.

Liao Lang was turning switches and pressing buttons on the control panel with feigned carelessness. The big screen grew brighter and brighter, in its depths some faint, blurred outlines appeared here and there in the field of vision. All movement on the screen then ceased, the fluid outlines of a big patch became clear-cut and filled almost the whole screen.

After a few more manipulations on the control panel the onlookers saw before them the skeleton of an unknown animal showing through a hazy glow. The wide paws with their long claws were bent under the body, the long tail was curled in a loop. An outstanding feature of the skeleton was the unusual thickness of the huge bones with curved ends and ridges to which the animal's mighty muscles had been attached. The skull with jaws clamped tight was grinning with its front teeth. It was seen from above and looked like a bone slab with a rough, broken surface. Liao Lang changed the depth of focus and the degree of enlargement until the whole screen was filled with the head of the ancient reptile that had lived two hundred million years before on the banks of a river that had once flowed there.

The top of the skull consisted of extraordinarily thick- no less than twenty centimetres-plates of bone. There were bony ridges over the eye-sockets and there were similar excrescences over the temporal hollows and on the convex bones of the skull. From the back part of the skull there rose a big cone with the opening of a tremendous parietal eye. Liao Lang gave a loud gasp of admiration.

Darr Veter could not take his eyes off the clumsy, heavy skeleton of the ancient beast that had been compelled to live *as* a prisoner of unresolved contradictions. Increases in muscular power had led to thicker bones that were put to great strain and the heavier weight of the bigger bones again required a strengthening of the muscles.

This direct dependence led the evolution of archaic organisms into a complete deadlock until some important physiological mutation resolved the old contradictions and brought about a new evolutionary stage. It seemed unbelievable that such creatures were amongst the ancestors of man with his beautiful body capable of great activity and precise movements.

Darr Veter looked at the excrescences over the brows of the Permian reptile that betrayed its stupid ferocity and compared it with lithe, supple Veda with such bright eyes in her intelligent, lively face. What a tremendous difference in the organization of living matter! Involuntarily he squinted sideways, trying to get a glimpse of Veda's features through her helmet and when his eyes returned to the screen there was something else there. This was the wide, flat, parabolic head of an amphibian, the ancient salamander, doomed to lie in the warm, dark waters of a Permian swamp, waiting until something eatable came within its reach. Then, one swift leap, one snap of the jaws and again the same eternal, patient and senseless lying in wait. Darr Veter felt annoyed and oppressed by pictures of the endlessly long and cruel evolution of life. He straightened up and Liao Lang, guessing his mood, suggested that they return home to rest. It was hard for Veda, with her insatiable curiosity, to tear herself away from her observations until she saw that the scientists were hurrying to switch on the machines to take electron photographs so as not to waste power.

Veda was soon ensconced on a wide divan in the drawing-room of the women's hostel but Darr Veter remained for some little time walking up and down the smooth terrace in front of the houses, mentally reviewing his impressions.

The dew of the northern morning washed the previous day's dust off the grass. The imperturbable Liao Lang returned from his night's work and proposed sending his guests to the nearest aerodrome on an Elf, a small accumulator-driven car. There was a base for jumping jet aircraft a hundred kilometres to the south-east, on the lower reaches of the River Trom-Yugan. Veda wanted to get in touch with her expedition but there was no radio transmitter of sufficient power at the dig. Since our ancestors discovered the harmful influence of radioactivity and introduced strict regulation into the use of radio, directed radio communication has required much more complicated apparatus, especially for long-distance conversations. In addition to that the number of stations has been greatly reduced. Liao Lang decided to get in touch with the nearest herdsmen's watch tower. These watch towers had radio intercommunication and could also communicate directly with the centre of their district. A young girl student who proposed driving the Elf in order to bring it back, suggested calling in at a watch tower on the way so that the visitors could use the televisophone for their conversation. Darr Veter and Veda were glad of the opportunity. A strong wind blew the occasional wisps of dust away from them and ruffled the abundant, short-cropped hair of their driver. There was scarcely room for the three of them in the narrow car, Darr Veter's huge body made it a tight fit for the two women. The slim silhouette of the watch tower was visible in the distance against the clear blue of the sky. Very soon the Elf came to a standstill at the foot of the tower. A plastic roof was built between the straddling legs of the structure where another Elf was garaged. The guide bars of a tiny lift led up through this roof and took them one by one past the living quarters to the platform at the top of the tower where they were met by an almost naked young man. The sudden confusion displayed by their hitherto self-reliant driver gave Veda to understand that the reason for her having been so accommodating was a deep-rooted one.

The circular room with crystal walls swayed noticeably and the metal structure of the tower thrummed monotonously like a taut violin string. The floor and ceiling o? the room were painted in dark colours. On the narrow curved tables under the windows there were binoculars, calculating machines and notebooks. The tower, from its height of ninety metres, had a full view of the surrounding steppe as far as the limits of visibility of neighbouring towers. The staff maintained constant watch over the herds and kept records of fodder supplies. The milking labyrinths, through which the herds of milk cows were driven twice a day, lay in the steppe in green concentric rings. The milk which, like that of the African antelope, did not turn sour, was poured into containers and frozen on the spot after which it could be kept for a long time in the underground refrigerators. The herds were driven from one pasture to another with the aid of the Elfs kept at each of the watch towers. The observers were mostly young people who had not completed their education and they had plenty of time to study during their tour of duty. The young man led Veda and Darr Veter down a spiral staircase to living quarters suspended between the supports of the tower a few yards below the platform. The rooms were equipped with sound insulation and the travellers found themselves in absolute silence. Only the constant swaying of the room served to remind them that they were at a height that could be dangerous in the event of the slightest carelessness.

Another youth was working at the radio. The exotic hair-do and brightly coloured dress of the girl in the televisophone screen showed that he was talking to the central station; women working in the steppes wore short overall suits. The girl on the screen connected them with the zonal station and soon the sad face and tiny figure of Miyiko Eigoro, Veda's chief assistant, appeared on the screen. There was pleasurable astonishment in her slightly slant eyes, like those of Liao Lang, and her tiny mouth opened at the suddenness of it all. A second later, however, Veda Kong and Darr Veter were confronted with a passionless face that expressed nothing except businesslike attention. Darr Veter went back upstairs and found the girl student of palaeontology engaged in a lively conversation with the first youth; Veter went outside on to the verandah surrounding the circular room. The damp of early morning had long since given way to a noonday heat that robbed the colours of their freshness and levelled out irregularities in the ground. The steppe spread far and wide, under a burning clear sky. Veter again recalled his vague longing for the northern land of his ancestors. Leaning on the rail of the swaying platform he could feel how the dreams of ancient peoples were coining true, and feel it with greater strength than ever before. Stern nature had been driven to the far north by the conquering hand of man and the vitalizing warmth of the south had been poured over these great plains that had formerly lain frozen under a cold, cloudy sky.

Veda Kong entered the round room and announced that the radio operator had agreed to take them farther on their journey. The girl with the cropped hair thanked the historian with a long glance. Through the transparent wall they could see the broad back of Darr Veter, as he stood there lost in contemplation.

"Perhaps you were thinking of me?" he heard a voice say behind his back.

"No, Veda, I was thinking of one of the postulates of ancient Indian philosophy. It was to the effect that the world is not made for man and that man himself becomes great only when he understands the value and beauty of another life, the life of nature."

"That idea seems incomplete and I don't understand it.'" "I suppose I didn't finish it. I should have added that man alone can understand not only the beauty but also the dark and difficult sides of life. Only man possesses the ability to dream and the strength to make life better!"

"Now I understand,'" said Veda, softly, and after a long pause added, "You've changed. Veter."

"Of course, I've changed. Four months of digging with a simple spade amongst the stones and rotting logs of your *kurgans is* enough to change anybody. Like it or not, you begin to look at life more simply and its simple joys become dearer to you."

"'Don't make a joke of it, Veter, I'm talking seriously," said Veda with a frown. "When I first knew you, you had command over all the power of Earth, and used to speak to distant worlds; in your observatories in those days, you might well have been the supernatural being whom the ancients called God. And here, at our simple work, where you are the equal of everybody else, you have …". Veda stopped.

"What have I done?" he insisted, his curiosity aroused. "Have I lost my majesty? What would you have said if you'd seen me before I joined the Institute of Astrophysics? When I was an engine driver on the Spiral Way? That is still less majestic. Or a mechanic on the fruit-gathering machines in the tropics?" Veda laughed loudly.

"I'll disclose to you a secret of my youth. When I was in the Third Cycle School I fell in love with an engine driver on the Spiral Way and at that time I could not imagine anybody with greater power … but here comes the radio operator. Come along, Veter."

Before the pilot would allow Veda Kong and Darr Veter to enter the cabin of the jumping jet aircraft he asked for a second time whether the health of the passengers could stand the great acceleration of the machine. He stuck strictly to the rules. When he was assured that it would be safe he seated them in deep chairs in the transparent nose of an aircraft shaped like a huge raindrop. Veda felt very uncomfortable, the seat sloped a long way back because the nose of the aircraft was raised high above the ground. The signal gong sounded, a powerful ' catapult hurled the plane almost vertically into the air ; and Veda sank slowly into her chair as she would in some viscous liquid. Darr Veter, with an effort, turned his head to give Veda a smile of encouragement. The pilot switched on the engine. There was a roar, a feeling of great weight in the entire body and the pear-shaped aircraft was on its course, describing an arc at an altitude of twenty-three thousand metres. It seemed that only a few minutes had passed when the travellers, their knees trembling under them, got out of the plane in front of their houses in the Altai Steppes and the pilot was waving to them to get out of the way. Darr Veter realized that the engines would have to be started on the ground as there was no catapult there to propel the machine. He ran as fast as he could, pulling Veda after him. Miyiko Eigoro, running easily, came to meet them and the two women embraced as though they had been parted for a long time.

CHAPTER FIVE

THE HORSE ON THE SEA BED

The warm, transparent sea lay tranquil with scarcely a movement of its amazingly bright green-blue waves. Darr Veter went in slowly until the water reached his neck and spread his arms widely in an effort to keep his footing on the sloping sea bed. As he looked over the barely perceptible ripples towards the dazzling distant expanses he again felt that he was dissolving in the sea, that he was becoming part of that boundless element. He had brought his long suppressed sorrow with him, to the sea-the sorrow of his parting from the entrancing majesty of the Cosmos, from the boundless ocean of knowledge and thought, from the terrific concentration of every day of his life as Director of the Outer Stations. His existence had become quite different. His growing love for Veda Kong relieved days of unaccustomed labour and the sorrowful liberty of thought experienced by his superbly trained brain. He had plunged into historical investigations with the enthusiasm of a disciple. The river of time, reflected in his thoughts, helped him withstand the change in his life. He was grateful to Veda Kong for having, with the sympathy and understanding so typical of her, arranged the flying platform trips to parts of the world that had been transformed by man's efforts. His own losses seemed petty when confronted with the magnificence of man's labour on

Earth and the greatness of the sea. Darr Veter had become reconciled to the irreparable, something that is always most difficult for a man.

A soft, almost childish voice called to him. He recognized Miyiko, waved his arms, lay on his back and waited for the girl. She rushed into the sea, big drops of water fell from her stiff, black hair and her yellowish body took on a greenish tinge under a thin coating of water. They swam side by side towards the sun, to an isolated desert island that formed a black mound about a thousand yards from the shore. In the Great Circle Era all children were brought up beside the sea and were good swimmers and Darr Veter, furthermore, possessed natural abilities. At first he swam slowly, afraid that Miyiko would grow tired, but the girl slipped along beside him easily and untroubled. Darr Veter increased his speed, surprised at her skill. Even when he exerted himself to the full she did not drop behind and her pretty immobile face remained as calm as ever. They could soon hear the dull splash of water on the seaward side of the islet. Darr Veter turned on to his back, the girl swam past him, described a circle and returned to him.

"Miyiko, you're a marvellous swimmer!" he exclaimed in admiration; he filled his lungs with air and checked his breathing.

"My swimming isn't as good as my diving," the girl replied, and Darr Veter was again astonished.

"I am Japanese by descent," she explained. "Long ago there was a whole tribe of our people all of whose women were divers; they dived for pearls and gathered edible seaweed. This trade was passed on from generation to generation and in the course of thousands of years it developed into a wonderful art. Quite by accident it is manifested in me today, when there is no longer a separate Japanese people, language or country."

"I never suspected "

"That a distant descendant of women divers would become an historian? In our tribe we had a legend. There was once a Japanese artist by the name of Yanagihara Eigoro."

"Eigoro? Isn't that your name?"

"Yes, it is rare in our days, when people are named any combination of sounds that pleases the ear. Of course, everybody tries to find combinations from the languages of their ancestors. If I'm not mistaken your name consists of roots from the Russian language, doesn't it?"

"They aren't roots but whole words, Darr meaning 'gift' and Veter meaning 'wind.'"

"I don't know what my name means. But there really ' was an artist of that name. One of my ancestors found a picture of his in some repository. It is a big canvas, you can take a look at it in my house, it will be interesting for an historian. A stern and courageous life is depicted with extreme vividness, all the poverty and unpretentiousness of a nation in the clutches of a cruel regime!

Shall we swim farther?"

"Wait a minute, Miyiko. What about the women divers?"

"The artist fell in love with a diver and settled amongst that tribe for the rest of his life. His daughters, too, became divers who spent their lives at their trade in the sea. Look at that peculiar islet over there, it's like a round tank, or a low tower, like those they make sugar in."

"Sugar!" snorted Darr Veter, involuntarily. "When I was a boy these desert islands fascinated me. They stand alone, surrounded by the sea, their dark cliffs or clumps of trees hide mysterious secrets, you could meet with everything imaginable on them, anything you dreamed of."

Miyiko's jolly laugh was his reward. The girl, usually so reticent and always a little sad, had now changed beyond recognition. She sped on merrily and bravely towards the heavily breaking waves and was still a mystery to Veter, a closed door, so different from lucid Veda whose fearlessness was more magnificent trustfulness than real persistence.

Between the big offshore rocks the sea formed deep galleries into which the sun penetrated to the very bottom. These galleries, on whose bed lay dark mounds of sponges and whose walls were festooned with seaweed, led to the dark, unfathomed depths on the eastern side of the island. Veter was sorry that he had not taken an accurate chart of the coastline from Veda. The rafts of the maritime expedition gleamed in the sun at their moorings on the western spit several miles from their island. Opposite them was an excellent beach and Veda was there now with all her party; accumulators were being changed in the machines and the expedition had a day-off. Veter had succumbed to the childish pleasure of exploring uninhabited islands.

A grim andesite cliff hung over the swimmers; there were fresh fractures where a recent earthquake had brought down the more eroded part of the coast. There was a very steep slope on the side of the open sea. Miyiko and Veter swam for a long time in the dark water along the eastern side of the island before they found a flat stone ledge on to which Veter hoisted Miyiko who then pulled him up.

The startled sea birds darted back and forth and the crash of the waves, transmitted by the rocks, made the andesite mass tremble. There was nothing on the islet but bare stone and a few tough bushes, not a sign anywhere of man or beast.

The swimmers made their way to the top of the islet, looked at the waves breaking below and returned to the coast. A bitter aroma came from the bushes growing in the crevices. Darr Veter stretched himself out on a warm stone, and gazed lazily into the water on the southern side of the ledge.

Miyiko was squatting at the very edge of the cliff trying to get a better view of something far down below. At this point there were no coastal shallows or piled-up rocks. The steep cliff hung over dark, oily water. The sunshine produced a glittering band along the edge of the cliff, and down below, where the cliff diverted the sunlight vertically into the water, the level sea bed of light-coloured sand was just visible.

"What can you see there, Miyiko?" The girl was deep in thought and did not turn round immediately.

"Nothing much. You're attracted to desert islands and I to the sea bed. It seems to me that you can always find something interesting on the sea bed, make discoveries."

"Then why are you working in the steppes?"

"There's a reason for it. The sea gives me so much pleasure that I cannot stay with it all the time. You cannot always be listening to your favourite music and it is the same with me and the sea. Being away for a time makes every meeting with the sea more precious."

Darr Veter nodded his agreement.

"Shall we dive down there?" he asked, pointing to a gleam of white in the depths. In her astonishment Miyiko raised brows that already had a natural slant.

"D'you think you can? It must be about twenty-five metres deep there, it takes an experienced diver."

"I'll try. And you?"

Instead of answering him Miyiko got up, looked round until she found a suitable big stone which she took to the edge of the cliff.

"Let me try first. I'll go down with a stone although it's against my rules, but the floor is very clean, I'm afraid there may be a current lower down,"

The girl raised her arms, bent forward, straightened up and then bent backwards. Darr Veter watched her at her breathing exercises, trying to memorize them. Miyiko did not say another word but, after a few more exercises, seized hold of the stone and dived into the dark water.

Darr Veter felt a vague anxiety when more than a minute passed and the bold girl did not reappear. He, too, began looking for a stone, assuming that he would need one much bigger. He had just taken hold of an eighty-pound lump of andesite when Miyiko came to the surface. The girl was breathing heavily and seemed fatigued. "There," she gasped, "there's a horse." "What? What horse?"

"A huge statue of a horse, down there, in a natural niche. I'm going back to take a proper look."

"Miyiko, it's too difficult for you. Let's swim bade to the beach and get diving gear and a boat."

"Oh, no. I want to look at it myself, now! Then it will be my own achievement, not something done by a machine. We'll call the others afterwards."

"All right, I'm coining with you!" Darr Veter seized his big stone and the girl laughed.

"Take a smaller one, that one will do. And what about your breathing?"

Darr Veter obediently performed the necessary exercises and then dived into the water with the stone in his hands. The water struck him in the face and turned him with his back to Miyiko; something was squeezing his chest and there was a dull pain in his ears. He clenched his teeth, strained every muscle in his body to fight against pain. The pleasant light of day was rapidly lost as he entered the cold grey gloom of the depths. The cold, hostile power of the deep water momentarily overpowered him, his head was in a whirl, there was a stinging pain in his eyes. Suddenly Miyiko's firm hand seized him by the shoulder and his feet touched the firm, dully silver sand. With difficulty he turned his head in the direction she indicated; he staggered, dropped the stone in his surprise and shot immediately upwards. He did not remember how he got to the surface, he could see nothing but a red mist and his breathing was spasmodic. In a short time the effects of the high pressure wore off and that which he had seen was reborn in his memory. He had seen the picture for an instant only but his eye had seen and his brain recorded many details.

The dark cliffs formed a lofty lancet arch under which stood the gigantic statue of a horse. Neither seaweed nor barnacles marred the polished surface of the carving.

The unknown sculptor had endeavoured mainly to depict strength. The fore part of the body was exaggerated, the tremendous chest given abnormal width and the neck sharply curved. The near foreleg was raised so that the rounded knee-cap was thrust straight at the viewer while the massive hoof almost touched the breast. The other three legs were strained in an effort to lift the animal from the ground giving the impression that the giant horse was hanging over the viewer to crush him with its fabulous strength. The mane on the arched neck was depicted as a toothed ridge, the jowl almost touched the breast and there was ominous malice in eyes that looked out from under the lowered brow and in the stone monster's pressed-back ears.

Miyiko was soon satisfied that Darr Veter was unharmed, left him stretched out on a flat stone slab and dived once again into the water. At last the girl had worn herself out with her deep diving and had seen enough of her treasure. She sat down beside Veter and did not speak until her breathing had again become normal.

"I wonder how old that statue can be?" Miyiko asked herself thoughtfully.

Darr Veter shrugged his shoulders and then suddenly remembered the most astonishing thing about the horse.

"Why is there no seaweed or barnacles on the statue?" Miyiko turned swiftly towards him.

"Oh, I've seen such things before. They were covered with some special lacquer that does not permit living things to attach themselves to it. That means that the statue must belong approximately to the Fission Age."

A swimmer appeared in the sea between the shore and the island. As he drew near he half rose out of the water and waved to them. Darr Veter recognized the broad shoulders and gleaming dark skin of Mven Mass. The tall black figure was soon ensconced on the stones and a good-natured smile spread over the face of the new Director of the Outer Stations. He bowed swiftly to little Miyiko and with an expansive gesture greeted Darr Veter.

"Renn Bose and I have come here for one day to ask your advice."
"Who is Renn Bose?"

"A physicist from the Academy of the Bounds of Knowledge."

"I think I've heard of him, he works on space-field relationship problems, doesn't he? Where did you leave him?"

"On shore. He doesn't swim, not as well as you, anyway."

A faint splash interrupted Mven Mass. "I'm going to the beach, to Veda," Miyiko called out to them from the water. Darr Veter smiled tenderly at the girl.

"She's going back with a discovery," he explained to Mven Mass and told him about the finding of the submarine horse. The African listened but showed no interest. His long fingers were fidgeting and fumbling at his chin. In the gaze he fixed on Darr Veter the latter read anxiety and hope.

"Is there anything serious worrying you? If so, why put it off?"

Mven Mass was not loath to accept the invitation. Seated on the edge of a cliff over the watery depths that bid the mysterious horse he spoke of his vexatious waverings. His meeting with Renn Bose had been no accident. The vision of the beautiful world known as Epsilon Tucanae had never left him. Ever since that night he had dreamed of approaching this wonderful world, of overcoming, in some way, the great space separating him from it, of doing something so that the time required to send a message there and receive an answer would not be six hundred years, a period much greater than a man's lifetime. He dreamed of experiencing at first hand the heartbeat of that wonderful life that was so much like our own, of stretching out his hand across the gulf of the Cosmos to our brothers in space. Mven Mass concentrated his efforts on putting himself abreast of unsolved problems and unfinished experiments that had been going on for thousands of years for the purpose of understanding space I as a function of matter. He thought of the problem Veda Kong had dreamed of on the night of her first broadcast to the Great Circle.

In the Academy of the Bounds of Knowledge Renn Bose, a young specialist in mathematical physics, was in charge of these researches. His meeting with Mven Mass and their subsequent friendship was determined by a similarity of endeavour.

Renn Bose was by that time of the opinion that the problem had been advanced sufficiently to permit of an experiment, but it was one that could not be done at laboratory level, like everything else Cosmic in scale. The colossal nature of the problem made a colossal experiment necessary. Renn Bose had come to the conclusion that the experiment should be carried out through the outer stations with the employment of all terrestrial power resources, including the Q-energy station in the Antarctic.

A sense of danger came to Darr Veter when he looked into Mven's burning eyes and at his quivering nostrils.

"Do you want to know what I should do?" He asked this decisive question calmly.

Mven Mass nodded and passed his tongue over his dry lips.

"I should not make the experiment," said Darr Veter, carefully stressing every word and paying no attention to the grimace of pain that flashed across the African's face so swiftly that a less observant man would not have noticed it.

"That's what I expected!" Mven Mass burst out. "Then why did you consider my advice to have any importance?"

"I thought we should be able to convince you." "All right, then, try!

We'll swim back to the others.

They're probably getting diving apparatus ready to examine the horse!"

Veda was singing and two other women's voices were accompanying her.

When she noticed the swimmers she beckoned to them, motioning with the fingers of her open hand like a child. The singing stopped. Darr Veter recognized one of the women as Evda Nahl, although this was the first time he had seen her without her white doctor's smock. Her tall, pliant figure stood out amongst the others on account of her white, still untanned skin. The famous woman psychiatrist had apparently been busy and had not had time for sunbathing. Evda's blue-black hair, divided into two by a dead straight parting, was drawn up high above her temples. High cheek-bones over slightly hollow cheeks served to stress the length of her piercing black eyes. Her face bore an elusive resemblance to an ancient Egyptian sphinx, the one that in very ancient days stood at the desert's edge beside the pyramid tombs of the kings of the world's oldest state. The deserts have been irrigated for many centuries, the sands are dotted with groves of rustling fruit-trees and the sphinx itself still stands there under a transparent plastic shade that does not hide the hollows of its time-eaten face.

Darr Veter recalled that Evda Nahl's genealogy went back to the ancient Peruvians or Chileans. He greeted her in the manner of the ancient sun worshippers of South America.

"It has done you good to work with the historians," said Evda, "thank Veda for that." Darr Veter hurriedly turned to his friend Veda, but she took him by the hand and led him to a woman with whom he was not acquainted.

"This is Chara Nandi! All of us here are guests of hera and Cart Sann's, the artist, you know they have been living on this coast for a month already. They have a portable studio at the other end of the bay."

Darr Veter held out his hand to the young woman who looked at him with huge blue eyes. For a moment his breath was taken away, there was something about the woman that distinguished her from all others, something that was not mere beauty. She was standing between Veda Kong and Evda Nahl whose natural beauty was refined, as it were, by exceptional intellect and the discipline of lengthy research work but which nevertheless faded before the extraordinary power of the beautiful that emanated from this woman who was a stranger to him.

"Your name has some sort of resemblance to mine," began Darr Veter. The corners of her tiny mouth quivered as she suppressed a smile. "Just as you yourself are like me!"

Darr Veter looked over the top of the mass of thick, slightly wavy black hair that came level with his shoulder and smiled expansively at Veda. "Veter, you don't know how to pay compliments to the ladies," said Veda, coyly holding her head on one side.

"Does one have to know that deception is no longer needed?"

"One does," Evda Nahl put in, "and the need for it will never die out!" "I'd be glad if you'd explain what you mean," said Darr Veter, knitting his brows.

"In a month from now I shall be giving the autumn lecture at the Academy of Sorrow and Joy, and it will contain a lot about spontaneous emotions, but in the meantime…" Evda nodded to Mven Mass who was approaching them.

The African, as usual, was walking noiselessly and with measured tread. Darr Veter noticed that the tan on Chara's cheeks became tinged with pink as though the sun that had permeated her body were bursting out through her tanned skin. Mven Mass bowed indifferently.

"I'll bring Renn Bose here, he's sitting over there on a rock."

"We'll all go to him," suggested Veda, "and on the way we'll meet Miyiko. She's gone for the diving apparatus. Chara Nandi, are you coming with us?"

The girl shook her head.

"Here comes my master. The sun has gone down and work will soon begin." "Posing must be hard work," said Veda, "it's a real deed of valour! I couldn't."

"I thought I couldn't do it, either. But if the artist's idea attracts you, you enter into the creative work. You seek an incarnation of the image in your own body, there are thousands of shades in every movement, in every curve! You have to catch them like musical notes before they fly away."

"Chara, you're a real find for an artist!"

"A find!" A deep bass voice interrupted Veda. "And if you only knew how I found her! It's unbelievable!"

Artist Cart Sann raised a big fist high in the air and shook it. His straw-coloured hair was tousled by the wind, his weather-beaten face was brick-red and his strong hairy legs sank into the sand a though they were growing there.

"Come along with us, if you have time," asked Veda, "and tell us the story."

"I'm not much of a story-teller. But still, it's an amusing tale. I'm interested in reconstructions, especially in the reconstruction of various racial types such as existed in ancient days, right up to the Era of Disunity. After my picture *Daughter of Gondwana* met with such success I was burning with ambition to reincarnate another racial type. The beauty of the human body is the best expression of race after generations of clean, healthy life. Every race tin the past had its detailed formulas, its canons of beauty I that had been evolved in days of savagery. That is the way we, the artists, understand it, we who are considered to be lagging behind in the storm of the heights of culture. Artists always did think that way, probably from the days of the palaeolithic cave painter. But I'm getting off the track.... I had planned another picture, *Daughter of Thetis,* of the Mediterranean, that is. It struck me that the myths of ancient Greece, Crete, Mesopotamia, America, Polynesia, all told of gods coming out of the sea. What could be more wonderful than the Hellenic myth of Aphrodite, the goddess of love and beauty. The very name, Aphrodite Anadiomene, the Foam-Born, she who rose from the sea.... A goddess, born of foam and conceived by the light of the stars in the nocturnal sea-what people ever invented a legend more poetic "

"From starlight and sea-foam," Veda heard Chara whisper. She cast a side glance at the girl. Her strong profile, like a carving from wood or stone, was like that of some woman of an ancient race. The small, straight, slightly rounded nose, her somewhat sloping forehead, her strong chin and, most important of all, the great distance from the nose to the high ear-all these features typical of the Mediterranean peoples at the time of antiquity were reflected in Chara's face.

Unobtrusively Veda examined her from head to foot and thought that everything in her was just a little "too much." Her skin was too smooth, her waist too narrow, her hips too wide. And she held herself too straight so that her firm bosom became too prominent. Perhaps that was what the artist wanted, strongly defined lines?

A stone ridge crossed their path and Veda had to correct the impression she had only just received: Chara Nandi jumped from boulder to boulder with an unusual agility, *as* though she were dancing.

"She must have Indian blood in her," decided Veda. "I'll ask her later on."

"My work on the *Daughter of Thetis*," the artist continued, "brought me closer to the sea, I had to get a feeling for the sea since my Maid of Crete, like Aphrodite, would arise from the waves and in such a manner that everybody would understand it. When I was preparing to paint the *Daughter of Gondwana* I spent three years at a forestry station in Equatorial Africa. When that picture was finished I took a job as mechanic on a hydroplane carrying mail around the Atlantic-you know, to all those fisheries and albumin and salt works afloat on big metal rafts in the ocean.

"One evening I was driving along in the Central Atlantic somewhere to the west of the Azores where the northern current and the counter-current meet. There are always big waves there, rollers that come one after another. My hydroplane rose and fell, one moment almost touching the low clouds and next minute diving deep into the trough between the rollers. The screw raced as it came out of the water. I was standing on the high bridge beside the helmsman. And suddenly ... I'll never forget it!

"Imagine a wave higher than any of the others that raced towards us. On the crest of this giant wave, right under the low ceiling of rosy-pearl clouds stood a girl, sunburned to the colour of bronze. The wave rolled noiselessly on and she rode it, infinitely proud in her isolation in the midst of that boundless ocean. My boat was swept upwards and we passed the girl who waved us a friendly greeting. Then I could see that she was standing on a surf board fitted with an electric motor and accumulator."

"I know the sort," agreed Darr Veter, "it's intended for riding the waves."

"What amazed me most of all was her complete solitude -there was nothing but low clouds, an ocean empty for hundreds of miles around, the evening twilight and the girl carried along on the crest of a giant wave. That girl "

"Was Chara Nandi," said Evda Nahl. "That's obvious, but where did she come from?"

"She was not born of starlight and foam!" chuckled Chara, and her laughter had a surprisingly high, resonant note to it, "merely from the raft of an albumin factory. We were moored on the fringe of the Sargasso Sea where we were cultivating Chlorella " and where I was working as a biologist."

"Be that as it may," said Cart Sann, "but from that moment for me you were a daughter of the Mediterranean, born of foam. You were fated to be the model for my future picture. I had been waiting a whole year." "May we come and look at it?" asked Veda Kong. "Please do, but not during working hours. You had better come in the evening. I work very slowly and cannot tolerate anybody's presence when I am painting." "Do you use colours?"

"Our work has changed very little during the thousands of years that people have painted pictures. The laws of optics and the human eye have remained the same. We have become more receptive to certain tones, new chromokatoptric colours" with internal reflexions contained in the paint layer have been invented, there are a few new methods of harmonizing colours, that's all; on the whole the artist of antiquity worked in very much the same way as I do today. In some respects he did better. He had confidence and patience-we've become more dashing and less confident of ourselves. At times strict *nalvete* is better for art. But I'm digressing again! It's time for us to go. Come along, Chara!"

They all stood still and watched the artist and his model as they walked away.

"Now I know who he is," murmured Veda, "I've seen the *Daughter of Gondwana*."

"So have I," said Evda Nahl and Mven Mass together.

"Gondwana, is that from the land of the Goods in India?" asked Darr Veter.

"No, it is the collective name for the southern continents. In general it is the land of the ancient black race."

"And what is this Daughter of the Black People like?"

"It is a simple picture. There is a plateau, the fire of blinding sunlight, the fringe of a formidable tropical forest and in the foreground, a black-skinned girl, walking alone. One half of her face and her firm, tangibly hard, cast-metal body is drenched with blazing sunlight, the other half of her is in deep, transparent half-shadow. A necklace of white animal's teeth hangs from her neck, her short hair is gathered at the crown of her head and covered with a wreath of fiery red blossoms. Her right arm is raised over her head to push aside the last branches of a tree that bar her way, with her left hand she is pushing a thorny stalk away from her knee. In the halted movement, in the free breathing, and in the strong sweep of the arm there is carefree youth, young life merging with nature into a single whole that is as change able as a river in flood…. This oneness is to be understood as knowledge, the intuitive understanding of the world. In her dark eyes, gazing over a sea of bluish grass towards the faintly visible outlines of mountains, there is a clearly felt uneasiness, the expectation of great trials in the new, freshly discovered world!" Evda Nahl stopped.

"It isn't exactly expectation, it is tormenting certainty. She feels the hard lot of the black people and tries to comprehend it," added Veda Kong. "But how did Cart Sann manage to convey the idea? Perhaps it is in the raising of the thin eyebrows, the neck inclined slightly forward, the open, defenceless back of her head…. And those amazing eyes, filled with the dark wisdom of ancient nature…. The strangest thing of all is that you feel, at the same time, carefree, dancing strength and alarming knowledge."

"It's a pity I haven't seen it," said Darr Veter. "I must go to the Palace of History and take a look at it. I can imagine the colours but I can't imagine the girl's pose."

"The pose?" Evda Nahl stopped, threw the towel from her shoulders, raised her right arm high over her head, leaned slightly backward and turned half facing Darr Veter. Her long leg was slightly raised as though making a short step and not completing it, her toes just touching the ground. Her supple body seemed to blossom forth. They all stood still in frank admiration.

"Evda, I could never have imagined you like that!" exclaimed Darr Veter, "you're dangerous. You're like the half exposed blade of a dagger!"

"Veter, those clumsy compliments again," laughed Veda, "why half and not fully exposed?"

"He's quite right," smiled Evda Nahl, relaxing to her normal self, "not fully. Our new acquaintance, Chara Nandi, is a fully drawn and gleaming blade, to use the epic language of Darr Veter."

"I can't believe that anybody can compare with you!" came a hoarse voice from amongst the boulders. Only then did Evda Nahl notice the red hair cut ere *brosee* and the blue eyes that were gazing at her adoringly with a look such as she had never before seen on anybody's face.

"I am Renn Bose!" said the red-headed man, bashfully, as his short, narrow-shouldered figure appeared from behind a boulder.

"We were looking for you," said Veda, taking the physicist by the hand, "this is Darr Veter."

Renn Bose blushed and the freckles on his face and neck stood out even more prominently than before.

"I stayed up there for some time," said Renn Bose, pointing to a rocky slope. "There *is* an ancient tomb there."

"It is the grave of a famous poet who lived a very long time ago," announced Veda.

"There's an inscription on the tomb, here it is." The physicist unrolled a thin metal sheet with four rows of blue symbols on it.

"Those are European letters, symbols that were in use before the world linear alphabet was introduced. They had clumsy shapes that were inherited from the still older pictograms. But I know that language."

"Then read it, Veda!"

"Be quiet for a few minutes!" she demanded and they all obediently sat down on the rocks. Very soon Veda stood before the seated people and read her improvised translation:

Thoughts and events and our dreams are all fleeting,
Vanquished by time like a ship lost at sea...
Leaving this world on my journey of journeys,
Earth's dearest obsession I'm talting with me...

"That's exquisite!" Evda Nahl rose to her knees. "A modern poet couldn't have said anything better about the power of time. I should like to know which of Earth's obsessions he thought the best and took with him in his last thoughts."

"He no doubt thought of a beautiful woman," said Renn Bose, impetuously gazing at Evda Nahl. Or did she imagine it?

A boat of transparent plastic containing two people appeared in the distance.

"Here comes Miyiko with Sherliss, one of our mechanics, he goes everywhere with her. Oh, no," Veda corrected herself, "it's Frith Don himself, the Director of the Maritime Expedition. Good-bye, Veter, you three will want to stay together so I'll take Evda with me!"

The two women ran down to the gentle waves and swam together to the island. The boat turned towards them but Veda waved to them to go on. Renn Bose, standing motionless, watched the swimmers.

"Wake up, Renn, let's get down to business!" Mven Mass called to him. The physicist smiled in shy confusion.

A stretch of firm sand between two ridges of rock was turned into a scientific auditorium. Renn Bose, using fragments of seashells, drew and wrote in the sand, in his excitement he fell flat, his body rubbing out what he had written and drawn so that he had to draw it all again. Mven Mass expressed his agreement or encouraged the physicist with abrupt exclamations. Darr Veter, resting his elbows on his knees, wiped away the perspiration that broke out on his forehead from the effort he was making to understand. At last the red-headed physicist stopped talking, and sat back on the sand breathing heavily.

"Yes, Renn Bose," said Darr Veter after a lengthy pause, "you have made a discovery of outstanding importance."

"I did not do it alone. The ancient mathematician Geiaenberg propounded the principle of indefiniteness, the impossibility of accurately defining the position of tiny particles. The impossible has become possible now that we understand mutual transitions, that is, we know the repagular calculus." At about the same time scientists discovered the circular meson cloud in the atomic nucleus, that is, they came very near to an understanding of anti-gravitation."

"We'll accept that as true. I'm not a specialist in bipolar mathematics," particularly the repagular calculus which studies the obstacles to transition. But I realize that your work with the shadow functions is new in principle, although we ordinary people cannot properly understand it unless we have mathematical clairvoyance. I can, however, conceive of the tremendous significance of the discovery. There is one thing …" Darr Veter hesitated.

"What, what is there?" asked Mven Mass, anxiously.

"How can we do it experimentally? I don't think we can create a sufficiently powerful electromagnetic field "

"To balance the gravitational field and obtain a state of transition?" inquired Renn Bose.

"Exactly. Beyond the limits of the system, space will remain outside our influence."

"That's true, but, as always in dialectics, we must look for a solution in the opposite. Suppose we obtain an anti-gravitational shadow vectorally and not discretely."

"Ah! But how?"

Swiftly, Renn Bose drew three straight lines and a narrow sector with an arc of greater radius intersecting them.

"This was known before bipolar mathematics. Two thousand and five hundred years ago it was called the Problem of the Fourth Dimension. In those times there was a widespread conception of multidimensional space; the shadow properties of gravitation, however, were unknown and people attempted to find an analogy with electromagnetic fields which led them to believe that points of singularity meant that matter had disappeared or had been changed into something that could be named but could not be explained. How could they have had any conception of space with their limited knowledge of the nature of phenomena? But our ancestors could guess- you sec, they realized that if the distance from, say, star A to the centre of Earth along line OA is twenty quintillion kilometres, then the distance to the same star by vector OB will equal zero ... in practice, not zero but approaching it. They said that zero time would be achieved if the velocity of motion were equal to the velocity of light. Remember that the cochlear calculus[2]" has been only recently discovered!"

"Spiral motion was known thousands of years ago," Mven Mass remarked cautiously, interrupting the scientist. Kenn Bose dismissed the remark disdainfully.

"They knew the motion but not the laws! It's like this, if the gravitational field and the electromagnetic field are two sides of one and the same property of matter and if space is a function of gravitation, then the function of the electromagnetic field is antispace. The transition from one to the other yields the vector shadow function, zero space, which is known in everyday language as the speed of light. I believe it to be possible to achieve zero space in any direction. Mven Mass wants to visit the planet of Epsilon Tucanae-it's all the same to me as long as I can set up the experiment! As long as I can set up the experiment!" repeated the physicist, lowering his short white eyelashes wearily.

"You will need not only the outer stations and Earth's energy, as Mven Mass pointed out, but some sort of an installation as well. Such an installation cannot be simple or easily erected."

"In that respect we're lucky. We can use Corr Yule's installation near the Tibetan Observatory. Experiments for the investigation of space were carried out there a hundred and seventy years ago. There will have to be some adjustments and, as far as volunteers to help me are concerned, I can get five, ten, twenty thousand any time I like. I have only to call for them and they will take leave of absence and come."

"You seem to have thought of everything. There is only one other consideration, but it is the most important- the danger of the experiment. There may be the most unexpected results; in conformity with the law of big numbers we cannot make a preliminary attempt on a small scale. We must take the extraterrestrial scale from the start."

"What scientist would be afraid of risk?" asked Renn Bose, shrugging his shoulders.

"I wasn't thinking of personal risk! I know that there will be thousands of volunteers as soon as they are required for some dangerous and novel enterprise. The experiment will also involve the outer stations, the observatories, the whole system of installations that has cost mankind a tremendous amount of labour. These are installations that have opened a window into the Cosmos, that have put mankind in contact with the life, knowledge and creative activity of other populated worlds. This window is mankind's greatest achievement: do you think that you, or I, or any other individual or group of individuals has the right to take the risk of closing it, even for a short time? I would like to know whether you feel that you have that right and on what grounds?"

"I have and on good grounds," said Mven Mass, rising to his feet. "You have been at archaeological excavations -do not the billions of unknown skeletons in unknown graves appeal to us? Do they not reproach us and make demands of us? I visualize billions of human lives that have passed, lives in which youth, beauty and the joy of life slipped away like sand through one's fingers-they demand that we lay bare the great mystery of time, that we struggle against it! Victory over space is victory over time, that is why I'm sure that I'm right, that's why I believe in the greatness of the proposed experiment!"

"My feelings are different," said Renn Bose. "But they form the other side of the same thing. Space still cannot be overcome in the Cosmos, it keeps the worlds apart and prevents us from discovering planets with populations similar to ours, prevents us from joining them in one family that would be infinitely rich in its joy and strength. This would be the greatest transformation since the Era of World Unity, since the days when mankind finally put an end to the separate existence of the nations and merged into one, in this way making the greatest progress towards a new stage in the conquest of nature. Every new step in this direction is more important than anything else, more important than any other investigations or knowledge."

Renn Bose had scarcely finished when Mven Mass spoke again.

"There is one other thing, a personal one. In my youth I had a collection of old historical novels. There was one story about your ancestors, Darr Veter. Some great conqueror, some fierce destroyer of human life of whom there were so many in the epochs of the lower forms of society, launched an attack against them. The story was about a strong youth who was madly in love. His girl was captured and taken away-'driven off'"" was the word used in those days. Can you imagine it? Men and women were bound and driven off to the country of the conqueror like cattle. The youth was separated from his beloved by thousands of miles. The geography of Earth was unknown, riding and pack animals were the only means of transport. The world of those days was more mysterious and vast, more dangerous and difficult to cross than Cosmic space is for us today. The young hero hunted for his dream, for years he wandered terribly dangerous paths until he found her in the depths of the Asian mountains. It is difficult to define the impression I had when I was younger, but it still seems to me that I, too, could go through all the obstacles of the Cosmos to the one I loved!"

Darr Veter smiled wanly.

"I can understand your feelings but I cannot get clear for myself what logical grounds there are for comparing a Russian story to your urge to get into the Cosmos. I understand Renn Bose better. Of course, you warned us that this was personal ".

Darr Veter stopped. He sat silent so long that Mven Mass began to fidget.

"Now I understand why it was that people used to smoke, drink, bolster themselves up with drugs at moments of uncertainty, anxiety or loneliness. At this moment I feel just as alone and uncertain-I don't know what to say to you. Who am I to forbid a great experiment? But then, how can I permit it? You must turn to the Council, then...."

"No, that won't do." Mven Mass stood up and his huge body was tensed as though he were in mortal danger. "Answer us: would you make the experiment? As Director of the Outer Stations, not as Renn Bose, he is different "

'No!" answered Darr Veter, firmly. "I should wait."

"What for?"

"The erection of an experimental installation on the Moon;'

"And power for it?"

"The lesser gravity of the Moon and the smaller scale of the experiment will make only a few Q-stations necessary."

"But that would take hundreds of years and I should never see it!"

"You wouldn't, but as far as the human race is concerned it doesn't matter whether it's now or a generation later."

"But it's the end for me, the end of my dream! And for Renn "

"To me it means that it's impossible to check up my work experimentally and make corrections-it means I cannot continue!"

"One mind is not enough. Ask the Council."

"Your ideas and your words are the Council's decision given in advance. We have nothing to expect from them," said Mven Mass softly.

"You're right. The Council will refuse."

"I shan't ask you anything else. I feel guilty, Renn and I have put the heavy burden of decision upon you."

"That is my duty as one older in experience. It is not your fault that the task seems magnificent and extremely dangerous. That is what upsets me so much, makes it hard to bear."

Renn Bose was the first to suggest returning to the temporary dwellings of the expedition. The three downcast men plodded through the sand, each in his own way feeling the bitter sorrow of having to reject an experiment such as had never before been tried. Darr Veter cast occasional side glances at his companions and felt that it was harder for him than for them. There was a bold recklessness in his nature that he had had to fight against all his life. It made him something like an old-time brigand-why had he felt such joy and satisfaction in his mischievous battle with the bull? In his heart he was indignant, he was full of protest against a decision that was wise but not bold.

CHAPTER SIX

THE LEGEND OF THE BLUE SUNS

Dr. Louma Lasvy and Eon Thai, the biologist, dragged their heavy weight slowly towards him from the ship's sick bay. Erg Noor went to meet them.

"Nisa?" "Alive, but…. "

"Dying?"

"Not yet. She is totally paralysed. Her respiration is extraordinarily low. Her heart is functioning-one beat in a hundred seconds. It is not death but it is absolute collapse which may last a long, an indefinitely long time."

"Is there any possibility that she may regain consciousness and suffer?" "None whatever."

"Are you sure?" The look in the commander's eyes was sharp and insistent, but the doctor was not at all put out. "Absolutely sure!"

Erg Noor looked inquiringly at the biologist. He nodded his affirmation.

"What do you intend to do?"

"Keep her in an even temperature, absolute repose and weak light. If the collapse does not progress… what does it matter … let her sleep till we reach Earth. Then she can go to the Institute of Nerve Currents. The injury is due to some form of current, her spacesuit was holed in three places. It is a good thing that she was scarcely breathing!"

"I noticed the holes and sealed them with my plaster," said the biologist.

In silent gratitude Erg Noor squeezed his arm above the elbow.

"Only ..." began Louma, "we'd better get her away from high gravitation as quickly as we can ... and ... at the same time there's danger, not so much in the acceleration of the take-off as in the return to normal gravitation."

"I see, you're afraid the pulse will get even slower. But the heart is not a pendulum that accelerates its oscillations in a field of high gravitation, is it?"

"The rhythm of impulses in the organism, in general, follows the same laws. If the heartbeats slow down to, say, one in two hundred seconds, then the brain will not get a sufficient supply of blood, and "

Erg Noor fell into such deep thought that he forgot that he was not alone: he suddenly came to himself and sighed deeply.

His companions waited patiently.

"Would it not be a way out if the organism were to be submitted to higher pressures in an atmosphere enriched with oxygen?" asked the commander cautiously, and by the satisfied smile of the faces of Louma Lasvy and Eon Thai he knew that the idea was the right one.

"Saturate the blood with the gas under increased pressure, good Of course, we must take precautions against thrombosis and-let her heart beat once in two hundred seconds, it will come right later."

Eon's smile showed his white teeth under a black moustache and gave his stern face a look of youthfulness and reckless merriment.

"The organism will remain paralysed but will live," said Louma with relief. "Let's go and get the chamber ready. I want to use the big silicolloid hood that we took for Zirda. We can get a floating armchair inside it to make a bed for her during the take-off. After acceleration ceases we can make her a proper bed."

"As soon as you're ready report to the control tower. We're not staying here a minute longer than necessary ... we've had enough of the darkness and weight of the black world!"

The crew hurried to their various sections of the ship, each of them struggling against excess weight as best he could.

The signals for the take-off resounded like a song of victory.

With feelings of such absolute relief as they had never before experienced the people of the expedition entrusted themselves to the soft embraces of the landing chairs. A take-off from a heavy planet is a difficult and dangerous undertaking. The acceleration necessary to escape its gravity would strain the very limit of human endurance and the slightest mistake on the part of the pilot might lead to the death of them all.

There was a deafening roar of the planet motors as Erg Noor directed the spaceship at a tangent to the horizon. The levers of the hydraulic chairs were pressed lower and lower under the influence of growing weight. In a moment the levers would reach the limit and then, under the pressure of acceleration the frail human bones might be broken as they would be on an anvil. The commander's hands, lying on the buttons that controlled the ship's machinery, were unbearably heavy. But his strong fingers were at work and *Tantra*, describing a huge, flattened arc, rose higher and higher out of thick darkness into the transparent blackness of infinity. Erg Noor kept his eyes fixed on the red line of the horizontal leveller-it wavered in its unstable equilibrium, indicating that the ship showed a tendency to stop its climb and travel on the downward arc. The heavy planet had still not given up its prisoner. Erg Noor decided to switch on the anameson motors whose power was sufficient to lift the spaceship from any planet. Their ringing vibration made the whole ship shudder. The red line rose about half an inch above the zero line. A little more....

Through the upper inspection periscope the commander saw that *Tantra* was covered with a fine layer of blue flame that flowed slowly towards the stern of the vessel. The atmosphere had been passed! In empty space vestigial electric currents, following the law of superconductivity, flowed along the vessel's hull.

The stars had again become needles of light and *Tantra*, escaping, flew farther and farther from the dread planet. The burden of gravity decreased with every minute. The body became lighter and lighter, the artificial gravitation machine began to hum and after so many days under the pressure of the black planet terrestrial gravity seemed indescribably small. The people jumped up from their chairs. Ingrid, Louma and Eon performed intricate passages from a fantastic dance. The inevitable reaction, however, soon set in and the greater part of the crew fell into a brief sleep that gave temporary repose. Only Erg Noor, Pel Lynn, Pour Hyss and Louma Lasvy remained awake. The spaceship's temporary course had to be worked out to avoid the belt of ice and meteoroids by describing an arc perpendicular to the plane of rotation of star T's system. After this the ship could be brought up to its normal subphotonic speed and work could be begun on the computation of the real course.

The doctor kept watch over Nisa's condition after the takeoff and the return to normal terrestrial gravity. She was soon able to reassure all those who were awake by her report that the pulse had reached a constant of one beat in a hundred and ten seconds. This was not mortal as long as there was an excess supply of oxygen. Louma Lasvy proposed using a tiratron,[21] an electronic cardiac exciter, and neurosecretory stimulators.[22]

The walls of the ship whined for fifty-five hours from the vibration of anameson motors until, at last, the speedometer showed that they had attained a speed of nine hundred and seventy million kilometres an hour, very close to the safety limit. In the course of a terrestrial 24-hour day their distance from the iron star increased by more than 20,000 million kilometres. It is difficult to describe the relief felt by all thirteen members of the expedition after their severe trials-the murdered planet, the loss of *Algrab* and the awful black sun. The joy of liberation was not complete, one member of the expedition, young Nisa Creet, lay motionless in a special partition of the sick bay in a cataleptic half sleep and half death.

The five women on the ship, Ingrid, Louma, the second electronic engineer, the geologist, and lone Marr, the teacher of rhythmic gymnastics (who was also keeper of the food stores, radio operator and collector of scientific material), gathered as though for an ancient funeral rite. Nisa's body, divested of all clothing and washed with the special solutions TM and AS, had been laid out on a thick hand-stitched carpet of the softest Mediterranean sponges. This carpet was placed on a pneumatic mattress under a dome of transparent, rosy-hued silicolloid. An accurate air-condition controller would keep the necessary temperature, pressure and composition of the air inside the hood constant for many years. Soft rubber blocks kept Nisa fixed in one position which Louma intended to change once a month. She was more afraid of bed-sores than of anything else-they could come from absolute motionlessness. Louma, therefore, decided that a watch had to be kept over Nisa's body and herself refused to take her periods of long sleep during the first year or two of the journey. Nisa's cataleptic state continued. The only improvement Louma could effect was an increase in pulse-beats to one a minute. Little as this was, it was sufficient to enable them to stop the oxygen saturation which was harmful to the lungs....

Four months passed. The spaceship was following its real, computed course home, avoiding the belt of free meteoroids. The crew, worn out with their adventures and hard toil, were sunk in a seven-months' sleep. This time there were four instead of the three people awake on board: Erg Noor and Pour Hyss, whose tour of duty it was, were joined by Louma Lasvy and Eon Thai.

The commander, after having got out of a graver situation than any spaceship commander had ever been in before, felt very lonely. The four years' journey back to Earth seemed endless to him. He did not deceive himself -they were endless because he could hope to save his fearless auburn-haired astronavigator, whom he had come to love, only on Earth.

For a long time he put off doing what he would otherwise have done on the day after the take-off-running through the electronic stereofilms from *Parus*-he had wanted to see them together with Nisa and with her hear the first news from those wonderful worlds, the planets of the blue star of the terrestrial night sky. He had wanted Nisa to share with him the pleasure of seeing the boldest romantic dreams of the past and present coming true- the discovery of new stellar worlds, the future distant islands of human civilization. But at last they were brought out....

The films had been taken at a distance of eight parsecs from the Sun eighty years before and, although they had been lying in the open ship on the black planet of star T they were in excellent condition. The hemispherical stereo-screen took the four members of *Tantra's* crew back to where blue Vega shone high above them.

There were many sudden changes of subject-the screen was filled by the dazzlingly blue star which was followed by casual, minute-long pictures of life on board the ship. The 28-year-old commander of the expedition, unbelievably young for his post, worked at the computers while still younger astronomers made observations. The films showed obligatory daily sport and dances that the young people had brought to acrobatic perfection. A mocking voice announced that the biologist had maintained the championship all the way to Vega. That girl with short, flaxen hair, was demonstrating the most difficult exercises twisting her magnificently developed body into all sorts of improbable poses.

As they looked at the perfectly natural images with all the normal colour tones on the hemispherical screen, they forgot that these happy, vigorous young astronauts had long before been devoured by the foul monsters of the black planet.

The terse chronicle of expedition life soon passed. The light amplifiers in the projector began to hum; so brightly did the blue star glow that even this pale reproduction forced people to put on protective glasses. The star was almost three times our Sun in diameter and mass-colossal, greatly flattened and madly rotating with an equatorial speed of three hundred kilometres a second, a ball of indescribably luminous gas with a surface temperature of 11,000° C. and a corona of rosy-pearl flame spreading millions of kilometres around it. It seemed as though Vega's rays would crush everything they met in their path as they thrust out their mighty million-kilometre long spears into space. The planet nearest to the blue star was hidden in their glow, but no ship from Earth or from any of her neighbours on the Great Circle could plunge into that ocean of fire. The visual image was followed by a vocal report on observations that had been made and the almost phantom lines of stereometric drawings showed the positions of Vega's first and second planets.

Parus could not approach even the second planet whose orbit was a hundred million kilometres from the star.

Monstrous protuberances flew out of the depths of an ocean of transparent violet flame, the stellar atmosphere, and stretched like all-consuming arms into space. So great was Vega's energy that the star emitted light of the strongest quanta, the violet and invisible parts of the spectrum. Even when human eyes were protected by a triple filter it aroused the horrible effect of an invisible but mortally dangerous phantom. They could see photon storms flashing past, those that had managed to overcome the star's gravitation. Their distant reverberations shook and tossed *Parus* dangerously. The cosmic ray meters and instruments measuring other non-elastic radiations refused to function. Dangerous ionization began to grow, even inside the well-protected ship. They could only guess at the extent of the furious radial energy that poured out into the emptiness of space in a monstrous stream.

The commander of *Parus* navigated his ship cautiously towards the third planet-a big planet with but a thin layer of transparent atmosphere. It looked as though the fiery breath of the blue star had driven away the cover of light gases for they trailed in a weakly glowing tail behind the planet on her dark side. They recorded the destructive evaporation of fluorine, poisonous carbon monoxide, and the dead density of the inert gases-nothing terrestrial could have lived for a second in that atmosphere.

The great heat of the blue sun made inert mineral substances active. Sharp spears, ribs, vertical battlemented walls of stone, red like fresh wounds or black like empty pits, rose out of the bowels of the planet. On the plateaux of lava, swept by violent gales, there were fissures and abysses belching forth molten magma like streaks of blood-red fire.

Dense clouds of ash whirled high into the air, blindingly blue on the illuminated side and impenetrably black on the dark side. Streaks of lightning thousands of miles long struck in all directions, evidence of the electric saturation of the dead atmosphere.

The awful violet phantom of the huge sun, the black sky, half covered by the pearly corona, and below, on the planet, the crimson contrasting shadows on a wild chaos of rock, the fiery crevices, cracks and circles, the constant flashes of green lightning-all this had been picked up by the stereotelescopes and the electron films had recorded it with unimpassioned, inhuman precision.

Behind the machines, however, were the emotions of the travellers, the protest of reason against the senseless power of destruction and the piling up of dead matter, the consciousness of the hostility of this world of furious cosmic fire. The four viewers, hypnotized by the sight, exchanged glances of approval when a voice announced that *Parus* would move on to the fourth planet.

The human selection of events reduced the time factor and in a few seconds the outer planet of Vega appeared under the spaceship's keel telescopes; in size it was comparable with Earth. *Parus* descended sharply, the crew had evidently decided to explore the last planet in the hope that they would find a world, if not beautiful, then at least fit to bear life.

Erg Noor caught himself mentally repeating those words-"at least." Most likely those who navigated *Parus* had similar ideas as they studied the planet's surface through their telescopes.

"At least"-with those two syllables they bade farewell to the dream of the beautiful worlds of Vega, of the discovery of pearls of planets on the far side of outer space for the sake of which people of Earth had voluntarily agreed to forty-five years of imprisonment in a spaceship.

Carried away by the pictures passing before his eyes, Erg Noor did not think of that immediately. In the depths pf the hemispherical screen he raced over the surface of he fantastically distant planet. To the great grief of the travellers, of those who were dead and those still living, The planet turned out to be like our nearest neighbour in he solar system, the planet Mars, which they had known since childhood. The same thin envelope of transparent as with a blackish-green, permanently cloudless sky, the same level surface of desert continents with chains of eroded mountains. The difference was that on Mars there "was a searing cold night and very sharp changes in the daytime temperature. There were shallow swamps on Mars, like huge puddles, that had evaporated until they were almost dry, there were rare and scanty rains and hoarfrosts, faint life in the form of gangrenous plants and peculiar apathetic burrowing animals.

Here, however, the raging flames of the blue sun kept the temperature of the planet so high that it breathed heat like Earth's hottest deserts. What little vapour there was rose to the upper layer of the atmosphere and the huge plains were overshadowed by vortices of hot currents in the constantly disturbed atmosphere. The planet rotated at high speed, like the others. The cold of night had broken the rocks up into a sea of sand; orange, violet, green, bluish or dazzlingly white patches of sand drowned parts of the planet that from a distance had the appearance of seas of imaginary vegetation. The chains of eroded mountains, higher than those on Mars but just as lifeless, were covered with a shining black or brown crust. The blue sun, with its powerful ultra-violet radiation, had destroyed the minerals and evaporated the lighter elements.

It seemed that the light, sandy plains were radiating flames. Erg Noor recalled that at the time when only a small part and not the majority of Earth's population had been scientists, many artists and writers had dreamed of people on other planets who had adapted themselves to life at high temperatures. It was a poetic and beautiful notion, it increased faith in the power of the human race -people on the fire-breathing planets of the blue sun meeting their terrestrial brethren! Erg Noor, like many others, had been impressed by a picture he had seen in the museum of the eastern sector of the southern inhabited zone: a hazy horizon on a plain of crimson sand, a grey, burning-hot sky and under it faceless human figures in temperature suits throwing blue-black shadows of improbably clear definition. They stood at the corner of some metal structure that was at white heat in dynamic poses that showed their amazement. Beside the structure stood an undraped female figure with her red hair hanging loose. Her light-coloured skin gleamed more brightly than the sand in the glaring light, blue and vermilion shadows stressed every line of her tall and graceful figure, the symbol of the victory of beautiful life over the forces of the Cosmos. Beautiful, that was the most important thing of all. For even the adaptation of animal life that reduced it to a formless devourer with but a faint spark of life in it, might be termed a victory.

It was a bold and quite unreal dream that contradicted the laws of biological development, laws that were far better known in the Great Circle Era than they had been when the picture was painted.

Erg Noor gave a shudder as the surface of the planet rushed towards him. The unknown pilot of *Parus* was bringing his ship down. Sand cones, black cliffs, deposits of some shining green crystals flashed past. The spaceship was flying in a regular spiral round the planet from pole to pole. There was not a sign of water or at least of the most primitive vegetable life. Again that "at least" how accommodating the human mind could be! Then came the nostalgia of loneliness, the feeling that the ship was lost in the dead distance, was in the power of the flaming blue star. Erg Noor could feel the hopes of those who took the film, who were watching the planet, could feel them as though they were his own. If there had only been at least the remains of some past life! How well known is this thought to all those who have flown to dead ^planets without water or atmosphere, who have searched in vain for ruins, for the remains of towns and buildings in the accidental shapes of the crevices, in the details of the lifeless rocks and in the precipices of mountains that had never known life.

The earth of that distant world, scorched, churned up by violent storms, without any trace of a shadow, flashed swiftly across the screen. Erg Noor, recognizing the collapse of an ancient dream, strove to imagine how such an incorrect conception of the planets of the blue sun could have arisen.

"Our terrestrial brothers will be disappointed when they know this," said the biologist, softly, moving closer to the commander. "For many thousands of years millions of people on Earth have gazed at Vega. On summer evenings in the north all young people, all those who loved and dreamed, turned their eyes to the sky. In the summer Vega, bright and blue, stands almost in the zenith, how could one not admire it? Many centuries ago people knew quite a lot about the stars. But by some strange freak of thought they did not suspect that almost every slowly rotating star with a strong magnetic field had its planets in the same way as almost all planets have their satellites. They did not know of this law but when they were overtaken by bitter loneliness they dreamed of fellow-beings in other worlds, and, more than elsewhere, on Vega, the blue sun. I remember translations from some of the ancient languages of beautiful poems about semi-divine people from the blue star...."

"I dreamed about Vega after the *Parus* communication," confessed Erg Noor, turning to Eon Thai, "and in my hope that my dream would come true I read my own meaning into that communication. Today it is obvious that thousands of years of longing for distant, beautiful worlds have impaired my vision and that of many clever and serious people."

"How do you understand the *Parus* communication now?"

"Quite simply. 'Vega's four planets quite lifeless. Nothing more beautiful than our Earth, what happiness to return.' "

"You're right," exclaimed the biologist, "why didn't we think of it before?"

"Perhaps somebody did, but not we astronauts and not the Council. That is to our honour-bold dreams and not sceptical disappointment bring victory in life."

The flight round the planet, as shown on the screen, was over. It was followed by the records made by the robot station that had been put out to study surface conditions on the planet. Next came a loud explosion as the geological bomb [23] was dropped. The huge cloud of mineral dust thrown up by the bomb explosion reached the keel of the spaceship where powerful suction pumps drew samples into the filtering side-channels of the vessel. Several samples of mineral dust from the sands and mountains of the scorched planet were put into silicolloid test-tubes and samples of the upper layers of the atmosphere were put into quartz containers. *Parus* set off on its long journey back home, a journey it was not fated to finish. Now the terrestrial sister ship of *Parus* was carrying back to the people of Earth everything that the lost travellers had won at the cost of such patient endeavour.

The remaining records-six reels of observations-were to be specially studied by Earth's astronomers and the moat important details broadcast round the Great Circle.

Nobody wanted to see films about the later history of *Parus*, the hard struggle to repair the damaged ship and the battle with star T; nobody wanted to hear the last sound spool as their own experiences were still too fresh. They decided to leave the examination of the remainder until the time came for the whole crew to be awakened. Leaving the commander alone in the control tower the others went away for a brief rest.

Erg Noor's dreams had collapsed and he no longer thought of them. He tried to estimate the value of those few pitiful crumbs of knowledge the two expeditions, his and *Parus*', would bring back to mankind at such terrific cost. Or did they seem pitiful only on account of his disappointment?

For the first time Erg Noor began to think of beautiful Earth as an inexhaustible treasure-house of refined, cultured human beings who had an insatiable thirst for knowledge now that they had been relieved of the terrible worries and dangers that nature and primitive society had inflicted them with. The sufferings of the past, the searchings and failures, the mistakes and disappointments still remained in the Great Circle Era but they had been carried to a loftier plane of creative activity in science, art and building. Knowledge and creative labour had freed Earth from hunger, over-population, infectious diseases and harmful animals. The world no longer had to fear the exhaustion of fuel and useful chemical elements, premature death and debility had been eliminated. Those crumbs of knowledge that *Tantra* would bring home would also be a contribution to the mighty stream of knowledge that made for constant progress in the organization of society and the study of nature.

Erg Noor opened the safe that housed *Tantra*'s records and took out the box containing the piece of metal from the spiral spaceship on the black planet. The heavy piece of sky-blue metal lay flat on his palm. Although he had put off the analysis of this precious sample for the huge laboratories on Earth, he knew that neither on Earth not-on any of the planets of the solar system or neighbouring stars was any such metal to be found. The Universe was made up of similar simple elements that had long before been systematized in the Mendeleyev Table. Consequently no new element-no metal-could be discovered; but in the processes of the creation of elements, natural or artificial, countless isotope variations, possessing vastly different physical properties, could emerge. Then again, directed recrystallization changed the properties of elements to a great extent. Erg Noor was convinced that this piece of the hull of a spaceship from worlds inconceivably far away was a terrestrial metal whose atoms had been completely rearranged. This would be something, perhaps the most important thing after news of Zirda's ruin, that he would take bade to Earth and the Great Circle.

The iron star was very close to Earth and a visit to its planet by a specially prepared expedition would not now, after the experience of *Purus* and *Tantra,* be particularly dangerous, no matter what multitude of black crosses and medusae there might be in that eternal darkness. They had been unfortunate in their opening of the spiral spaceship. If they had had time to ponder over the tiling they would have realized then that the gigantic spiral tube was part of the spaceship's propulsion system.

In his mind the commander went over the events of hat fateful last day. He remembered Nisa spread over him like. a shield after he had fallen unconscious near the roonster. Youthful emotions that combined the heroic loyalty of the ancient women of Earth and the frank and *wise* courage of the modern world had not had time to develop in her to the full....

Four Hyss appeared silently from behind him to relieve she commander at his post. Erg Noor went through the library-laboratory but did not go on to the central dormitory cabin; instead he opened the heavy side-bay door ; The diffused light of an earthly day was reflected from the silicolloid cupboards containing drugs and instruments, from the X-ray, artificial respiration and blood-circulation apparatus. He drew back a heavy curtain that reached up to the ceiling and entered the semi-darkness of the sick-room. The faint illumination, like moonlight, acquired warmth in the rosy crystal of the silicolloid. Two tiratron stimulators were kept permanently switched on in case of sudden collapse; they clicked away almost soundlessly, keeping the paralyzed patient's heart beating. In the rosy-silver light inside the hood Nisa was stretched out motionless and seemed as though she were sunk in calm, sweet slumber. A hundred generations of the healthy, clean and full life of her ancestors had produced the strong and supple lines of the female body that approached the acme of artistic perfection-the most beautiful creation of Earth's powerful life.

Everything moves and develops in a spiral and Erg Noor could see in his imagination that magnificent spiral of the common ascent as applied to life and to human society. Only now did he realize with surprising clarity that the more difficult the conditions for the life and work of organisms as biological machines, the harder the path of social development, the tighter the spiral is twisted and the closer to each other are its turns, the slower the process and more standardized and similar are the forms that emerge. By the laws of dialectics, however, the more imperceptible the ascent, the more stable is that which has been achieved.

He had been wrong in his pursuit of the wonderful planets of the blue sun and he had been teaching Nisa wrongly! They should not fly to new worlds in search of some uninhabited planet that chance made suitable for life, but man should advance deliberately, step by step, through his own arm of the Galaxy in a triumphal march of knowledge and the beauty of life. Such as Nisa....

In a sudden burst of deep sorrow Erg Noor dropped to his knees in front of the astronavigator's silicolloid sarcophagus. The girl's breathing was not perceptible, her eyelashes cast blue shadows on her cheeks and her white teeth were just visible through her slightly parted lips. On her left shoulder, at the base of her neck and near the elbow there were pale, bluish marks-the places where the injurious currents had struck her.

"Can you see me, do you remember anything in your sleep?" asked Erg Noor in agony, in an outburst of grief; he felt his own willpower becoming softer than wax, it was difficult for him to breathe and there was a catch in his throat. The commander strained his interlocked fingers until they turned blue in his effort to transmit his thoughts to Nisa, to make her hear his impassioned call to life and Happiness. But the girl with the auburn curls lay as immobile as a statue of pink marble carved to perfection from a living model.

Dr. Louma Lasvy entered the sick bay softly and sensed the presence of somebody else in the silent room. Cautiously withdrawing the curtain she saw the kneeling figure of the commander as motionless as a memorial to the millions of men who have mourned their loved ones. This was not the first time she had found Erg Noor there and her heart was moved with pity for him. He rose gloomily to his feet. Louma went over to him and whispered in anxious tones:

"I want to speak to you."

Erg Noor nodded and went out, blinking as he entered the lighted part of the sick bay. He did not sit down on the chair Louma offered him but remained leaning against the upright of a mushroom-shaped irradiation apparatus. Louma Lasvy stood up in front of him to her full, lint not very great, height, trying to make herself look taller and more important for the impending talk. The commander's looks gave her no time for preparations.

"You know," she began uncertainly, "that present-day neurology has discovered the process by which emotions emerge in the conscious and subconscious divisions of the psyche. The subconscious yields to the influence of inhibiting drugs administered through the ancient spheres of the brain that control the chemical regulation of the organism, including the nervous system and, to some extent, higher nervous activity "

Erg Noor raised his brows. Louma Lasvy felt that she was speaking in too great detail and too long.

"I want to say that medicine is able to affect those brain centres that control the strong emotions. I could…." Understanding flashed up in Erg Noor's eyes and developed into a slight smile.

"You propose affecting my love for Nisa and relieving me of suffering?" he asked brusquely.

The doctor nodded in affirmation, afraid to spoil the tenderness of her sympathy with words that would inevitably be schematic.

Erg Noor stretched out his hand gratefully but shook his head in refusal.

"I would not give up the wealth of my emotions, no matter how much suffering they cause me. Suffering, so long as it is not beyond one's strength, leads to understanding, understanding leads to love and the circle is complete. You're very kind, Louma, but it isn't necessary!"

And the commander disappeared through the door with his usual swift gait.

Hurrying, as they would have done in an emergency, the electronic and mechanical engineers erected the televisophone screen for the reception of terrestrial transmissions. After thirteen years the screen was being erected in the library of the central control tower as the ship was now in a zone where radio waves, dispersed by Earth's atmosphere could be received.

The voices, sounds, forms and colours of their native Earth cheered the travellers up and also served to increase their impatience-the great length of the Cosmic journey was becoming intolerable.

The spaceship sent out a call to Artificial Earth Satellite No. 57 on the usual wavelength used for long-distance Cosmic journeys and impatiently awaited an answer from this powerful station that served as a link between Earth and the Cosmos.

At last the call signals from the spaceship reached Earth.

The whole crew of the ship were awake and did not leave the receivers. They were returning to life after thirteen terrestrial and nine dependent years in which there had been no contact with their native planet! They listened eagerly to reports from Earth, and they took part in the discussion of important questions raised on the world radio network by anybody who wished to do so.

Quite by chance they picked up a proposal from the soil scientist Heb Uhr that gave them material for a six-weeks' discussion and very intricate calculations.

"Discuss Heb Uhr's proposal!" thundered the voice of Earth. "Let everybody who is working in that field; who has any similar ideas or objections, say his word!"

This, the usual formula, had a pleasant sound for the travellers. Heb Uhr had proposed to the Astronautical Council a plan for the systematic exploration of the reachable planets of the blue and green stars. He believed these to be special worlds with extraordinarily strong power emanations that might chemically stimulate mineral compounds that are inert under terrestrial conditions to struggle against entropy, that is, give them life. Special forms of life from minerals that are heavier than gas would be active in high temperatures and in the intense radiation of stars in the higher spectral classes. Heb Uhr was of the opinion that the failure of the Sirius expedition, the failure to find life there, was to be expected since that rapidly rotating star was a binary that did not possess a powerful magnetic field. Nobody disputed with Heb Uhr the fact that binary stars could not be regarded as the originators of planetary systems in the Cosmos, but the essence of the proposal called forth very lively opposition from *Tantra's* crew.

The astronomers, headed by Erg Noor, compiled a report which was transmitted as being the opinion of the first people who had seen Vega in the film taken by *Parus*.

People on Earth listened with delight and admiration to the voice from the approaching spaceship.

Tantra opposed the dispatch of the expeditions suggested by Heb Uhr. The blue stars really did emanate tremendous energy per unit of their planets' surfaces, sufficient to ensure the life of heavy compounds. Any living organism, however, was at once both an energy filter and a dam which, in its struggle against the Second Law of Thermodynamics, functioned only by means of the creation of a complex, by means of the great complication of simple mineral and gas molecules. Such complications could only occur in a process of tremendously active development, which, in turn, entailed the lengthy stability of physical Conditions. Stable conditions did not exist on the planets of high-temperature stars which rapidly destroyed complicated compounds in bursts and vortices of powerful radiation. Nothing there could exist for long despite the fact that minerals acquired the most stable crystal structure with a cubic atomic pattern.

Tantra was of the opinion that Heb Uhr was merely repeating the one-sided assertions of the ancient astronomers who had not understood the dynamics of planet development. Every planet lost the lighter substances that were carried away into space and dispersed. The loss of light elements was especially great in cases where there was great heat and great light pressure from the blue suns.

Tantra gave a long string of examples and concluded that the process of "increasing weight" on the planets of the blue stars did not permit the emergence of living forms.

Satellite 57 transmitted Tantra's objections direct to the Council observatory.

At last the moment came that Ingrid Dietra and Kay Bear, like all other members of the expedition, had been awaiting so impatiently. *Tnntra* began to reduce her speed from her subphotonic velocity, had passed the ice belt of the solar system and was approaching the spaceship station on Triton. High velocity was no longer necessary: travelling at a speed of 900 million kilometres an hour, they would have reached Earth from Neptune's satellite. Triton, in less than five hours. The acceleration of the spaceship, however, took so long that she would have overshot the Sun and travelled far away from it into space if she had set out from Triton.

In order to economize the precious anameson and save the ship from carrying unwieldy equipment, communications inside the solar system were effected by ion planet-ships. Their speed did not exceed 800,000 kilometres an hour for the inner planets and 2,500,000 kilometres an hour for the most distant outer planets. The usual trip from Neptune to Earth took two and a half to three months.

Triton was a very big satellite, only a little smaller than the huge third and fourth satellites of Jupiter, Ganymede and Callisto, or the planet Mercury. It therefore possessed a thin atmosphere consisting mainly of nitrogen and carbon monoxide.

Erg Noor lauded the spaceship at the appointed place at the satellite's pole, far from the broad domes of the station buildings. On a ledge of the plateau, near a cliff that was honeycombed with underground premises, stood the gleaming glass building of the quarantine sanatorium.

Here the travellers were subjected to a five-week quarantine in complete isolation from all other people. In the course of this time skilled doctors would study their bodies to make sure that no new infection had taken root. The danger was too great to be ignored: every person who had landed on another planet, even on an uninhabited one, had to submit to this inspection no matter how long he had afterwards been confined to the spaceship. The interior of the ship itself was also inspected by the sanatorium's scientists before the station gave permission for the journey to Earth. Those planets that had been studied long before and had been colonized by man, such as Venus and Mars, as well as some of the asteroids, had their own quarantine stations where travellers were examined before the ships left.

Confinement *in* the sanatorium was easier than in the spaceship. There were laboratories in which to work, concert halls, combined baths using electric currents, music, water and wave oscillations, daily walks in light protective suits in the hills near the sanatorium, and, lastly, there was contact with Earth, not always regular, but, still, Earth was only five hours away!

Nisa's silicolloid sarcophagus was carried into the sanatorium with every possible precaution. Erg Noor and the biologist Eon Thai were the last to leave *Tantra*. They moved easily even though wearing weights to prevent their making sudden leaps in the low gravitation on the satellite.

The floodlights around the landing field were extinguished. Triton was moving across Neptune's daylight side. Dull as the greyish light reflected by Neptune was, the giant mirror of the planet, only 35,000 kilometres away from Triton, dispelled the gloom and gave the satellite a bright twilight like that of a spring evening in the northern latitudes of Earth. Triton revolved about Neptune in the opposite direction to the planet's revolution, that is, from east to west, once in about six terrestrial days so that the "daytime" twilight lasted about seventy hours. In that time Neptune revolved about its Own axis four times and at the moment of their arrival the shadow of the satellite was noticeable as it crossed the nebulous disc.

Almost simultaneously the commander and the biologist noticed a small ship standing near the edge of the plateau. This was not a spaceship with its stern half broader than the bows and with high stabilizer ribs. Judging by the sharp bows and slim hull it must have been a planetship hut its contours differed in the thick ring at the stern and the long, distaff-shaped structure on top.

"There's another ship here in quarantine?" half asked, half asserted Eon. "Can the Council have changed its rules?"

"Not to send out stellar expeditions before a previous one has returned?" asked Erg Noor in his turn. "We have kept to our schedule but the report we should have sent to Earth from Zirda was two years late."

"Perhaps it is an expedition to Neptune," suggested the biologist. They soon covered the two kilometres to the sanatorium and climbed up to a wide terrace faced with red basalt. The tiny disc of the Sun, easily visible from the pole of the non-rotating satellite, shone brighter than any other star in the black sky. The bitter frost, --170° C., felt like the ordinary cold of a northern winter on Earth through their heated protective suits. Huge flakes of snow, frozen ammonia or carbon monoxide, fell slowly through the still atmosphere, giving their surroundings the serene appearance of Earth during a snow-fall.

Erg Noor and Eon Thai stared hypnotized at the falling snowflakes as did their distant ancestors in the northern lands for whom the first snow-fall meant the end of the farm year. And this unusual snow also meant the end of their journey and their labours.

The biologist, in response to a subconscious impulse, held out his hand to the commander.

"Our adventures are over and we are still alive and well-thanks to you!"

Erg Noor made an abrupt gesture repelling his hand. "Are we all well? And thanks to whom am I alive?" Eon Thai was not put out.

"I'm sure Nisa will be saved! The doctors here want to begin treatment immediately. Instructions have been received from Grimm Schar himself, you know, the head of the General Paralysis Laboratory."

"Do they know what it is?"

"Not yet. But Nisa has obviously been struck by some sort of current that condenses in the nerve nodes of the autonomous systems. When we find out how to put a stop to its extraordinarily long action the girl will be cured. We have discovered the functioning of persistent psychic paralysis that was considered incurable for centuries, haven't we? This is something similar caused by an outside exciter. We'll carry out some experiments on my prisoners, whether they are dead or alive, then … my arm will also begin to function again!"

The commander felt ashamed and frowned; in his great sorrow he had forgotten how much the biologist had done for him. Not at all decent in a grown man! He took the biologist's hand and they expressed their warm friendship in man's age-old handshake.

"Do you think the lethal organs of the black jelly-fish and that-that cross-shaped abomination are of the same order?" asked Erg Noor.

"I don't doubt it, my arm tells me that. Adaptation to life in these black creatures, inhabitants of a planet rich in electricity, has taken the form of the accumulation and transformation of electric energy. They are obviously beasts of prey but we still don't know whom they prey on."

"But do you remember what happened to us all when Nisa "

"That's another thing. I have thought a lot about that. When that awful cross appeared it radiated infrasonic waves of tremendous strength that broke down our willpower. Sounds in that black world are also black and we cannot hear them. This monster dulls the consciousness with infrasonic effects, and then uses a sort of hypnosis much stronger than that once used by the now extinct big terrestrial snakes, like the anaconda, for example. That was what nearly finished us-if it had not been for Nisa "

Erg Noor looked at the distant Sun that was at that moment also shining on Earth. The Sun is man's eternal hope, has been since the prehistoric days when man dragged out a pitiful existence in the teeth of ruthless nature. The Sun is the incarnation of the bright forces of the intellect driving away the darkness and the monsters of the night. And a joyful spark of hope went with him for the rest of his journey.

The Director of the Triton Station came to see Erg Noor at the sanatorium to tell him that Earth wanted to speak to him. The Director's appearance in a building that was in strict quarantine meant that their isolation was over and that *Tantra* would be able to complete her thirteen-year journey. Erg Noor came back looking more business-like than ever.

"We are leaving today. I have been asked to take six people from the planetship *Amat* with us; the ship is remaining here to organize the mining of new mineral deposits on Pluto. We are taking back the expedition and the material they collected on Pluto.

"These six people re-equipped an ordinary planetship for the performance of a deed of great valour. They dived into the depths of hell, down through Pluto's thick atmosphere of neon and methane, they flew through blizzards of ammonia snow, every second bringing fresh risks of collision with gigantic needles of frozen water as hard as steel. They managed to find a region where there are mountains.

"The mystery of Pluto has been solved at last-it is a planet that does not belong to our solar system but one that was captured by the Sun during its passage through the Galaxy. This accounts for Pluto's density being much greater than that of any other planet. The explorers discovered strange minerals on this alien world but more important still, on one ridge they found an almost completely ruined structure that told of an inconceivably ancient civilization. The research data must, of course, be checked. The intelligent working of building materials has still to be proved. But still, an amazingly valorous deed has been done. I am proud that our spaceship will carry the heroes back to Earth and I am all impatience to hear their stories. Their quarantine was over three days ago."

Erg Noor stopped, exhausted by such a lengthy speech.

"But there is a serious contradiction in this!" shouted Pour Hyss.

"Contradiction is the mother of truth!" Erg Noor answered calmly, making use of an old proverb. "It's time to get *Tantra* ready."

The tried and tested spaceship got away from Triton very easily and described a huge arc perpendicular to the plane of the ecliptic. It was impossible to get directly to Earth--any ship would have been destroyed in the wide asteroid and meteoroid belt, a zone filled with the fragments of the burst planet Phaeton that once existed between Mars and Jupiter and was exploded by the gravitation of the giant of the solar system.

Erg Noor increased acceleration. He did not intend to take his expedition back to Earth by the normal seventy-two day route but to use the colossal power of the spaceship to make the journey in fifty hours with a minimum expenditure of anameson.

Transmission from Earth raced through space to *Tantra* and the planet greeted the victory over the gloom of the iron star and over the gloom of icy Pluto. Specially written songs and symphonies in honour of *Tantra* and *Amat* were performed.

The Cosmos resounded with triumphant melodies. Stations on Mars, Venus and the asteroids called the ship, their chords merging with the general chorus of homage to the heroes.

"*Tantra… Tantra…*" came, at last, the voice from the Council's control post. "You may land on El Homra!"

The Central Cosmic Port was situated where there had formerly been a desert in North Africa and the spaceship made its way there through the sun-drenched atmosphere of Earth.

CHAPTER SEVEN

SYMPHONY IN F-MINOR,
COLOUR TONE 4.75M

The wall of the broad verandah facing south towards the sea was made of sheets of transparent plastic. The pale diffused light from the ceiling complemented rather than rivalled the moonlight, softening its dense black shadows. Almost the whole maritime expedition had gathered on the verandah, only the very youngest members of the expedition were still frolicking in the moonlit sea. Cart Sann, the artist, was there with his beautiful model. Frith Don, the Director of the expedition, shook back his long, golden hair as he told the people about the horse Miyiko had found. When they made tests of the material from which it was made in order to calculate the weight to he lifted they got the most unexpected results. Under the superficial layer of some alloy the statue was pure gold. If the horse were cast solid then its weight, after allowance had been made for water displacement, would be four hundred tons. Special vessels with powerful salvage gear had been sent for-an unexpected development from a pleasant afternoon's swim enjoyed by Miyiko Eigoro and Darr Veter. Somebody asked how so much valuable metal could have been used so foolishly. One of the older historians recalled a legend discovered in the historical archives telling of the disappearance of the gold reserves of a whole country, and that at a time when gold was the monetary expression of labour values. Certain criminal rulers, guilty of tyranny and the impoverishment of the people, had been forced to flee to another country-in those days there were obstacles called frontiers preventing contact between nations-and before absconding they gathered together the entire gold reserve and cast a statue from it and placed it in the busiest square of the country's chief city. Nobody was able to find the gold. The historian presumed that in those days nobody had been able to find the precious metal under the layer of the cheap alloy.

The story caused some excitement. The find of a large quantity of gold was a fine gift to mankind. Although the heavy metal had long ceased to serve as a symbol of value it was still very necessary in electrical instruments, medicines and, especially, for the manufacture of anameson.

In a small group in a corner outside the verandah sat Veda Kong, Darr Veter, the artist, Chara Nandi and Evda Nahl. Renn Bose sat down bashfully beside them after his fruitless attempts to find Mven Mass.

"You were right when you said that artists, or rather, art in general, must always inevitably lag behind the rapid advance of knowledge and technique," said Darr Veter.

"You didn't understand me," objected Cart Saun. "Art has already corrected its errors and understood its duty to mankind. Art has ceased to create oppressive monumental forms, to depict brilliance and majesty that do not exist in reality, for all that was purely superficial. Art's most important duty has become the development of man's emotional side, since only art can rightly attune the human psyche and prepare it for the acceptance of the most complicated impressions. Who does not know how wonderfully easy it is to understand something when you have been pretuned by music, colour or form, and how inaccessible the human spirit is when you try to force a way into it. You historians know better than anybody else how much mankind has suffered through a lack of understanding of the necessity to train and develop the emotional side of the psyche."

"There was a period in the past when art craved abstract forms," Veda Kong put in.

"Art craved abstract forms in imitation of the intellect that had gained priority over everything else. Art, however, cannot find expression in the abstract, with the exception, of course, of music, and that occupies a special place and *is* concrete in its own way. Art in those days was on the wrong track."

"What do you believe to be the right track?"

"I believe that art should be a reflection of the struggle and anxieties of life in people's feelings, at times it should illustrate life but under the control of a common purposefulness. This purposefulness, in other words, is beauty, without which I cannot see happiness or a meaning for life. Without it art can easily degenerate into mere fanciful invention, especially if the artist has an insufficient knowledge of life and of history."

"I have always wanted art to help conquer and change he world and not merely to sense the world," added Darr Veter. I "I agree with that, but with one proviso," said Cart Sann. "Art shouldn't treat the outside world alone; it's more important to treat of man's inner world, his emotions, his education. With an understanding of all contradictions "

Evda Nahl placed her strong, warm hand on Darr Veter's.

"What dream have you renounced today?" At first Veter wanted to put her off, but realized that with Evda equivocation was impossible. And so he pretended to be absorbed in the artist's discourse.

"Those who have seen the mass art of the past," continued the artist, "cinema films, recordings of theatre shows, exhibitions of pictures, know how. marvellously refined, elegant, purged of all superfluities our present-day spectacles, dances and pictures seem by contrast. I am not comparing them with the periods of decay, of course."

"He's clever but too verbose," whispered Veda Kong. "It's difficult for an artist to express in words or formulas those complicated phenomena that he sees and selects from his environment," Chara Nandi said in his defence and Evda Nahl nodded approvingly.

"What I want to do is something like this," continued Cart Sann, "I want to collect into one image the pure grains of the wonderful genuineness of feeling, form and colour scattered among many people. I want to restore the ancient images by the highest expression of the beauty of each of the races of the distant past that have gone into the makeup of mankind today. The *Daughter of Gondwana is* unity with nature, a subconscious knowledge of the connections between things and phenomena, a complex of senses and feelings interlaced with instincts.

"The *Daughter of Thetis,* the Mediterranean, has strongly developed emotions that are fearlessly expansive and infinitely varying; here there is a different degree of the union with nature, through emotions, the power of Eros-that is how I imagine her. The ancient civilizations of the Mediterranean, the Cretan, Etruscan, Hellenic and Proto-Indian-gave rise to the type of man who, alone of all others, could have created that civilization that stemmed from the rule of woman. I had the best of luck when I discovered Chara: she is by pure accident a combination of the traits of ancestors from amongst the Graeco-Cretans of antiquity and the later peoples of Central India."

Veda smiled at the correctness of her guess and Darr Veter whispered to her that it would be hard to find a better model.

"If my Daughter of the Mediterranean turns out a success then I must go on to the third part of the plan- I must paint the golden- or flaxen-haired northern woman, with her calm and transparent eyes, tall, somewhat slow in her movements, her glance straightforward as she looks out at the world like one of the ancient Russian, Scandinavian or English women. Only when that is finished shall I be able to start on the synthesis, the image of the present-day woman in which I shall have to portray the best features of each of those ancestors."

"Why do you only paint 'daughters' and no 'sons'?" asked Veda, smiling mysteriously.

"Is there any need for me to explain that by the laws of physiology the beautiful is always more finished and more refined in woman?" frowned the artist.

"When you are ready to paint your third picture, your *Daughter of the North,* take a good look at Veda Kong," began Evda Nahl, "you'll hardly...."

Andromeda

The artist rose swiftly to his feet.

"D'you think I'm blind? I am struggling against myself to prevent that image becoming part of me at a time when I am full of another. But Veda…."

"Is dreaming of music," continued Veda. "What a pity there is only a solar piano here and it's silent at night."

"Is that the piano with a system of semi-conductors that works from sunlight?" asked Renn Bose, leaning over the arm of his chair. "If it is, I can switch it over to use the, current of the receiver."

"Will it take long?" asked Veda, pleased at the opportunity.

"It would take about an hour."

"Then don't bother. The news broadcast on the world circuit begins in an hour and we want to see and hear it. We've been busy the past two evenings and haven't switched on the receiver."

"Then sing us something, Veda," asked Darr Veter. "Cart Sann has the eternal stringed instrument, the one that dates back to feudal society in the Dark Ages."

"Guitar," guessed Chara Nandi.

"Who'll play? I'll try myself, perhaps I can manage."

"I'll play." Chara Nandi volunteered to go for the guitar.

"We'll run together," suggested Frith Don. Chara roguishly tossed back her mass of black hair. Sherliss pulled a lever moving back the side wall of the verandah giving them a view of the eastern corner of the bay. Frith Don ran with long strides. Chara ran with her head thrown back and soon fell behind but in the end they arrived at the studio together, plunged into the un-lighted entrance and a second later reappeared to skim along the edge of the sea, stubborn and swift-footed. Frith Don was the first to reach the verandah but Chara vaulted over the open side partition and was first in the room. Veda clapped her hands in admiration. "But Frith Don won last year's decathlon!" "And Chara Nandi was graduated from the Higher School of Dance, both departments. Ancient and Modern," retorted Cart Sann, in the same tone.

"Veda and I studied dancing too, but only in the lower grades," sighed Evda Nahl.

"Everybody passes the lower grade nowadays," said the artist teasingly. Chara ran her fingers lightly over the strings, sticking out her small, firm chin. The guitar hummed low, pensive notes. The young woman's high-pitched voice combined longing and challenge. She sang a new song, one that had just come from the southern zone, a song of an unfulfilled dream. Veda's low contralto joined in and became the beam around which Chara's voice coiled and quivered. It was a magnificent duet, the two singers were absolute opposites and yet they complemented each other perfectly. Darr Veter turned his gaze from one to the other unable to decide to whom the singing was most becoming-Veda, who stood leaning her elbows on the receiver and her head bowed under the weight of a mass of blonde hair that glittered silver in the moonlight, or Chara, leaning forward with the guitar on her round, bare knees, with a face tanned by the sun in which the white of her teeth and the bluish whites of her eyes stood out in sharp contrast.

The song finished, Chara picked idly at the strings. Darr Veter clenched his teeth-she was strumming the song that had once separated him from Veda, a song that was now painful to her, too.

She plucked at the strings spasmodically, the chords following each other and dying before they could merge. It was a jerky melody, like the splashes of waves falling on the beach, spreading over the sand for an instant and then rolling back, one after another, to the black depths of the sea. Chara was quite unaware of anything, her clear voice gave life to the words of love that flew out into the icy void of the Cosmos from star to star, trying to find, to understand, to feel where he was ... he who had gone into the Cosmos for the great deed of discovery-he would never return-let it be so, if only for one moment .she could know what was happening to him, help him with a whispered word, a kind thought, a greeting!

Veda remained silent and Chara felt there was something wrong, she broke off the song, jumped up, tossed the guitar to the artist and went over to where the fair-haired woman was standing, her head bowed guiltily.

Veda smiled.

"Dance for me, Chara."

The latter nodded obediently but Frith Don stopped her.

"The dances can wait, there's a transmission beginning now.

On the roof of the building a telescopic pipe was put up on which there were two metal sheets at right angles to each other surmounted by a circular structure with eight hemispheres arranged around its circumference. The room was filled with the mighty sounds of the world information service.

"The discussion of the project introduced by the Academy of Directed Radiation continues," said a man on the screen. "The project provides for the substitution of electronic recording for the linear alphabet. The project is not being universally supported. The chief objection is the intricacy of the reading apparatus. The book will cease to be a friend to accompany men everywhere. Despite all its apparent advantages the project will probably be rejected!"

"It's been discussed for a long time," said Renn Bose.

"A big contradiction," answered Darr Veter, "on the one hand, there is the tempting simplicity of the writing and, on the other, the difficulty of reading."

The man on the screen continued:

"Yesterday's report is confirmed-Cosmic Expedition No. 37 has been heard from. They are returning "

Darr Veter was staggered by the strength of his own contrasting emotions. Out of the corner of his eye he saw Veda Kong slowly rise to her feet, her eyes opening wider and wider. With the keen ears of a lover Darr Veter caught the sound of her spasmodic breathing.

"... from the direction of square four hundred and one the ship has just come out of the negative field at one-hundredth of a parsec from Neptune's orbit. The expedition has been delayed through an encounter with a black sun. There have been no losses of life! The speed of the ship.'" said the news reader in conclusion, "is about five-sixths of the absolute unit. The expedition is expected at Triton in eleven days! ... Listen for reports of their marvellous discoveries!"

The broadcast continued. There were other items of "news but nobody listened to them any more. They crowded round Veda, congratulating her. She smiled, her cheeks were burning but there was anxiety hidden deep down in her eyes. Darr Veter also approached. Veda felt the firm pressure of his hand and met his eyes, direct and sincere. Not for a long time had he looked at her like that and she understood the sadness of his former attitude towards her and she realized that at that moment he read something else in her face besides joy.

Darr Veter slowly released her hand, smiled in a way all his own, inimitably open and frank, and walked away. Her companions from the expedition were excitedly discussing the news. Veda remained inside the circle of people but watched Darr Veter out of the corner of her eye. She saw Evda Nahl go up to him and a moment later they were joined by Renn Bose. "We must find Mven Mass, he still doesn't know the news!" exclaimed Darr Veter, as though he had suddenly remembered. "Come along with me, Evda. And what about you, Renn?"

"I'll come too," said Chara Nandi as she came up.

"May I?"

They went down towards the gently lapping waves. Darr Veter stopped, turned his face to the cool breeze and sighed deeply. Turning round he met Evda Nahl's eyes.

"I'm going away without returning to the house," he said in answer to her unasked question. Evda took him by the arm. For some time they walked on in silence.

"I've been thinking... must you?" whispered Evda, "but I suppose you must, I suppose you're right. If Veda ..." Evda stopped, but Darr Veter squeezed her hand understandingly and pressed it to his cheek. Renn Bose followed on their heels, carefully edging away from Chara who, with a slightly mocking smile, ogled him with her big eyes and swayed her body exaggeratedly as she walked with long steps beside him. Evda laughed a scarcely audible laugh and suddenly offered the physicist her free arm. Rcnn Bose seized it with a predatory movement that seemed funny in that bashful fellow.

"Where are we to look for your friend?" asked Chara, stopping at the edge of the water. Darr Veter looked round in the bright moonlight and saw fresh footprints on the strip of wet sand. They were made at exactly the same intervals and the soles were turned outward symmetrically with such precision that the footprints seemed to be the work of a machine.

"He went that way," said Darr Veter pointing towards some big boulders.

"Yes, those are his footprints," confirmed Evda Nahl.

"Why are you so sure?" asked Chara, doubtfully. "Look at the regularity of the paces, that's how primitive hunters walked... or those who have inherited their traits. It seems to me that Mven, despite all his learning, is closer to nature than any of us ... although ... I don't know about you, Chara." Evda turned to the girl who was pondering over something.

"Me? Oh, no!" She pointed forward and exclaimed, "There he is!"

The huge figure of the African, shining like polished black marble in the moonlight, appeared on the nearest boulder. Mven Mass was shaking his fists energetically as though he were threatening somebody. The powerful muscles of his mighty body rose and fell and rolled beneath his gleaming skin.

"He's like the spirit of the night from the children's tales," whispered Chara excitedly. Mven Mass noticed the people approaching him, jumped down from his rock and soon appeared before them with his clothes on. In a few words Darr Veter explained what had happened and Mven Mass expressed a desire to see Veda Kong.

"Go over there with Chara," said Evda, "and we'll stay down here for a little while." Darr Veter made a gesture of farewell and saw by Mven's face that he had understood. A burst of something like childishness egged Mven on to whisper words of farewell that had long since gone out of usage. Darr Veter was touched by this gesture and walked away, deep in thought, accompanied by the silent Evda. Renn Bose hesitated for a while in some confusion and then followed behind Mven Mass and Chara.

Darr Veter and Evda walked down as far as the cape that protected the bay from the open sea. From there they would see the lights round the huge disc-shaped rafts of the maritime expedition.

Darr Veter pushed a transparent plastic boat off the sand and stood by the water in front of Evda, even more massive and powerful than Mven Mass. Evda stretched up on tiptoes to give her friend a parting kiss.

"Veter, I'll be with Veda," she said, as though answering his thoughts. "We'll go back to our zone together and there we'll await your arrival. Let me know where you fix yourself up, I'll always be glad to help you."

For a long time Evda followed the boat with her eyes as it crossed the silvery sea.

Darr Veter went as far as the second raft where the mechanics were still working in a hurry to set up the accumulators. In response to Veter's request they lit three green lights in the form of a triangle. An hour and a half later, the first helicopter that came that way hung over the raft, the roar of its engines rumbling over the sleepy sea. Darr Veter entered the lift it lowered; for a second he could be seen against the illuminated bottom of the aircraft and then disappeared through the hatch. By morning he reached his permanent abode near the Council observatory which he had not had time to change for another. Darr Veter opened the air-taps in both his rooms and in a few minutes all dust had vanished. He pulled his bed out of the wall and, tuning his bedroom in to the smell and sounds of the sea that he had lately become accustomed to, was soon sound asleep.

He awoke with a sensation that the beauty of the world had been lost. Veda was far away and would remain far away … now … until …. But he must help her and not complicate matters!

In his bathroom a whirling column of cold electrified water burst upon him. Darr Veter stood under the column of water so long that he began to shiver. Feeling refreshed he went to the televisophone, opened its mirror doors and called up the nearest Registrar of Vacancies. The face of the registrar, a young man, appeared on the screen. He knew Darr Veter and greeted him with a scarcely perceptible shade of respect that was considered the hallmark of politeness.

"I want to get some hard and lengthy job, with tough physical labour," said Darr Veter, "something like the Antarctic mines!"

"All the jobs there are taken!" answered the registrar, in tones of sincere regret. "All the miner's jobs on Venus, Mars and even Mercury have been filled too. You know that the young people are always anxious to go where the work is hardest."

"That's true but I can no longer place myself in that fine category. What is there now? I want a job immediately."

"There are the diamond workings in Central Siberia," began the registrar slowly, glancing at a list that Darr Veter could not see, "that is, if you want mine work. Then there are some jobs on the rafts of the oceanic food-packing plants, at the solar pumping station in Tibet, but that's easy work. There are some other places, but nothing particularly hard!"

Darr Veter thanked him and asked for some time to think things over and asked him to keep the place open in the diamond workings.

He switched off the Registrar of Vacancies and tuned in to Siberia House, the centre for geographical information concerning that country. His televisophone was switched on to a memory machine that showed him the latest records and he saw pictures of extensive forests go floating past him. The boggy, scanty, larch forests growing on permafrost that had once occupied the region were gone for ever, giving place to such giants as Siberian cedars and American sequoias, trees that had formerly been in danger of extinction. Their gigantic red trunks made a magnificent fence round hills covered with ferroconcrete caps. Steel tubes, thirty feet in diameter, crawled from under the caps and curved over ridges to the nearest rivers that they sucked entirely into their huge scoops. Monstrously huge pumps roared dully. Billions of gallons of water were driven into the volcanic chimneys where the diamonds were found; the water whirled and raged as it washed the clay away and then found its way out again leaving behind tons of diamonds on the grids of the washing chambers. In long, well-lit buildings people were watching the dials of the sorting machines. The brilliant stones were sifted like grain through the calibrated holes of a screen into boxes. The pumping station operators were keeping constant watch over the calculating machines that computed the ever-changing resistance of the rock, the pressure and expenditure -of water, the depth of the shaft and the expulsion of solid matter. Darr Veter thought that though the joyful picture of sun-bathed forests did not suit his mood at that moment, the concentrated activity of the work at the pumps might suit him and he switched off Siberia

House. Immediately the call signal rang out and the Registrar of Vacancies appeared on the screen.

"I'd like to give you something more concrete to think about. We have received a request for somebody to fill a vacancy that has just occurred in the submarine titanium mines off the west coast of South America. This is the hardest work available today, but if you take it you'll have to go there immediately."

That last piece of information rather upset Darr Veter. "But I shan't have time to pass the tests at the nearest station of the Academy of the Psychophysiology of Labour," he said.

"The sum of the annual tests that were obligatory for your former work is sufficient to exempt you from them."

"Inform them that I'm coming and give me the coordinates!" answered Darr Veter immediately.

"Western section of the Spiral Way, seventeenth southern branch.

Station 6L, Point KM40. I'll inform them."

The serious-looking face disappeared from the screen. Darr Veter gathered together all the little trifles that belonged to him personally and filled a box with films containing the photographs and voices of his nearest relatives and friends and the most important records of his own thoughts. He took a chromoreflex reproduction of an old Russian picture from the wall and from the table he took a bronze statuette of the actress Bello Galle, which he kept because it bore a resemblance to Veda Kong. All these things and his few clothes he packed into an aluminium box with some letters and figures embossed on the lid. Darr Veter dialled the coordinates he had been given, opened a hatch in the wall and pushed the box into it. The box disappeared, taken up by an endless belt. Then he checked up on his rooms. Long before the Great Circle Era special cleaners and charwomen had been abolished. The work was now done by every person in his own place, something he could do because of his sense of absolute orderliness and discipline and because domestic and public buildings were designed more conveniently and fitted with means to clean and air them automatically.

When he had finished his examination he pulled down the lever at the door which immediately informed the Housing Bureau that his rooms had been vacated. Outside, on an external gallery glazed with sheets of milk-coloured plastic, the sun's warmth made itself felt, but on the flat roof the sea breeze was as cool as ever. The light footbridges thrown from one high latticed building to another seemed to be soaring in the air and tempting the onlooker to a leisurely saunter along them. Darr Veter, however, no longer belonged to himself. Through the tubular tunnel of the automatic descent he made his way to the underground electromagnetic mail tunnel and a tiny truck took him with switchback-like movements to the Spiral Way station. Darr Veter did not travel north, to the Behring Straits, where he could get on the intercontinental arch of the Spiral Way. To reach South America by this route, especially as far south as the seventeenth branch, would take four days and nights. In the northern and southern inhabited zones there were helicopter lines that handled heavy cargo round the planet, crossing the oceans and short-circuiting the brandies of the Spiral Way. Darr Veter travelled by the Central Branch as far as the southern inhabited zone hoping there to be able to convince the Director of Transport that he was urgent cargo. Apart from saving thirty hours by going this way he would be able to see Diss Ken, the son of Grom Orme, President of the Astronautical Council, who had selected him as his mentor.

Diss Ken had come to the end of his school years and in the following year would begin his twelve Labours of Hercules; in the meantime he was working in the Watchers' Service of the West African swamps.

Every youth wanted to enter the Watchers' Service- to keep a look-out for sharks in the ocean, for harmful insects, vampires and reptiles in the tropical swamps, for disease microbes in the living zones, for epizoons and forest fires in the savanna and forest zones-hunting down and destroying all harmful life left over from the old world that in some mysterious way kept reappearing in remote corners of the planet. The struggle against harmful forms of life never ceased for a moment. Microorganisms, insects and fungi reacted to new and most radical chemical destroyers by the development of new, impervious forms. People learned to make proper use of strong antibiotics without generating dangerous and stable bacteria only after the Era of Disunity.

"If Diss Ken has been appointed to the Swamp Watchers' Service," thought Darr Veter, "he must be a serious young man."

Diss Ken, Groin Orme's son, like all children in the Great Circle Era, had been brought up away from his parents in a school on the sea-shore in the northern zone. There, too, he had passed the first tests made by a local station of the Academy of the Psychophysiology of Labour. When young people were allotted work the psychological specifics of youth-the urge to go farther, an exaggerated sense of responsibility and egocentrism-were taken into consideration.

The huge coach ran on smoothly and silently. Darr Veter went up to the top deck where there was a transparent roof. Far below, on either side of the Spiral Way, buildings, canals, forests and mountain tops swept past. The brightly gleaming, transparent domes of buildings marked the narrow belt of automatic factories at the junction of the agricultural and forestry belts. The rugged shapes of the huge servicing machines could be clearly seen through the glass walls of the buildings.

The monument erected to Zhinn Cahd, the inventor of a cheap method of manufacturing artificial sugar, flashed past and then the arches of the Spiral Way cut across the forests of the tropical agricultural zone. Plantations of trees stretching away into infinite distance showed every conceivable shade of leaf and bark and great variety in the shape and height. Harvesting, pollination and calculating machines crawled along the smooth narrow roads that separated the plantations: countless cables formed a giant cobweb. There was a time when a field of ripe, golden corn had been the symbol of abundance. In the Era of World Unity, however, the economic inefficiency of annual crops was realized and, after all farming had been transferred to the tropical belt, the hard labour involved in the annual cultivation of herbage and bush plants became unnecessary. In the Great Circle Era perennial trees that did not take too much out of the soil and were impervious to climatic changes, became the chief crop.

Bread, berry and nut trees, yielding thousands of different kinds of fruit rich in proteins, produced up to a hundred kilograms of food each. Forests of these trees ran round the planet in two belts covering thousands of millions of acres-true belts of Ceres, the ancient Goddess of Agriculture. Between these two belts lay the equatorial forestry zone, an ocean of humid tropical forests that supplied the whole world with its timber-white, black, violet, pink, golden and grey wood with a silky grain, wood as hard as Lone or as soft as an apple, wood that sank like a stone and wood that floated like cork. The forests also yielded dozens of kinds of resin cheaper than the synthetic varieties, possessing valuable technical or medicinal properties.

The tops of the forest giants were level with the permanent way and waved and surged on both sides like a green ocean. In the dark depths of these forests, in cosy-looking glades, stood houses on metal piles and beside them mechanical spider-like monsters capable of turning these stands of 80-metre trees into stacks of logs and planks.

To the left appeared the rounded summits of the famous equatorial mountains. On one of them, Kenya, was the installation for the maintenance of communications with the Great Circle. The ocean of trees moved away to the left, making way for a stony plateau. Blue cube-shaped buildings appeared on both sides.

The train stopped and Darr Veter stepped out on to the extensive, glass-paved square of the Equator Station. Near the foot-bridge that stretched over the grey tops of the Atlas cedars, stood a white truncated pyramid of porcelain-like aplite from the River Lualaba, surmounted by the statue of a worker of an age long past. The luxuriant silver foliage of trees brought from South Africa surrounded the pedestal whose sides gleamed dazzlingly bright in the sunshine. In his right hand he held a gleaming sphere with four transmitting antennae jutting out from it, his left was stretched out towards the pale equatorial sky. The man's body, straining backwards as though to launch the sphere into the sky, was the expression of inspired effort. The figures of people in strange clothing arranged around the pedestal at the feet of the central figure increased the impression of effort. This was a monument to the builders of the first man-made Earth satellites, people who had performed miracles of inventiveness, labour and courage.

[margin note: Eurocentrism?]

Ivan Efremov

Darr Veter could never look at these sculptured faces without a feeling of excitement. He knew that the first people to build artificial Earth satellites and reach the threshold of the Cosmos had been Russians, that amazing nation from whom Darr Veter was descended, the people who had taken the first steps towards building the new social order and towards the conquest of the Cosmos....

That day, as usual, Darr Veter made his way to the monument to look once more at the carvings of the heroes of ancient times and to seek in them similarities and differences in comparison with the people of his own day and with himself ....

Two tall, youthful figures appeared through the trees, stopped and then one of them rushed to Darr Veter. He placed his arms round Veter's shoulders and took a stealthy look at the familiar features of that well-known face: the big nose, wide chin, the unexpectedly mirthful turn of the lips that did not seem to fit in with the rather grim expression of the steel-grey eyes under their joined brows.

Darr Veter cast a glance of approval over the son of a famous man who had built bases on the planets of the Centaurus system and had been elected President of the Astronautical Council for five three-year periods in succession. Groin Orme must have been at least 130 years old -three times the age of Darr Veter-but his son was very young.

Diss Ken called over his friend, a dark-haired boy.

"This is Thor Ahn, my best friend, the son of Zieg Zohr, the composer," he said. "We're working together in the swamps and we want to do our Labours of Hercules together and after that we want to continue working together."

"Are you still interested in the cybernetics of heredity?" asked Darr Veter.

"Oh, yes! Thor has got me even more interested-he's a musician, like his father. He and his girl-friend dream of working in a field where music helps us understand the development of living organisms, that is, they want to study the symphony of their structure "

"It's all very indefinite, the way you put it," said Veter, frowning.

"I don't know enough yet," answered Diss in confusion, "perhaps Thor can tell you better than I."

The other lad blushed but stood up to the test of the penetrating glance.

"Digs wanted to tell you about the rhythms of the mechanism of heredity. As the living organism develops from the original cell it attunes itself by chords of molecules. The primordial paired spiral develops along lines analogous to the development of a musical symphony, or, to put it another way, to the logical development in an electronic computing machine."

"Really!" exclaimed Darr Veter in exaggerated astonishment. "Then you will reduce the entire evolution of all living and non-living matter to some sort of a gigantic symphony?"

"The plan and internal rhythm of which are determined by basic physical laws. We have only to understand how the programme is built up and where the information of the musico-cybernetic mechanism comes from," insisted Thor Ahn with the unconquerable confidence of youth.

"Whose idea is it?"

"My father's, Zieg Zohr's. He recently published his 13th Cosmic Symphony in F-minor, Colour Tone 4.75 m

"I'll most certainly hear it! I love blue tones…. Now about your immediate plans, your Labours of Hercules. Do you know what has been allotted you?"

"Only the first six."

"Of course, the other six will be allotted when the first half has been done," Darr Veter recalled.

"Clean out the lower tier of the Kon-I-Gut caves in Central Asia so that visitors can go there." began Thor Ahn.

"Build a road to Lake Mental across the steep mountain ridge," continued Diss Ken, "renew a grove of old bread trees in the Argentine, explain the causes for the appearance of big octopuses in the region of the recent lift near Trinidad "

"And destroy them!"

"That's five, what's the sixth?"

The two lads turned somewhat bashful.

"We are both proficient at music," began Diss Ken, blushing, "and … we have been asked to collect material on the ancient dances of the Island of Bali and resuscitate them musically and choreographically."

"By that do you mean select girls to dance them and form a troupe?" laughed Darr Veter.

"Yes," admitted Thor Ahn, unwillingly.

"An interesting job. But that's a group job, like the road to the lake, isn't it?"

"Yes, we've got a good group. Only ... they want you to be their mentor, too. It would be fine if you only agreed!"

Darr Veter doubted his abilities with regard to the last of the six tasks. The lads, however, their faces beaming, danced for joy and assured him that "Zieg Zohr himself" had promised to guide the sixth task.

"In a year and four months I'll find myself something to do in Central Asia," said Darr Veter, pleased at the happy faces of the two youngsters.

"It's a good thing you're not Director of the Outer Stations any more," exclaimed Diss Ken, "I never thought I'd be working with such a mentor! ..." The lad suddenly blushed so furiously that his forehead was covered with tiny beads of perspiration and Thor even moved away from him with an expression of reproach. Darr Veter hurried to help Grom Orme's son over his *faux pas*. "Have you got plenty of time?"

"No, we were given three hours off and we brought a man here who is ill with a fever he caught in our swamps." "Is there still fever here? I thought...." "It's very rare and only occurs in the swamps," put in Diss, very hurriedly, "that's what we're here for!"

"So we still have two hours left. Let's go into the town, you'll probably want to go to News House."

"Oh, no. We'd like you to ... answer our questions- we have got them ready and you know how important it is when we are selecting our life's work."

Darr Veter gave his consent and the three of them went to the Guest Hall and sat in one of its cool rooms fanned with an artificial sea breeze.

Two hours later another coach took Darr Veter farther on his way; tired out he dozed on a sofa on the lower deck. He woke up when the train stopped in the City of Chemists. A huge structure in the form of a star with ten glazed glass-covered radial buildings stretching from it rose up over an extensive coal-field. The coal that was extracted here was processed into medicines, vitamins, hormones, artificial silk and fur. The waste products went for the manufacture of sugar. In one of the rays of the Star the rare metals germanium and vanadium were extracted from the coal-there was no end to the things that could be got out of that valuable black mineral!

One of Darr Veter's old friends who worked as a chemist in the fur ray came to the station to meet him. Once, long before, there had been three happy young mechanics working on the fruit-gathering machines in Indonesia. Now one of them was a chemist in charge of a laboratory in a big factory, the second had remained a fruit-grower and bad invented a valuable new pollination process and the third, Darr Veter, was once more returning to Mother Earth, only deeper down this time, into the mines. The friends spent no more than ten minutes together, but even such a meeting was much pleasanter than meetings on the TVP.

He had not much farther to go. The Director of the latitudinal air lines listened to his persuasion with the friendly helpfulness that was typical of the Great Circle Era. Darr Veter flew across the ocean and arrived on the western section of the Spiral Way south of the seventeenth branch, at the dead end of which he transferred to a hydroplane to continue his journey.

High mountains came right down to the sea. The gentler slops at the foot were terraced with white stone to hold the soil and were planted with rows of southern pines and Widdringtonia in alternate avenues of bronze and bluish-green needles. High up the bare rocks, there were clefts to be seen in which waterfalls sent up clouds of water dust. Buildings painted bright orange or yellow with bluish-grey roofs stretched at intervals along the terraces.

Jutting out into sea there was an artificial sand-bank at the end of which stood a wave-washed tower. It stood at the edge of the continental shelf which in those parts ended in a submarine cliff a good thousand metres deep. From the tower an extremely thick concrete pipe, strong enough to withstand the pressure in the depths of the ocean, led down vertically. At the bottom the pipe rested on the summit of a submarine mountain that consisted almost entirely of pure rutile or titanium dioxide. The processing of the ore was done under the water, inside the mountain. All that reached the surface was slabs of pure titanium and waste products that spread far into sea, turning the water a muddy yellow. The hydroplane tossed on the yellow waves in front of the landing stage on the southern side of the tower, and Darr Veter waited his opportunity to jump on to the spray-soaked platform. He went upstairs to the railed gallery where several people, not on duty, gathered to welcome the newcomer. Darr' Veter had imagined the mine to be in complete isolation but the people who met him were not at all the anchorites his own mood had led him to expect. The faces that greeted him were happy even if they were somewhat tired from their exacting work. There five men and three women-so women worked there, too!

Before ten days had passed Darr Veter had settled down to his new job.

The mine had its own power plant-in the depths of the abandoned workings on the mainland there was an old nuclear power station type E, or type 2, as it used to be called, which did not have a harmful fall-out and was, therefore, useful for local stations.

A most involved complex of machines was housed in the stone belly of the submarine mountain and moved forward as it bit into the friable reddish-brown mineral. The most difficult work was at the bottom of the installation where the ore was automatically extracted and crushed. The machine received signals from the central control post in the upper storey where all the data on the work of the cutting and crushing apparatus, on the changing hardness and viscosity of the extracted rock as well as information from the flotation tables were accumulated. Depending on the changing metal content in the ore, the crushing and washing arrangements were accelerated or decelerated. The work had to be done by mechanics as the entire control could not be passed over to cybernetic machines owing to the small area protected from the sea.

Darr Veter was given the job of mechanic, testing and setting the lower assembly. He spent his daily tours of duty in semi-dark rooms, packed with indicator dials, where the pump of the air conditioning system could scarcely cope with the overwhelming heat made worse by the increased pressure due to the inevitable leakage of compressed air.

After work Darr Veter and his young assistant would make their way to the top, stand for a long time on the balcony breathing in the fresh air, then take a bath, eat and go each to his own room in one of the houses at the pithead. Darr Veter had tried to renew his study of the new cochlear branch of mathematics but, as time went on, he began to fall asleep more and more quickly, waking up only in time for work. As the months passed he began to feel better. He seemed to have forgotten his former contact with the Cosmos. Like all other workers at the titanium mines he got pleasure out of seeing off the rafts that transported the ingots of titanium. Since the polar ice-caps had been reduced, storms all over the planet had decreased in violence so that many cargoes could be transported on sea-going rafts, either pulled by tugs or self-propelled. The staff of the mines changed but Darr Veter, with two other mining enthusiasts, stayed for another term.

Nothing goes on for ever in this changing world and in the mine the ore crushing and washing assembly had to atop work for an overhaul. It was then that Darr Veter made his first visit to the mine chamber beyond the tunnelling shield where he had to wear a special suit to protect him from the heat and pressure and from sudden streams of poisonous gas that burst out of cracks in the rocks. The brilliantly illuminated brown rutile walls gleamed with a special diamond-like lustre of their own and gave off flashing red lights like the infuriated glower of eyes hidden in the mineral. It was exceptionally quiet in the chamber. The hydro-electric spark rock-drill and the huge discs radiating ultra-short waves stood motionless for the first time in many months. Geophysicists who had only just arrived, were busy under the shields setting up their instruments, so as to take advantage of the stoppage to check the contours of the mineral deposit.

On the surface it was autumn, a period of calm, hot days in the south. Darr Veter went up into the mountains and felt very strongly the loneliness of those masses of stone that had stood poised between sea and sky for thousands of years. The dry grass rustled and from down below came the faint sounds of the surf beating against the shore. His tired body asked for rest but his brain grasped hungrily at impressions of the world that came fresh to him after long, arduous labour underground.

The former Director of the Outer Stations, breathing deeply the odour of heated rocks and desert grasses, recalled the little island in a distant sea where the golden horse had been hidden. And he had faith in his intuitive feeling that there was much that was good still ahead of him, and that the better and stronger he himself was the more of the good there would be.

Sow a fault and reap a habit.
Sow a habit and reap a character.
Sow a character and reap your fate ...

was the way the old saw went. Yes, he thought to himself, man's greatest fight is against egoism. This is a fight that cannot be fought by sentimental rules and pretty but helpless morals but by the dialectic realization that egoism is not the outcome of some forces of evil but is a natural instinct of primitive man that played an important role in his life as a savage and had been his means of self-preservation. This is why strong, outstanding individuals often have egoism highly developed and find it difficult to combat. The victory over egoism is, however, essential, probably the most important thing in modern society. This accounts for the time and effort that are expended on the upbringing of young people and the care with which the structure of every person's heredity is studied. In the great mixture of races and peoples that forms the single family of our planet today, the most unexpected traits of character belonging to distant ancestors suddenly emerge out of the depths of heredity. There are the most amazing deviations of a psychology acquired at the time of the great calamities in the Era of Disunity, when engineers were not careful enough in their use of nuclear energy and did great hereditary harm to many people. There was a time when genealogies were

Andromeda

drawn up for predatory conquerors who called themselves noble and high born; this was done to enable them to place themselves and their families above all others. Today we understand the great importance of genealogy in life-in the selection of a profession, for medical treatment, etc. Darr Veter had formerly possessed a long genealogy, but today such things are no longer necessary. The study of ancestors has been replaced by the direct analysis of the structure of heredity mechanisms which is much more important in view of greater longevity. Ever since the Era of Common Labour people have been living to the age of 170 and now it is clear that even 300 is not the limit...."

The rattle of stones awakened Darr Veter out of his complicated and vague reverie. Coming down the valley from above were two people, an operator from the electro-smelting section, a reticent and bashful young woman and an excellent pianist, and an engineer from the surface workings, lively and small in stature. They were both flushed from their rapid walk, greeted Darr Veter and would have passed on, but he stopped them in response to something he suddenly remembered.

"I've been wanting to ask you a long time," lie said, turning to the young woman. "Can you play something for me-the 13th Blue Cosmic Symphony in F-Minor. You've often played for us but you've never played that even once."

"Do you mean Zieg Zohr's Cosmic?" she asked and when Darr Veter answered with a nod of confirmation she burst out laughing.

"There aren't many people on the planet who could play that piece for you. A solar piano with a triple keyboard is not enough and it hasn't been transposed yet... and probably never will be. Why don't you ask the House of Higher Music to play a recording for you? Our receiver is universal and has power enough!"

"I don't know how," muttered Darr Veter, "before, I never "

"I'll do it for you this evening," she said and, holding out her hand to her companion, continued her way down the valley.

For the rest of the day Darr Veter could not rid him-elf of the feeling that something important was going to happen. It was probably the same feeling that had come over Mven Mass on his first night's work at the observatory. With a peculiar impatience he waited for eleven o'clock, the time the House of Higher Music had appointed for the transmission of the symphony.

The electro-smelting operator undertook the role of Master of Ceremonies and seated Darr Veter and other music lovers in the focus of the hemispherical screen and opposite the sound reproducer in the music room. She turned out the lights, explaining that with them on it would be difficult to follow the colour scheme of the symphony that could only be properly performed in a special hall and must, in this transmission, of necessity be confined to the limits of the screen.

The screen flickered faintly in the darkness and the noise of the sea could just be heard. Somewhere, incredibly far away, a low note sounded, a note so rich in tone that it seemed almost tangible. It grew in volume, shattering the room and the hearts of the listeners and then suddenly became softer, rose to a higher note and was broken and scattered in a million crystal fragments. Tiny orange sparks appeared in the dark atmosphere. It was like that flash of primordial lightning whose discharge on Earth, millions of centuries ago, had fused simple carbon compounds to form the more intricate molecules, the basis of organic matter and life.

A wave of alarming and dissonant sounds flooded the room, a thousand-voiced chorus of will-power, yearning and despair to complement which vague shadows of purple and vermillion came in hurried flashes and died away again.

In the movement of the short and strongly vibrant notes a circular arrangement could be felt and was accompanied by' an irregular spiral of whirling grey fire in the heights. Suddenly the whirling chorus of sounds was severed by long notes, proud and resonant, filled with impetuous force.

The vague fiery outlines of space were pierced by clear lines of blue fiery arrows that flew into the bottomless void beyond the edges of the spiral and were drowned in the darkness of horror and silence.

Darkness and silence-on this note ended the first movement of the symphony.

The audience, slightly staggered, did not have time to pronounce a single word before the music began again. Extensive cascades of powerful sounds were accompanied by dazzling opalescences that covered the whole spectrum; they fell, weakening as they grew lower, and glowing fire died away to their melancholy rhythm. Again something narrow and vehement broke through the falling cascades and again blue lights began their rhythmic, dancing ascent.

Astounded, Darr Veter caught in the blue sounds an urge towards ever more complicated rhythms and forms and thought that the primitive struggle of life against entropy could not be better expressed. Steps, dams, filters holding back the cascades that were falling to lower levels of energy …. To retain them for one moment and in that moment to live! So, so and so-there they were, those first splashes of the complicated organization of matter.

Blue arrows resolved into a round dance of geometric figures, crystal and lattice forms that grew more complicated to the accompaniment of various combinations of minor tercets, fell apart, were again combined and then suddenly dissolved in the grey twilight.

The third movement began with the measured tread of bass notes in time with which blue lanterns were lit and extinguished as they moved off into the void of infinite space and time. The surge of tramping basses increased, their rhythm grew faster until they merged into a broken, ominous melody. The blue lights were like flowers swaying on thin stems of fire-they bowed their heads sadly under the flood of low, thundering and blasting notes and were extinguished in the distance. But the lines of lights or lanterns became denser and their stems were thicker. Then two fiery strips marked a road leading into immeasurable blackness and the resonant golden voices of life floated into the immenseness of the Universe, warming fcwith a glorious warmth gloomy, indifferent, ever-moving [patter. The dark road changed to a river, a gigantic stream f blue flames in which splashes of multicoloured fire made K pattern that was constantly changing and becoming more Intricate.

! The higher combinations of rounded, regular curves and spherical surfaces were of a beauty equal to that of "the contradictory quartal chords, in the succession of which a complicated resonant melody increased rapidly, whirling more powerfully and expansively in the rhythmical advance of the low rumble of time.

Darr Veter's head was in a whirl and he could no longer follow all the shades of music and colour and was able to grasp only the general outline of the gigantic idea. The blue ocean of high notes, pure as crystal, glowed with a beaming, unusually powerful, joyful and clear colour. The tone rose higher and higher and the melody itself began rotating furiously in an ascending spiral until it broke off in flight, in a blinding flash of fire.

The symphony was over and Darr Veter realized what lie had been missing all these long months. He needed work that was closer to the Cosmos, closer to the tirelessly unwinding spiral of human urge forward into the future. He went straight from the music room to the telephone room and from there called the Central Employment Bureau of the northern living zone. The young clerk who had sent him to work in the mines was pleased when he recognized him.

"They called for you from the Astronautical Council this morning," he said, "but I could not get in touch with you. I'll put you through now."

The screen grew blank and then the light came on again and Mir Ohm, the senior of the four secretaries of the Council, appeared. His face wore a very serious look and, Darr Veter thought, a look mingled with sadness.

"There has been a great catastrophe! Satellite 57 has perished! The Council is calling you for a most difficult job. I'll send an ion-powered planetship for you. Be ready to leave!"

Darr Veter stood motionless in amazement in front of the already empty screen.

CHAPTER EIGHT

RED WAVES

The wide verandah of the observatory was open to the winds that brought the perfume of flowering plants from the hot African cost across the sea, a perfume that aroused an urgent yearning in a man's soul. Mven Mass could not compose himself into the state of clarity and firmness, when no doubts remained, that was essential on the eve of a decisive experiment. Renn Bose had reported from Tibet that the Corr Yule installation had been reconstructed and was ready. The four observers on Satellite 57 had willingly agreed to risk their lives if that would help in carrying out an experiment such as Earth had never before known.

The experiment, however, was being mounted without the permission of the Council and without an extensive preliminary discussion of all possibilities. This made it seem like the secret manufacture of weapons in the darkest eras of man's history and gave it a flavour of cowardly secrecy not common to people of today.

It is true that the great objective they hoped to reach Seemed to justify the means, but... they had to remain pure in spirit! The old human conflict between the end and the means of its attainment had arisen: and the experience of thousands of generations teaches mankind that there is a certain boundary limiting the means to an end that must not be overstepped.

The case of Beth Lohn gave the African no rest. Thirty-two years before, one of Earth's leading mathematicians, Beth Lohn, had discovered that certain signs of displacement in the interaction of strong power fields could be explained by the existence of parallel dimensions. He carried out a series of interesting experiments involving the disappearance of objects. The Academy of the Bounds of Knowledge found an error in his computations and produced an explanation of the observed phenomena that differed from his in principle. Beth Lohn, with his powerful mind hypertrophied at the expense of an underdeveloped sense of moral values and uninhibited desires, was a man of great strength and equally great egoism who decided to continue his experiments in his own way. To get convincing proofs he drew into the work courageous young volunteers who were willing to sacrifice themselves in the service of science. The people in Beth Lohn's experiments disappeared as completely as the things had done and, contrary to the hopes of the ruthless mathematician, not one of them made his presence known from "the other side" of the other dimension. When Beth Lohn had sent a group of twelve people into "non-existence," in other words had destroyed them, he was arraigned before the court. He succeeded in proving that he really believed his victims to be alive and somewhere in another dimension and that he had only acted with their consent; he was condemned to exile, spent ten years on Mercury and then, on returning to Earth, went to the Island of Oblivion, out of resentment for our world. Mven Mass felt that Beth Lohn's story was very much like his own; there, too, a secret experiment undertaken for objectives rejected by science had been forbidden and this was an analogy that Mven Mass did not like.

In two days' time there would be a transmission round the Great Circle and after that he would be free for eight days for the experiment!

Mven Mass threw back his head to look at the sky. The stars seemed brighter and nearer than usual. Many of them he knew by their ancient names, knew them as old friends-and were they not, indeed, the age-old friends of man that had shown him his ways, given him lofty ideas and encouraged him to dream?

A not very bright star inclining to the northern horizon was the Pole Star or Gamma Cephei. In the Era of Disunity the Pole Star had been in Ursa Minor, the Little Bear, but the revolution of the fringe of the Galaxy, and of the solar system with it, was in the direction of Cepheus. Cygnus, the Swan, one of the most interesting constellations in the northern sky, stretching through the Milky Way, had its long neck turned to the south. In this constellation there was a most beautiful binary star that the ancient Arabs had named Albireo. It was afterwards discovered that there were really three stars, the binary Albireo I and Albireo II, a huge blue star with an extensive planetary system. They were almost as far from us as Deneb, the huge star in the Swan's tail with a luminosity equal to 4,800 of our suns. Only eight years before this a direct answer had been received from the inhabited worlds of the Dencb system to a message transmitted in the second year of the Great Circle Era. During the last transmission our trusty friend 61 Cygni had received a message of warning from Albireo II some 400 years after it had been sent but which was nevertheless of great interest. A famous Cosmic explorer from Albireo II whose name was transmitted in terrestrial sounds as Vlihh oz Ddiz, had been lost in the vicinity of the Lyra Constellation where he met one of the greatest dangers of the Cosmos, an Ookr star. Terrestrial scientists have placed these stars in class E so called in honour of Einstein, the greatest physicist of ancient days, who predicted their existence although it was long disputed; the limit for the mass of a star was even determined and given the name of the Chandrasekhar Limit. But that ancient astronomer based his calculations exclusively on the mechanics of gravitation and thermodynamics and did not take into consideration the intricate electromagnetic structure of the giant stars. It was precisely these forces that conditioned the existence of E stars that in size rival the huge red M class giants like Antares or Betelgeuse but their density is greater, something like that of our Sun. The terrific gravitation of such bodies prevented radiation so that light could not leave the star and travel through space.

These inconceivably gigantic and mysterious masses had existed in space for an infinitely long time, secretly drawing into their inert ocean everything that came within reach of the inescapable tentacles of their gravity.

There were periods of the lengthy accumulation of matter that later ended with the heating of the surface of the star until it reached class O", that is, reached a temperature of 100,000° C.; at last there came the final explosion that hurled into space new stars with new planets, in the way the Crab Nebula once exploded and spread until it had a diameter of fifty billion kilometres.

There was a similar idea in ancient Indian religious mythology; the periods of the deity's inert repose were called the Nights of Brahma which alternated with his Days, the periods of creative activity.

The explosion was equal in force to the explosion of a quadrillion of the murderous hydrogen bombs made in the Era of Disunity.

The presence in space of absolutely dark stars of the E class could only be guessed by their gravitation and a spaceship whose course lay in the vicinity of the monster was doomed. The invisible infrared stars of the T class also constituted a danger to spaceships; the same applied to dark clouds of big particles or absolutely cold bodies of the TT class.

Mven Mass stood thinking that the establishment of the Great Circle that linked up all the worlds inhabited by reasoning beings had been the greatest of all revolutions for Earth and, consequently, for all inhabited planets. Firstly, this had been a victory over time, over the shortness of the span of human life, that had prevented us and our thinking brothers in other worlds from penetrating into the farther depths of space. The transmission of information around the Great Circle was the transmission into an indefinite future since human thought, transmitted in this form, would continue its journey through space until it reached the farthest regions. The study of the most distant stars had become possible because the receipt of information from any place where there were planets that understood the Circle was only a matter of time. Only recently Earth received a message from the huge but very distant star known as Gamma Cygni;

the star is 2,800 parsecs from us and a message takes over 9,000 years to reach Earth but that which had been received was understandable and could be deciphered by those members of the Great Circle whose thought processes are similar. It *is* another matter if a message should come from globular stellar systems or clusters that are older than our flat systems.

The same is true of the centre of the Galaxy-in its axial star-cloud there is a colossal zone of life on millions of planet systems that do not know the darkness of night for they are illuminated by the radiation of the centre of the Galaxy! Incomprehensible communications have been received from there, pictures of intricate structure that cannot be expressed by any of our concepts. The Academy of the Bounds of Knowledge has been trying, unsuccessfully, to decipher them for eight hundred years. And yet, perhaps.... The African's heart missed a beat at the suddenness of the idea-reports from the nearer planet systems, members of the Great Circle, dealt with the *internal* life of each of the inhabited planets, its science, technology, its works of art while the distant, ancient worlds of the Galaxy showed the *external.* Cosmic movement of their science and life. How they rearranged the planetary systems to suit themselves.... How they sweep space clear of meteoroids that interfere with spaceships and dump them, together with cold planets unsuited to life, into their central sun in order to lengthen the duration of its radiation or with the intention of increasing its heating effect. If that is not enough, perhaps they rearrange neighbouring planetary systems where the best conditions of life for gigantic civilizations are created....

Half ironically, half seriously, Mven Mass got in touch with the Repository of Great Circle Records and selected the catalogue number of a distant message. The screen of his viewer was filled with strange pictures that had reached Earth from the globular cluster Omega Centauri. This cluster is the second nearest to the solar system and is only 6,800 parsecs removed. Light from its bright stars travelled through outer space for 22,000 years before reaching the eye of earthbound man.

A dense blue haze spread in even layers that were pierced by vertical black cylinders rotating fairly rapidly. The contours of the cylinders were scarcely perceptible-from time to time they contracted until they were like squat cones with their bases joined. Then the blue haze would break up into fiery crescents that revolved madly about the axes of the cones. Blackness retreated into the heights, liuge, dazzlingly white columns grew up and from behind them faceted points, green in colour, formed diagonal curtains....

Mven Mass rubbed his forehead in an effort to grasp anything that made sense.

On the screen the pointed green blades wound in spirals around the white columns and suddenly showered down in a stream of gleaming metal globes that lay in the form of a broad, circular belt. The belt began to grow in width and in height. Mven Mass smiled and switched off the record, returning to his former contemplation....

Owing to the absence of populated worlds, or rather, to the absence of contact with them in the higher latitudes of the Galaxy, the people of Earth were still unable to get out of the equatorial belt of the Galaxy where space is darkened by fragments of matter and dust. We could not rise above the gloom in which our star and its neighbours are plunged. It was, therefore, difficult for us to learn about the Universe, even with the aid of the Great Circle.

Mven Mass turned his eyes to the horizon, to the Coma Berenices Constellation lying below Ursa Major and under the Canes Venatici. This was the North Pole of the Galaxy-in this direction lay the whole expanse of extragalactic space in the same way as at the opposite point of the sky, in the Piscis Anstrinus Constellation, near the well-known star Fomalhaut, lay the South Pole of the galactic system. In the outer region of the Galaxy, where our Sun is situated, the width of the branch of the spiral galactic disc is no more than 600 parsecs. Perpendicular to the plane of the galactic equator it was enough to cover a distance of 300-400 parsecs to rise above the level of the Galaxy's gigantic stellar wheel. This route could not be covered by a spaceship but it was well within reach of Circle transmissions ... but ... so far not a single planet of any of the stars in those areas had joined the Circle.

These eternal riddles and unanswered questions would have been turned into nothing if another revolution, the greatest in science, could be achieved-if time could be conquered, if we could learn to overcome any distance in any span of time and enter the endless expanses of the Cosmos as its master. Then our Galaxy and other stellar islands would be no farther away from us than the tiny islands of the Mediterranean, against which the sea was splashing down below in the darkness of night. This was justification for the desperate experiment planned by Renn Bose and being put into effect by him. by Mven Mass, Director of the Outer Stations. If only they could have a better scientific basis to their experiment and obtain the sanction of the Council....

The lights of the Spiral Way changed colour from orange to white-2 a.m. the traffic peak. Mven Mass remembered that next day there would be the Fete of the Flaming Bowls to which Chara Nandi had invited him. The Director of the Outer Stations could not forget the reddish-bronze girl with her precisely supple movements that he had met on the beach. She was like a flower of sincerity and strong passions, rare enough in an epoch when feelings had been disciplined.

Mven Mass went back to his study, called the Institute of Metagalactics, that worked at night, and asked them to send him stereotelefilms of a few galaxies next evening. Having obtained their consent he went up to the roof of the inner building where he kept his long-range leaping apparatus. Mven Mass was very fond of this unpopular sport and had achieved a fair degree of skill. He strapped the helium container to his body, leaped agilely into the air and for a second switched on a tractor propeller that was driven by a light accumulator. He described an arc about 600 metres long and, landing on a ledge of the Catering House, repeated the jump. In five such leaps he reached a small garden under a limestone cliff where he landed on an aluminium tower, removed the apparatus and slid down a pole to the ground and so to his hard bed standing under a huge plane-tree.

The African fell asleep to the rustling of the leaves of the giant tree.

The Fete of the Flaming Bowls got its name from the well-known poem by the poet-historian Zann Senn in which he describes the ancient Indian custom of selecting the most beautiful women to carry swords and bowls containing flaming aromatic incense to heroes about to set out for the performance of great deeds. Swords and bowls were no longer in use but remained as the symbol of heroism. Heroic deeds had grown to countless numbers amongst the bold and energetic population of the planet. A tremendous capacity for work, possessed in the past by only those few people who were known as geniuses, depended entirely on the physical strength of the body and an abundance of hormone stimnlators. Correct physical training for thousands of years had made the average person on the planet the equal of the heroes of antiquity, insatiable in his desire for heroic deeds, love and knowledge.

The Fete of the Flaming Bowls was the women's spring festival. Every year in the fourth month after the winter solstice or, according to the old calendar, in April, the most beautiful women on Earth took part in dances, singing and gymnastics. The finest shades of beauty of the various races that showed in the mixed population of the planet were to be seen here in inexhaustible variety like the facets of a precious stone; they gave endless pleasure to their audiences which included everybody from scientists and engineers, tired out with their meticulous labours, to inspired artists and the still youthful pupils of the Third Cycle schools.

No less beautiful was the Festival of Hercules, the men's autumn festival celebrated in the ninth month. At this festival young men coming of age reported on the Herculean labours they had performed. Later it became the custom on these occasions to review all the noteworthy deeds and achievements of the past year. And so the festival had become a general one, celebrated by both men and women, and lasting three days-the Day of Useful Excellence, the Day of Higher Art, and the Day of Scientific Audacity and Fantasy. One year Mven Mass had been elected hero of the first and third days.

Veda Kong sang a number of songs. Mven Mass appeared the gigantic Solar Hall of the Tyrrhenian Stadium during her performance. He found the ninth sector of the fourth radius where Evda Nahl and Chara Nandi were sitting and stood there in the shadow of an arcade listening to Veda's low deep voice. She was dressed in white. Her blonde head thrown back and her face turned to the upper galleries of the hall, she was singing a song of joy and to the African she seemed the very incarnation of spring. Every member of the audience pressed one of the four buttons in front of him. The golden, blue, emerald or red lights flickering on the ceiling showed the artist to what extent the performance had been appreciated and took the place of the noisy applause of former days.

Veda finished singing and was awarded by a bright cluster of gold and blue lights amongst which the very few green ones were completely lost. Her face flushed with excitement as usual, she ran to her friends. At that moment they were joined by Mven Mass whom they heartily welcomed.

The African looked round the stadium in search of his teacher and predecessor but Darr Veter was nowhere to be seen.

"Where have you hidden Darr Veter?" he asked jokingly, turning to the three women.

"And where have you hidden Renn Bose?" Evda Nahl replied, and the African hastily avoided her penetrating glance.

"Veter is digging holes in South America," said the more kindhearted Veda and a shadow passed over her face. With a protective gesture Chara Nandi pulled Veda towards her, pressing her cheek against Veda's. The faces of the two women were vastly different but possessed a gentle tenderness which lent them similarity.

Chara's eyebrows; straight and low under a high forehead, resembled the outline of a soaring bird and were in perfect harmony with her long narrow eyes. Veda's eyebrows slanted upwards.

"A bird flapping its wings," thought the African. Chara's thick, shining; black hair lay on her neck and shoulders contrasting sharply with Veda's fair hair, piled high on her head.

Chara glanced at the clock in the domed roof and got up. Her dress astounded the African. On the girl's smooth shoulders lay a platinum chain leaving her high neck open. The chain was fastened below her throat by a gleaming red tourmaline.

Her firm breasts, like wide upturned bowls carved with a very delicate chisel, were almost completely exposed. Between them, stretching from the tourmaline clasp to her belt ran a narrow strip of dark purple velvet. Similar strips, running across the middle of each breast, were held taut by the chain and joined on her bare back. The girl's very narrow waist was encircled by a white belt besprin-kled with black stars and fastened by a platinum buckle in the form of a crescent, from which a strip of dark purple velvet hung down to her knees. Attached to her belt behind was what seemed like half a long skirt of heavy white silk, also decorated with black stars. The dancer wore no jewels with the exception of glittering buckles on her tiny black slippers.

"It will soon be my turn!" said Chara calmly making her way towards the arcade exit; she glanced at Mven lass and disappeared, accompanied by whispered questions and thousands of curious glances.

The stage was occupied by a gymnast, a beautifully proportioned girl no more than eighteen years old. In the golden floodlights, to the recitative of the music, she went through an amazingly rapid succession of leaps, springs and turns, balancing with unbelievable equilibrium to slow, lyrical passages of music. The audience awarded her performance with a multitude of golden lights and Mven Mass thought that it would not be easy for Chara Nandi to dance after such a successful number. He looked anxiously at the faceless multitude of people opposite and suddenly noticed the artist Cart Sann sitting in the third sector. The latter greeted him with a gaiety that the African felt out of place-who, if not the artist who had painted Chara's picture as the *Daughter of the Mediterranean,* should have been perturbed at the outcome of her performance.

The African was just thinking that after his experiment he would go to see the *Daughter of the Mediterranean* when the lights overhead were extinguished. The transparent floor of organic glass gleamed with the cherry-red light of hot iron. Streams of red light poured out from under low footlights around the stage. The lights moved back and forth keeping time with the marked rhythm of the melody and merging with the resonant song of the violins and the low hum of bronze strings. Mven Mass was somewhat staggered by the power and tempestuousness of the music and did not immediately notice Chara as she appeared in the centre of that flaming floor and began her dance at a Speed that took the onlookers' breath away.

Mven Mass was afraid of what might happen if the music demanded still greater acceleration of the dance. She danced not only with her legs and arms-the girl's entire body responded to the blazing fire of the music with equally searing flames of life. The African thought that if the women of ancient India had been like Chara, then the poet had been right in likening them to flaming bowls and in giving that name to the women's fete.

Chara's reddish sunburn turned to a bright copper in the glow of the stage and the floor. Mven Mass's heart beat wildly. The woman he had seen on the fabulous planet of Epsilon Toucanis had skin of just that colour. At that time, also, he had learned there existed such a thing as the inspiration of a body capable of employing its movements, its delicate changes of beautiful forms, to express the most profound shades of feeling, fantasy and passion, to express a prayer for happiness.

Up to that moment he had known nothing but the urge to overcome the unattainable distance of ninety parsecs but now Mven Mass realized that flowers just as beautiful as the carefully nurtured picture of the distant planet were to be found in the inexhaustible treasure-house of terrestrial beauty. But his long-cherished urge to achieve an unattainable dream did not pass so quickly. Chara's likeness to the red-skinned daughter in the world of Epsilon Toucanis only served to strengthen the determination of the Director of the Outer Stations. If so much joy was to be felt from one Chara Nandi what would the world be like where the majority of the women were like her?!

Evda Nahl and Veda Kong, excellent dancers themselves, were staggered at this, the first of Chara's dances that they had seen. Veda, anthropologist and specialist in the history of the ancient races, had come to the decision that in the past the women of Gondwana, the southern countries, had exceeded the men in number because men were often killed hunting dangerous wild beasts. Later when the despotic states of the Ancient East were established in the densely populated countries of the south, the men continued to be killed in wars, by religious excesses and by the whims of the despots. The daughters of the south went through a period of the strictest selection that developed the finer points of adaptation. In the north, where the population was scantier and nature less bounteous, there had not been such despotism in the Dark Ages. More men survived, women were more valued and lived a more dignified life.

Veda followed Chara's every gesture and conceived the idea that in all her movements there was an amazing duality-they were at once gentle and predatory. The gentleness came from the graceful movements and unbelievable suppleness of the body and the predatory impression was created by the abrupt changes, turns and poses that followed each other with the elusive rapidity that is natural in the wild beast. This feline litheness had been achieved by the dark-skinned daughters of Gondwana in the thousands of years of the struggle for existence through which the debased and enslaved women of the southern continents had lived ... but in Chara it was harmonically combined with the small firm features of a Creto-Hellenic face.

The dissonant sounds of some percussion instruments merged in a short, slower adagio. The urgent, ever swifter rhythm of the rise and fall of human emotions was expressed in the dance by the alternation of movements full of meaning and their almost complete cessation when the dancer turned into a motionless statue. Slumbering emotions were aroused, flared up stormily, wilted in their exhaustion, died and were born again, stormy and untasted-life, fettered and struggling against the inevitable march of time, against the clear-cut, merciless definiteness of duty and fate. Evda Nahl felt that the psychological basis of the dance was something so near to her that her cheeks became flushed and her breathing quickened.

Mven Mass did not know that the composer had written the ballet suite specially for Chara Nandi, but he was no longer afraid of the wild tempo when he saw how well the girl was coping with it. Scarlet waves of light embraced her copper body, gave off crimson splashes from her strong legs, were drowned in the dark whirls of velvet and turned the white silk to the pink of dawn. Her arms, raised and thrown back, slowly ceased their motion over her head. Suddenly, without any finale, the music broke off in a stormy clangour of high notes and the red lights came to a standstill and were extinguished. The high dome of the building was flooded with its usual light. The tired girl bowed her head and her thick hair covered her face. The thousands of golden lights were followed by a dull noise. The audience were doing Chara the greatest of all honours-they were thanking her by standing up and stretching their clasped hands towards her. Chara, who, before the performance, had not known a tremor, lost her self-possession, threw back the hair from her face and ran away, after a glance towards the upper galleries. Mven Mass knew then why the artist had been so calm-he knew his model.

The Master of Ceremonies announced an *entr'acte*. Mven Mass hurried to look for Chara while Veda Kong and Evda Nahl went out on to the gigantic opaque glass staircase, a thousand metres wide, that led from the stadium straight down to the sea. The evening twilight, lucid and warm, tempted the two women to bathe, following the example of thousands of other spectators from the fete.

"No wonder I was attracted to Chara Nandi the moment I saw her," said Evda Nahl. "She's a remarkable artist. Today we have seen the Dance of the Power of Life, in which is incorporated the best of everything that constitutes the foundation of the human soul and is frequently its ruler. That must contain something of the erotic dances of the ancients!"

"Now I understand Cart Sann, for beauty really is more important than we think. Beauty is the happiness and the meaning of life-how well he said that! And your definition is a true one!" agreed Veda, kicking off a shoe and putting her foot into the warm water that splashed against the steps.

"It is a true one if the psychic forces are born of a healthy body full of energy," Evda Nahl corrected her as she removed her clothes and jumped into the transparent water. Veda swam after her and they went together to a huge rubber island that shone silver about a mile away from the stadium. The flat surface of the island, level with the water, was surrounded by rows of shelters in the shape of shells of mother-of-pearl plastic, big enough to screen three or four people from the sun and wind and to isolate them from their neighbours.

The two women lay down on the soft, swaying floor of a "shell," breathing deeply of the eternally fresh smell of the sea.

"You've got beautifully tanned since I met you on the beach!" said Veda looking at her companion. "Have you been at the seaside or does it come from sunburn pills?"

"SB pills," admitted Evda, "I've been in the sun for only two days, yesterday and today. I haven't got such wonderful skin as Chara Nandi."

"Don't you really know where Renn Bose is?" continued Veda.

"I know approximately and that is sufficient to worry me!" answered Evda Nahl, softly.

"Do you really want..." began Veda and then stopped but Evda lifted her lazily closed eyelids and looked her straight in the eyes.

"It seems to me that Renn Bose is somehow ... helpless, like an undeveloped boy," Veda objected, hesitantly, "and you're so strong, you have an intellect that is the equal of any man's. One always feels that inside you there is a steel rod, your will-power "

"Renn Bose told me the same. But you're wrong in your estimation of him, you're as one-sided as Renn Bose himself. He is a man with a bold and powerful intellect and a terrific capacity for work. Even today there are few to equal him on our planet. It is the comparison of his other qualities with his great talents that makes them seem undeveloped because they are just about the average or even puerile, perhaps. You were right in calling Renn a boy, he is, but at the same time he's a hero in the true sense of the word. Take Darr Veter-there's something boylike in him, too, but with him it's just a superabundance of physical strength and not the lack of it, like it is with Renn."

"What do you think of Mven?" Veda inquired, "now that you know him better."

"Mven Mass is a splendid combination of the cold intellect and the archaic fury of desires. He is a man of great ability and is highly educated but at the same time he is the high priest of nature's elemental forces!"

Veda Kong burst out laughing. "How can I learn to give such precise character studies?!"

"Psychology is my line," said Evda, shrugging her shoulders. "But let me ask you a question. Do you know that Darr Veter is a man that I like very much?"

"You're afraid of half-formed decisions?" Veda blushed. "No, this time there will be no fatal half-way decisions and insincerity. Everything is as clear as crystal…." Under the penetrating glance of the psychiatrist, Veda continued:

"Erg Noor … our ways parted long ago. I could not give way to a new feeling as long as he was in the Cosmos. I could not draw myself away and so weaken the strength of my hopes, my faith in his return. Now it is only a case of precise calculation and confidence. Erg Noor knows everything but is going his own way."

Evda Nahl placed her slender arm round Veda's shoulder. "So it's Darr Veter?"

"Yes," answered Veda, firmly.

"Does he know?"

"No. Later, when Tantra arrives…. Isn't it time for us to go back?"

"I have to leave the fete," said Evda Nahl, "my holiday is finished. I have a big job to do in the Academy of Sorrow and Joy, and I must see my daughter before I go there."

"Is she a big girl?"

"Seventeen. My son is older. I have done the duty of every woman who is normally developed and has normal heredity-two children, no less! Now I want a third one-but I want him grown up!" Evda Nahl smiled and her serious face was lit up with the tenderness of love, her bow-shaped upper lip lifted slightly.

"I imagine a fine, big-eyed boy with such a loving and ever-astonished mouth … with freckles and a snub nose," said Veda, slyly, looking straight in front of her. Her companion, after a short pause, asked her;

"Have you got any new job yet?"

"No, I'm waiting for *Tuntra*, then there will be a big expedition."

"Then come with me to visit my daughter," suggested Evda, and Veda gladly consented.

The whole of one wall of the observatory was taken up with a seven-metre hemispherical screen for the demonstration of films and photos taken by powerful telescopes. Mven Mass switched on a general view of a section of the sky near the North Pole of the Galaxy, the meridional strip of constellations from Ursa Major to Corvus and Centaurus. In this part, in Canes Venatici, Coma Berenices and Virgo there were many galaxies, islands of stars in the form of flat wheels or discs. An especially large number of them had been discovered in Coma Berenices-separate galaxies, of regular and irregular form, showing different degrees of revolution and projection, some of them inconceivably far away, at a distance of thousands of millions of parsecs, often forming whole "clouds" of tens of thousands of galaxies. The biggest of the galaxies are anything from 20,000 to 50,000 parsecs in diameter, like the stellar island or Galaxy NN 89105 + SB 23, in the old days known as M 31, or the Andromeda Nebula. This little, faintly gleaming, nebulous cloud could be seen from Earth with the naked eye. Long before this people had discovered the secret of this cloud. The nebula proved to be a gigantic, wheel-shaped stellar system one and a half times the size of our huge Galaxy. The study of the Andromeda Nebula, despite the fact that it was 450,000 parsecs distant from terrestrial observers, did much to help gain knowledge of our own Galaxy.

Mven Mass remembered from childhood the magnificent photographs of the various galaxies that had been obtained by means of electron inverted pictures or by radio telescopes such as the gigantic Pamir and Patagonia installations, each of them almost 400 kilometres in diameter, that penetrated even deeper into the Cosmos. The galaxies, monster clusters of billions of celestial bodies separated by distances of millions of parsecs, had always aroused in him an irrepressible desire to know the laws of their constitution, the story of their origin and their further evolution. The main thing that intrigued every inhabitant of Earth was the possibility of there being life on the countless planetary systems in these islands of the Universe, the question of the fires of thought and knowledge that burned there, of human civilizations in those infinitely distant spaces of the Cosmos.

Andromeda

Three stars appeared on the screen that the ancients had named Alpheratz, Mirach and Almak, (α, β, γ Andro-medae), arranged in an ascending straight line. On either side of this line were the two galaxies close to each other, the Andromeda Nebula or M 31, and the beautiful spiral of M 33 in the Triangnlum Constellation. Mven Mass changed the metal film.

He was now looking at the galaxy known in ancient days as M 51, in the Canes Venatici, 800,000 parsecs away. This was one of the few galaxies that we see "flat," our line of sight being perpendicular to the plane of the "wheel." It has a very bright, dense core made up of countless millions of stars from which two spiral arms stretch out, each of them with similarly dense star clusters at the beginning. Their long ends seem to get fainter and more nebulous until they disappear into the darkness of space, stretching for tens of thousands of parsecs from each other in opposite directions. Between the arms, or main branches, there are short streams of stellar condensations and clouds of luminous gas alternating with black "voids," accumulations of dark matter; the bright arms are all curved like the blades of a turbine.

The huge galaxy NGK 4565 in the Coma Berenices Constellation was a very beautiful one. At a distance of a million parsecs it was seen edgeways. Leaning over to one side, like a soaring bird, the galaxy spread its thin disc, apparently consisting of spiral branches, over a huge area; the central core was a greatly oblate spheroid that burned brightly and had the appearance of a solid gleaming mass. It could be clearly seen that the islands of stars were so flat that the galaxy could be compared to a thin wheel belonging to some clockwork mechanism. The edges of the wheel were indistinct, they seemed to merge into the bottomless void. Our Sun is located on just such an edge of a galaxy together with a tiny speck of dust called Earth that, linked by the power of knowledge with many inhabited worlds, is spreading the wings of human thought over the infinity of the Cosmos!

Mven Mass then switched the projector over to the galaxy NGK 4594 in the Virgo Constellation; this galaxy, also visible in its equatorial plane, had always interested him. It stood at a distance of ten million parsecs from Earth and resembled a thick lentil of burning stellar material wrapped in a layer of luminescent gas. A thick black line, a condensation of dark material, cut the lentil along its equator. The galaxy looked like a mysterious lantern shining out of an enormous abyss.

What worlds were hidden there, in a galaxy whose total radiation was brighter than that of other galaxies and averaged that of an F class star? Were there any mighty inhabited planets there? Was thought there also grappling with the mysteries of nature?

The fact that the huge clusters of stars did not answer made Mven Mass clench his fists. He realized the terrific distances involved-light from the galaxy he was looking at travelled thirty-two million years to reach Earth. Sixty-four million years would be required to exchange information!

Mven Mass selected another reel and on the screen there appeared a big, bright, round patch of light amongst dispersed, faint stars. An irregular black strip cut the patch in two, making the brightly gleaming fiery masses on either side of it still brighter by contrast and thickening towards its ends and overshadowing an extensive field of the burning gas that formed a ring round the bright patch. This was a picture of colliding galaxies in the Cygnus Constellation that had been obtained by the most remarkably ingenious technical set-ups. This collision of giant galaxies, each equal in size to our Galaxy or to the Andromeda Nebula, had long been known as a source of radio emanation, probably the most powerful in the part of the Universe that we could probe. Rapidly moving gas streams of colossal size set up electromagnetic fields of such inconceivable power that they sent out news of the titanic catastrophe to all ends of the Universe. Matter itself sent out this alarm signal from a radio station with a power of a quintillion megawatts. So great was the distance to the galaxies, however, that the picture on the screen showed its state millions of years before. The present state of these two galaxies, passing one through the other, will be known on Earth such a long time after that we cannot say whether terrestrial man will continue to exist so unimaginably long.

Mven Mass jumped up and leaned on the table with both hands so hard that the joints cracked.

Andromeda

Transmission periods of millions of years, covering tens of thousands of human generations and which actually amount to that "never" that is killing to scientific thought, could disappear at the wave of a magic wand-Renn Bose's discovery and their joint experiment!

Inconceivably distant points of the Universe would be within reach!

Astronomers in ancient days believed the galaxies to be moving apart. The light that reached terrestrial telescopes from distant stellar islands had been changed, light oscillations had lengthened, turning to red waves. This reddening of the light was taken as evidence that the galaxies were receding from the observer. People in the past were accustomed to a direct, one-sided conception of phenomena and they created the theory of a Universe that was moving apart or exploding, not realizing that they saw only one side of the magnificent process of destruction and creation. It was this one aspect-dispersion and destruction, that is, the transition of energy to a lower level in accordance with the second law of thermodynamics-that was conceivable to us and was recorded by instruments constructed to sharpen our senses. The other aspect-accumulation, concentration and creation-was outside man's concepts because life acquired its strength from energy diffused by the stars, the suns, and our conception of the surrounding Universe took shape on the basis of this. Man's mighty brain, however, penetrated even into the hidden processes of the creation of worlds and of our Universe. But in those distant times it still seemed that the greater the distance to a galaxy the greater the speed of its motion away from the terrestrial observer. As man penetrated farther into outer space he found galaxies with velocities close to that of light. The end of the visible Universe was the point where galaxies seemed to have reached that velocity although actually no light from them could have reached us and we should not have seen them....

We now know why the light from these galaxies is red. As is usually the case in science there proved to be more than one cause-it is not only due to their recession from us. The only light that reaches us from distant stellar islands is that radiated by their brightest centres. These huge masses of matter are encircled by annular electromagnetic fields that strongly affect light rays, not only by their intensity but also on account of the area they cover; they gradually slow down the light waves until they become longer red waves. In very ancient times astronomers knew that light from very dense stars turns red, the spectral lines shifting towards the red end, so that the star seems to be receding like, for example, the second component of Sirius, the white dwarf Sirius B. The farther away the galaxy, the more centralized is the radiation that reaches us and the stronger the concentration at the red end of the spectrum.

During a very long journey through space light waves, on the other hand, are "shaken up" and the light quanta lose part of their energy. This phenomenon has now been studied-the red waves may also be fatigued "old" waves of ordinary light. Even light waves that penetrate everywhere "grow old" from their journey over tremendous distances. What hope had man of overcoming such distances unless he attack gravitation itself by means of its opposite, following Renn Bose's calculations?

His anxiety was fading away! He was doing the right thing by carrying out the unprecedented experiment!

Mven Mass, as usual, went out on the observatory veran-dah and began walking swiftly up and down. The distant galaxies still shone in his tired eyes, galaxies that sent waves of red light to Earth like signals calling for help, like appeals to the all-conquering thought of man. Mven Mass laughed softly and confidently. These red rays would become as familiar to man as those at the Fete of the Flaming Bowls that had wrapped Chara Nandi's body in the red light of life-Chara, who had appeared to him unexpectedly as the copper daughter of Epsilon Tucanae, the girl of his impossible dreams.

And he would direct Renn Bose's vector precisely at Epsilon Tucanae, not merely in the hope of seeing that wonderful world, but also in honour of her, of its terrestrial representative!

CHAPTER NINE

A THIRD CYCLE SCHOOL

Third Cycle School No. 410 was situated in Southern Ireland. Broad fields, vineyards and oak groves ran down the slopes of the green hills to the very sea. Veda Kong and Evda Nahl arrived when the children were still in class; they walked along a corridor running round class-

rooms on the perimeter of a circular building. The day was dull with a drizzle of rain so that all classes were being held indoors instead of out in the open as was more usual.

Veda Kong felt like a schoolgirl again as she crept up to listen at the entrances to the classrooms which, as in the majority of schools, were without doors and shut off by overlapping projecting walls. Evda Nahl joined in the game and the two women peeped into class after class in an attempt to find Evda's daughter and remain unnoticed themselves.

In the first classroom they saw a drawing in blue chalk covering the whole length of one wall: it showed a vector that was encircled by a spiral unfolding along it. Two sections of the spiral were encircled by transverse ellipses in which a system of rectangular coordinates was inscribed.

"Bipolar mathematics!" exclaimed Veda in mock horror.

"This is something more than that! Wait a minute!" said Evda.

"Now that we know something about the shadow functions of the cochlear, or spiral progressive movement, that occurs along the vector,"-the elderly teacher with deep-set, blazing eyes, thickened one of the lines with his chalk -"we are close to understanding the repagular calculus. The name of the calculus comes from the ancient Latin word 'repagulum,' a barrier or obstacle, and it is the transition from one quality to another, seen in a two-sided aspect." The teacher pointed to an extensive ellipse across the spiral. "In other words, it is the mathematical analysis of mutually transitional phenomena "

Veda Kong disappeared behind the outjutting wall, pulling her companion after her.

"That's something new! It's from that branch of mathematics Renn Bose was talking to us about down on the seashore."

"The school always gives its pupils the newest of everything and discards whatever is outworn. If new generations repeat old conceptions how can we expect to ensure rapid progress? As it is, a terrible amount of time elapses before a child takes its place in the relay race of knowledge. It takes dozens of years for a child to become fully educated and ready to undertake gigantic tasks. This pulsation of the generations, where you take one step forward and nine-tenths backward-backward while the next shift in the relay is learning-is that most difficult of all biological laws for man, the law of death and renascence. Much of what we learned in mathematics, physics and biology is already out of date. Your history is different, it grows old more slowly because it is very old itself."

They glanced into another room. The schoolmistress, Standing with her back to them, and the interested children, did not notice them. The attentive faces of the pupils -they were young men and women seventeen years of age, in the higher classes of the Third Cycle School-and their burning cheeks told how thrilled they were with the lesson.

"We, the human race, have passed through many trials," the voice of the teacher resounded with her excitement, "and the most important thing in your school history is the study of the historic mistakes made by man and their consequences. We have passed through the stage of the unbearable complication of life and things used by man and have arrived at extreme simplicity. The complication of life led dialectically to the simplification of spiritual culture. There must not be any unnecessary thing to tie man up, his experiences and perceptions are finer when he leads a simple life. Everything relating to everyday life is studied by the best brains as befits important scientific problems. We have followed the general line of development of the animal kingdom which was directed towards the liberation of attention by making movements automatic and developing reflexes in the work of the nervous system. The automation of the productive forces of society created an analogous reflex system of control in production economy and released many people for what is now man's chief occupation-scientific research. Nature has provided us with a big brain capable of scientific inquiry although at first it was only used to search for food and investigate its edibility."

"Very good!" whispered Evda Nahl and at that moment noticed her daughter. The girl did not suspect anything and sat staring in contemplation at the corrugated glass that prevented the pupils from seeing what was going on outside the classroom.

Veda Kong was curious to compare her with her mother. They had the same long straight hair, the daughter's plaited with a blue thread and tied up in two big loops. Both had the same oval face, narrow at the chin and somewhat babyish from the too high forehead and the high cheekbones protruding below the temples. A snow-white sweater of artificial wool stressed the dark paleness of the girl's skin and the acute blackness of her eyes, eyebrows and eyelashes. A necklace of red coral harmonized with the girl's unquestionably original appearance.

Evda's daughter, like all other pupils, wore wide shorts, hers differing only in a red fringe that was stitched into the seams.

"An American Indian ornament," whispered Evda Nahl in answer to her friend's inquiring glance.

Evda and Veda just had time to step back into the corridor when the teacher left the room followed by several pupils, Evda's daughter amongst them. The girl stopped suddenly in her tracks as she noticed her mother, her pride and an example to be followed.

Although Evda did not know it, there was a circle of her admirers in the school, youngsters who had decided to take the same road in life as she had taken.

"Mother!" whispered the girl, casting a shy glance at her mother's companion and clinging to Evda.

The teacher stopped and then came over to them, giving them a nod of greeting.

"I must inform the school council," she said, disregarding Evda's gesture of protest, "we must gain something from your visit."

"Better take advantage of her visit," said Evda as *she* introduced Veda Kong.

The history teacher blushed deeply and looked like a young girl.

"That's fine!" she said, trying to keep her tone businesslike. "The school is about to graduate the senior groups and a word from Evda Nahl to send them on their way coupled with a review of the ancient cultures and races from Veda Kong will be something for our youth to remember! Won't it, Rhea?"

Evda's daughter clapped her hands. The teacher ran with the light gait of a gymnast to the subsidiary premises, contained in a long straight building.

"Rhea, can you cut out the polytechnics lesson today and come for a walk?" Evda suggested to her daughter. "I shan't be able to see you again before you have to choose your matriculation tasks. Last time we didn't come to a decision."

Rhea did not answer but took her mother's hand. In each of the school cycles the lessons were interspersed with polytechnics. At the moment they were to have one of Rhea's favourite occupations, the grinding of optical lenses, but what could be more interesting or more important than her mother's arrival?

Veda went away to a little observatory that she could see in the distance, leaving mother and daughter alone. Rhea, clasping her mother's strong arm like a child, walked beside her wrapped in thought.

"Where's your little Kay?" asked Evda and the girl grew noticeably sad. Kay had been a ward of hers-the older school-children paid regular visits to first- and second cycle schools in their vicinity to help with the teaching and upbringing of wards they had selected. Integrated help for the teachers was absolutely essential to ensure thoroughness of education.

"Kay was promoted to the second cycle and has gone far away from here. It's such a pity ... why do they move us from place to place every four years, when we are promoted to the next cycle?"

"The psyche is wearied and becomes sluggish where there is a uniformity of impressions and perception becomes duller. The efficiency of teaching and upbringing grows less year by year. That is why the twelve years of schooling are divided into three four-year cycles and you move to another school after every cycle, each time to a different part of the planet. It is only the babies in the zero cycle, from one to four years, that do not need any change of place and conditions of upbringing."

"And why does each cycle have separate schools and separate living quarters?"

"As you little people grow up and are trained you become qualitatively different beings. If different age groups live together it makes their training more difficult and is annoying to the youngsters themselves. We have reduced the differences to a minimum by dividing the children into three age groups, but this is still not a perfect system.

The first cycle, for example, obviously needs splitting into two groups, and that will soon be done. But let us talk first about your affairs and your dreams for the future. I shall have to deliver a lecture to all of you and may be able to answer your questions."

Rhea began to confide her innermost thoughts to her mother with the frankness of a child of the Great Circle Era who had never experienced hurtful ridicule or misunderstanding. The girl was the incarnation of youth that as yet knew nothing of life but was full of contemplative anticipation. At the age of seventeen the girl was finishing school and starting her three-year period of matriculation tasks, working amongst adults. After the tasks her interests and abilities would be clearly defined. A two-year higher education would follow that would give her the right to independent work in the chosen field. In the course of a long life a man or woman had time to take higher educational courses in five or six different fields, changing work from time to time, but a great deal depended on the choice of the first difficult tasks-the Labours of Hercules, or matriculation tasks. They were chosen after long contemplation and always following the advice of older people.

"Have you passed the graduation psychological tests yet?" asked Evda. "Yes. I got 20 and 24 in the first eight groups, 18 and 19 in the tenth and thirteenth and even 17 in the seventeenth!" exclaimed Rhea proudly.

"That's wonderful!" said Evda in pleased tones. "Everything is open to you. Have you stuck to the choice you made for the first task?"

"Yes, I'm going to be a nurse on the Island of Oblivion, and then all our circle are going to work at the Jutland Psychological Hospital."

Rhea told her mother about the circle of her "followers." Evda had plenty of good-natured jokes to make about these zealous psychologists but nevertheless Rhea persuaded her mother to be mentor for the members of the group who were also at the time selecting their tasks.

"I shall have to live here until the end of my holiday," laughed Evda, "and what will Veda Kong do?"

The girl suddenly remembered her mother's companion.

"She's very nice," said Rhea, seriously, "and almost as beautiful as you are!"

"She's much more beautiful!"

"No, I know … and it's not because you're my mother," said the girl, bashfully. "Perhaps she's better at first glance but you have a spiritual tabernacle within you that Veda Kong hasn't yet got. I don't say she won't have, it's just that she hasn't built it yet… but she'll build it and then "

"Then she'll outshine your mother like a moon outshines the stars." Rhea shook her head.

"And are you going to stand still? You'll go farther than she!"

Evda passed her hand over the girl's smooth hair and looked down into her upturned face.

"Isn't that enough eulogy, daughter? We're wasting time!"

Veda Kong walked slowly down an avenue that led her deeper into a grove of broad-leaved maples, whose heavy moist foliage rustled dully. The first wraiths of the evening mist were making an effort to rise from a nearby meadow but they were instantly dispersed by the wind. Veda Kong was pondering over the mobile tranquillity of nature and thinking that the sites for the schools were always so well chosen. The development of a keen perception of nature and a sensitive communion with nature were an important part of the child's training. Dulled interest in nature is, in actual fact, an impediment to man's development, for one who has forgotten how to observe will soon lose the ability to generalize. Veda thought about the ability to teach, the most important of all competencies in the age when they had at last learned that upbringing was more important than education and was the only way to prepare the child for the difficult job of being a real man. The basis, of course, is provided by inherent abilities but they might easily be left undeveloped, without that chiselling of the human spirit that is done by the pedagogue.

Veda's mind turned back to those distant days when she had been a third cycle schoolgirl, a mass of contradictions, burning with the desire to sacrifice herself and at the same time judging the world by herself alone, with all the egocentrism of healthy youth. How much the teachers did for her in those days-in truth there is no loftier profession in this world of ours than that of teacher!

The future of mankind is in the hands of the teacher for it is only by his efforts that man rises ever higher and becomes more and more powerful, coping with the most arduous of all tasks, that of overcoming himself, his greedy self-love and his unbridled desires.

Veda Kong turned towards a small bay surrounded by pines where she could hear the sounds of youthful voices; soon she came upon a dozen boys in plastic aprons busily trimming an oak beam with axes, instruments that had been invented as far back as the stone age. The young builders greeted the historian respectfully and explained to her that they wanted to build a vessel without the aid of automatic saws and other machinery, in the same way as the heroes of ancient days had done. The ship, when built, was to take them to the ruins of Carthage, a trip they wanted to make during their vacation, accompanied by the teachers of geography, history and polytechnics.

Veda wished them success and intended to continue on her way. A tall, thin lad with absolutely yellow hair stepped forward.

"You came here with Evda Nahl, didn't you? Then may I ask you a couple of questions?"

Veda laughingly consented.

"Evda Nahl works at the Academy of Sorrow and Joy. We have studied the social organization of our planet and of several other worlds, but we have not been told the significance of that Academy."

Veda told them of the great census conducted by the Academy to compute sorrow and happiness in the lives of individuals and investigate sorrow by age groups. It was followed by an analysis of sorrow and joy for all the stages of the historical development of mankind. No matter what qualitative differences there may have been in emotions, the sum totals, investigated by big number stochastic [24] methods, showed some important regularities. The Councils that directed the further development of society did their utmost to correct any worsening and ensure improvement. Only when joy predominated, or at least counterbalanced sorrow, was it considered that society was developing successfully.

"And so the Academy of Sorrow and Joy is the most important?" asked another boy, one with bold eyes. The others smiled and the boy who had first spoken to Veda Kong explained what they were laughing at.

"Oil is always looking for what is most important. He dreams about the great leaders of the past "

"That's a dangerous thing to do," smiled Veda. "As an historian I can tell you that the great leaders were people who were themselves tied hand and foot and very dependent."

"Tied up by the conventionalism of their actions?" asked the yellow-haired boy.

"Exactly. But you must remember that that was in the unevenly and spontaneously developing ancient societies of the Era of Disunity or even earlier. Today, leadership [a invested in each of the

Councils and is expressed by the fact that the action of all the others is impossible without it."

"What about the Economic Council? Without that Council nobody can undertake anything big," Oil objected cautiously, somewhat abashed but still not confused.

"That's true because economics are the only real basis of our existence. But it seems to me that you don't have quite the right idea of what constitutes leadership. Have you studied the cytoarchitectonics[25] of the human brain?"

The boys said that they had.

Veda took a stick from one of them and in the sand drew circles to represent the administrative bodies.

"Here in the centre is the Economic Council. We will draw direct links from it to the consultative bodies: the ASJ, the Academy of Sorrow and Joy, the APF, the Academy of Productive Forces, the ASP the Academy of Stochastics and Prognostication, the APL, the Academy of the Psychophysiology of Labour. There is lateral connection with the Astronautical Council, a body that functions independently. From the latter there is direct communication with the ADR, the Academy of Directed Radiation, and the Outer Stations of the Great Circle. Further...."

Veda drew an intricate diagram in the sand *and* continued.

"Isn't that just like the human brain? The research and registration centres are the sensory nerve centres. The Councils are the associative centres. You know that all life consists of the dialectics of attraction and repulsion, the rhythm of dispersal and accumulation, excitation and inhibition. The chief inhibition centre is the Economic Council that translates everything into the actual possibilities of the social organism and its objective laws. Our brain and our society, both of which are persistently advancing, have this dialectic interplay of opposing forces brought into harmonic action. There was a time, long ago, when this was incorrectly termed cybernetics, or the science of control, in an attempt to reduce the most intricate interplay of inhibitions to the relatively simple functioning of a machine. That attempt, however, was due to ignorance; the greater the knowledge we acquired the more complicated we found the phenomena and laws of thermodynamics, biology, and economics, and simplified conceptions of nature or the processes of social development disappeared for ever."

The boys listened to Veda spellbound.

"What is the chief thing in such a social structure?" she asked the lover of "chiefs" and "leaders." He was so put out that he could not think of an answer and the first boy came to his rescue.

"Its forward movement!" he answered, boldly.

"A prize for such an excellent answer!" exclaimed Veda admiringly; she looked at herself and then took an enamel brooch, depicting an albatross over the blue sea, from her left shoulder. She offered it to the lad on the palm of her hand. He was shyly hesitant.

"As a reminder of today's talk and… of forward movement!" Veda insisted and the lad took the albatross.

Holding up the blouse that was slipping from her shoulder Veda made her way back through the park. The brooch had been a present from Erg Noor and her sudden urge to give it away meant o lot- amongst other things it meant a strange desire to get rid of the past as quickly as possible, to get rid of what had been or was being left behind….

The entire population of the school-town gathered in the round hall in the centre of the school building. Evda Nahl, in a black dress, stood on the central dais, illuminated from above, calmly studying the rows of people in the audience. The people maintained perfect silence, listening to her clear but not loud voice. Screaming loudspeakers were used only for safety precautions and large halls had ceased to be necessary since the stereoscopic televisophone (TVP) had come into general use.

"Seventeen is the turning point in life. Soon you will pronounce the traditional words at a meeting of the Irish Educational Division:

"You, my elders, who have called me to a life of endeavour, accept my ability and my desire, accept my labour and teach me by day and by night. Hold out to me the hand of help, for the road is a hard one, and I will follow you.'

"A very great deal is understood between the lines of this ancient formula and that is what I am going to talk about today.

"From childhood you have been taught the philosophy of dialectics that long ago, in the secret books of the ancients, was called the *Secret of Duality*. It was believed that its power could only be achieved by the initiated-mentally and morally lofty and strong individuals. From childhood you have looked upon the world through the laws of dialectics and its mighty strength is now at everybody's service. You have been born into a well-ordered society created by countless generations of unknown toilers and those who struggled for a better life in the dark ages of cruelty and tyranny. Five hundred generations have passed since the formation of the first society with a division of labour. In the course of that time the various races and nations of the globe have mingled. Every one of us has drops of blood, or, as we should say today, the mechanics of heredity, in him from each of those peoples. A tremendous amount of work has been done to purge heredity of the consequences of the incautious handling of radioactive materials and from the diseases that were formerly widespread and interfered with it.

"The upbringing of the new man is an elaborate task involving personal analysis and a very cautious approach to each individual. The time has gone beyond recall when society could be satisfied with people who had been brought up casually, whose insufficiencies were excused by heredity or by man's inherent nature. Every badly brought up person is today a reproach to the whole community, a grave mistake made by a large number of people.

"You, who have not yet freed yourselves of the egocentrism of youth or of an overestimation of your own ego must get a clear understanding of how much depends on your own selves, to how great an extent you are the creators of your own freedom and of an interest in life. Many roads are open to each of you and this freedom of choice carries with it full responsibility for that choice.

Gone for all time are the back-to-nature dreams of the uncultured, dreams of the freedom of primitive society and primitive relations. Humanity, a union of gigantic masses of people, was faced with the final choice-either submit to social discipline, lengthy teaching and training, or perish; there was no other way to live on our planet, generous as her nature is. The puny philosophers who dreamed of nature did not understand her or love her as she should be loved-if they had they would have known her merciless cruelty.

"The man of the new society was inevitably faced with the necessity of disciplining his desires, will and thoughts. The struggle against the personal, against the 'I' that is man's most dangerous enemy, is essential for the good of society and for the maximum expansion of his own intellect. This method of training mind and will is today obligatory for every one of us as is the training of the body. The study of the laws of nature and of society with its economics has replaced desire by definite knowledge. When we say 'I want to' we mean 'I know that it can be done.'

"There is one other enemy amongst you, an enemy against whom we fight from the time the child makes *its* first steps on earth; that is, a crudeness of perception that sometimes seems to be primitive naturalness. Crudeness means that the key to measure and understanding has been lost and, consequently the key to love, since a measure of understanding is a degree of love. Thousands of years ago the Hellenes said, *metron ariston,* the mean is the most lofty. Today we still say that the basis of culture is an understanding of moderation in all things.

"As the cultural level improved the striving for the crude pleasures of property grew weaker and there was less craving for a quantitative increase in the amount of property owned, which once acquired, soon began to pall and leave the owner still unsatisfied.

"We have taught you the greater pleasure of austerity, the pleasure of helping one another, the genuine joy of work that sets the heart on fire. We have helped you liberate yourselves from the power of petty strivings and petty things and carry your joys and disappointments to a higher sphere, the sphere of creative activity.

"Good physical training, the clean, regular lives of dozens of generations have rid you of the third enemy of the human psyche, indifference, the empty and indolent spirit that arises out of a morbid insufficiency of energy in the body. You are going out in the world to work charged with the necessary energy, with a balanced, healthy psyche which, by virtue of the natural ratio of emotions, possesses more good than evil. The better you are, the better and more elevated society will be-the two conceptions are interrelated. You will create a high spiritual milieu as an integral part of society and society will elevate you. The social milieu is the most important factor in the training and teaching of the individual. Man today is training and learning his whole life long, so that society is constantly progressing."

Evda Nahl stopped and smoothed her hair with her hand, using exactly the same gesture as Rhea who sat there in front, never once taking her eyes off her mother.

"At one time people called their urge to comprehend reality a mere dream," she continued. "You will dream in that way all your lives and will know joy in knowledge, in movement, in struggle and in labour. Never pay any attention to the falls that follow flights of the spirit because they are the regular turns of the spiral of motion that we find in all matter. The reality of liberty is stern but you have been prepared for it by the discipline of your schooling and upbringing; you, therefore, are permitted all the changes of activity that constitute happiness because you are conscious of your responsibility. The dream of tranquil inactivity has not been justified by history because it is against the nature of man the fighter. There always have been and still are specific difficulties in every epoch, but a regular and rapid ascent to the heights of knowledge and emotion, science and art has become the good fortune of all mankind!"

Evda Nahl finished her lecture and went down to the front row of seats where Veda Kong greeted her as they had done Chara at the fete. All those present stood up and repeated the gesture, in this way expressing their admiration for an incomparable art.

CHAPTER TEN

TIBETAN EXPERIMENT

The Corr Yule installation on the flat top of a high -I mountain was no more than a thousand metres from the Astronautical Council's Tibetan Observatory. It stood at a height of nearly 4,000 metres where the only trees that would grow were a dark-green leafless variety with branches bending inwards towards the top brought from Mars. Although the light-yellow grass in the valleys waved in the wind these rigid iron-limbed strangers from another world stood motionless. The slopes were covered with streams of stones, the remnants of eroded rocks. The fields, patches and strips of snow gleamed with that special whiteness that belongs to mountain snow under a clear sky.

A tower built of steel tubes supporting two latticed arches stood behind crumbling diorite walls belonging to a ruined monastery that had been built with astounding audacity at that great height. On the arches lay an inclined parabolic spiral of beryllium bronze dotted with the gleaming white spots of rhenium contacts and open to the sky. Close beside it lay a second spiral with the open end turned to the ground to form a cover over eight huge cones made of the greenish borason amalgam. Energy was brought to the installation by branches of the main pipe, six metres in diameter. The valley was crossed by a line of pylons with directing rings, a temporary line from the observatory's main that was used when transmissions requiring the energy of all the world's stations were in progress. Renn Bose, scratching his tousled head, reviewed with a pleased air the changes that had been made in the former installation. It had all been done by volunteers in an incredibly short time. The most difficult job had been the digging of deep, open trenches in the hard stone of the mountain without the use of big mining machines. But that was all over and the volunteer workers, justly believing themselves entitled to see the great experiment as a reward for their labours, had moved to some distance from the installation and found a place for their tents on the mountain slope to the north of the observatory.

Mven Mass, who was in control of all communications with the Cosmos, sat on a cold boulder opposite the physicist and, shivering slightly from the cold, told him the latest news from the Great Circle. Satellite 57 had been used recently for communication with spaceships and planetships and had not been working for the Circle. Mven Mass also told him of the death of Vlihh oz Ddiz near star E at which the weary physicist showed more interest.

"The high gravitational tension of star E will lead to its becoming overheated in its further evolution. It is becoming a violet super-giant of tremendous power that is overcoming colossal gravitation. The red end of the spectrum is missing altogether and, despite the strength of the gravitational field, the waves of light rays are shortened and not lengthened."

"They become very short violet or even ultra-violet," agreed Mven Mass.

"That's not all. The process goes farther. The quanta become bigger until at last the transition takes place- there is a zero field and antispace-the other side of the movement of matter that is unknown to us on earth owing to the insignificant scale of everything we have. We could not achieve anything like it even if we were to burn up all the hydrogen in all the water on Earth."

Mven Mass made a lightning mental calculation.

"If we translate fifteen thousand trillion tons of water into the energy of the hydrogen cycle on the principle of the relativity of mass-energy we should get roughly a trillion tons of energy. The Sun gives off 240 million tons a minute so that it would be equal to no more than the Sun's radiation for ten years."

Renn Bose gave a smile of satisfaction.

"And how much does a blue super-giant radiate?"

"I can't compute it at once. But you can judge for yourself. In the Greater Magellanic Cloud there is a cluster, NGK 1910, near the Tarantula Nebula … excuse me, I'm accustomed to using the old names and numbers for heavenly bodies!"

"It doesn't matter at all!"

"Cluster 1910 is only 70 parsecs in diameter but it contains no less than a hundred super-giant stars. And the Tarantula Nebula is so bright that if it could be moved closer to us like, for example, the Orion Nebula that everybody knows so well, it would be as bright as our Moon. In that area there is the binary blue super-giant in the Dorado, with clear-cut hydrogen lines in the spectrum and dark lines at the violet end. It is greater than Earth's orbit in diameter and its luminosity is about half a million of our suns! Is that the sort of star you mean? In that same cluster there are stars bigger in size, with a diameter equal to Jupiter's orbit, but they are only just beginning to warm up."

"We'll leave the super-giants alone. For thousands of years people have been looking at the annular nebulae in Aquarius, Ursa Major and Lyra, not realizing that they have before them neutral fields of zero gravitation, which, according to the repagulum law, is the transition from gravitation to antigravitation. It was there that the riddle of zero space was hidden."

Renn Bose jumped up from where he had been sitting on the doorstep of the control room, a shelter built of huge blocks of cast stone.

"I'm sufficiently rested. We can begin now."

Mven Mass' heart was beating fast and he was almost choking from excitement. His breathing was deep and irregular. Renn Bose remained quite calm, the feverish gleam of his eyes alone betraying the concentration of thought and will-power that the physicist had achieved in order to begin his dangerous experiment.

Andromeda

Mven Mass squeezed Renn Bose's tiny hand in his huge palm. A nod of the head and Mven's tall figure was striding downhill along the road to the observatory. The cold wind howled wildly down from the ice-bound mountain giants that stood guard over the road. Mven Mass shivered and involuntarily hurried his footsteps although, actually, there was no need for haste. The experiment was to begin at sunset.

Mven Mass established radio communication with Satellite 57, using the lunar waveband. The reflectors and directors set up on the station were fixed on Epsilon Tucanae for the few minutes of the satellite's revolution from 33° north latitude to the South Pole during which the star was visible.

Mven Mass took his place at the control desk in the underground room, a place very similar to that at the Mediterranean Observatory.

For the thousandth time he looked through the sheets of data on the planet of the star Epsilon Tucanae, again systematically checked up the orbit of the planet and again got in touch with Satellite 57 and gave instructions that at the moment when the field was switched they must very slowly change direction along an arc four times greater than the parallax of the star.

The time passed slowly. Mven Mass could not rid himself of thoughts of Beth Lohn, the criminal mathematician. Renn Bose appeared on the TVP screen seated at the control desk of his installation. His stiff hair was sticking up more than usual.

The dispatchers at the power stations had been warned and reported their readiness. Mven Mass' hand moved towards the switches on his desk but a motion from Renn Bose in the screen stopped him.

"We must warn the reserve Q station on the Antarctic. We have not got sufficient power."

"I've done that, they're ready."

The physicist pondered for a few more seconds.

"On the Chukotka Peninsula and on Labrador there are F-energy stations. If you were to talk to them and ask them to switch in at the moment of the field inversion … I'm afraid the apparatus is imperfect "

"I've done that."

Renn Bose beamed and waved his hand.

The colossal column of energy reached Satellite 57. The excited young faces of the observers appeared in the hemispherical screen at the observatory.

Mven Mass greeted the courageous young people, checked up on the direction of the column to make sure that it would reach and follow the satellite. Then he switched all the energy over to Renn Bose. The physicist's head disappeared from the screen.

The indicators on the energy collector turned their needles to the right showing a constant growth in the condensation of power. The signals burned brighter and with a whiter light. As Renn Bose switched in one field radiator after another the intensity indicators fell in jerks towards zero. The sound of a muffled gong from the experimental station made the African start, but he knew what to do: with a movement of a lever he switched in the Q station and its power surged into the dying eyes of the indicators, bringing life to their falling needles. Scarcely had Renn Bose switched on the common inverter, however, than the needles again dropped to zero. Almost instinctively Mven Mass switched in both F stations.

It seemed to him that the measuring instruments had been extinguished-a peculiar pale light filled the room. Sounds ceased. Another second and the shadow of death crossed the consciousness of the Director of the Outer Stations, dulling his senses. He struggled against a nauseating dizziness, squeezing the edges of the desk in his hands and sobbing from the effort and from a terrible pain in his spine. The pale light began to grow brighter on one side of the underground room, but from which side, Mven Mass could not determine, or had forgotten. Perhaps it came from the screen, or from the direction of Renn Bose's installation….

Suddenly it seemed that a waving curtain had been torn asunder and Mven Mass heard clearly the splashing of waves. An indescribable perfume, one that could not be remembered, reached his widely dilated nostrils. The curtain moved to the left and in the corner the former grey hangings were still trembling. High copper mountains materialized before his eyes with remarkable reality; they were surrounded by turquoise trees and the violet waves of the sea splashed at Mven Mass' feet. The curtain moved still farther to the left and he saw his dream. A red-skinned woman sat on the upper platform of the staircase leaning on the polished surface of a white stone table, staring at the ocean. Suddenly she saw something and her widely placed eyes were filled with astonishment and admiration. The woman stood up with magnificent elegance and stretched out her open hand to the African. She was breathing spasmodically and in that moment of delirium she reminded Mven Mass of Chara Nandi.

"Offa alii cor." Her gentle, melodious and strong voice penetrated to Mven Mass' heart. He opened his mouth to answer her but in place of his vision there was a green flame and a shattering whistle filled the room. As the African lost consciousness he felt some soft, invincible power folding him in three, rotating him like the blade of a turbine and then flattening him out against something solid. Mven Mass' last thought was of the fate of Satellite 57, the station and Renn Bose....

The observatory staff and the builders who were some distance away saw very little. Something flashed across the profound Tibetan sky that dimmed the brightness of the stars. Some invisible power crashed down on to the mountain on which the experimental station was situated. Then came a whirlwind that swept up a mass of stones. A black stream, some five hundred metres in diameter that seemed to have been fired from a gigantic hydraulic gun raced towards the observatory building, swept upwards, turned back and again struck the mountain, smashing the entire installation and scattering the fragments. An instant later everything was quiet again. The dust-filled air was saturated with the odour of hot stones and burning mixed with a strange aroma similar to that of the flowering coast of a tropical sea.

At the site of the catastrophe the people saw that a wide furrow with molten edges had been ploughed across the valley, and that the side of the mountain facing it had been torn clean away. The observatory building had not been touched. The furrow stretched as far as the southeastern wall where it had destroyed the transformer chamber built against it; it ended at the dome of the underground chamber cast from a four-metre thick layer of molten basalt. The basalt was polished as though it had been worked on a grinding machine. Part of it remained untouched and that had saved Mven Mass and the underground chamber from complete destruction.

A stream of molten silver hardened in a hollow-the melted fuses of the power receiver!

Emergency lighting cables were soon connected and when the searchlight from the lighthouse on the highway threw out its beam an appalling sight met the eyes of the onlookers-the whole of the metal structure of the experimental installation was spread along the furrow in a gleaming thin coating making the ground shine as though it had been chromium-plated. A piece of the bronze spiral had been pressed into the precipice formed where the side of the hill had been cut away as clean as with a knife. The rocks had melted into a glassy mass, like sealing wax under a hot stamp. The turns of the spiral of reddish metal with its white rhenium tooth-like contacts were embedded in the rock and gleamed in the electric light like a flower done in enamel. One glance at that piece of jewellery two hundred metres in diameter was sufficient to arouse fear of the unknown force that had operated there.

When the fallen boulders had been cleared away from the entrance to the underground chamber rescue workers found Mven Mass on his knees with his head resting on the bottom step. The Director of the Outer Stations had apparently made an effort to escape the moment he regained consciousness. There were doctors amongst the volunteers who had been working there and his powerful organism aided by no less powerful medicines soon recovered. Mven Mass got to his feet, still trembling and staggering and had to be supported on both sides.

"Renn Bose?"

The faces of the people surrounding the scientist darkened at this question, and the Director of the observatory said harshly:

"Renn Bose has been badly disfigured. He is hardly expected to live." "Where is he?"

"He was found at the bottom of the eastern slope of the mountain. He must have been hurled out of the installation building.

There is nothing left on top of the mountain, even the ruins have been wiped off the face of the earth!"

"Is Renn Bose still lying there?"

"He must not be touched. Some bones have been crushed, some ribs broken and his stomach injured."

"What's wrong with it?"

"His stomach has been split open and his insides have fallen out."

Mven Mass' legs gave way under him and he clutched spasmodically at the necks of those supporting him. His will and his mind, however, were functioning clearly.

"Renn Bose must be saved at all costs. He is the greatest of all scientists "

"We know. There are five doctors there. They have erected a sterilized operation tent over him. Two men who have volunteered to give blood are lying beside him. The tiratron, the artificial heart and liver are already working."

"Then help me to the telephone room. Switch on to the world network and call the information centre in the northern zone. How are things on Satellite 57?"

"We called the satellite but got no answer." "Are the telescopes in working order?"

"Yes, they are."

"Look for the satellite in the telescope and examine it through the electronic inverter to get the maximum magnification."

The night operator at the northern information centre looked into his screen and saw a face smeared with blood, the eyes gleaming feverishly. He had to study the face for some time before he recognized Mven Mass who, as the Director of the Outer Stations, was a person well known throughout the planet.

"I want Grom Orme, President of the Astronautical Council and Evda Nahl, psychiatrist."

The operator nodded his head and began fiddling with the switches and vernier scales of the memory machines. The answer came back in a minute.

"Grom Orme is preparing some papers and is spending the night at the Council. Shall I call the Council?"

"Yes, call them. And Evda Nahl?"

"She's at School No. 410 in Ireland. If you need her I can try to call her to …"-here the operator looked up at a diagram-" … to telephone station No. 5654SP!"

"She's badly needed. It is a matter of life or death!"

The operator looked up from his diagrams.

"Has there been an accident?"

"A very serious accident."

"Then I'll hand everything over to my assistant and get busy on your call alone. Wait for me."

Mven Mass dropped into an armchair that had been pushed towards him, in an effort to gather his thoughts and regain his strength. The Director of the observatory came running into the room.

"The situation of Satellite 57 has been ascertained. There is no satellite."

Mven Mass jumped to his feet as though he had not received any injuries.

"A piece of the bow which acts as a quay for the reception of ships, has survived," continued the staggering report, "and is still in the same orbit. There are probably some smaller pieces but they have not yet been discovered."

"So the observers "

"They must have been killed!"

Mven Mass clenched his fists and sank back into the chair. A few minutes of oppressive silence followed, then the screen lit up again.

"Grom Orme is at the Council transmitter," said the operator and turned a handle. The screen showed a huge, dimly-lit hall and then the well-known head of the President of the Astronautical Council appeared. The narrow seemingly streamlined face, the big aquiline nose, the deep-set eyes under sceptically raised brows, the questioning twist of the tightly pressed lips…. Under Grom Orme's glance Mven Mass hung his head like a naughty boy.

"Satellite 57 has just been destroyed," began the African, plunging straight into his confession as he would into dark water. Grom Orme started and his face seemed even sharper.

"How could that have happened?"

Briefly and precisely Mven Mass told him everything, not hiding the illegality of the experiment or in any way sparing himself. The President's brows knitted together, deep lines appeared at the corners of his mouth but his glance remained calm.

"Wait a moment, I'll see about aid for Renn Bose. Do you think that Ahf Noot "

"Oh, if you could get Ahf Noot!"

The screen went dark. There was a long wait and Mven Mass forced restraint upon himself with the last of his strength. He would be all right, soon… ah, here was Grom Orme.

"I found Ahf Noot and have given him a planetship. He will require an hour to prepare his apparatus and his assistants. In two hours he'll be at your observatory. Make the necessary arrangements for the handling of heavy cargo. Now about you-did the experiment succeed?"

The question took Mven Mass by surprise. He did not doubt that he had seen Epsilon Tucanae. Was this, however, real contact with an inaccessibly distant world? Or had it been a combination of the deadly effect of the experiment on his organism and the burning desire to see that had produced a very clear hallucination? Could he announce to the whole world that the experiment had been a success, that fresh efforts, new sacrifices and further expenditure to repeat it would be justified? Could he say that the method adopted by Renn Bose was more successful than that of his predecessors? For fear of risking anybody else's life they had foolishly carried out the experiment alone, just the two of them. But what had Renn seen? What could he tell them? … Would he ever be able to talk … if he had seen! … Mven Mass stood up still straighter. "I have no proof that the experiment was successful. I don't know what Renn Bose saw "

Undisguised sorrow was expressed on Grom Orme's face. A minute before that he had only been attentive, now he had become stern.

"What do you propose to do?"

"Please permit me to hand over the station to Junius Antus immediately. I am no longer worthy to direct it. Then, I'll remain with

Renn Bose to the end..." he stammered and then corrected himself, "... until the end of the operation. Then ... then I'll go away to the Island of Oblivion to await trial. I have already condemned myself!"

"Possibly you are right. Some of the circumstances are not yet clear to me so I must reserve my judgement. Your actions will be examined at the next meeting of the Astronautical Council. Whom do you consider the most fitting successor to your post-firstly for the work of rebuilding the satellite?"

"I don't know a better candidate than Darr Veter!" The President of the Council nodded his consent. For some time he continued looking at the African as though he intended saying something, but instead he just made a gesture of farewell. The screen was extinguished just in time, for at that moment everything went hazy in Mven Mass' head.

"You tell Evda Nahl yourself," he whispered to the observatory Director who was standing near by; then he fell, made several attempts to get up and lost consciousness.

A little man with Mongoloid features, a merry smile and unusually imperative in his words and actions became the centre of attention at the Tibetan Observatory. The assistants that had come with him obeyed him with that glad willingness with which faithful soldiers had probably followed the great captains of ancient days. The authority of their teacher, however, did not suppress their own ideas and enterprise. They constituted a very harmonious little group of strong people worthy to give battle to man's most terrible and implacable enemy-death!

When Ahf Noot learned that Renn Bose's heredity record had still not been received he gave vent to exclamations of indignation, but was just as quickly calmed when he was told that it was being prepared by Evda Nahl herself and that she would bring it in person.

The Director of the observatory asked quietly what the card was needed for and in what way Renn's distant ancestors could help. Ahf Noot screwed up his eyes slyly as though he were about to divulge a great secret.

"Accurate knowledge of the heredity structure of every person is needed both for an understanding of his psychological structure and to help make predictions in that field; it also provides important data on his neuro-physiological peculiarities, the resistance factor of his organism, immunity, selective sensitivity to traumas and allergy to medicines. The choice of treatment cannot be precise without an understanding of the heredity structure and the conditions under which his ancestors lived."

The Director wanted to ask more questions but Ahf Noot stopped him. "I've given you a sufficient answer for independent thought. I have no time for more!"

The Director muttered some apology which the surgeon did not wait to hear.

A portable operating theatre was erected at the foot of the mountain: water, electricity and compressed air were laid on. A huge number of workers offered their services and the building was ready in three hours. Ahf Noot's assistants selected fifteen doctors from amongst the volunteer builders to service the surgical clinic that had been so rapidly built. Renn Bose was carried under a transparent plastic shield that had been fully sterilized and had had sterilized air blown through it by means of special filters. Ahf Noot and four of his assistants entered the first section of the operating theatre and remained there several hours where they were subjected to waves of bactericides and air saturated with antiseptic emanations until their very breath became sterilized. In the meantime Renn Bose's body was subjected to deep freezing. Then their swift and confident work began.

The shattered bones and torn blood vessels were joined by means of tantalum hooks and plates that did not irritate the living tissues. Ahf Noot sorted out the injured intestines and stomach: they were quickly freed of the mortified parts, stitched up and placed in a jar of healing solution B 314 that was prepared in conformity with the somatic properties of the human organism. He then started on his hardest job. From under the ribs he removed the blackened liver, pierced with fragments of the rib bones, and, while his assistants held it suspended in position, he confidently treated the fine hairs of the autonomous nerves of the sympathetic and parasympathetic systems and pulled them into position behind it. The slightest harm done to these finer branches of the nerves might lead to serious, irreparable damage. With a lightning-like movement the surgeon cut through the portal vein and joined the tubes of artificial blood vessels to the two ends. Then he did the same with the artery and placed the removed liver in a jar of solution B 314. After an operation lasting five hours all Renn Bose's injured organs were in separate jars. Artificial blood flowed through his body, pumped by the patient's own heart and an auxiliary double-heart, a tiny automatic pump. Now they had to wait for the healing of the removed organs. Ahf Noot could not simply replace the liver with another from the planet's surgical fund because that would require further investigation and the condition of the sick man would not permit of any delay. One of the surgeons stayed with the outstretched body (it looked just like an anatomized corpse) until the next shift of surgeons had undergone their sterilization.

The doors of the protective walls built round the operation theatre opened noisily and Ahf Noot, squinting and stretching himself like a beast of prey awakened from its slumber, appeared in the company of his blood-smeared assistants. Evda Nahl, tired and pale, met him. and handed him Renn Bose's heredity record. Ahf Noot snatched at it eagerly, glanced through it and heaved a sigh of relief.

"I think everything will be all right. Come on and get some sleep."

"But... suppose he wakes up?"

"Come along. He can't wake up. Do you think we are so foolish that we did not take care of that?" "How long must we wait?"

"Four or five days. If the biological investigation is accurate and the calculations are correct we shall then be able to make another operation, putting all the organs back. After that, consciousness...." "How long can you stay here?"

"About ten days. The catastrophe fortunately coincided with a break in my teaching work. I'll take advantage of the opportunity to have a look at Tibet, I've never been here before. It is my fate to live where there are moat people, in the inhabited zone!"

Evda Nahl gazed at the surgeon in admiration. Ahf Noot smiled gloomily.

"You're looking at me in the same way as people used to look at an

image of a god. That does not befit the cleverest of my pupils!"

"I really am seeing you in a different way. This is the first time in my life that a person dear to me has been in the hands of a surgeon and I can well understand the emotions of those who have come in contact with your art-knowledge combined with unexcelled skill!"

"All right! Admire us, if you must. I shall have time to perform not only a second but even a third operation on your physicist."

"What third operation?" asked Evda Nahl, immediately on the alert. Ahf Noot, however, squinted cunningly and pointed to the pathway leading to the observatory. Mven Mass, his head bowed, was hobbling down.

"Here's another unwilling admirer of my art. Have a talk with him, if you can't sleep, that is. I must sleep."

The surgeon disappeared round an irregularity in the hill in the direction of the temporary home of the doctors. From afar Evda Nahl could see how haggard the Director of the Outer Stations had grown and how much he had aged: but then, Mven Mass was no longer Director. She told him everything she had learned from Ahf Noot and the African heaved a sigh of relief.

"Then I'll go away in ten days' time."

"Are you doing the right thing, Mven? I'm still suffering too much from shock to be able to think over what has happened, but it doesn't seem to me that your guilt is so great as to require such condemnation."

Mven Mass frowned painfully.

"I was carried away by Renn Bose's brilliant theories. I had no right to apply all Earth's power to the first attempt."

"Renn Bose showed you that an attempt would be useless with less power," she objected.

"That's true, but we should have made indirect experiments first. I was insanely impatient and did not want to wait years. Don't waste words-the Council will confirm my decision and the Control of Honour and Justice will not annul it."

"I'm a member of the Control of Honour and Justice myself!"

"And apart from you there are ten other people. Since my case concerns the whole planet there will be a decision by the Joint Controls of North and South-twenty-one people besides you."

Evda Nahl laid a hand on the African's shoulder.

"Let's sit down, Mven, you're weak on your legs. Did you know that when the first doctors looked at Renn they decided to call a death concilium?"

"I know, they were two short. All doctors are conservative, and according to an old rule that they haven't got down to changing, there must be twenty-two people to decide to give a patient an easy death."

"Until recently the death concilium consisted of sixty doctors!"

"That is a relic of the days when there was a fear of the right to put a patient out of his suffering being misused; in those days doctors used to condemn the sick to long and useless suffering and their relatives to senseless moral torment, even when there was not the slightest hope and death would have been a quick and easy release. But still, you see how useful tradition has been in this case, they were two short and I was able to get Ahf Noot, thanks to Grom Orme."

"That's what I wanted to remind you of. Your own concilium of social death so far consists of only one man!"

Mven Mass took Evda's hand and raised it to his lips and she permitted him this gesture of great and intimate friendship. She was, at the moment, the only friend of a strong man oppressed by moral responsibility. The only one? And if Chara had been in her place? No... to receive Chara now the African would need great spiritual uplift and he still had not found strength enough for that. Let everything go its own way until Renn Bose recovered and the Astronautical Council held its meeting.

"Do you know what the third operation is that Renn has to undergo?" asked Evda, to change the subject. Mven Mass thought for a moment and then recalled a conversation he had had with Ahf Noot.

"Noot wants to take advantage of Renn's being opened up to cleanse his organs of accumulations of entropy. It is usually done by physiochemotherapy and takes a long time, but it can be done in conjunction with such extensive surgery much more quickly and thoroughly."

Evda Nahl thought over everything she knew of the basis of longevity, the cleansing of the organism of entropy. Man's fish, saurian and arboreal ancestors have left contradictory vestiges of ancient physiological structures in his organism each of which has its own specific way of forming entropic remnants of their activity. Thousands of years of study of these ancient centres of entropy accumulation, formerly the cause of senility and sickness, have resulted in the elaboration of cleansing by chemical and ray treatment and of methods of stimulating the aging organism with wave baths.

In nature living beings are freed of accumulated entropy through being born of different individuals coming from different places and possessing different lines of heredity. This juggling with heredity in the struggle against entropy and the absorption of fresh strength from the surrounding world is one of the most difficult riddles of science that biologists, physicists, palaeontologists and mathematicians have been battling with for thousands of years. But the struggle has been worth it, expectation of life is now almost two hundred years and, more important still, that exhausting period of decay in old age has been eliminated.

Mven Mass guessed the psychiatrist's thoughts.

"I have been thinking of the new and great contradiction of our lives," said the African. "I mean the power of biological medicine that fills the body with new strength and the constantly increasing creative labour of the brain that burns a man up so quickly. How complicated everything is in the laws of our world."

"That's true and explains why we are lagging behind with the development of man's third system of signals," agreed Evda Nahl. "Thought-reading greatly facilitates communication between individuals but requires a great expenditure of energy and weakens the inhibitory nerve centres. This latter effect is the most dangerous."

"And still the majority of the people, the real workers, live only half the possible number of years owing to their tremendous nervous tension. As far as I can understand, medicine cannot combat this except by forbidding people to work. But, then, who will give up his work for the sake of a few extra years of life?"

"Nobody, naturally, because people only fear death and try to hang on to life when their lives have been passed in isolation and in sorrowful expectation of joys never experienced," said Evda Nahl pensively; despite herself she could not help remembering that people live longer on the Island of Oblivion than anywhere else.

Mven Mass once again understood her unspoken thoughts and grimly suggested that they return to the observatory to rest. Evda consented.

Two months later Evda Nahl found Chara Nandi in the upper hall of the Palace of Information, whose tall columns gave it the appearance of a Gothic cathedral. The rays of the sun, slanting down from high windows, crossed at half the height of the hall creating a warm glow above and soft twilight below.

The girl stood leaning against a column, her hands folded behind and her legs crossed. Evda Nahl, as usual, could not help admiring her simple attire-a short grey dress trimmed with blue and with a very low-cut bodice.

Chara glanced over her shoulder as Evda approached and her sorrowful eyes lit up.

"What are you doing here, Chara? I thought you were practising a new dance to surprise us with."

"Dances are a thing of the past," said Chara, seriously. "I'm choosing a job in a field I'm acquainted with. There is a vacancy at a factory growing artificial leather somewhere in the South Seas near Celebes and another at the station developing perennial plants in the old Atakama Desert. I was happy working in the Atlantic Ocean, everything was so clear and bright and joyful there from the power of the sea and an unthinking contact with it… I enjoyed skilful play in competition with the waves, the big waves that are always there waiting for you and, as soon as you've finished work "

"I, too, have only to give way to melancholy to recall my first work in the psychological sanatorium in New Zealand where I was just an ordinary nurse. And Renn Bose, today even, after his terrible accident, says that he was happiest when he was working on helicopter traffic control. But, Chara, surely you know that's just weakness! It's only fatigue from the tremendous strain that was necessary for you to keep at the high artistic level you have achieved. It is going to be worse later on when your body ceases to be so splendidly charged with vital energy. But as long as it remains what it is, please give us the pleasure of admiring your skill and your beauty."

"You don't know how it is with me, Evda. Every new dance I prepare is a matter of joyful search. I realize that I shall once more be giving people something good, something that brings them joy and reaches to the very depths of their emotions and that is what I live by. The moment comes when my plan is put into effect and I give myself up entirely to one burst of passion, to furious, flaming voluptuousness. I suppose this is transmitted to the audience and accounts for the enthusiasm with which the dance is received. I give all of myself to you all!"

"And then what next? A sudden anticlimax?"

"Yes! I'm just like a song that has flown away and vanished into thin air, I'm an exile from a vanished world that nobody wants and to whom nothing is left but the admiration of naive youth. I do not create anything that is registered by the intellect!"

"You do more than that, you leave something in the hearts of people!"

"That's all very immaterial and transient-I was thinking of myself!"

"Have you ever been in love, Chara?"

The girl lowered her eyelashes and her chin stuck out.

"Would that be like me?" she answered with another question.

Evda Nahl shook her head.

"I mean that tremendous big emotion that you, but not everybody, are capable of."

"I know what you mean, the poverty of my intellectual life leaves me a richness of emotion "

"That's the right idea in essence but I would explain it differently; you are so gifted emotionally that the other side docs not necessarily have to be poor, although, of course, it will naturally be weaker by the law of contradictions. We're talking too much in the abstract and

I have an urgent matter to talk to you about, something that directly concerns our conversation. Mven Mass "

The girl flinched and Evda Nahl felt that she was inwardly putting up barriers against her. She took Chara under the arm and led her to a side gallery of the hall where the dark wooden panelling harmonized beautifully with the blue-gold of the stained glass in the arched windows.

"Chara, my dear, you are an earthly, light-loving flower transplanted on to the planet of a double star. There are two suns in the sky, one blue and the other red, and the flower does not know which one to turn to. You are a daughter of the red sun, why do you turn to the blue?" Strongly but gently Evda drew the girl to her shoulder and Chara suddenly snuggled up to her. The famous psychiatrist stroked the girl's thick, somewhat harsh hair, thinking all the time how thousands of years of training had changed man's petty private joys for something greater and common to all. But how far they still were from victory over the loneliness of the soul, especially in a soul complicated by a gamut of feelings and impressions, nurtured by a body rich in life. Aloud she said:

"Mven Mass-do you know what's happened to him?"

"Of course, the whole planet is talking about his unsuccessful experiment!"

"And what do you think?" "I think he was right!"

"So do I. That's why we have to get him off the Island of Oblivion. A month from now there will be the annual meeting of the Astronautical Council. His misdeeds will be discussed and the Council's decision will be handed over to the Control of Honour and Justice that constitutes the guardian of every person on the planet. I have every reason to hope for a lenient verdict, but Mven Mass must be here. A man whose emotions are quite as strong as yours must not remain long on the island, especially as he is alone!"

"Am I really so much of an ancient woman that I build up plans for my life to depend on what a man is doing, even if it is the man I've chosen myself?"

"Chara, my child, don't! I've seen you together and I know what you mean to him and he to you. Don't blame him for not having seen you, for having hidden from you. Think what it would mean to a man, one of the same type as yourself, to come to you whom he loves-yes, it's true, Chara-badly defeated and liable to judgement and exile. Could he have come to you, one of the world's beauties?"

"That's not what I was thinking of, Evda. Does he need me now that he is weary and broken? I'm afraid he may not have the strength necessary for a great flight of the spirit, not intellectual, but emotional this time, for such love as I believe we are both capable of. If he doesn't possess strength enough he might lose faith in himself a second time and that would be too much for him. That's why I thought that it would be better for me to be … in the Atakama Desert!"

"You're right, Chara, but only from one side. You have forgotten his loneliness and the unnecessary self-condemnation of a great and passionate man who has nothing to support him once he has left our world. I would go there myself but I have Renn Rose on my hands, he's just pulling through, and, as he's badly wounded, he comes first. Darr Veter's been appointed to build the new satellite and that's his share in helping Mven Mass. I'm making no mistake when I tell you quite seriously to go to him, ask nothing of him, not even a tender glance, no plans for the future, no love … only give him your support, dispel his doubts in his own right and then bring him back to our world. You have strength enough to do that, Chara. Will you go?"

The girl was breathing fast, she raised her childishly trusting eyes to the older woman and there were tears in them.

"I'll go today!"

Evda Nahl kissed Chara heartily.

"You're right, you must hurry. We'll go to Asia Minor together on the Spiral Way. Renn Bose is in a surgical sanatorium on the Island of Rhodes and I'll send you on to Deir-es-Sohr where there is a helicopter base belonging to the technical and medical first-aid service on the Australia and New Zealand route. I can imagine the pleasure it will give the pilot to take the famous dancer Chara- alas, not the biologist Chara!-to any place she wants to visit."

The chief conductor of train 116/78 invited Evda Nahl and her companion to pay a visit to the central control room. A corridor, covered with a silicolloid hood, ran along the whole length of the huge cars. Mechanics walked up and down this corridor, from one end of the train to the other, watching instruments indicating the temperature of the axles, the strain on the springs and frame of each of the cars. Geiger counters kept a check on lubrication and brakes. The two women went up a spiral staircase and walked along the corridor until they came to a big cabin high up over the streamlined nose of the first car. In a crystal ellipsoid twenty-two feet above the railway line sat two mechanics one on either side of the pyramidal hood of the electronic robot driver. Parabolic screens showed them everything that was going on on both sides and behind the train. The whiskers of the antenna that trembled on the roof belonged to an apparatus that should give warning of anything appearing on the line of the Spiral Way for the next 50 kilometres although the circumstances under which anything could appear would be very extraordinary.

Evda and Chara sat down on a sofa against the bade wall of the cabin placed half a metre higher than the seats of the mechanics and allowed themselves to be hypnotized by the railway lines racing swiftly towards them. The gigantic railway crossed mountain ranges, was carried over the plains along huge embankments and crossed narrow waters and bays by viaducts built deep in the water. The forest planted on the sides of the colossal cuttings and embankments formed a continuous carpet owing to the train's uniform speed of 200 kilometres an hour, a carpet that was reddish, light or dark green depending on the trees of the district-pines, eucalypti, or olives. The calm waters of the Archipelago were set in motion on both sides of the bridge by the movement of the air as it was cut by the ten-metre-wide train. The big ripples ran out fanwise, darkening the transparent blue water.

The two women sat in silence, watching the line and wrapped up, each in her own thoughts and cares. So they sat for four hours on end. Another four hours were spent in the comfortable chairs of the saloon on the second storey amongst the other passengers until they parted near the coast of Asia Minor. Evda transferred to an electrobus that would take her to the nearest port and Chara continued her way to the East Taurus station, the junction of the First Meridian

Branch. Another two hours and Chara found herself on a hot plain, in a haze of hot dry air. Here on the edge of the former Syrian Desert was the airport Deir-es-Sohr, where spiral helicopters, dangerous in inhabited areas, could land and take off.

Chara Nandi would never forget the weary hours she spent at Deir-es-Sohr waiting for the plane to come in. Time and again she thought over her words and her actions, trying to imagine her meeting with Mven Mass; she built up plans for the search for him on the Island of Oblivion, where everything was blurred in the procession of uneventful days.

At last she was on her way: below spread the endless fields of thermo-elements in the Nefud and Rub-el-Hali deserts, huge stations for the conversion of sunshine into electric power. They were arranged in straight rows and had blinds that shielded them at night and from the dust; built on consolidated sand dunes, on plateaux cut away with a slope to the south and over a labyrinth of filled-in wadis, they stood there as a monument to man's terrific struggle for energy, a struggle that had begun when the ancient coal and oil resources were exhausted, after the first failures with atomic energy, when mankind came to the conclusion that the chief source of energy would have to be that of the sun in two forms-hydroelectric power stations and sun stations. When new forms of energy, P, Q and F energy were discovered, the necessity for severe economy disappeared. A whole forest of windmotors stood motionless along the southern coast of the Arabian Peninsula, another reserve power capacity for the northern living zone. In an instant the helicopter had crossed the barely noticeable line of the coast and was airborne over the Indian Ocean. Five thousand kilometres was an insignificant distance for the swift aircraft. Very soon Chara Nandi, followed by good wishes and hopes for a speedy return, left the helicopter, stepping wearily on her shaky legs.

The director of the landing field sent his daughter with a tiny flat-bottomed motor-boat to take Chara to the Island of Oblivion. The two girls were frankly delighted with the high speed of the tiny boat as it skimmed the big waves of the open sea. They went straight to a big bay on the east coast of the island where there was a medical station belonging to the Great World.

Coconut palms, their feathered leaves bowed over the wavelets lapping gently against the shore, welcomed Chara to the island. The medical station was deserted, all its workers having gone inland to destroy ticks discovered on certain rodents in the forest.

There was a stable at the station. Horses were still bred for work in places like the Island of Oblivion or at sanatoria where helicopters could not be used on account of the noise or electric cars on account of the absence of roads. Chara slept for a while, changed her clothes and then went to look at the rare and beautiful animals. There she met a woman who was skilfully operating two machines-a feed distributor and a stable-cleaning machine. Chara helped her with her work and the woman answered her questions. Chara asked her the best way to look for somebody on the island. The woman advised her to join one of the destroyer caravans that travelled all over the island and knew the place much better than the local inhabitants. Chara approved of this idea.

CHAPTER ELEVEN

THE ISLAND OF OBLIVION

The hydroplane was crossing Palk Strait against a strong head wind, leaping over the flat-topped rollers. Two thousand years before there had been a ridge of coral reefs and shallows there known as Adam's Bridge. Recent geological processes had created a deep gulf in place of the ridge and deep waters now divided the lovers of repose from a mankind that was surging ever forward.

Mven Mass stood against the rail, his feet placed wide apart, peering at the Island of Oblivion as it gradually grew in size on the horizon. This huge island, washed by warm currents, was a natural paradise. In man's primitive religious conceptions paradise had been a happy refuge after death where there were no cares or labour. The Island of Oblivion was also a happy asylum for those who were not attracted by the feverish activity of the Great World and who did not want to work on the same level as other people.

Here in the lap of mother nature, they lived out their years in the peace and calm known to the ancient cultivator of the soil, fisherman or herdsman.

Although mankind had given their weaker brothers a large area of wonderfully fruitful land, the primitive economy of the island could not fully guarantee the population against famine especially in periods of drought or other calamities that were so common where the productive forces were poorly developed. The Great World, therefore, was constantly allotting part of its reserve supplies to the Island of Oblivion.

Foodstuffs, preserved to last for many years, medicines, means of biological protection and other necessities were shipped to the island through three ports on the north-western, southern and eastern coasts. The three chief local governors also lived in the north, east and south and were known as the Directors of Animal Husbandry, Agriculture and Fisheries respectively. These people, elected by the islanders themselves, were always noted for their strong character. Some of them might have become pitiless tyrants if it had not been for the constant watch kept by the Economic and Health Councils and by the Control of Honour and Justice.

Not only on the island, but also in the Great World it occasionally happened that men of the hated category of "bulls" tried to enter into conspiracies and organize rebellions but the detachments of the Destroyer Battalions were as ruthless in dealing with wilful murderers as they were with sharks, bacteria and poisonous reptiles.

As he gazed at his future asylum Mven Mass began to wonder whether he, too, was a "bull", but he put the thought aside in disgust. A "bull" was a strong and energetic man but one completely unaffected by the sufferings of others, a man who thought only of his own, usually unworthy, pleasures. People who, in the past obtained such characters from an unfortunate combination of inherited qualities had to keep themselves in hand and in training throughout their lives in order to be worthy members of the new society. The sufferings, quarrels and misfortunes of mankind in the distant past had always been aggravated by such people who, in various guises, proclaimed themselves the sole holders of the truth, the rulers who claimed the right to suppress all those whose opinions did not agree with theirs, the right to eradicate all other ways of thought or of life. Since then mankind has avoided the slightest sign of the absolute in opinions, desires and tastes and had become more wary of the "bulls" than of anything else. They, the "bulls," ignoring the inviolable laws of economics, with no thought for the future, lived only for the present. The wars and disorganized economy of the Era of Disunity had led to the plundering of the planet. In those days forests were felled, supplies of coal and oil that had accumulated in the course of millions of years were burned up, the atmosphere was polluted by carbon monoxide and other filth that belched out of improperly constructed factories, beautiful and harmless animals were annihilated, and this went on until the world at last arrived at the communist structure of society, the only system that could ensure man's continued existence. Great difficulties were left for the descendants. In the Era of Unity the most complicated reorganization of the world had to be undertaken in countries whose trees had degenerated into bushes and their cattle into dwarfs. The earth had been littered with rubbish of all sorts-broken glass, paper, rusty iron-and the rivers and sea-coasts had been polluted by waste oil and chemicals. Only when the water, air and earth had been properly cleansed did man see his planet in its present form where he could go anywhere barefoot without fear of hurting his feet.

But had not he, Mven Mass, who had been less than two years in an important post, destroyed an artificial satellite built by thousands of people employing miracles of the engineer's art? Four competent scientists, any of whom might have become a Renn Bose, had been killed and Renn Bose himself had been saved with the greatest difficulty. Again the figure of Beth Lohn, hiding somewhere in the mountains and valleys of the Island of Oblivion, arose before his eyes, this time arousing great sympathy in him. Before he had left, Mven Mass had seen photographs of the mathematician, and had remembered his energetic face with its massive jaw and sharp eyes, deep-sunk and close to each other-he remembered his whole athletic frame....

The hydroplane engineer came over to Mven Mass. "There's heavy surf. We shan't be able to put in to the coast, the waves are beating over the mole. We'll have to make for the southern port."

"There's no need to. You have life rafts. I can put my clothes on one and swim ashore."

The engineer and helmsman looked at Mven Mass with respect. Surf-capped white waves piled up on the shallows and poured down in heavy, thundering cascades. Closer to the shore a disorderly swirl of waves whipped the sand and foam together and raced far up the low beach. The warm, fine rain that fell from the low-hanging clouds was swept at a slant by the wind and mixed with the wisps of foam.

Some grey figures were dimly visible on the beach through the veil of haze.

The engineer and the helmsman exchanged glances as Mven Mass stripped and packed up his clothes. Those who went to the Island of Oblivion were no longer under the guardianship of society where everybody protected everybody else and helped him. Mven Mass' personality aroused the involuntary respect of the helmsman and he decided to warn him of the great danger he was running. The African waved his hand carelessly. The engineer brought him a small hermetically sealed case.

"Here is a month's supply of concentrated foods, take it with you."

Mven Mass thought for a second then put the case and his clothes in the waterproof chamber, buckled the flap tightly and with the little raft under his arm put his leg over the rail.

"Swing her round!" he commanded. The hydroplane leaned over in a sharp turn. Mven Mass, thrown far away from the tiny vessel, began his furious fight with the waves. Those on the boat saw him rise on the crest of a wave, disappear into a trough and reappear on another crest.

"With his strength he'll manage it all right," said the engineer, with a sigh of relief. "We're drifting, we must get away from here."

The screw raced and the little vessel jumped forward and lifted up on a wave that ran counter to it. Mven Mass' dark figure appeared at full height on the beach and merged with the haze of rain.

Across the sandy beach, beaten hard by the waves, a group of people wearing nothing but loin-cloths came to meet him. They were dragging a huge, madly writhing fish in triumph. When they noticed Mven Mass they stopped and greeted him in friendly manner.

"A new one from that world," said one of the fishermen with a smile. "He swims well. Come and live with us!"

Mven Mass gave the fishermen a frank, friendly look and shook his head.

"It would be hard for me to live here on the sea-coast and always be looking at the expanse of water and thinking of my beautiful lost world. I'm going into the interior, on to the plateau where the herdsmen live."

One of the fishermen with a lot of grey in his thick beard that apparently was here considered an adornment to a man, laid his hand on the newcomer's wet shoulder.

"Could you have been compelled to come here?"

Mven Mass gave a bitter smile and tried to explain what had brought him there.

The fisherman looked at the newcomer sadly and with sympathy.

"We do not understand each other. Go your way," he said, pointing to the south-east, where the blue terraces of distant mountains could be seen through a break in the clouds. "It is a long way and there is no other means of transport here than…" and the islander slapped the powerful muscles of his legs.

Mven Mass was glad to get away as quickly as possible and with long, swinging steps went up the winding path that led to some low hills.

The way to the centre of the island was a little more than two hundred kilometres and Mven Mass was in no hurry. Why should he be? Wearisome days, not filled by any sort of useful labour, dragged on slowly. At first, when he had not fully recovered from the catastrophe, his tired body demanded repose, the tranquillity of nature. If he had not been conscious of the tremendous loss he had suffered he would have enjoyed the silence of the deserted, wind-swept plateaus and the blackness and primordial silence of hot, tropical nights.

But as day followed day, the African, wandering about the island in search of some work to interest him, began to yearn for the Great World. The peaceful valleys with their groves of hand-cultivated fruit-trees no longer gave him pleasure nor was he lulled by the almost hypnotic gurgle of the pure mountain streams on whose banks he could now sit for countless hours in the heat of the afternoon or on a moonlit night.

Countless hours ... why should he count that which was of no use to him there, time? He bad as much as he wanted, an ocean of time but he felt that his own, individual time was so insignificant. One brief and soon-forgotten moment! That was what happened to the lives of our stone age ancestors, lives full of courage and real heroism.

Only then did Mven Mass feel how well the island had been named-the Island of Oblivion! The stupid namelessness of the ancient ways of life, the doings and feelings of man! Deeds were forgotten by descendants because they were performed for the satisfaction of individual needs and did not make the life of the community easier and better, did not brighten life with creative art.

Mven was accepted into a company of herdsmen in the centre of the island and for two months pastured herds of buffalo at the foot of a huge mountain bearing the clumsily long name it had been given by the people who inhabited the island in ancient days.

For a long time he boiled his black porridge in a sooty pot and a month before he had had to seek fruits and nuts in the forest in competition with the greedy monkeys who threw their shells and peelings at him. That had happened when he had given the food he brought from the hydroplane to an old couple in a distant valley in accordance with the rule of the Great Circle World and its greatest joy: first give pleasure to others. Then he had discovered what it meant to have to seek food in unpopulated desert places. What a senseless waste of time.

Mven Mass got up from the stone on which he had been sitting and glanced round. The sun was setting behind the edge of the plateau and the wooded, rounded top of a hill rose up before him.

Below in the twilight murmured a swift rivulet flowing between growths of tall, feathered bamboos. Half a day's journey on foot or on the back of a buffalo at an even slower pace, stood the almost six-thousand-year-old ruins of the ancient capital of the island. Other bigger and better preserved cities had also been abandoned. Mven Mass took no interest in them so far.

The herd lay like black boulders in the dark grass. Night fell quickly. The stars came out in their thousands to twinkle in the black sky. This was the darkness to which the astronomer was accustomed ... the well-known outlines of the constellations ... the bright lights of the bigger stars. From there he could see the fatal Tucana - but how weak human eyes are! Never again would he see the magnificent spectacle of the Cosmos, the spirals of the gigantic galaxies, the mysterious planets and blue suns. All these were now only points of light immeasurably distant. Did it matter any more whether they were stars or lanterns hanging on a crystal sphere, as the ancients used to think. To the unaided eye it was all the same!

The African scraped together the brushwood he had made ready. There was another article that had become necessary, a small lighter. Perhaps soon he would follow the example of some of the local inhabitants and inhale narcotic smoke to make the endlessly lengthy days seem shorter.

Tongues of flame played amongst the sticks, driving away the darkness and extinguishing the stars. The big animals were snuffling peacefully near by. Mven Mass stared pensively into the fire.

Had this bright planet of ours become a gloomy home for him?

No, his proud renunciation was nothing more than the self-confidence of ignorance. Ignorance of his own self, an underestimation of the loftiness of the full creative life he had lived, a misunderstanding of his love for Chara. It would be better to sacrifice his life for one hour of some worth-while deed for the Great World than to live here a whole century.

On the Island of Oblivion there were about two hundred medical centres where doctor volunteers from the Great World provided the local inhabitants with everything modern medicine could offer. The youth of the Great World also served in the Destroyer Battalions that prevented the island from becoming a breeding ground for the ancient diseases and for harmful animal life. Mven Mass deliberately avoided meeting these people so that he should not feel himself an outcast from the world of beauty and knowledge.

At dawn Mven Mass was relieved by another herdsman. He was free for two days and decided to go to a small town to get a cloak as the nights in the mountains were chilly.

It was a calm, hot day when Mven Mass left the plateau and descended to the wide plain, a veritable sea of pale lilac and golden-yellow flowers over which countless brightly coloured insects were hovering. Puffs of a light breeze made the tops of the plants wave and the flowers gently brushed their heads against Mven Mass' bare knees as he walked through them. When he reached the middle of the huge field he stood still for a moment to enjoy the simple and joyful beauty of that aroma-filled natural garden. Bending down, the African passed the palms of his hands pensively over the wind-rocked flowers, and felt he was reliving a childhood dream.

A faint, rhythmical tinkle reached his ears. Mven Mass raised his head and saw a girl walking along swiftly, up to her waist in flowers. She turned to one side and Mven Mass looked admiringly at her graceful figure in the midst of that sea of flowers. A feeling of deep regret seized him: that could have been Chara if… if things had turned out differently.

His scientist's sharp powers of observation told him at once that the girl was worried. She kept looking back and increased her pace without reason as though she were afraid she were being followed. Mven Mass changed his direction and quickly caught up with the girl.

The girl stopped. A brightly-coloured shawl was wrapped tightly round her body with the ends crossed and the hem of her red skirt was wet with dew. The thin bracelets on her bare arms tinkled more loudly as she threw back from her face a lock of hair that the wind had tousled. Her sorrowful eyes were looking out in concentration from under short curls that fell carelessly on her cheeks and forehead. The girl was breathing heavily, apparently from her long walk. A few beads of perspiration showed on her pretty, tanned face. She made a few uncertain steps towards Mven Mass.

"Who are you and where are you hurrying to?" he asked. "Perhaps you are in need of help?"

The girl stared intently at him and then answered, hurriedly and jerkily:

"I'm Onar from the 5th Settlement. But I don't need help."

"I think you do! You're tired and something *is* bothering you. What can be threatening you? Why do you refuse my help?"

The girl looked at him and her eyes beamed, pure and profound, like those of a woman of the Great World.

"I know who you are! You are the big man from there," and she waved her hand in the direction of Africa and the sea. "You are kind and credulous."

"You be the same! Is somebody after you?"

"Yes!" gasped the girl in despair, "he's chasing after me!"

"Who is he that dares to make you fear him and to chase after you?"

The girl blushed and hesitated.

"There's one man who wants me to be his "

"But surely you can choose for yourself whether to respond or not, can't you? How can he compel you to love him? Let him come here and I'll tell him "

"Oh, no! He also came from the Great World, but a long time ago, and he's strong, only he's not like you, he's terrible!"

Mven Mass laughed a carefree laugh. "Where are you going?"

"To the 5th Settlement. I've been to the town and I met "

Mven Mass nodded his head and took the girl by the hand. She allowed her fingers to remain in his big hand and together they went along a side path leading to the settlement.

On the way the girl, from time to time looking back apprehensively, told him that the man who was persecuting her was always accompanied by two other strong and evil men who were in every way obedient to him.

Her fear to speak frankly made Mven Mass indignant. He had been trained from childhood by history lessons, through books, films and music to hate all those who oppressed people, all the secret organizations that had existed in the past, everything that was hidden from the conscience and judgement of the people, everything that meant bloodshed and unhappiness. He could not tolerate the existence of oppression, even if it were only occasional, on their well-ordered earth!

"Why don't your people do something?" exclaimed Mven Mass, "and why doesn't the Control of Honour and Justice know about it? Don't your schools teach you history and don't you know what even tiny centres of brute force may lead to?"

"We're taught… we know …" answered Onar, mechanically, looking straight in front of her. The flowery plain had come to an end and the path disappeared among the bushes in a sharp bend. Two men jumped out at the bend, barring the road to them. The girl snatched her hand away frantically, whispering, "I'm afraid for you, go away, man from the Great World!"

"Seize her!" came an imperative voice from behind the bushes. In the Great Circle Era nobody spoke so roughly. Mven Mass instinctively thrust the girl behind him and began to try his persuasion on these incomprehensibly wild people, but he stopped talking when he realized that his words did not reach them.

The broad-shouldered young men ran up to him and tried to push him away from the girl but Mven Mass stood as firm as a rock.

Then one of them gave him a lightning-like blow in the face with his fist. Mven Mass staggered. Never in his life had he seen deliberate, spiteful blows struck for the purpose of causing hurt, to stun and insult a man.

The other man punched him in the kidneys and through the ringing in his ears Mven Mass heard Onar's pitiful cry. Fury overcame him and he threw himself on his enemies, trying to crush them. Two deadly blows in the stomach and the jaw brought the African to the ground. Onar dropped to her knees, covering him with her body but her enemies seized her with a howl of triumph. They pulled her elbows bads behind her and she straightened up in pain, her head thrown back. Hands filthy from earth and Mven Mass' blood squeezed her helplessly writhing body and the girl sobbed, her face purple with anger.

"Bring her here!" came the loud voice again. An elderly man of tremendous height came out of the bushes. He was naked to the waist and athletic muscles rippled under the grey hair that covered his torso.

Mven Mass, however, had already recovered. He had had more serious tussles during his youth when he was performing his Labours of Hercules and had fought against sharks and octopuses, beings not bound by human laws. He tried to remember all he had been taught about hand-to-hand fighting with the monsters.

Mven Mass remained on the ground for a few second? to get his breath and then with one powerful leap reached the men who were dragging Onar away. One of them turned to meet the attack and Mven punched him exactly on a nerve centre. He fell to the ground with a bestial howl and a moment later was followed by his companion, brought down by a well-placed kick. The girl was free. Mven stood face to face with the third man, the leader of the gang, who was lifting his hand to strike. He cast one glance at his fury-distorted face to note the spot where he would deliver him one crushing blow- and staggered back. He recognized that powerful face that had so long tormented him in his dreams when he was wondering about his right to carry out the Tibetan experiment.

"Beth Lohn!"

Lohn stood still, staring at the unknown dark-skinned man who had now lost all his customary good nature.

The two confederates jumped up, still writhing with pain and wanted to attack again but the mathematician waved them back imperiously.

"Beth Lohn, I have thought a lot about the possibility of meeting you, believing you to be my companion in misfortune" exclaimed Mven Mass, "but I never expected the meeting would be like this!"

"Like what?" asked Beth Lohn insolently, hiding the wrath that burned in his eyes.

Mven Mass waved the question aside. "What is the use of empty words? In that world you did not use them and acted, even if criminally, for the sake of a great idea. For the sake of what are you acting here?"

"For my own sake, for myself alone!" said Beth Lohn contemptuously, spitting the words through his teeth. "I have considered others and the common good long enough. Now I realize that it is all of no use to a man. Some of the wise men in ancient times knew it, too."

"You never did think of others, Beth Lohn," Mven Mass said, interrupting him. "Giving way to your own desires in everything you have become what you are now -rapist, deceiver, an animal, almost!"

The mathematician made as if to attack Mven Mass but restrained himself.

"Is it proper for a man of the Great World to lie? I have never been a deceiver."

"What about them?" Mven Mass pointed to the two young men who were listening to the conversation in bewilderment. "Where are you taking them? What are you leading them to-the narcotic bullets of the Destroyer Battalion? You know very well that brute force, apparent power over other people, is the way to repudiation and death."

"I did not deceive them in any way. They came of their own free will "

"You, with your powerful intellect and will-power made use of the weakness of the human spirit, of their willingness to submit, a factor that was responsible for many of the calamities of the ancient world. In the old days men could avoid responsibility by laying the blame on the stronger, by submitting blindly and obediently and then laying the blame for their own ignorance, laziness and weak will on to God, an idea, a military or political leader. Was that the same thing as reasonable obedience to a teacher of our world? What you want is to train people who are loyal to you in the same way as oppressors of the past did, you want human robots."

"Enough, you talk too much."

"I see that you've lost too much and I want "

"And I don't want! Get out of my way!"

Mven Mass did not budge. With his head bent, he stood confidently and threateningly in front of Beth Lohn and could feel the girl's trembling shoulder against his back. That shiver enraged him far more than the blows he had received.

The former mathematician stood stock still, staring straight at the African, straight into black eyes that were burning with rage.

"Go!" he said with a loud gasp, stepping back from the path and ordering his companions to do the same. Mven Mass again took

Andromeda

Onar by the hand and led her through the bushes; he could feel Beth Lohn's stare of hatred following him.

At a bend in the path Mven Mass stopped so suddenly that Onar bumped into him.

"Beth Lohn, let's go back to the Great World together!"

The mathematician burst out laughing with his former abandon but Mven's sharp ear caught a note of bitterness behind his bravado.

"Who are you to suggest such a thing? Do you know?..."

"Yes, I know. I have also carried out a forbidden experiment and killed people I should have protected.... My path in science was close to yours and we, you and I and others, are already on the eve of victory! People need you, but not such as you are today."

The mathematician stepped up to Mven Mass and lowered his eyes, then suddenly turned away and contemptuously spat out coarse words of refusal over his shoulder. Mven Mass continued his way along the path without a word.

The 5th Settlement was about six miles away. The African learned that the girl lived quite alone and advised her to go to the east coast, to a seaside village where she would not meet the brutal Beth Lohn again.

Formerly a famous scientist, he had become a tyrant to the quiet little settlements of the mountain district that lived such a secluded life. In order to avoid any evil consequences Mven Mass decided to go into the settlement at once and ask for the three men to be kept under observation.

Mven Mass said good-bye to Onar on the outskirts of the settlement. The girl told him that there were rumours that tigers had appeared in the forests that covered the round-topped mountain; they had either escaped from the reservation or were still living in the dense jungles that surrounded the island's highest mountain. She grasped his hand and implored him to take care of himself and not go through the mountains at night. Mven Mass made his way back quickly and as he thought over everything that had happened he could see the girl's last look, a look that was filled at once with both anxiety and loyalty such as were rarely met with in the Great World. For the first time in his life Mven Mass thought of the true heroes of the distant past, people who had remained good in face of humiliation, wrath and physical suffering, something that required indomitable courage and fortitude. For the first time in his life he realized that the people of ancient times whose life seemed so hard to his contemporaries had also known the meaning of happiness, hope and creative activity, at times, perhaps, even to a greater extent than was the case in the Great Circle Era.

It was almost with anger that Mven Mass recalled the theoreticians of those days who based their prophecy that mankind would not improve in a million years on a false understanding of the slowness of the mutation of species in nature.

If they had loved people more and had understood the dialectics of development such ridiculous ideas would never have entered their heads.

The sunset turned red the clouds that lay on the rounded spur of a gigantic mountain. Mven Mass jumped into a stream to wash off the dirt and blood of battle.

Refreshed and calm at last he sat down on a flat stone to dry himself and rest. He would not be able to get to the town before nightfall but he expected to be able to cross the mountain when the moon came up. As he sat contemplating the water gurgling over the stones he suddenly felt that somebody's eyes were fixed on him but could not see anybody. The same feeling that unseen eyes were watching him was still with him when he crossed the stream and began to climb the slope.

Mven Mass walked quickly along the cart road leading to a plateau about 1,800 metres high, passing from terrace to terrace in order to cross a wooded spur which was the shortest way to the town. The thin crescent of the new moon would light the way for no more than an hour and a half and it would be very difficult to ascend a steep mountain path in the dark.

Mven Mass, therefore, had to hurry. Occasional low trees cast shadows that made black lines on the dry moonlit earth. Mven Mass kept a sharp look-out in order not to stumble over the countless roots that lay in his way but all the time he was thinking deeply.

From somewhere far away to the right, where the slope was gentler and lay in deep shadow, came a menacing growl that made the earth tremble as it carried over the ground. It was answered by a low roar from amongst the patches and strips of moonlight in the forest. These sounds had a strength in them that penetrated deep into a man's soul, arousing a long forgotten feeling of fear and doom in the victim selected by an invincible beast of prey. To counteract the ancient fear, in the African's heart there burned the no less ancient fury of battle, inherited from countless generations of nameless heroes that had defended the rights of the human race to live amongst mammoths, lions, giant bears, savage bulls and ruthless wolf-packs in exhausting days spent in hunting and nights spent in fear-filled defence. Mven Mass stood still, looking round and holding his breath. Nothing moved in the silence of the night but when he walked on a few steps along the path, he was certain that he was being followed. Tigers!-was it possible that Onar's information was really correct?

He began to run, trying to decide what to do when the animals, there were clearly two of them, attacked him.

It was senseless to try to escape up a tall tree that a tiger could climb better than a man. What was there to fight with? There was nothing at hand but stones, lie could not even break a decent club off the branches of trees as hard as iron. When the growls came from behind him and close at hand he realized that he was lost. The dusty branches of the trees that now overshadowed the path stifled him, he wanted to gain courage for the last few moments from the eternal depths of the starry sky, to the study of which all his past life had been devoted. Mven Mass ran on with long strides. Fate favoured him for he came to a place in the forest where there was a big, open glade. In the centre of the glade he noticed a heap of big boulders, ran to it, seized a thirty-kilogram sharp-cornered block of stone and turned towards the forest. He could now see vaguely moving, phantom-like figures. They were striped and were easily lost amongst the shadows of the scanty trees. The moon was already so low that its edge touched the tree-tops. The lengthened shadows lay across the glade like paths and the huge cats were crawling along them towards Mven Mass. He felt approaching death in the same way as he had done in the underground chamber at the Tibetan Observatory. This time it was not coming from inside him but from outside, it gleamed in the green flame of the animals' phosphorescent eyes. Mven Mass breathed in a puff of wind that came through the heated air, glanced up at the shining glory of the Cosmos, straightened his back and raised the big stone above his head.

"I'm with you!" A tall shadow spread across the glade from the darkness of the slope threateningly brandishing a knotted branch. For a moment the astounded Mven Mass forgot all about the tigers-he recognized the mathematician. Beth Lohn, out of breath from his headlong race stood beside Mven Mass, gasping spasmodically. The giant cats had at first drawn back but now they began steadily approaching the men. The tiger on his left was no more than thirty paces away and had drawn up its hind legs to spring.

"Quicker!" a loud shout resounded across the glade. As the pale flashes of grenade-throwers came from three points behind Mven's back he dropped his stone in his surprise at the suddenness of it. The nearer tiger reared up on its hind legs to full height, the paralyzing grenades burst like the beating of drums and the animal lay stretched out on its bade. The other leaped towards the forest but from there three figures on horseback appeared. A glass bomb with a powerful electric charge struck the tiger on the forehead and he stretched out with his heavy head in the dry grass.

One of the horsemen rode forward. Never before had the working dress worn by people of the Great World seemed so elegant to Mven Mass-wide shorts and shirt of strong, artificial blue linen open at the neck and with breast pockets.

"Mven Mass, I felt that you were in danger!"

Could he fail to recognize that high-pitched voice that was still full of alarm! Chara Nandi! The African forgot to answer her and stood rooted to the spot until the girl sprang from her horse and ran to him. She was followed by her five companions whom Mven Mass could not get a glimpse of because the moon had hidden behind the trees; the wind died down and stifling darkness enveloped the glade and the forest. Chara's hand found Mven's elbow. He took her thin wrist and laid her hand on his chest where his heart was beating wildly. Chara's fingertips stroked a bulging muscle and that gentle caress gave Mven Mass a sense of tranquillity such as he had never known before.

"Chara, this is Beth Lohn, my new friend." He turned round and found that the mathematician had disappeared.

"Beth Lohn, don't go away!" he shouted with all his might into the darkness.

"I'll come back!" a powerful voice answered from a distance and this time there was no bitter insolence in it.

One of Chara's companions, a youth of medium height, apparently the leader of the group, took a lantern that was hanging behind his saddle. A faint light together with an unseen radio ray rose into the air and Mven Mass guessed that they were expecting an aircraft of some sort. All five were little more than boys, members of a Destroyer Battalion who had chosen, as one of their Labours of Hercules, the security service that fought against dangerous animals on the Island of Oblivion. Chara Nandi had joined them in her search for Mven Mass.

"You're mistaken if you think we're so astute," said the leader when they were sitting in a circle round the lantern and Mven Mass began asking the inevitable questions, "a girl with an ancient Greek name helped us." "Onar!" exclaimed Mven Mass. "Yes, Onar. Our detachment was approaching the 5th Settlement from the south when the girl came running up to us on the verge of collapse. She confirmed the rumour about the tigers that had brought us here and persuaded us to ride after you immediately as there was a danger that they might attack you when you were crossing the mountain. As you see we were only just in time. A cargo helicopter will come soon and we'll send your temporarily paralysed enemies to a reservation. If they really turn out to be man-eaters they'll be killed. But such a rare animal must not be destroyed until it has been tested."

"What sort of test?" The boy raised his brows.

"That's outside our competency. To begin with they'll probably be given a tranquillizer.... Now and again people who have too much misapplied energy and strength have to be dealt with in that way, too." "How is it done?" asked Mven Mass. "I know of a case of an unbelievably brutal athlete here who forgot his social duties and obligations. He was given an injection to lower vital activity and bring his physical strength down to the level of his weak will and intellect thus balancing the two sides of his being. In the last three years he has learnt a lot-your enemies will be taught in the same way."

A loud rumble interrupted the youth. A huge, dark mass came slowly down to them. A blinding light flooded the whole glade. The striped cats were enclosed in soft containers such as were used for fragile goods. The big airship, poorly visible in the darkness, disappeared, leaving the glade to the calm light of the stars. One of the five lads had gone off with the tigers and Mven Mass had been given his horse.

Mven's horse and Chara's walked along side by side. The path led down to the valley of the River Galle at whose mouth, on the sea-coast, the medical station and Destroyer Battalion base were situated.

"This is the first time I've been to the sea since I came to the island," said Mven Mass, breaking the silence. "Until now it has seemed to me that the sea is a wall that I'm forbidden to cross and which marks off my world."

"The island has been a new school for you," said Chara joyfully but half-questioningly.

"Yes, in a short time here I've experienced a lot and have done some new thinking. All these ideas I've had on my mind for a long time...."

Mven Mass told her about his fears that man, by repeating the mistakes of the past, even if in a much less ugly form, is developing in a too rational, too technical manner. It seemed to Mven that on the planet of Epsilon Tucanae there was a mankind very much like ours and very beautiful in body that had paid greater attention to the perfection of the emotional side of the psyche.

"I've suffered a great deal from this sense of imperfect harmony with life," answered the girl after a pause. "I've always wanted more of the old and much less of what is around me. I dreamed of the epoch that had not expended the strength and feelings accumulated in the primitive period, the Age of Eros in Mediterranean

Antiquity. It would be a good thing for the Great World to set up a reservation for the Life of Antiquity where we could rest and acquire emotional strength. I have always tried to arouse a real strength of feeling in my audiences but, I'm afraid, only Evda Nahl has fully understood me!"

"And Mven Mass!" added the African, seriously, telling her how she had appeared to him as the copper-coloured daughter of Tucana. The girl raised her face and in the timid light of early dawn Mven Mass saw eyes so big and profound that he felt a slight dizziness, moved away from her and laughed.

"There was a time when our ancestors in their novels about the future imagined us as weakly, rickety beings with overgrown skulls. Despite the millions of animals that were tormented and slaughtered in the name of science they did not come any nearer to an understanding of the brain mechanism of man and simply because they used a knife where the most delicate measuring instruments in the molecule and atom range were needed. We now know that strong intellectual activity requires a powerful body, full of vital energy and that that body will produce strong emotions that we have so far learned only to suppress and, by suppressing them, make ourselves the poorer!"

"We are still chained to the intellect," agreed Chara. "A lot has been done but the intellectual side continues to advance while the emotional lags behind and that is what must be looked after-so that emotion should not demand an intellectual chain but that reason should at times need emotion's chains. I have come to regard this as so important that I intend to write a book about it."

"Oh, of course," exclaimed Chara enthusiastically, but grew timid and continued, "very few great scientists have devoted themselves to research into the laws of the beautiful and the fullness of emotions-I'm not talking about psychology."

"I can understand you," answered the African, admiring the girl who, in her confusion, had raised her proud head higher to the rays of the rising sun that again gave her skin the colour of burnished copper. Chara sat easily and lightly on the big black horse that walked in step with Mven Mass' roan.

"We are lagging behind!" exclaimed the girl slackening her reins and urging her horse forward. The African overtook her and they cantered together along the smooth old road. They soon caught up with the others, reined in their horses and again Chara turned to Mven Mass.

"What about that girl, Onar?"

"She must go to the Great World. You said yourself that she had remained on the island quite by chance because she was attached to her mother who came here and died recently. It would be good for Onar to work with Veda, women's gentle and sensitive hands are needed at the excavations…. And there are thousands of other jobs for which they are needed … and Beth Lohn, the new Beth Lohn who will come back with us, he'll find her in a new way."

Chara frowned and the bird that flew over her eyes spread its wings still more widely.

"And you won't leave your stars?"

"Whatever the decision of the Council may be I shall continue my study of the Cosmos. But first I have to write "

"About the stars of the human soul?"

"Quite right, Chara! So great is their variety that it takes my breath away." Noticing that the girl was smiling gently at him, Mven Mass stopped, "Don't you agree?"

"Of course I do. I was thinking about your experiment. You did it out of your passionately impatient desire to give people the fullness of the world. In that you were an artist and not a scientist."

"And Renn Bose?"

"He's different. For him the experiment was another step forward in his research but one that science required."

"You don't blame me, Chara?"

"No! Nor do many other people, the majority, I'm sure!"

Mven Mass took the reins in his left hand and held out his right to Chara. They entered the tiny group of houses around the station.

The waves of the Indian Ocean beat rhythmically at the foot of the cliff. In the sounds they made Mven Mass could hear the rhythmic beat of the basses in Zieg Zohr's symphony depicting life reaching out into the Cosmos. There was one powerful note, a strong F, the basic note in terrestrial nature, that sang over the sea and compelled man to respond with his entire soul, merging with the nature that gave him birth.

The sea was transparent, shining, cleansed of the relics of the past, of predatory sharks, poisonous fish, molluscs and medusae in the same way as the life of present-day man has been cleansed of the evil and fear of past centuries. But somewhere in the distant corners of the boundless ocean the seeds of harmful life have survived and we have the Destroyer Battalions to thank for keeping our ocean waters safe and clean.

And is it not true that in the same way there suddenly arises savage stubbornness, the self-confidence of the cretin, the egoism of the beast in the transparent soul of youth? If man today does not submit to the authority of society that is directed towards wisdom and goodness but, instead, is guided by his own accidental ambition and individual passions, courage is turned into bestiality, creative activity into cruel cunning while loyalty and self-abnegation become the bulwark of tyranny, cruel exploitation and abasement. The surface layer of discipline and social culture is easily torn off, only one or two generations of poor living are needed. Mven Mass had glanced into the face of the beast there, on the Island of Oblivion. If he is not restrained, if he has his way, a monstrous despotism will come into being that will crush everything underfoot and bring back that ruthless arbitrariness that held mankind enslaved for so many centuries.

The most astounding thing in world history is the emergence of that undying hatred for knowledge and beauty that is typical of all vicious ignoramuses. This mistrust, fear and hatred are to be found in all human communities, beginning with fear of the primitive witches and witch-doctors and continuing up to the beating o(those thinkers who were ahead of their time in the Era of Disunity. The same thing occurred on other planets with highly-developed civilizations that had not succeeded in protecting their social systems from the arbitrary action of small groups of people, oligarchies, that emerged suddenly and cunningly in the most diverse forms. Mven Mass recalled that the same thing had been reported over the Great

Circle about other inhabited worlds where the highest achievements of science were used to intimidate, for torture and punishment, for thought-reading and turning the masses into obedient semi-idiots ever ready to fulfil the most monstrous orders. A cry for help from such a planet had reached the Circle and flown on into space many hundreds of years after the people who sent it and their cruel rulers had perished.

Our planet is now at a stage of development when such horrors are inconceivable. But man's spiritual development is still insufficient and people like Evda Nahl are working on the problem.

"How can you get so deep in thought?" came Chara's voice from behind. "The artist Cart Sann said that wisdom is the combination of knowledge and feelings," as she walked along the girl threw off her bathrobe, "and so we'll be wise!"

Chara ran past the African and dived from the height into the noisy swirl below. Mven Mass saw her jump forward, turn a somersault, spread her arms and disappear into the waves. The lads from the Destroyer Battalion, bathing down below, were suddenly silent. A cold shiver of admiration verging on fright ran down Mven's back. The African had never dived from such a crazy height but he now stood without a tremor on the edge of the cliff and took off his clothes. He later remembered that in hazy momentary thoughts Chara seemed like an ancient goddess to him, a goddess that could do anything. If she could, then so could he!

A faint cry of warning from the girl arose out of the waves but Mven Mass did not hear it as he dived down. The flight was blissfully long. Mven Mass, a skilled diver, entered the water perfectly and his dive carried him a long way down. The water was so amazingly transparent that the sea bed seemed dangerously close. He twisted his body upwards and the impact of unspent inertia was so terrific that for a moment everything ceased to exist for him. With the velocity of a rocket Mven Mass flew to the surface, rolled over on to his back and lay rocked by the waves. When he opened his eyes he saw Chara swimming towards him, the paleness of fright dulling the bronze of her sunburn. There was both reproach and admiration in her eyes.

"Why did you do that?" she whispered, hardly breathing.

"Because you did. I'll follow you anywhere to build my Epsilon Tucanae on our Earth!"

"Will you come back to the Great World with me?"

"Yes!"

Mven Mass turned over to swim farther and gave a shout of amazement. The astounding transparency of the ' water that had played such a nasty trick on him seemed even greater out there, farther from the beach. He and Chara seemed to be floating at a dizzy height over the sea bed every detail of which showed as clearly through the pure water as it would through the air. Mven Mass was brimming over with courage and triumph such as people experience when they get outside the bounds of terrestrial gravitation. Journeys across the ocean in a storm, leaps into the black gulf of the Cosmos from artificial satellites aroused similar feelings of boundless daring and success. Mven Mass in a single spurt swam up to Chara, whispered her name and read a fervent response in her clear and courageous eyes. Their hands and lips joined over the crystal gulf.

CHAPTER TWELVE

THE ASTRONAUTICAL COUNCIL

The Astronautical Council, like the planet's central brain, the Economic Council, had for centuries possessed its own building for scientific conferences. It was believed that specially designed and decorated rooms would attune the assembled scientists to the Cosmos and in this way facilitate their rapid mental transition from matters terrestrial to matters astral.

Chara Nandi had never before been inside the main hall of the Council building. She was excited when she and Evda Nahl entered that strange, egg-shaped hall with its curved, parabolic ceiling and its rows of seats arranged in ellipses. The hall was drenched in a bright, transparent light that seemed to have been collected from some other star brighter than the Sun. All the lines of the walls, ceiling and seats converged at the end of the huge hall that seemed to be their natural focal point. At that point there was a dais with a screen, a rostrum and seats for the members of the Council who conducted the meetings.

The dull gold panels of the walls alternated with relief maps of the planets. On the right-hand aide there were maps of the solar system and on the left the planets of neighbouring stars that had been studied by the Council's expeditions. A second series under the pale-blue dome of the ceiling carried diagrams of other inhabited stellar systems done in radiant colours; these had been received from the Great Circle.

Chara's attention was drawn to an old, faded picture over the rostrum that had apparently been restored several times. A violet-black sky occupied the entire upper half of the huge canvas. The tiny crescent of an alien moon cast a deathly white light on the uplifted stern of an ancient spaceship harshly silhouetted against the ruddy glow of a setting sun. The rows of ugly blue plants, coarse and dry, seemed to be made of metal. A man in a light spacesuit was dragging his feet through deep sand. He was looking back at the wrecked ship and the dead bodies of his companions. The eyeglasses of his mask reflected only the setting sun but by some trick of infinite skill the artist had managed to put into them an expression of the hopeless despair of loneliness in a strange world. Something living, formless and disgusting, was crawling over a nearby sand hummock. There was a title under the picture in big letters, as brief as it was expressive: *Left Alone!*

So impressed was she by the picture that the girl did not at first notice a wonderful architectural feature of the hall: the seats spread out fanwise and were arranged in steps so that a separate gangway to each seat was provided from galleries running under the rows of chairs. Each row was cut off completely from its higher and lower neighbours. Only when she sat down with Evda did Chara notice the ancient craftsmanship of the chairs, reading desks and barriers, all of which were made from real pearl-coloured African wood. Nobody today would waste so much time and effort on something that could be cast and polished in a few minutes. Perhaps it was due to the love of old things that lives in all people that Chara found the wood warmer and more full of life than plastic. Gently she stroked the curved arms of her chair, all the time looking round the hall.

As usual many people had gathered in the hall although powerful transmitters would carry telepictures of the proceedings over the whole planet. Mir Ohm, Secretary of the Council, opened the proceedings by the usual reading of brief announcements that had accumulated since the last meeting. Not a single unattentive face.

not a single person occupied with his own thoughts, could have been found amongst the hundreds in the hall. A tactful attention to everything was a typical feature of the people of the Great Circle Era. Nevertheless Chara missed the first communication as she continued looking round the hall and reading citations from famous scientists written under the planet maps. She liked most of all an appeal to be receptive to natural phenomena written under the map of Jupiter: "Look how we are surrounded by facts that we do not understand-they thrust themselves upon us but we neither see nor hear the great things hidden in their faint outlines and awaiting discovery." In another place, farther to the left, an inscription said: "The curtain hiding the unknown cannot be lifted easily-it is only after persistent labour, retreats and deviations that we begin to fathom true meanings and new boundless horizons open up before us. Never try to avoid that which at first seems useless and inexplicable, incomprehensible "

There came a movement on the rostrum and the lights in the hall went out. The strong, calm voice of the Council Secretary quivered with excitement.

"You will now see that which was but recently considered impossible, a photograph of our Galaxy taken from the side. More than a hundred and fifty thousand years ago-one and a half galactic minutes-the inhabitants of planetary system…." Chara let the, to her, meaningless figures go, "in the Centaurus Constellation sent an appeal to the inhabitants of the Great Magellanic Cloud, the only extra-galactic stellar system near us that we know to contain worlds inhabited by intelligences capable of communicating with our Galaxy through the Circle. We still cannot give the exact coordinates of the Magellanic planetary system but we have received their transmission, a photograph of the Galaxy. Here it is!"

On the huge screen a wide cluster of stars, narrowing towards the ends, gleamed with a distant silver light. The profound darkness of space drowned the edges of the screen. The same blackness filled the gaps between the smaller spiral branches with their ragged tips. A pale glow spread over a ring of spherical clusters, the oldest stellar systems in our universe. Flat stellar fields alternated with clouds and strips of black condensed matter. The photograph had been taken from an awkward angle, the Galaxy was taken diagonally and from above so that the central core was a scarcely visible burning convex mass in the centre of a thin lentil-shaped cluster. Obviously if we wanted to get a complete picture of our Galaxy we should have to ask more distant galaxies that were situated at a higher galactic latitude. Not once since the inception ot the Great Circle had any of the galaxies shown signs of intelligent life.

The people of Earth watched the screen intently. For the first time man could look at his stellar Universe from the side and from a terrific distance in space.

It seemed to Chara that the entire planet was holding its breath as it looked at its Galaxy in millions of screens on all six continents and on all the oceans wherever islands of human life and labour were scattered.

"That is the end of the news received by our observatories and not previously broadcast in the world news circuit," announced the Secretary in a calm voice. "We will now go over to projects submitted for general discussion.

"Juta Gay's proposal to create an atmosphere for Mars suitable for human respiration by means of the extraction of the light gases from deep-lying rocks deserves attention as it is supported by sound calculations. The air so produced will be sufficient for breathing and for the heat insulation of our settlements which will then be able to come out of their glass houses. Many years ago, after oceans of oil and mountains of hard carbohydrates were discovered on Venus, automatic installations had been set working there to create an artificial atmosphere under a gigantic dome of transparent plastic. These installations enabled man to plant vegetation and build factories to provide tremendous quantities of everything organic chemistry could produce.

"We usually announce new proposals ourselves," continued Mir Ohm, "but today you will hear an almost finished piece of research. Its author, Eva Djann, will give you material that will require most careful thought."

The Secretary laid aside a metal sheet and smiled in a friendly way. At the end of the row of seats nearest to the rostrum Mven Mass appeared; in his dark-red costume he looked at once gloomy, solemn and calm. As a sign of respect for the assembly he raised his folded hands above his head and then sat down.

Mir Ohm left the rostrum to make way for a young woman with short, golden hair and green eyes that had a look of permanent surprise in them. Grom Orme, the President of the Council, stood beside her.

Eva Djann began speaking in a suppressed voice and was so shy that she seemed afraid to make the slightest movement. She started from the well-known fact that southern vegetation is distinguished by its blue foliage. This is a colour that is typical of ancient forms of vegetable life on Earth. An investigation of plant life on other planets had shown that blue foliage belongs to an atmosphere that is either more transparent than that of Earth or to one that is subjected to greater ultra-violet radiation from its luminary than Earth is from the Sun. It had long been known, she said, that the Sun, whose red radiation is stable, shows great instability at the blue and ultraviolet end of the spectrum. About two million years earlier there had been a sharp change in the Sun's ultraviolet radiation that had continued over a lengthy period. It was then that the blue foliage appeared, the birds and beasts of the open spaces acquired black protective covering and birds that nested in the open began laying blade eggs.

At this time Earth's axis lost its stability owing to changes in the electromagnetic regime of the solar system. For a long time astronomers had based their calculations on the mechanics of gravitation alone and had paid no attention to electromagnetic equilibrium which is much more changeable than gravitation.

There had long been in existence schemes for the transfer of seas into depressions on the continents in order to bring about a shift of Earth's axis. If this problem be approached from the standpoint of the electromagnetic forces of the system and not as a problem in elementary mechanics it would be more easily and cheaply achievable. It would be remembered, she continued, that in the early days of space travel the creation of artificial gravitation had required such a tremendous expenditure of power that it had been practically impossible. Since the discovery of meson forces, however, our spaceships had been equipped with simple and reliable artificial gravity installations. And Renn Bose's experiment had indicated a way of by-passing gravitation.

Eva Djann stopped. A group of six people, the heroes of the Pluto Expedition, seated in the centre of the hall, applauded her by extending their folded hands. The young woman's cheeks flushed for a moment before the screen lit up with the phantom contours of stereometric drawings.

"I realize that the problem is one that can be developed on a wider scale and that we can then think of changing the orbits of planets and bringing Pluto nearer to the Sun. But so far I have in mind only the shifting of the planet's axis of rotation to improve climatic conditions on the continental hemisphere. Renn Bose's experiment showed the possibility of the inversion of the gravitational field in its second aspect, that is, in the aspect of the electromagnetic field, with subsequent vectoral polarization in these directions," she pointed to geometric figures on the screen that had become elongated and were rotating, "Earth's axis of rotation would lose its stability and the planet could be turned in the desired direction for the better illumination of the continents."

Rows of parameters that had been computed by machines beforehand now appeared on the long glass under the screen and everybody who could understand them saw that Eva Djann's project was, at any rate, not without sound foundation.

Eva Djann stopped the movement of the drawings and symbols and, her head bowed, left the rostrum. Her audience exchanged glances and whispered amongst themselves. The young commander of the Pluto Expedition, exchanging a scarcely perceptible glance with Grom Orme, mounted the rostrum.

"There is no doubt that Renn Bose's experiment will have a trigger action and set off a chain of important discoveries. It seems to me to be leading us to distant vistas of science that were formerly unattainable. It was the same way with the quantum theory-the first approach to an understanding of the repagulum or mutual transition with the subsequent discovery of the antiparticle and the antifield. Then came the repagular calculus that scored a victory over the principle of indefiniteness proposed by the ancient mathematician Geisenberg. And, lastly, Renn Bose made the next step, the analysis of the space-field system, leading to an understanding of antigravitation and antispace, or, by the repagulum law, to zero space. All the formerly unaccepted theories have, in the long run, become the foundations of science!

"In the name of the Pluto exploration group I propose transmitting the problem over the universal information network for general discussion. The inclination of Earth's axis would reduce the expenditure of energy for the warming of the polar regions, would smooth out the polar fronts and increase the planet's water supply."

"Is the question now being submitted to the vote clear to everybody?" asked Grom Orme.

A large number of green lights flashed up in answer to the question.

"All right, we'll begin," said the President and pushed his hand under the book-rack in front of his seat. There were three buttons there connected with a calculating machine, the one on the right signalled "yes," the middle one, "no" and the one on the left "abstain." Every member of the Council sent a signal which the others could not see. Evda Nahl and Chara also pressed buttons working a separate machine which counted the votes of the audience to control the correctness of the Council's decision.

A few seconds later large symbols appeared on the demonstration screen-the problem had been accepted for discussion by the whole planet.

Grom Orme took the floor.

"For a reason that I shall not disclose until the case is over, we shall now examine the action of Mven Mass, the former Director of the Outer Stations of the Astronautical Council and will then decide the question of the 38th Cosmic Expedition. Does the Council believe that I have sufficient motives for my request?"

Green lights signalled unanimous consent.

"Does everybody know the details of what happened?"

Again a flash of green lights.

"That will speed up our business! I will ask Mven Mass, the former Director, to outline his motives for an action that had such dire results. The physicist, Renn Bose, has not yet sufficiently recovered from his injuries and has not been sent for as a witness. He is not answerable for the experiment."

Groin Orme noticed a red light burning at Evda Nahl's seat.

"Attention everybody! Evda Nahl wants to make an additional statement about Renn Bose."

"I would like to speak in his place." "What are your motives?"

"I love him!"

"You may speak after Mven Mass."

Evda Nahl extinguished the red light and sat down.

Mven Mass appeared on the rostrum. Calmly, in no way excusing himself, he told of the results that were expected from the experiment, related what had actually happened and the vision in which he did not quite believe. Their foolish hurry in carrying out the experiment on account of the secretiveness and illegality of their action, left them no time to devise special recording machines, they had relied on the usual memory machines and they had been destroyed in the first instant. Another mistake had been the conduct of the experiment through the satellite. They ought to have attached an old planetship to Satellite 57 and set up instruments on it to orientate the vector. He, Mven Mass, was guilty in all respects. Renn Bose made the arrangements for the ground installations but the transmission of the experiment into the Cosmos was exclusively the competency of the Director of the Outer Stations.

Chara clenched her fists, Mven Mass' self-accusation seemed weighty enough to her.

"Did the observers on the satellite know that a catastrophe was the possible outcome?" asked Grom Orme.

"Yes, they were warned and willingly gave their consent."

"I am not surprised that they consented, thousands of young people take part in dangerous experiments that are carried out every year on the planet and it sometimes happens that they arc killed. And new volunteers come to the fore undaunted," said Grom Orme, grimly "to do battle with the unknown. When you, however, warned the young people, you were showing that you suspected that such an outcome was possible. Nevertheless you carried out a risky experiment without even taking the necessary steps to ensure that definite results would be obtained."

Mven Mass lowered his head in silence and Chara suppressed a profound sigh, feeling Evda Nahl's hand on her shoulder.

"Outline the motives that led you to undertake the experiment," said the President after a pause.

Mven Mass spoke again, this time with impassioned excitement. He said that from early youth he had always regarded as a reproach the millions of nameless graves of people defeated by inexorable time, and that he could not allow this opportunity to pass, for the first time in the history of this and neighbouring worlds, of making an attempt at the conquest of space and time, of erecting the first landmarks on that great path, a path which many great minds would follow.... He did not believe that he had the right to postpone, perhaps for a century, this experiment, merely because he was subjecting a few people to danger and himself to great responsibility.

Mven Mass spoke and Chara's heart beat faster in pride for her fiance elect. Now the African's guilt did not seem so great.

Mven Mass returned to his place and stood there waiting, in view of all.

Evda Nahl handed over a record of Renn Bose's speech. His weak, gasping voice filled the hall through the amplifiers. The physicist exonerated Mven Mass. As he did not know all the implications of the experiment the Director of the Outer Stations could do nothing but trust him, Renn Bose, and he had convinced him that success was certain. The physicist, however, did not consider that he was in any way to blame, either. Every year, he said, important experiments are mounted and some of them have a tragic end. Science is a struggle for the happiness of man and it demands its victims in the same way as any other struggle. Cowards who are afraid to risk their own skins never know the fulness and joy of living, nor do such scientists ever make any advances.

Renn Bose concluded with a brief explanation of the experiment and an analysis of the mistakes and expressed his confidence in future successes. The tape recorder stopped.

"Renn Bose did not say anything about his observations during the experiment," said Grom Orme, raising his head and addressing Evda Nahl. "You wanted to speak in his place."

"I expected that question and for that reason asked for the floor," answered Evda. "Renn Bose lost consciousness a few seconds after the F station was switched in and did not see anything else. On the verge of consciousness he noticed and remembered only the readings of the instruments that indicated zero space. Here is his record from memory."

A few figures appeared On the screen and were immediately copied down by many people.

"Allow me to add on behalf of the Academy of Sorrow and Joy," said Evda, "that a poll of public opinion taken since the catastrophe gives the following "

A series of eight-figure numbers flashed on the screen in columns headed *condemnation, exoneration, doubt with regard to the scientific approach* and *accusation of haste*. The total was undoubtedly in favour of Mven Mass and Renn Bose: the faces of those present brightened up.

A red light was switched on at the far end of the hall and Groin Orme gave the floor to Pour Hyss, the astronomer of the 37th Cosmic Expedition. He spoke loudly and temperamentally, waving his long arms and stretching his neck so that his Adam's apple was prominent.

"A group of us, astronomers, condemn Mven Mass. The conduct of an experiment without the sanction of the Council, was an act of cowardice that gives rise to the suspicion that his action was not as selfless as it would appear from what has been said."

Chara burned with indignation and only remained in her seat in obedience to Evda Nahl's cold glance. Pour Hyss finished his speech.

"Your accusation is a serious one but not clearly worded," said Mven Mass when the President gave him the floor, "will you please explain what you mean by cowardice and selfishness?"

"Immortal fame should the experiment succeed-that is the thought of self that underlies your experiment. And I say cowardice because you were afraid that you would not get permission for the experiment and conducted it hastily and in secret!"

Mven Mass' face expanded in a smile, he spread his arms like a child and sat down without speaking again. Pour Hyss was the very picture of malignant triumph. Evda Nahl again asked for the floor.

"I do not see any grounds for Pour Hyss' suspicions. His statement was made too hurriedly and too maliciously for the solution of such a grave question. His views on the secret motives underlying people's actions belong to the Dark Ages. Only people of the distant past could speak in that way about immortal fame. They did not know the joy and fulness of real life, they did not feel that they were particles of mankind engaged in collective creative activity, they were afraid of inevitable death and clung to the faintest hope of immortality. Pour Hyss, a scientist, an astronomer, does not understand that only those remain alive in the memory of mankind whose ideas, will and achievements remain active and once their activity has ceased the people are forgotten. It is a long time since I came into contact with such a primitive understanding of immortality and fame and am amazed to find it in a cosmic explorer."

Evda Nahl stretched herself to full height and turned towards Pour Hyss who cringed in his chair illuminated by a large number of red lights of disapproval.

"Let us put aside all absurdity," continued Evda Nahl, "and examine the action of Mven Mass and Renn Bose by the criterion of human happiness. They were advancing along an untrodden path. I do not possess sufficient knowledge in their field but it is obvious, even to me, that their experiment was premature. In that respect both are guilty and are responsible for considerable material losses and for the loss of four human lives. This, by the laws of Earth, constitutes a crime, but it was not committed for personal gain and, therefore, does not merit heavy punishment. The noble aspirations of the chief accused, Mven Mass, should be regarded as an extenuating circumstance."

Evda Nahl returned slowly to her place. Groin Orme asked if anyone else wished to speak but nobody responded.

The members of the Council asked the President to propose final judgement. The thin, wiry figure of Grom Orme leaned forward on the rostrum and his piercing glance penetrated to the back of the hall.

"The circumstances on which we have to give judgement are quite simple. I do not hold Renn Bose in any way responsible. What scientist would not take advantage of such possibilities, placed at his disposal, especially if he were certain of success? The disastrous failure of the experiment will serve as a lesson. There has, however, been something gained that will, to a certain extent, recompense us for the material losses; the experiment will help solve a number of problems that the Academy of the Bounds of Knowledge has only just begun to think about.

"We have long since given up petty economies when it comes to the solution of great problems or the employment of our productive forces and have abandoned the tendency to utilitarian adaptation typical of the old economic system. Problems that arise during the reconstruction of production processes or during research are solved on a grand scale. Even today, however, the moment of success is sometimes incorrectly understood because there are people who forget that the laws of development are immutable. It seems to them that progress must be endless....

"The wisdom of a leader lies in his ability to recognize the highest permissible level at a given stage and in his ability to stop, wait or change his course. Mven Mass has proved incapable of such leadership. The Council made a wrong choice and the Council are as much responsible as the man they selected. In the first place I am at fault myself, since I supported the proposal of two members of the Council to invite Mven Mass for the post.

"I propose that the Council exonerate Mven Mass as having acted from the highest motives but forbid him to occupy any post in the governing bodies of the planet. I should also be removed from my position as President of the Council and sent to make good the damage done by my unfortunate selection-I should help build the new satellite."

Grom Orme cast a glance round the hall and saw the sincere regret expressed on many faces. The people of the Great Circle Era, however, did not try to persuade one another but respected other people's decisions and trusted to their correctness.

Mir Ohm discussed the matter with the other members of the Council and the calculating machine announced the result of the voting. Grom Orme's proposal was accepted without dissension but with the proviso that he conduct the present meeting to the end of the session.

He bowed and his face, controlled by his iron will, did not change its expression.

"I must now explain my reason for postponing the discussion of the Cosmic Expedition," continued the President in a calm voice. "It was obvious that the matter would end favourably and I think the Control of Honour and Justice will agree with us. I may now ask Mven Mass to take his seat in the Council as we are faced with a serious discussion. His knowledge is essential to us for the correct solution of our problems, especially as Erg Noor cannot participate in today's discussion."

Mven Mass walked over to the Council seats and green lights of good-will flashed up all over the hall, lighting his way.

The maps of the planets moved noiselessly aside and their place was taken by grim black charts with the stars shown in coloured lights, the blue lines of the interstellar routes proposed for the next century linking them up. The President of the Council was a changed man. His cold passionless attitude had vanished, a warm glow lit up his greyish cheeks, his steel-grey eyes grew darker. Grom Orme mounted the rostrum.

"Every Cosmic expedition is a long-cherished dream; it is a new hope that is carefully nurtured for many years, it is another step upward in the great ascent. It is also the labour of millions of people for which there must be due recompense, a very substantial economic or scientific gain, otherwise our forward movement would cease and there would be no further victories over nature. That is why we enter into such detailed discussions and make such careful calculations before a new ship shoots off into interstellar space.

"It was our duty to send out the 37th Cosmic Expedition to learn the fate of Zirda instead of continuing our own exploration. To compensate for this we have been able to discuss the 38th Expedition more thoroughly.

"A number of events that occurred last year have brought changes that necessitate a re-examination of the route and objectives of the expedition that had been approved by previous Councils and by a planet-wide discussion. The discovery of methods of processing alloys under high pressure at absolute zero temperature gives us material of higher durability for the hulls of the ships. Anameson motors have been improved and are now more economical which, of course, increases the ship's radius of activity. The spaceships *Aella* and *Tintagelle* that had been earmarked for the 38th Expedition are now out of date in comparison with the newly built *Lebed,* a round-hulled vessel of the vertical type with four stability keels. Longer flights are becoming possible.

"Erg Noor, now back from the 37th Expedition, has informed us of his meeting with a black star of the T class, on whose planet his expedition discovered a spaceship of unknown construction. Efforts made to enter it nearly cost the whole party their lives but they managed to bring back a piece of the metal of its hull. It is a substance that we do not know, here on Earth, although it resembles the 14th isotope of silver discovered on the planets of the very hot Os class star long since known by the name of Zeta Carinae.

"The spaceship is a disc, convex on both sides, with a crudely spiral surface, a design that has been discussed by the Academy of the Bounds of Knowledge.

"Junius Antus has been through the information records of the Great Circle for the entire eight hundred years since we joined it. A spaceship of this type cannot be built by science and engineering that follow our line of development and are at our present level of knowledge. Such ships are unknown in those worlds of the Galaxy with whom we have exchanged information.

"A disc spaceship of such gigantic proportions is undoubtedly a visitor *from* some inconceivably distant planet, perhaps, even, from some extragalactical world. It could have continued its journey millions of years after the death of its crew before landing on the planet of the iron star in our desert region on the fringe of the Galaxy.

"There is no need for me to enlarge on the importance of a study of that ship by a special expedition to star T."

Grom Orme switched on the hemispherical screen and the hall disappeared. The records of the memory machines moved slowly across the screen.

"This is a recently received communication from planet CR 519,1 will omit the detailed coordinates for the sake of brevity, about their expedition to the Achernar system."

The positions of the stars seemed peculiar and even the most experienced eye could not recognize well-known heavenly bodies. The screen showed patches of dully luminous gas, dark clouds and, lastly, huge dead planets that reflected the light of a terrifically bright star.

Achernar had a diameter only three and a half times that of our Sun but its luminosity was 280 times greater: it was an indescribably bright blue star belonging to spectral class B^5. The spaceship that had made the record had travelled a long way to one side, dozens of years' journey, perhaps.

Another star appeared on the screen, a bright green star of class S. It grew in size, became brighter and brighter as the spaceship from another world drew nearer to it. The surface of a new planet then appeared. It showed a country of high mountains clothed in every possible shade of green. Deep canyons and steep slopes were marked by dark green, almost black shadows, the gentler slopes and valleys were bathed in greens in which a blue tint predominated, the snow on the mountain tops and high plateaux was aquamarine and there were also patches of yellowish green where the sun had scorched the earth. Rivers the colour of malachite ran down slopes to lakes and seas hidden beyond the mountains.

Next came a plain dotted with round hills that stretched as far as a sea that from a distance looked like a gleaming sheet of green iron. Blue trees carried masses of dense foliage and the glades were bright with purple strips and patches of unknown bushes and grasses. Gold-green rays came in a mighty stream from the amethyst heavens. The earthlings were dazzled by the beauty of the planet. Mven Mass searched his encyclopaedic memory for the exact coordinates of the green star.

"Achernar is Alpha Eridani, it is high up in the southern sky not far from Tucana ... distance-21 parsecs ... the return of a spaceship with the same crew ia impossible," were the thoughts that flashed through his mind.

The screen was switched off and the sight of the closed hall, adapted for contemplation and conferences by Earth-dwellers, seemed suddenly strange to behold.

"That green star," the voice of the President continued, "with an abundance of zirconium in its spectrum, is slightly larger than our Sun." Here Grom Orme gave the coordinates of the zirconium star very rapidly.

"There are two planets in its system," he continued. "They are twins revolving opposite each other at a distance from the star that ensures them about the same amount of energy as Earth receives from the Sun.

"The depth and composition of the atmosphere and the amount of water are similar to those of Earth. These are the preliminary data obtained by the expedition sent out from planet CR 519. The same report speaks of the absence of intelligent life on the twin planets. Higher forms of intelligent life transform nature to such an extent that it is visible even from a spaceship flying at a great height. We must assume that higher forms of life have not been able to develop or have not yet developed there. This is unusually favourable to us. If there were higher forms of life there the planets would be closed to us. In year 72 of the Great Circle Era, over seven centuries ago, our world discussed the question of settling a planet with higher forms of intelligent life even if they had not reached our level of civilization. It was then decided that any invasion of such a planet would only lead to acts of violence due to the profoundest misunderstandings.

"We now know how great is the diversity of worlds in our Galaxy. There are blue, green, yellow, white, red and orange stars; they are all of the hydrogen-helium type but their mantles and cores are of different composition- carbon, cyanogen, titanium, zirconium-and they have different kinds of radiation, high or low temperatures and atmospheres of different composition. There are planets whose volume, density, depth and composition of atmosphere and hydrosphere, distance from their sun, conditions of rotation all differ very greatly. We also know that our planet, with water covering seventy per cent of its surface in combination with its proximity to a sun that pours a tremendous amount of energy on to it, enjoys conditions favouring the development of powerful living organisms, a rich variety of biological forms that are undergoing constant transformation, a case that is not often met with in the Universe.

"Life on our planet, therefore, developed more quickly than in other worlds where it is hampered by a shortage of water or solar energy or by insufficient dry land. And more quickly, too, than on the planets that have too much water! In the Circle transmissions we have seen the evolution of life on the planets that are under water, life that is crawling desperately upwards on stems of plants sticking out of the water.

"Our planet also has large expanses of water and the area of the continents is relatively small for the accumulation of solar energy through food plants, trees or simply by means of thermoelectric installations.

"In the earliest periods of Earth's history life developed more slowly in the swamps of the low-lying continents of the Palaeozoic Era than it did on the high land of the Cainozoic where there was a struggle for water as well as for food.

"We know that for an abundant and powerful life there must be a certain ratio of land to water and our planet is very close to the optimum in its composition. There are not many such planets in the Cosmos and every one of them is an invaluable acquisition for mankind as new land where man can settle and continue to develop.

"Man has long since ceased to fear the catastrophic over-population that at one time greatly disturbed our distant ancestors, but still we persist in our exploration of the Cosmos, extending the region settled by our people, for this, too, is progress, this, too, is an unavoidable law of development. So great are the difficulties involved in settling on a planet with physical properties differing from those of Earth that there have long been projects in existence to settle man in the Cosmos on gigantic, specially constructed installations, something like our artificial satellites magnified many times over. You will remember that an island of this type was built on the eve of the Great Circle Era, *Nadir*, situated more than 18 million kilometres from Earth. A small colony of people still live there but the failure of such closely confined and restricted quarters to satisfy the needs of human life if it is to spread boldly throughout the Cosmos is so obvious that we can only express amazement at our ancestors even though we admire the audacity of their engineering.

"The twin planets of the green zirconium star are very similar to ours. They are unsuitable or difficult to settle for the fragile inhabitants of planet CR 519 who discovered them and passed the information on to us in the same way as we pass our discoveries on to them.

"The green star is situated at a greater distance from our planet than any spaceship has yet covered. If we reach the planets of that star we shall have moved far out into the Universe. We shall move forward, not on the tiny world of an artificial island but on big planets where there is every opportunity for the organization of comfortable life and for mighty technical achievements.

"You now see why I have taken up so much of your time with a detailed description of the planets of the green star-they seem to me to be important objectives for exploration. The distance of seventy light years is feasible for a spaceship of the *Lebed* type and I think that we should, perhaps, send the 38th Cosmic Expedition to Achernar?"

Grom Orme finished at that point and returned to his place, pushing over a switch on the rostrum as he did so.

A small screen rose up before the audience and on it appeared the head and shoulders of Darr Veter, a massive figure known to many of those present. The former Director of the Outer Stations smiled as he was silently greeted with flashing green lights.

"Darr Veter is now in the Arizona Radioactive Desert from where he is sending groups of rockets 57,000 kilometres into space to build a satellite," explained Grom Orme. "He wishes to speak and give his opinion as a member of the Council."

"I propose the simplest possible solution," came his jolly voice to which the portable transmitter had added some metallic tones. "We should send out three expeditions and not just one!"

The members of the Council and the visitors were taken completely by surprise. Darr Veter was no orator and did not take advantage of the effective pause.

"Our first plan was to send both spaceships of the 38th Expedition to the triple star EE7723 "

Mven Mass immediately pictured the triple star that had been known as Omicron 2 Eridani in olden times. It was situated less than five parsecs from the Sun and was a system of yellow, blue and red stars with two lifeless planets which in themselves were of no interest. The blue star in this system was a white dwarf as big as one of the larger planets but with a mass half that of the Sun. The average specific weight of matter in that star was 2,500 times greater than of Earth's heaviest metal, iridium.

Gravitation, electromagnetic fields, thermal processes and the creation of heavy chemical elements on that star were of colossal interest and the importance of studying them at close quarters was very great, especially as the 10th Cosmic Expedition that had been sent to Sirius had been lost but had managed to send a warning of the danger. Sirius, a double blue star and near neighbour of the Sun, also possessed a white dwarf of lower temperature and larger dimensions than Omicron 2 Eridani and with a density twenty-five times that of water. It proved impossible to reach this near star owing to gigantic streams of meteorites crossing each other and encircling the star; they were so widely dispersed that it was found impossible to determine the area over which these treacherous fragments were spread. It was then that the expedition to Omicron 2 Eridani had first been mooted, 315 years before....

"... now, after the experiment made by Mven Mass and Renn Bose, it is of such importance that it cannot be rejected.

"But then, the study of a strange spaceship from a far distant world may give us knowledge that will by far exceed that acquired at the first examination.

"We may ignore former safety regulations and send the ships out separately. *Aella* can be sent to Omicron 2 Eridani and *Tintagelle* to star T. They are both first class spaceships like *Tantra* that managed alone against overwhelming odds."

"Romanticism!" said Pour Hyss loudly and unceremoniously but cringed in his seat when he noticed the disapproval of the audience.

"Yes, it is, it's genuine romanticism!" exclaimed Darr Veter, jauntily. "The very romanticism that was not properly appreciated in the past when it was killed by literature, education and experience. Romanticism is nature's luxury but in a well-ordered society it is indispensable! A craving for something new, for frequent changes, is engendered in every person by a superfluity of physical and spiritual strength. From this emerges a particular attitude to the phenomena of life, a desire to see more than the even tread of humdrum everyday existence, the expectation that life will provide a greater quota of trials and impressions.

"I can see Evda Nahl in the hall," continued Darr Veter, "and she'll tell you that romanticism is not only psychology but physiology as well! It is the task of our epoch to make romanticists of all the inhabitants of the planet. But let me continue: let us send the new spaceship *Lebed* to Achernar, to the green star, because we shall only know the result in a hundred and seventy years' time. Grom Orme is right in saying that the exploration of similar planets and the establishment of bases for advance into the Cosmos is our duty to posterity."

"We have anameson supplies for two ships only," objected Mir Ohm, the Council Secretary. "It will take ten years to build up supplies for a third ship without interfering with our economy. I must also remind you that a large part of our production potential is going into the restoration of the satellite."

"I have foreseen all that," answered Darr Veter, "and propose, if the Economic Council will agree, to appeal to the population of the planet. Let everybody abandon all pleasure trips and holiday journeys for one year, let us switch off the television cameras in our aquariums and in the ocean depths, let us stop bringing precious stones and rare plants from Venus and Mars and stop the factories producing clothing and ornaments. The Economic Council can tell you better than I what must be stopped in order to economize energy to make anameson. Which of us would refuse to curtail his needs for one year only in order to make a wonderful gift to our children-two new planets in the vitalizing rays of a green sun so pleasant to terrestrial eyes!"

Darr Veter spread out his arms as he appealed to the whole world, knowing that thousands of millions of eyes were on him; he nodded and disappeared, leaving a nickering bluish light behind. Out there, in the Arizona Desert, a dull thunder shook the earth periodically as the rockets bore their loads way out beyond the blue vault of heaven. In the Council hall the whole audience rose to their feet and raised their left hands as an open expression of agreement with the speaker.

The President of the Council turned to Evda Nahl.

"Will our visitor from the Academy of Sorrow and Joy please let us know her opinion from the standpoint of human happiness?"

Evda Nahl went to the rostrum again.

"The human psyche is so organized that it is incapable of lengthy excitation or frequent repetitions of excitation. This constitutes its defence against the rapid exhaustion of the nervous system. Our distant ancestors almost annihilated mankind by ignoring the fact that frequent rest is physiologically essential to man. We were at first afraid of repeating the mistake and began to take too much care of the psyche because we did not understand that the best way to get rid of impressions and to rest is to be found in work. A change of employment is essential but that is not all-there must be a regular alternation of work and rest. The heavier the work the longer must be the rest and it will be seen that the harder the task performed the greater the pleasure it will bring, the more fully the worker will be absorbed in his task.

"We may speak of happiness as a constant sequence of work and rest, of difficulties and pleasures. The longevity of man has widened the bounds of his world and he feels the urge to get out into the Cosmos. The struggle for the new-that's where we find real happiness! From this we may conclude that the dispatch of a spaceship to Achernar would bring more direct happiness to mankind than any two other expeditions because the planets of the green sun will make a gift of a new world to our senses while the investigation of the physical phenomena of the Cosmos, despite all its significance, is so far perceived only by the intellect. In the struggle to increase the sum of human happiness, the Academy of Sorrow and Joy would no doubt find the expedition to Achernar the most beneficial, but if it is possible to dispatch all three expeditions, so much the better!"

The excited audience rewarded Evda Nahl with a shower of green lights. Grom Orme rose to speak.

"The question and the Council's decision have already been made clear so that my speech will, apparently, be the last. We are going to ask mankind to curtail consumption for the year 809 of the Great Circle Era. Darr Veter did not mention the golden horse dating back to the Era of Disunity that the historians found. These hundreds of tons of pure gold can be used for the production of anameson so that a supply sufficient for the flights will soon be ready. For the first time in world history we are sending out three simultaneous expeditions to different stellar systems and for the first time we are trying to reach worlds that are seventy light years away!"

The President closed the meeting requesting only the members of the Council to remain. A demand for all requirements had to be drawn up for the Economic Council and a request had to be made to the Academy of Stochastics and Prognostication to investigate all possible hazards on the way to Achernar.

Weary Chara plodded along behind Evda wondering how it was that the famous psychiatrist's pale cheeks were as fresh as ever. The girl wanted to be alone as quickly as possible so that she could quietly enjoy the exoneration of Mven Mass. It had been a red-letter day! It is true the African had not been crowned as a hero in the way Chara had secretly hoped; he had been removed from the list of leaders for a long time, if not for ever. But he had been allowed to remain in society! Was not the wide and tortuous road of love, research and labour open to them both?

Evda Nahl forced the girl to go to the nearest dining-room. Chara stared at the menu so long that Evda decided to take action, and called the numbers of the dishes and the index of their table into the speaking tube. They sat down at a little oval table for two in the centre of which a trapdoor opened almost immediately and a container with their order appeared. Evda Nahl offered Chara a glass containing the opalescent invigorating drink Lio but was herself satisfied with a glass of cold water and a baked pudding of chestnuts, walnuts and bananas served with whipped cream. Chara ate a dish made from the minced meat of the rapt, a bird that has replaced both the domestic fowl and game birds in the modern cuisine. After Chara had eaten, Evda let her go and watched her as she ran down the staircase, with a grace that was astonishing even in the Great Circle Era, passing between statues of black metal and lanterns on posts of the most whimsical shapes.

CHAPTER THIRTEEN

ANGELS OF HEAVEN

Erg Noor held his breath as he followed the manipulations of the skilled laboratory workers. The mass of instruments reminded him of a spaceship's control tower, but the huge area of the room with its big, bluish windows, immediately took his mind off the Cosmic ship.

On a metal table in the middle of the room stood a special chamber made of thick sheets of rutholucite, a material that is transparent to visible and to infrared rays. A network of pipes and wires encircled the brown enamel water-tank from the spaceship in which the two black jelly-fish from the planet of the iron star were still imprisoned.

Eon Thai, erect as though doing gymnastics but with his arm still helplessly hanging in a sling, looked from a distance at the slowly revolving drum of a recording instrument. Above the biologist's black brows there appeared beads of perspiration.

Erg Noor licked his dry lips.

"Nothing there. There can't be anything left but dust after five years' journey," said the astronaut hoarsely.

"If so, that's bad luck for Nisa and me," answered the biologist, "we shall probably have to fumble for years to find out the nature of our injuries."

"Do you still think that the 'medusae' and the 'crosses' have the same organs for killing victims?"

"I do. Grimm Schar and all the others have come to the same conclusion. Before that I had the most unexpected ideas. I imagined that the black cross had nothing at all to do with the planet "

"I thought so, too; if you remember, I spoke about it. I got the idea that it was a being from the disc-shaped spaceship and was on guard over it. If you think about it seriously there's no reason to guard an invincible fortress from the outside, is there? When we tried to open the disc we had proof of the foolishness of such ideas."

"My idea was that the 'cross' wasn't alive but was just a robot placed there to guard the spaceship."

"That's what I thought. But now, of course, I've given up all such ideas. The black cross is a living being engendered by the world of darkness. The beasts probably live down below, on the plain. This one came from the direction of the gap in the cliffs. The medusae are lighter and more mobile, they live on the platean where we landed. The connection between the black cross and the spiral disc is a pure coincidence due to the fact that our protective arrangements did not reach the far corner of the plain and it was all the time in the shadow behind the disc."

"And do you think the lethal organs of the 'cross' and the 'medusa' are identical?"

"Yes. Animals living in similar conditions should evolve similar organs. The iron star is a sun that radiates heat and electricity. The whole atmosphere of the planet is strongly saturated with electricity. Grimm Schar believes that the animals gathered energy from the atmosphere and created condensations like our fire-balls. Do you remember how the brown lights moved along the tentacles of the medusae?"

"The cross had tentacles, too, but there was no…." "Simply because nobody had time to take note of them. The nature of the injury to the nerve column accompanied by paralysis of the higher centre concerned--we all agree on this-is the same in my case and Nisa'8. That is the chief proof and the main hope!" "Hope?" Erg Noor showed signs of agitation. "Of course. Look at this," said the biologist showing him the regular line of the recording instrument. "The sensitive electrodes placed in the trap with the jelly-fish do not show anything. The monsters had a full charge of energy when they went in there and it could not have escaped from the tank after it was sealed. I do not think that the insulation of the cosmic food containers could be broken down, it's much stronger than our light biological spacesuits. If you remember, the 'cross' that injured Nisa did not do you any harm. Its supersonic waves penetrated into the super-protective spacesuit you wore and broke down your will-power but the paralyzing chargea were powerless to inflict harm. They penetrated Nisa'B light spacesuit in the same way as the jelly-fish's penetrated mine."

"You mean that the charges of globular lightning or whatever it is that went into the tank should still be there, is that it? But the instruments don't record anything."

"That's why I say there is hope: it means that the jelly-fish have not been reduced to dust. They "

"Now I understand. They have sealed themselves up in something like a cocoon!"

"That's it. Such forms of adaption are widespread among living organisms that have to go through long periods of unfavourable climatic conditions-like the long, icy nights of the black planet and the hurricanes at 'sunrise' and 'sunset.' As these conditions on the planet alternate very quickliy I imagine the jelly-fish can come out of their state of lethargy as quickly as they go into it. If our assumptions are correct it will be fairly easy to restore the lethal propensities of the black medusae."

"By providing the temperature, atmospheric, lighting and other conditions of the black planet, I suppose?"

"Yes, we've made all the calculations and preparations. Soon Grimm Schar will be here and we'll start filling the tank with a mixture of neon, oxygen and nitrogen until the pressure reaches three atmospheres. But first let's make sure of our ground."

Eon Thai conferred with his two assistants. Some sort of a machine began crawling slowly towards the brown tank. The sheet of rutholucite that formed the front of the protective housing moved to one side opening up a passage for the machine.

The electrodes inside the tank were changed for micro-mirrors with cylindrical lamps to provide light for them. One of the assistants stood at the remote control panel: a concave surface appeared on the screen; it was covered with a sort of granular coating that reflected light very dully-this was the interior wall of the tank.

"X-rays won't be of much use," said Eon Thai, "the insulation is too thick. We'll have to use a more complicated method."

The revolutions of the mirror revealed, on the bottom of the tank, two white masses of irregular spherical shape and with a spongy, fibrous surface. The balls bore some resemblance to the fruit of the bread-tree that had shortly before been developed and were about 70 centimetres in diameter. "Switch the televisophone on to Grimm Schar's vector," said the biologist to an assistant. The scientist, *as* soon as he was sure of the correctness of the general assumptions, hurried to the laboratory. He screwed up his eyes near-sightedly, but merely from habit and not from weak sight, and looked over the apparatus. Grimm Schar did not have the impressive appearance and imperative character one would expect in a prominent scientist. Erg Noor remembered Renn Bose, whose bashful, boyish appearance was also deceptive and belied the greatness of his mind.

"Open the welded seam," ordered Grimm Schar. A mechanical hand cut through the hard enamel mass without moving the heavy lid. Hoses with the gaseous mixture were attached to the stop-cocks. A strong infrared ray projector took the place of the iron star.

"Temperature ... pressure ... electrical charge ..." called out an assistant reading off the dials of the instruments.

Half an hour later Grimm Schar turned to the astronauts.

"Let's go to the rest-room, there's no way of guessing how long those capsuled beasts will take to revive. If

Eon's right it won't be long. The assistant will call , "

The Institute of Nerve Currents was situated far from the inhabited zone, on the fringe of the steppe reservation. At the end of summer the earth was dry and the wind had a peculiar rustle to it that came through the open windows together with a faint odour of sun-dried grasses.

The three scientists, seated in comfortable armchairs, kept silent as they stared out of the windows over the tops of wide-spreading trees towards the haze of the distant horizon. From time to time one or the other of them would close his tired eyes but the waiting was too tense for anybody to doze. This time, however, the patience of the scientists was not too severely tried. Before three hours had passed the screen giving direct communication with the laboratory lit up and an assistant appeared, scarcely able to contain himself.

"The lid's moving!"

In an instant all three of them were in the laboratory.

"Shut the rutholucite chamber tight, check up on its hermetic sealing!" ordered Grimm Schar. "Arrange planet conditions in the chamber."

The powerful pumps hissed faintly, the pressure regulators whistled and in a moment the transparent cage was filled with the atmosphere of the world of darkness.

376

"Increase gravitation, humidity and atmospheric electricity," continued Grimm Schar. The laboratory was filled with the acrid odour of ozone.

Nothing happened. The scientist knitted his brows as he studied the instruments and tried to imagine what had been omitted.

"They need darkness!" came Erg Noor's measured tones.

Eon Thai even jumped in the air.

"How could I have forgotten? Grimm Schar, you haven't been on the blade planet, but I have!"

"The polarizing shutters!" ordered the scientist instead of answering him.

The light went out. The laboratory was illuminated only by the lights in the instruments. The assistants pulled blinds over the control desk and complete darkness ensued. Here and there faint stars twinkled-the luminous dials of some indicators.

The breath of the black planet wafted in the faces of the astronauts bringing with it memories of the awful but thrilling days of hard struggle.

There was silence for some minutes that was broken only by the cautious movements of Eon Thai who was tuning in the demonstration screen for infrared reception and arranging the polarizing shield so that light from the screen would not be reflected.

First came a faint sound and then a heavy thud as the lid from the tank fell down inside the chamber. It was followed by the familiar flickering of brown lights as the tentacles of the black monster appeared over the edge of the tank. With a sudden jump it leaped upwards spreading darkness over the whole area of the rutholucite chamber and banged against the transparent ceiling. Thousands of brown stars spread over the body of the jellyfish, its black cloak bulged and formed a dome as if the wind were blowing from below and then rested on the floor of the chamber with all its tentacles gathered in a bunch. The second monster rose out of the tank like another black phantom, its swift and silent movement inspiring fear in the onlookers. Here, however, within the walls of the experimental chamber and surrounded by remote-controlled instruments, the spawn of the planet of darkness was powerless.

Instruments measured, photographed, drew intricate curves, determined the nature of the animals and broke down their structure into various physical, chemical and biological indicants. The human intellect gathered these qualitatively different data together again and mastered the structure of the awe-inspiring monsters in order to subordinate them to himself.

As hour after hour passed almost unnoticed Erg Noor became sure of victory.

Eon Thai was becoming more and more radiant, Grimm Schar grew as vivacious as his youthful assistants.

At last the scientist approached Erg Noor.

"You may go now with an easy heart. We shall stay here until the investigation is finished. I'm afraid to switch on visible light as these black medusae can't hide from it here as they would on their own planet. They must first be made to tell us all we want to know."

"And how long will it take to find out?"

"In three or four days our investigation will have become exhaustive for the level of knowledge we possess. We can already imagine how their paralysing organs function."

"And will you be able to cure ... Nisa ... Eon?" "Yes!"

Only then did Erg Noor realize what a heavy burden he had been bearing since that black day. Day or night... what did it matter! Wild joy filled the whole of that man of great restraint. He had difficulty in overcoming a mad desire to throw Grimm Schar up into the air, to shake the little scientist and embrace him. Erg Noor was astounded at himself, began to calm down and a minute later had returned to his normal state of concentration.

"Your studies will be a tremendous help to the future expedition that will have to fight against the black jellyfish and crosses!"

"Of course! We shall know the enemy now. But is there going to be another expedition to that world of heavy weight and darkness?"

"I don't doubt it."

The warm morning of a northern autumn was just beginning.

Erg Noor, without his usual hustle, was walking barefoot on the soft grass. In front of him, at the forest fringe, the green wall of the cedars was interspersed with already leafless maples that looked like columns of thin smoke. On the reservation man did not interfere with nature-there was beauty in the disorderly growths of tall grasses, in their mixed, contradictory, pleasant and pungent odours.

A cold stream barred his way and Erg Noor turned on to a footpath. The ripples caused by the wind on the sunlit surface of the transparent water gave it the appearance of an undulating network of wavy golden lines thrown on the pebbles of the river-bed. Unnoticeable strands of moss and water-weeds floated on the water casting shadows that ran like blue patches along the bottom. On the far bank big pale-blue harebells swayed in the wind. The aroma of damp meadows and red autumn leaves promised the joy of labour to man, for tucked away in a far corner of his heart everyone had hidden something of the experience of the first ploughman.

A bright yellow oriole alighted on a branch and emitted its mocking self-confident whistle.

The clear sky over the cedar forest was turned to silver by the far-spreading wing of a cirrus cloud. Erg Noor dived into the gloom of the forest with its odours of cedar needles and resin, came out on the other side, climbed a hill and wiped his bare head that the dew had wetted. The forest reservation that surrounded the Nerve Clinic was not a big one and Erg Noor soon came to a road. The stream had been diverted into a series of basins of milk-coloured glass, keeping them filled with water. Several men and women in bathing costumes ran round a bend in the road and raced on between rows of brightly coloured flowers. The autumn water could hardly have been warm but the runners, encouraging one another with laughter and jokes, sprang into the basins and in a jolly crowd swam down the cascade from basin to basin. Erg Noor smiled in spite of himself. It was rest time at some local factory or farm.

Never before had our planet seemed so beautiful to him who had spent the greater part of his life in the close quarters of a spaceship. He was filled with profound gratitude to all people, to Earth's nature, to everything that had helped to save Nisa, his astronavigator with the auburn curls. Today she had come to meet him in the clinic gardens. After a consultation with the doctors they had arranged to go away together to a polar sanatorium for nervous disorders. As soon as the scientists had managed to break the chain of paralysis and put an end to the persistent inhibition of the cerebral cortex caused by the discharge of the "cross" beast's charge through its tentacles, Nisa had become quite healthy. She had only to regain her former energy after such a long cataleptic sleep. Nisa was alive and well! It seemed to Erg Noor that he would never be able to think of that without an impulse of joy somewhere inside him.

He saw the solitary figure of a woman coming rapidly towards him from a side path. He would have recognized her among thousands-Veda Kong, the Veda who had been so much in his thoughts before it had become clear that their paths in life were different. Erg Noor was accustomed to the diagrams of the computing machines and his thinking followed the same lines-he saw a steep arc sweeping upwards into the heavens-his own urge-while Veda's path of life and work left her hovering over the planet to delve into the depths of centuries passed and gone. The lines diverged until they were far apart.

Erg Noor knew every tiny detail of Veda's face but he was suddenly surprised to notice the resemblance she bore to Nisa Greet. The same narrow face with eyes placed wide apart, the same high forehead with the long upward sweep of the eyebrows, the same expression of gentle irony in her big mouth. Even their noses were both slightly snub, softly rounded and a bit long, just as though they were sisters. The only difference was that Veda always had a direct and pensive look while Nisa Greet would throw her head back in youthful exuberance or would lower her forehead and knitted brows to meet an obstacle.

"Are you examining me?" asked Veda, surprised.

She held out both hands to Erg Noor who took them and pressed them to his cheeks. Veda shivered and pulled herself away. The astronaut gave a weak smile.

"I wanted to thank those hands for having nursed Nisa. She ... I know about everything! Somebody had to be in constant attendance and you gave up an interesting expedition. Two months "

"I didn't give it up, I was late for it, waiting for *Tantra*. The expedition had left by then, and well ... she's charming, your Nisa! We look alike but she's the real companion for the conqueror of the Cosmos and the iron stars, with her urge to get back into space and her loyalty."

"Veda!"

"I'm not joking, Erg, I mean it. Don't you feel that this is no time for jokes? We must make everything clear!"

"I find everything clear enough as it is! And I'm thanking you for Nisa, not for myself."

"Don't thank me. It would have been difficult for me if you'd lost Nisa, that's why "

"I understand but still I don't believe you because I know that Veda Kong could never be so calculating. And so my gratitude remains."

Erg Noor patted the young woman's shoulder and placed his fingers in the crook of her arm. They walked side by side along the deserted road in silence until Erg Noor spoke again.

"Who is he, the real one?" "Darr Veter."

"The former Director of the Outer Stations? So that's it!"

"Erg, you are saying words that mean nothing. I don't recognize you." "I suppose I must have changed. I can't imagine Darr Veter apart from his work and I thought that he was a Cosmic dreamer."

"He is. He dreams of the world of stars but he has proved able to combine the stars with an ancient farmer's love of Earth. He is a man of knowledge with the big hands of the simple mechanic."

Erg Noor involuntarily looked at his narrow hand with the long fingers of a mathematician and musician.

"If you only knew, Veda, how much I love our Earth at this moment!" "After the world of darkness and a long journey with paralysed Nisa? Of course, you do!"

"You don't believe that love for Earth can provide the basis of my life?"

"I don't. You're a real hero and will always be thirsting for deeds. You will carry that love like a full bowl from which you are afraid to spill a drop, carry it on Earth in order to give it to the Cosmos for the sake of that same Earth!"

"Veda, you'd have been burnt at the stake in the Dark Ages!"

"I've been told that before. Here's the fork.... Where are your shoes. Erg?"

"I left them in the garden when I came to meet you. I'll have to go back."

"Well, good-bye, Erg. My job here's finished and yours is just about to begin. Where shall we meet again? Perhaps it will be only before you leave on the new ship?"

"Oh, no, Veda. Nisa and I are going to a polar sanatorium for three months. Come and see us and bring Darr Veter with you."

"Which sanatorium? The 'Stone Heart' on the north coast of Siberia or 'Autumn Leaves' in Iceland?"

"It's too late for the northern polar regions. We're being sent to the southern hemisphere where the summer will soon begin. The 'White Dawn' in Grahamland."

"All right. Erg, we'll come if Darr Veter does not start out immediately to rebuild Satellite 57. There'll probably be a long time spent on getting materials together."

"That's a fine terrestrial man for you-almost a year in the sky!"

"Don't try to be smart. That's quite near compared with your tremendous spaces, the spaces that divided us."

"Do you regret it, Veda?"

"Why do you ask, Erg? There are two halves in each of us, one half is anxious to get at the new, the other half cherishes the old and would be glad to return to it. You know that and you also know that return never achieves its aim."

"But regret remains like a wreath on a beloved grave. Give me a kiss, Veda, my dear!"

The young woman obediently complied with the request, pushed the astronaut lightly aside and strode swiftly away to the main road where there was an electrobus service. Erg Noor watched her until the robot driver of the first bus to arrive stopped the vehicle and her red dress disappeared inside.

Veda also looked through the glass at Erg Noor as he stood there immobile. Her head was filled with the refrain of a song dating back to the Era of Disunity that had recently been reset to music by Arck Geer. Darr Veter had once repeated it to her in response to a gentle reproach from her.

And neither the angels in heaven above,
Nor the demons down under the sea,
Can ever dissever my soul from the soul
Of the beautiful Annabel Lee!

This was the challenge of a man of ancient days to the menacing forces of nature that had taken his beloved from him ... the challenge of a man who was not reconciled to his loss and did not want to make any concessions to fate!

The electrobus drew near the branch of the Spiral Way but Veda Kong was still standing by the window holding on to the polished hand-rails and humming the beautiful romance filled with such sweet sorrow.

"Angels-that's what religious Europeans in the old days called the imaginary spirits of heaven, the heralds who made known the will of the gods. *Angelas* meant 'herald' or 'messenger' in the ancient Greek language. It's a word that has been forgotten for centuries…." Veda shook off these thoughts while she was at the station but they returned to her in the coach of the Spiral Way train.

"The Heralds of Heaven, of the Cosmos-why, that's what we might call Erg Noor and Mven Mass and Darr Veter. Especially Darr Veter when he will be in the nearby, terrestrial heaven, building a satellite…." Veda smiled mischievously. "Then the demons down under the sea that's us, the historians," she said aloud, listening to the sound of her own voice, and laughed merrily. "Yes, that's right, the angels of heaven and the spirits of the under world! Only Darr Veter may not like it."

Low cedars with black needles, a variety impervious to frosts that had been developed for the subantarctic regions, sang solemnly and monotonously in the never-slackening wind. The cold, dense air flowed like a swift river, carrying that extraordinary purity and freshness with it that one associates with the open ocean and high mountain ranges. When the wind comes in contact with the eternal snows of the mountains, however, it is dry, it tends to burn, like sparkling wine. Here the breath of the ocean made its heavy touch felt as the wind wrapped the body in a humid mantle.

The building of the "White Dawn" Sanatorium stretched down to the sea in terraces, the rounded form of its glass walls resembling the huge ocean liners of ancient days. The pale vermilion tones of the walls, staircases and vertical columns were in sharp contrast to the domed masses of the chocolate and violet andesite cliffs, cut by blue and grey porcelain-like paths of cast syenite. The polar night in late spring, however, made all colours alike in its specially white light that seemed to come from the depths of the sky and the sea. The sun had hidden for an hour behind the plateau to the south. A majestic arc of light covered the southern half of the sky, reflected from the giant ice-cap of the southern continent that still remained on the high plateau of the eastern part to where it had been moved back by the will of man who had reduced it to one-quarter of its former mass. The icy white dawn, whose name the sanatorium bore, turned the whole countryside into a phantom world of light without shadows or reflections.

Four people were coming down the silvery porcelain path to the ocean. The faces of the two men who walked behind seemed carved out of grey granite and the big eyes of the two women were bottomless and mysterious.

Nisa Greet, pressing her face against the fur collar of Veda Kong's jacket, was arguing with the historian. Veda, making no effort to conceal her faint amazement was looking into that gentle face that outwardly resembled hers.

"I believe that the best gift a woman can make to the man she loves is to re-create him and in this way prolong the existence of her hero. Then another loving woman will create a new copy-why, it's almost like immortality!"

"Men feel differently about us," answered Veda. "Darr Veter once told me that he would not like to have a daughter that was too much like the woman he loved because it would be hard to go out of the world and leave her behind without him, without the cloak of his love and tenderness, leave her to a fate of which he would know nothing. That's just a relic of the jealousy and protection of the old days."

"I cannot bear the thought of parting with a tiny being that is mine to his last drop of blood," continued Nisa, full of her own thoughts, "of giving him up to the school as soon as I have finished nursing him."

"I can understand you although I do not agree," said Veda, frowning, as though the girl had touched a painful string in her heart. "One of mankind's greatest victories is the conquest of the blind instinct of maternity, the realization that only the collective upbringing of children by people trained and selected for the job can produce a man of our society. That insane maternal love of the past has almost died out. Every mother knows that the whole world is kind to her child and that he runs none of the dangers he formerly did. And so the instinctive love of the she-wolf that arose out of fear for her progeny has disappeared."

"I understand all that but only with my mind," said Nisa.

"I not only know it but feel it, I know that the greatest happiness is to bring joy to another and that is now possible for anybody, irrespective of age. That which was possible in former ages for parents and grandparents, and most of all for mothers.... Why must one always be together with the little one? That's also a relic of ancient days, when the woman was compelled to live" a narrow life and could not always be together with the man she loved. You'll always be together, as long as you love each other...."

"I don't know, but sometimes I feel an overpowering desire to have beside me a little one that is like him, it is so strong that I clench my hands in despair ... no, I don't know anything."

"There's Java, the Mothers' Island. Those who want to bring up their own children live there, those who've lost their dear ones, for example "

"Oh no! And I couldn't be a teacher, either, like those who have some special love for children. I feel that I have great strength and I've been into the Cosmos once already."

"You're the personification of youth, Nisa, and not only physically. Like all people who are very young you don't realize when you come up against contradictions that they are what go to make up life. You don't realize that the joy of love will most certainly bring anxiety, cares and sorrows that will be the greater, the stronger the love. And you think that you'll lose everything at the first blow struck by life."

As she uttered those last words Veda herself became aware that Nisa's restiveness and anxiety were not to be explained by youthfulness alone.

Veda had made a mistake common to many people, that of believing that spiritual traumas heal together with physical wounds. That, however, is not the case, for wounds to the psyche remain for a long, long time, hidden deep down in a physically healthy body, and they may open up at any moment from the most insignificant of causes. Such was Nisa's case-she had been paralysed for five years and it had left its impress in every cell of her body; even if the memory was subconscious it still remained-the horror of her meeting with the terrible cross that almost been the death of Erg Noor!

Nisa guessed what Veda was thinking about and answered her in a dull voice.

"Ever since the iron star there is a strange feeling that has never left me. Somewhere there is an empty place in my heart. It continues to exist together with confident joy and strength and does not exclude them and at the same time does not disappear. I can struggle against it only by means of something that will employ me entirely and will not leave me alone with ... Oh, now I know what the Cosmos is for a lonely man and have even greater respect for the first space travellers!"

"I think I can understand," said Veda. "I was once on the tiny Polynesian islands that are lost in the ocean. There, standing by the sea in a moment of loneliness, you are overcome by a profound sorrow that is like a nostalgic song merging with the deadly monotony of great distances. Perhaps that is a memory of the distant past, n memory of the primordial isolation of his consciousness telling man how weak and helpless he formerly was, shut up in his own little cage of a soul. The only cure was common work and common thoughts-a boat came, smaller, even, than the island, but it was enough to change the ocean. A handful of companions and a ship is a world of its own striving towards distant objectives that they can reach and subordinate to their will. The same is true of the Cosmic vessel, the spaceship. In that ship you are together with strong and brave companions! But alone in the Cosmos," Veda shuddered, "I don't suppose a man could stand it!"

Nisa clung still more closely to Veda.

"How well you said that, Veda! That's why I want everything at once "

"Nisa, I'm getting very fond of you. Now I can sense the meaning of your decision but at first I thought it was sheer madness. For a ship to be able to return from such a long flight your children will have to take your places on the return journey-two Ergs, or maybe, more."

Nisa squeezed Veda's hand and pressed her nose against her cheek, cold from the wind.

"Do you think you can stand it, Nisa? It's impossibly difficult!"

"What difficulties are you talking about, Veda?" asked Erg Noor, turning round on hearing her last exclamation. "Have you come to an agreement with Darr Veter? For the last half-hour he's been trying to persuade me to give the youth the benefit of my experience as an astronaut and not to set out on a flight from which I shall never return."

"Has he persuaded you?"

"No. My experience as an astronaut *is* still more necessary to pilot *Lebed* to her destination, up there," said Erg pointing to the bright starless sky, to the place where Achernar should be seen, lower than the Lesser Magellanic Cloud and just below Tucana and the Hydra, "to pilot her where no ship from Earth hag ever been before!"

As Erg Noor spoke those last words the edge of the rising sun came in a burst of fire over the horizon, its rays driving away all the mystery of the white dawn.

The four friends walked down to the water. A cold breeze came towards them from the ocean and the heavy swell of the stormy Antarctic seas came in mighty surfless rollers that raced up the beach. Veda Kong looked at the steel-grey water with interest, it grew rapidly darker in the depths and in the rays of the low sun took on the violet hue of the ice.

Nisa Greet was standing beside her in a blue fur coat and round cap from which her dark auburn curls escaped in profusion. The girl held her head up in her usual pose. Darr Veter could not help but admire her but frowned as he did so.

"Veter, don't you like Nisa?" exclaimed Veda with exaggerated indignation.

"You know I'm very fond of her," answered Darr Veter moodily, "but at the moment she seems to me so small and fragile in comparison with…."

"With what awaits me?" asked Nisa with a note of challenge in her voice. "Are you transferring the attack from Erg to me now?"

"I wasn't thinking of anything of the sort," answered Darr Veter, seriously and sadly, "but my grief is natural. A beautiful creature of my wonderful Earth must disappear into Cosmic void, into the darkness and frightful cold. It's not pity that I feel, Nisa, but grief over a loss!"

"You feel the same about it as I do," agreed Veda. "Nisa, a bright spark of life … and dead, icy space."

"You think I'm a delicate flower?" asked Nisa and there was a strange intonation to the question that made Veda hesitate to agree that that was what she did think.

"Who, more than I, enjoys the struggle against the cold?" and the girl took off her cap and her fur coat and shook out her auburn curls.

"What are you doing?" asked Veda, the first to guess her intention. She ran to get hold of the girl.

But Nisa ran to the edge of the cliff, threw her fur coat to Veda and stood poised over the water.

The cold waves closed over Nisa and Veda shivered as she tried to imagine the sensation of such a bath. Nisa calmly swam out to sea, cutting through the waves with strong strokes. As she rose on a crest she waved to those on shore, inviting them to join her in the water.

Veda Kong watched with growing admiration.

"Veter, Nisa would be a better mate for a polar bear than for Erg. How can you, a man of the north, admit yourself beaten?"

"I am a northerner by ancestry but still I prefer the warm southern seas," admitted Darr Veter plaintively as he walked unwillingly towards the edge of the sea. He took off his clothes and touched the water with his toe and then, ouch! he plunged into an approaching steel-grey wave. With three powerful strokes he reached the crest of a wave and dived into the trough of another. Darr Veter's reputation was saved by his many years of training and his habit of bathing all the year round. His breath was checked and there were red rings before his eyes. A few brisk dives and leaps in the water returned to him the ability to breathe freely. He returned shivering and blue with the cold and ran up the hill together with Nisa. A few minutes later they were enjoying the warmth of their fur clothes. It seemed that even the icy wind brought with it a breath of the coral seas.

"The more I get to know you, the more I'm convinced that Erg hasn't made any mistake in his choice," whispered Veda. "You, better than anybody else, will be able to encourage him in a moment of difficulty, to bring him joy and take care of him."

Nisa's cheeks, devoid of any sunburn, were flushed a rosy red.

At breakfast on a high crystal terrace that vibrated in the wind, Veda met the girl's gentle, pensive glance several times. All four ate in silence, unwilling to talk as people usually are on the eve of parting for a long time.

"It's hard to have to part from such people when you have only just got to know them," Darr Veter suddenly exclaimed.

"Perhaps you …" began Erg Noor.

"My free time is over. It's time for me to get up into the sky. Grom Orme's waiting for me!"

"And it's time for me to get down to work, too," added Veda. "I'm going down into the depths, into a recently discovered cave, a treasure repository of the Era of Disunity."

"*Lebed* will be ready to take off in the middle of next year and we're going to start preparations in six weeks from now," said Erg Noor, softly. "Who's directing the Outer Stations at the moment?"

"So far Junius Antus has been, but he doesn't want to give up his job with the memory machines and the Council has not yet confirmed the candidacy of Embe Ong, an engineer and physicist from the Labrador F station."

"I don't know him."

"Few people do, he's working for the Academy of the Bounds of Knowledge on questions of megawave mechanics."

"What may that be?"

"The powerful rhythms of the Cosmos, huge waves that spread slowly through space. The contradiction between colliding light velocities producing negative values greater than the absolute unit, for example, finds expression in the megawave. The problem has not yet been developed."

"And what is Mven Mass doing?"

"He's writing a book on emotions. He, too, has very little time left to himself, the Academy of Stochastics and Prognostication has appointed him to a consultative job in connection with the flight of your *Lebed*. As soon as they have enough material for him he'll have to give up his book."

"That's a pity, it's an important subject. It's time we had a proper understanding of the reality and strength of the world of emotions," said Erg Noor.

"I'm afraid Mven Mass is incapable of a cold analysis," said Veda.

"That's as it should be, if he were he wouldn't write anything outstanding," objected Darr Veter, as he rose to his feet to say good-bye.

"Till our next meeting!" Erg and Nisa held out their hands to him. "Hurry up and finish that job of yours or we shan't meet again."

"Yes, we shall," promised Darr Veter confidently. "Even if it's only in the El Homra Desert before the take-off."

"Before the take-off," repeated the astronauts.

"Come on, my angel of heaven," said Veda Kong as she took Darr Veter by the arm, pretending not to notice his knitted brows. "You're probably fed up with Earth?"

Darr Veter stood with his feet wide apart on the still shaky structure that formed the skeleton of the hull and looked down into the fearful abyss between the clouds. Our planet was there and its tremendous size could still be felt at a distance of five times its own diameter: he could see the grey outlines of the continents and the violet of the seas.

Darr Veter recognized outlines that had been familiar to him from childhood through pictures taken from satellites. There was the concave line with dark strips of mountains stretching across it. To the right the sea sparkled and directly under his feet was a narrow mountain valley. He was in luck that day-the clouds had parted directly over that part of the planet where Veda was living and working. At the foot of the vertical terraces of iron-coloured mountains there was an ancient cave that went deep into the earth in a number of extensive storeys. It was there that Veda was selecting from amongst the dumb and dusty fragments of past life those grains of historical truth without which the present could not be properly understood nor the future foreseen.

Darr Veter, leaning over the rail of a platform of corrugated zirconium bronze sent a mental greeting to the spot, roughly conjectured, that was fast disappearing under the wing of the cirrus clouds of intolerable brightness coming up from the west. The darkness of night stood like a wall sprinkled with shining stars. Layers of clouds floated by like gigantic rafts hanging one over the other. Below them the Earth's surface was rolling into the darkening abyss as though it were disappearing for ever into the absolute. A delicate zodiacal light clothed the dark side of the planet shedding its glow into Cosmic space.

There was a layer of light-blue clouds over the daylight side of Earth that reflected the powerful light of the blue-grey Sun. Anybody who looked at the clouds except through dark filters would be blinded as would anybody unprotected by the 800 kilometres of Earth's atmosphere who turned his face to the Sun. The harsh short-wave rays-ultra-violet and X-rays were irradiated in a powerful stream that was lethal to all living things. A constant downpour of cosmic particles was added to the stream. Newly-awakened stars or those that had collided at unimaginably great distances in the Galaxy sent deadly radiation out into space. Only the reliable protection of their spacesuits saved the workers from speedy death.

Darr Veter threw the safety line over to the other side and moved towards the radiant dipper of Ursa Major. A giant pipe had been fixed in position throughout the entire length of the future satellite. At either end acute-angled triangles rose up from it to support the discs radiating the magnetic field. When the batteries transforming the Sun's blue radiations into electricity were installed it would be possible to do away with lifelines and walk along the lines of force in the magnetic field with directional plates on the chest and back.

"We want to work at night." The voice of a young engineer, Cadd Lite, suddenly sounded in his space helmet. *"Altai* has promised to provide the light."

Darr Veter looked to the left and below where a bunch of cargo rockets, tied together, lay like sleeping fish. Above them, under a flat roof to protect it from meteorites and the Sun, floated the temporary platform built from the inner plating of the satellite where all the components brought by the rockets were stored and assembled. Workers crawling there like black bees suddenly turned to glow-worms when the reflecting surfaces of their space-suits moved beyond the shadow of the roof. A cobweb of ropes stretched from the gaping hatches in the sides of the rockets out of which big components were being unloaded. Higher still, directly over the hull of the satellite, a group of people in strange, often ridiculous, poses were busy round a huge machine. One ring of beryllium bronze with borason plating would have weighed at least a hundred tons on Earth. Here the huge mass was dangling beside the metal skeleton of the satellite on a thin wire rope whose only purpose was to keep all these components rotating round Earth at the same velocity.

The workers became confident and agile once they had become accustomed to the absence of weight or rather, to the negligible weights. These skilled workers, however, would soon have to be replaced by others. Lengthy periods of physical labour without gravitation lead to disturbances in blood circulation which might become chronic and make the sufferer a permanent invalid on his return to Earth. For this reason the shift on the satellite was one of fifty working hours after which the worker returned to Earth, going through reacclimatization at the Intermediate Station revolving round the Earth at a height of 900 kilometres.

Darr Veter directed the assembly of the satellite and tried to avoid physical exertion although, at times, he badly wanted to help hasten the completion of some job or another. He would have to hold out at a height of 57,000 kilometres for several months.

If he agreed to night work he would have to send his young workers back to the planet and call others before time. *Barion,* the construction job's second planetship was on the Arizona Plain where Groin Orme sat at the TVP screens and registration machine controls.

A decision to work through the entire icy Cosmic night would have reduced the time required for assembling the satellite by one half and Darr Veter could not let such an opportunity pass. As soon as they had obtained h's consent the workers came down from the platform, running about in all directions, making a still more complicated network of ropes. The planetship *Altai* that served as living quarters for the satellite builders and hung motionless, moored to one end of the satellite's main beam, suddenly cast off the hawsers that linked her main hatch with the satellite. A long stream of blinding flame shot out of her exhausts. The huge ship swung round swiftly and silently, not the slightest noise carrying through the emptiness of interplanetary space. The skilled commander of *Altai* needed no more than a few strokes of his engines to send the ship forty metres above the structure and turn with his landing lights directed at the assembly platform. Hawsers were again dropped between the ship and the satellite and the whole mass of objects suspended in space became motionless relative to each other as they continued their revolutions round the Earth at a speed of about ten thousand kilometres an hour.

The distribution of the cloud masses told Darr Veter that the construction job was passing over the Antarctic region of the planet and would, therefore, soon enter Earth's shadow. The improved heating system of the spacesuit could not fully guarantee its wearer against the bitter cold of Cosmic space and woe betide the careless traveller who exhausted his batteries. An architect-erector had been killed that way a month before when he hid from a meteorite shower in the cold shell of an open rocket. He did not live to reach the sunny side of the planet. Another engineer was killed by a meteorite- such occurrences could not be foreseen or prevented with any degree of certainty. The building of a satellite always claimed its victims and nobody knew who would be the next. The laws of stochastics, although only partly applicable to such tiny particles as individual people, said that he, Darr Veter, would most probably be the next because he would be there, at that height and open to all the vagaries of the Cosmos, longer than anybody else. There was an impudent little inner voice, however, that told Darr Veter that nothing could possibly happen to his magnificent person. No matter how ridiculous such confidence may have been for a mathematically minded man it never abandoned Darr Veter and helped him calmly balance himself on narrow girders and grilles on the open, unprotected hull of the satellite in the abyss of the black sky.

Structures on Earth were erected by special machines called *embryotecti* because they worked on the principle of the cybernetic development of the living organism. It goes without saying that the molecular structure of the living organism, effected by the hereditary cybernetic mechanism, was immeasurably more complicated.

Living organisms, however, could only grow in the conditions provided by warm solutions of ionized molecules while the *embryotecti* usually worked in polarized streams of electricity or light or in a magnetic field. The markings and keys on all the component parts painted in radioactive thallium gave the correct orientation to the machines assembling them precisely and at high speed. At the great height of the satellite there were not and could not be any such machines. The assembly of the satellite was an old-fashioned building job employing human hands. Despite the dangers involved the work seemed so interesting that it attracted thousands of volunteers. The psycho-physiological stations were scarcely able to examine the flood of volunteers desirous of informing the Council of their readiness to venture into interplanetary space.

Darr Veter reached the foundations of the solar machines that were arranged fanwise round a huge hub containing the artificial gravity apparatus and joined the battery he was carrying on his back to the terminals of the test circuit. A simple melody could be heard in the phones of his space helmet. Then he connected in parallel a glass plate with the thin gold lines of a drawing on it. It produced the same melody. Darr Veter turned a couple of vernier scales until points of time coincided and listened to make sure there was no difference in the melody or even in the tone of the tuning. An important part of the future satellite had been assembled faultlessly. They could now begin the erection of the radiation electric motors. Darr Veter straightened shoulders that were bent wearily under the weight of a spacesuit worn over a long period and turned his head to the right and to the left. The movement caused a creaking of the upper vertebrae that immobility in the space helmet had made stiff. It was a good thing that, so far, Darr Veter had proved impervious to the psychoses that affect those who work outside the terrestrial atmosphere-these included ultra-violet sleeping sickness and infrared madness-otherwise he would not have been able to bring his worthy mission to a successful conclusion.

Soon the outer walls of the hull would protect the workers from the effects of a feeling of loneliness in the Cosmos, alone over an abyss that had neither sky nor ground!

Altai sent out a small rescue rocket that shot past the construction job like an arrow. This was a tug going to fetch the automatic rockets carrying only cargo and halting at a given altitude. Just in time! The bundle of rockets, people, machines and building materials, floating in space, was passing over to the night side of the planet. The tug rocket returned pulling behind it three long, gleaming, blue fish-like rockets that weighed a hundred and fifty tons on Earth (without fuel).

The rockets joined their fellows around the assembly platform. In one leap Darr Veter reached the other side of the hull and was soon amongst the technicians supervising the unloading who were gathered in a circle. They were discussing the plan for the night work. Darr Veter consented but insisted that all personal batteries be changed for freshly charged ones with sufficient energy to keep the spacesuits warm for thirty hours and at the same time supply the electric lamps, air filters and radiotelephones.

The whole construction job was plunged in darkness as though it were at the bottom of the sea but the soft zodiacal light from the Sun's rays dispersed by the gases of the atmospheric zones still lit up the skeleton of the future satellite that was gripped in a frost of 180 degrees C. The superconductivity of the metal now hindered them even more than it did by day. The slightest amount of wear in the insulation of the instruments, batteries or accumulators surrounded the nearby objects with a blue glow from current flowing along their surfaces and which could not be canalised in any given direction.

The profound darkness of outer space came together with increasing cold. The stars burned fiercely like dazzlingly bright blue needles in the sky. The invisible and inaudible flight of the meteoroids was even more awe-inspiring at night. In the currents of the atmosphere over the dark globe down below there were variously coloured clouds of electric glow, spark discharges of tremendous length and sheets of dispersed light thousands of kilometres long. Down below, in the upper layers of the atmosphere there were gales of greater fury than anything known on Earth. Vigorous movements of energy continued in an atmosphere saturated by the radiations of the Sun and the Cosmos and made communication with the planet extremely difficult.

Suddenly something changed in that tiny world lost in the darkness and fearful cold. Darr Veter did not immediately realize that the planetship had switched on its searchlights. The darkness had become even blacker, the burning stars grew dull, leaving the platform and the hull in a sea of bright white light that divided them off from the gloom. A few minutes later *Altai* reduced the voltage and the light turned yellow and was less intense.

The planetship was economizing current from its accumulators. The squares and ellipses that went to make up the walls of the hull, the latticed trusses that reinforced the structure, the cylinders and pipes of the reservoirs again moved about, finding their places in the skeleton of the satellite as though in daylight.

Darr Veter felt for a cross beam, took hold of the handles of a roller car running on a ropeway, and with one hard push of his feet sailed up to *Altai*. Right in front of the planetship's hatch he pressed the brake lever in his hand and halted just in time to prevent his crashing into a closed door.

The air-lock was not kept at normal terrestrial pressure in order not to lose too much air with the coming and going of such a large number of workers. Darr Veter kept on his spacesuit until he was in a second, auxiliary air-lock, where he unscrewed his space helmet and battery.

Flexing a body that was weary of the spacesuit, Darr Veter walked firmly along the deck of the ship, enjoying a return to almost normal gravity. The artificial gravitation of the planetship worked constantly. It was inexpressibly pleasant to feel yourself standing firmly on the ground as a man should stand and not be like a flea floundering in an unsteady, treacherous gulf! Soft light and warm air and a comfortable chair tempted him to stretch out in it and relax without having to think. Darr Veter was experiencing the pleasures of his distant ancestors that had once astonished him in old novels. It was in this way that people entered a warm house, a mud hut or a felt tent after long journeys through cold deserts, wet forests or icy mountains. And now as then a thin wall separated him from a huge, dangerous world, hostile to man, a wall that retained the warmth and light, gave him a chance to rest, gather fresh strength and think over what he was to do next.

Darr Veter did not yield to the temptation of armchair and book. He had to contact Earth-the light burning all night at that height might cause alarm amongst those who were keeping the satellite under observation. It was also necessary to warn Earth that reinforcements would be needed ahead of time.

There was good communication that day and Darr Veter talked with Grom Orme on the TVP and not in coded signals; the TVP was an extremely powerful one, such as was fitted to every spaceship. The old chairman was pleased with the progress made and said he would immediately see about new workers and extra materials.

Darr Veter left the Altai's control tower and passed through the library that had been re-equipped as a dormitory with two tiers of bunks. Cabins, dining-rooms, the cook's galley, the side corridors and the forward engine room had all been fitted out with extra bunks. The planet-ship had been converted into a stationary base and was overcrowded. Scarcely able to drag his feet Darr Veter walked down the corridor panelled with plastics warm to the touch, and lazily opened and closed hermetically sealed doors.

He was thinking of astronauts who spent dozens of years inside such a ship without any hope of leaving it before the appointed time, a cruelly long one. He had been living there six months and every day had left the narrow confines to work in the oppressive spaces of interplanetary vacuum. He was already longing for his beautiful Earth with its steppes and seas and the teeming life of the big centres in the inhabited zones. But Erg Noor, Nisa Greet and twenty other people would have to spend ninety-two dependent years or a hundred and forty terrestrial years in a spaceship before it brought them back to their own planet. Not one of them could possibly live so long! Their bodies would be cremated and buried away on the distant planets of the green zirconium star!

Or they would die *en route* and their bodies enclosed in a funeral rocket would be sent out into the Cosmos just ,as the funeral boats of their ancestors swept out to sea carrying dead warriors away with them. But such heroes as those who undertook life-long imprisonment in a spaceship without the hope that they, personally, would return, were unknown in the history of mankind. No, he was wrong, Veda would have rebuked him! How could he have forgotten the nameless fighters for the dignity and freedom of man in distant epochs who undertook even greater risks-horrible tortures and life-long imprisonment in damp dungeons. Yes, these heroes had been stronger and more worthy even than his contemporaries preparing to make their magnificent flight into the Cosmos to explore distant worlds!

And he, Darr Veter, who had never been away from his native planet for any length of time, was a pygmy compared with them and by no means an angel of heaven, as his infinitely dear Veda Kong had called him!

CHAPTER FOURTEEN

THE STEEL DOOR

The robot tunneller had been working for twenty, days in the damp and gloom before it had finally cleared away the roof fall and bolstered up the ceiling. The road down into the cave was open and could be used as soon as it had been tested for safety. Other robots, small cars on caterpillar tracks, operated by Archimedean screws moved noiselessly down into the depths. At every hundred metres the instruments on the cars sent back reports on temperature, humidity and the content of the air. The cars cleverly overcame all obstacles and went down to a depth of four hundred metres. Following behind them Veda Kong and a group of historians descended into the treasure cave. Ninety years before that, when tests for subsoil waters were being made, indicators had shown a large quantity of metal amongst sandstone and limestone deposits that are not, in general, associated with metallic ores. It was soon discovered that the place coincided with a description of the site of a cave, Halovkul, that had been mentioned in old legends. The name had originally been *Hall of Culture* in a language now dead. During a terribly devastating war, people who had believed themselves the most advanced in science and culture, hid the treasures of their civilization in a cave. In those distant days secrecy and mystery were very widespread.

Veda was quite as excited as the youngest of her assistants as she slid down the wet, red clay that formed the floor of the sloping entrance tunnel.

Her imagination drew pictures of magnificent halls, hermetically sealed safes containing films, drawings and maps, cupboards of tape recordings or the recordings of memory machines, shelves with jars of chemical compounds, alloys and medicines, stuffed animals, now extinct, in air- and water-tight glass-cases, prepared plants and skeletons put together from the fossilized bones of the past inhabitants of Earth. She even dreamed of slabs of silicoll in which the pictures of the most famous artists had been cast, whole galleries of sculptures of mankind's best representatives, the most prominent people, skilful carvings of animals ... models of famous buildings, inscriptions about outstanding events perpetuated in stone or metal....

Lost in her dreams Veda Kong found herself in a huge cave between three and four thousand square metres in extent. The vaulted ceiling was lost in the darkness and long stalactites glistened in the electric light. The cave was truly magnificent and, in realization of Veda's dreams, machines and cupboards had been placed in the countless niches formed in the walls by the ribs and ledges of limestone. With shouts of joy the archaeologists spread around the perimeter of the cave: many of the machines standing in the niches, some of them retaining the polish on their glass and metal parts, were motor-cars of the type that pleased our distant ancestors to such an extent and were considered the highest technical achievement of human genius in the Era of Disunity. In that period, for some unknown reason, people built large numbers of vehicles capable of carrying only a few passengers. The construction of the cars reached a high level of elegance, the engines and steering mechanisms were very ingenious but in all else these vehicles were senseless. Hundreds of thousands of them filled the city streets and country roads carrying people who lived far from the places where they worked and hurried every day to reach their jobs and then get home again. The vehicles were dangerous to drive, killed a tremendous number of people every year and burned up millions and millions of tons of valuable organic substances accumulated in the geological past of the planet and in so doing poisoned the atmosphere with carbon monoxide. The archaeologists of the Great Circle Era were very disappointed when they discovered how much room had been devoted to these machines in the cave.

On low platforms, however, there were more powerful steam engines, electric motors, jet, turbine and nuclear motors. In glass show-cases covered with a coating of limestone there were vertical rows of instruments of all kinds, most likely they were TV receivers, cameras, calculating machines and other similar devices. This museum of machines, some of which had quite rusted away but others were in a good state of preservation, was of great historical value as it illustrated the technical level of civilization at a distant date, the majority of whose records had been lost in political and military disturbances.

Miyiko Eigoro, Veda's faithful assistant who had again given up her beloved sea for the damp and darkness of underground exploration, noticed the black opening of a gallery at the far end of the cave, behind a big limestone pillar. The pillar turned out to be the limestone-covered skeleton of a machine and at its foot lay a heap of plastic dust, the remains of the door that had once covered the entrance to the gallery. Advancing step by step, guided by the red cable of the scouting machines, the archaeologists got into the second chamber that was almost at the same level and was filled with hermetically sealed cupboards of metal and glass. A long English inscription in big letters ran round the vertical walls that had, in places, collapsed. Veda had to stop for a moment to decipher it.

With the boastfulness that was typical of the ancient individualists, the builders of the caves informed their descendants that they had reached the heights of knowledge and were preserving their magnificent achievements for posterity.

Miyiko shrugged her shoulders contemptuously.

"The inscription alone tells us that the Hall of Culture belongs to the end of the Era of Disunity, to the last years of the old type of social order. This foolish confidence in the eternal and unchanging continuation of their civilization, language, customs, morals and in the majesty of the so-called 'white man' is typical of the period!"

"You have a clear conception of the past, but it is somewhat one-sided, Miyiko. Through the grim skeleton of moribund capitalism I see those who struggled for a better future. Their future is our 'today.' I see countless men and women seeking light in a narrow impoverished life-they had strength enough to fight their way out of its captivity and goodness enough to help their friends and not harden their hearts in the suffocating morals of the world around them. And they were brave, recklessly brave."

"But it was not they who hid their culture here," objected Miyiko. "Just look, there is nothing but machines, technology, here. They wallowed in machines, paying no attention to their own moral and emotional degradation. They were contemptuous of the past and blind to the future!"

Veda thought that Miyiko was right. The lives of the people who had filled those caves would have been easier if they had been able to compare that which they had achieved with that which still had to be done before the world and society could be really transformed. Then their dirty, sooty planet, with its felled forests and litter of paper and broken glass, bricks and rusty iron, would have been seen in its real light. Our ancestors would have had a better understanding of what still had to be done and would not have blinded themselves with self-praise.

A narrow well, thirty-two metres deep, led down to the next cave. Veda sent Miyiko and two other assistants back for the gamma-ray apparatus to examine the contents of the cupboards and herself went to examine the third cave that had not been affected by lime and clay deposits. The low, quadrangular plate-glass show-cases were only misty from the damp that had penetrated into the cave. Pressing their faces against the glass the archaeologists saw the most remarkable articles of gold and platinum decorated with precious stones. Judging by the workmanship these ancient relics had been collected at a time when people still had more respect for the old than for the new, a habit that had come into being in very ancient days when people worshipped their ancestors. As Veda looked at the collection she felt the same disappointment in the people of olden days as she had done when she read the inscription on the wall: she was annoyed at the absurd self-confidence of the ancients who believed that their idea of values and their tastes would continue unchanged for dozens of centuries and would be accepted as canons by their descendants.

The far end of the cave merged into a high, straight passage that sloped down to an unknown depth. The instruments on the explorer cars showed a depth of three hundred and four metres from the surface at the beginning of the corridor. Huge crevices divided the ceiling into a number of separate limestone blocks that probably weighed several thousand tons each. Veda felt alarmed: her experience in the exploration of many underground premises told her that the rocks at the foot of the mountain chain were certain to be in a state of instability. The mass of rock may have been shifted by an earthquake or by the general rise of the mountains that had grown at least fifty metres higher in the centuries that had elapsed since the caves had been sealed. An ordinary archaeological expedition had no means at its disposal to strengthen such a huge mass. Only an objective of importance to the planet's economy would have justified the expenditure necessary for the job.

At the same time historical secrets hidden in the deep cave might be of technical value, they might consist of such things as forgotten inventions that would be of value in modern times.

It would have been nothing more than wise precaution to abandon all further exploration. But why should a historian be so very careful of his own person? When millions of people were carrying out risky experiments and doing risky jobs, when Darr Veter and his companions were working at a height of fifty-seven thousand kilometres above the Earth, when Erg Noor was preparing to start out on a voyage from which there would be no return! Neither of these men whom Veda admired would have hesitated ... nor would she!

They would take reserve batteries, an electronic camera, two oxygen apparatuses and would go alone, she and the fearless Miyiko, leaving their companions to study the third cave.

Veda advised her workers to take a meal to keep up their strength. They got out their travellers' cakes, slabs of pressed, easily assimilated proteins, sugars and preparations destroying the toxins of weariness mixed with vitamins, hormones and nerve stimulants.

Veda, nervously impatient, did not want to eat. Miyiko appeared some forty minutes later, she had been unable to resist the temptation of examining the contents of some of the cupboards with her gamma-rays.

The descendant of Japanese women divers thanked her principal with a glance and got herself ready in the twinkling of an eye.

The thin red cables stretched down the centre of the passage. The pale light emanating from the phosphorescent crowns worn by the two women was insufficient to penetrate the thousand-year-old darkness that lay ahead of them where the slope grew steeper. Big drops of cold water dripped steadily and dully from the roof. To the sides and below them they could hear the gurgle of streams of water running in the crevices. The air, saturated with moisture, was as still as death in that enclosed underground chamber. The silence was such as exists only in caves where it is guarded by the dead and inert matter of Earth's crust. Outside, no matter how great the silence may be, nature's hidden life, the movement of water, air and light may always be assumed.

Miyiko and Veda were unwittingly hypnotized by the cave that drew them into its black depths as though into the depths of a dead past that had been wiped out by time and lived only as figments of the imagination.

The descent was rapid although there was a thick layer of sticky clay on the floor. Blocks of stone fallen from the walls at times barred the way and had to he climbed over, the women crawling through the narrow space left between the fall and the roof. In half an hour Miyiko and Veda had descended another one hundred and ninety metres into the earth and reached a perfectly smooth wall at the foot of which the two explorer robots lay motionless. One flash of light was enough to show them that the smooth wall was a massive, hermetically sealed door of stainless steel. In the middle of the door were two convex circles with certain symbols on them, handles and gilded arrows. The lock opened when a pre-arranged signal had been selected. The two archaeologists knew of such safes belonging to an earlier period. After a short consultation Veda and Miyiko made a closer examination of the lode. It was very much like those malignantly clever constructions that people once used to keep other people's hands off their property-in the Era of Disunity people were divided in that way into "us" and "others." There had been a number of cases when an attempt to open such doors had caused an explosion or the emission of poisonous gases or deadly radiations, killing the unsuspecting investigators. The mechanism of such locks, made of non-oxidizing metals or plastics, was not affected by time: a large number of people had fallen victim to these steel doors before archaeologists had learned to render them harmless.

It was obvious that the door had to be opened with special instruments. They would have to go all the way back from the very threshold of the cave's main secret. Who could doubt that the locked door would hide the most important and valuable possession of the people of those distant times. Putting out their lamps and making do with the glow of their phosphorescent crowns, Veda and Miyiko sat down to rest and eat in order to be able to repeat their attempt.

"What can there be in there?" asked Miyiko with a sigh, never once taking her eyes off the door and its haughtily gleaming gold symbols. "It seems to be laughing at us... 'I won't let you in, I won't tell you anything!' "

"What did you see in the cupboards you gamma-rayed in the second cave?" asked Veda, driving away her primitive and useless chagrin at this unexpected obstacle.

"Drawings of machines, books printed on metal sheets instead of on the old-fashioned paper made from wood. Then there was something that looked like rolls of films. some sort of lists, stellar and terrestrial maps. In the first hall there are samples of machines and in the second there are the technical documents belonging to them and in the third there are, well, what can I call them? - historical relics and the valuables of the period when money still existed. It all follows the usual scheme.

"Where are the things that we regard as being valuable? The loftiest achievements of man's spiritual development-science, art, literature?" exclaimed Miyiko.

"I hope they're behind that door," answered Veda, calmly, "but I should not be at all surprised if there were weapons there."

"What? What did you say?"

"Weapons, armaments, the means of slaughtering masses of people in the shortest possible time. I don't think that such an assumption is either fantastic or pessimistic!"

Little Miyiko thought it over for a while and then said:

"Yes, that seems to be quite regular if you think of the object of this cache. The chief technical and material values of the Western civilization of those days are hidden here. What did they regard as fundamental? If the public opinion of the planet as a whole or even of nations or of a group of countries did not then exist? The necessity or the importance of anything at any given moment was decided by the ruling group of people who were not always competent to judge. That is why the things here were not really the most valuable possessions of mankind but those things that the given group deemed valuable. They tried to preserve chiefly machines and, possibly, weapons, not realizing that civilization is built up historically, like a living organism," added Miyiko, thoughtfully.

"Yes, by the growth and acquisition of working experience, knowledge, techniques, stores of materials, pure chemical substances and buildings. The restoration of high civilizations would have been impossible without highly durable alloys, rare metals, machines with a high productivity and great precision. If all these things were destroyed where would they be able to get them from and where would they get the experience and ability to build complicated cybernetic machines capable of satisfying the needs of thousands of millions of people?"

"It would have been just as impossible to return to a pre-machine age civilization, like that of antiquity, although some people did dream of it."

"Of course. Instead of the civilization of antiquity they would have been faced with a terrible famine. Those were individualist dreamers who did not want to understand that history does not turn back."

"I'm not insisting that there are armaments in there," said Veda, "but there is every reason to suppose there are. If the men who devised this cache made the mistake that was typical of their day in confusing culture and civilization and ignoring the absolute necessity of training and developing a man, they would certainly not have seen the vital necessity for preserving works of art, literature or research far removed from current needs. In those days science was divided into useful and useless sciences and no thought was given to their unity. There were branches of art and science that were regarded as being merely pleasant but by no means an essential or even useful accompaniment to the life of mankind. Here, in this cave, the most important things are preserved, that's why I think of weapons, no matter how foolish and naive that may seem to us today."

Veda stopped talking and stared at the door.

"Perhaps that's just a cipher lock and we can open it by listening to it with a microphone," she said, suddenly, walking over to the door. "Shall we risk it?"

Miyiko jumped between her friend and the door.

"No, Veda, why take such a foolish risk?"

"It seems to me that the roof of this cave is very insecure. We'll go away from here and we'll never have a chance to come back. Listen! ..."

A diffused and distant sound from time to time penetrated into the cave in front of the door. It came sometimes from below, sometimes from above.

Miyiko, however, was adamant, she stood with her back to the door and her arms outstretched.

"You think there are weapons in there, Veda. If there are they must be well protected. No, no ... it's an evil door, like many others."

Two days later a portable X-ray reflector screen to study the mechanism and a focussed high-frequency radiator for the molecular destruction of parts of the door were brought into the cave. They did not, however, have time to set their apparatus to work.

Suddenly an intermittent roar resounded through the caves. Strong earth tremors underfoot sent the people who were in the third cave running instinctively to the exit.

The noise increased until it became a dull rumble. The whole mass of fissured rock was apparently settling along the line of the fault at the foot of mountains.

"Save yourselves, everybody get out," shouted Veda and her people ran to the robot cars, directing them towards the entrance to the second cave.

Hanging on to the cables of the robots they scrambled out of the well. The noise and the tremors of the stone walls followed close on their heels and, at last, overtook them. There came a fearful crash as the walls of the second cave tumbled into the abyss that had formed where the wall had been seconds before. The air blast literally carried the people together with a shower of dust and rubble into the first cave. There the archaeologists threw themselves on the floor and awaited death.

The clouds of dust began to subside. Through the dusty haze it could be seen that the stalagmites and the niches had not changed their form. The former grave-like silence returned to the caves.

Veda came to and stood up, trembling from the reaction. Two of her assistants took hold of her but she shook them off impatiently.

"Where's Miyiko?"

Her friend was leaning against a low stalagmite carefully wiping the dust from her neck, ears and hair.

"Almost everything has been lost," she said in answer to an unasked question. "The impassable door will remain closed under a four-hundred-metre thick layer of stone. The third cave has been completely destroyed but the second can be excavated. There and in this cave are the things of greatest value to us."

"You're right." Veda licked her dry lips. "We were wrong in dallying and being over-careful. We should have foreseen the fall."

"You had only unfounded instinct to go on. But there's nothing to worry about, we would hardly have tried to prop up those masses of rock for the sake of very doubtful treasures behind that closed door. Especially if it is full of worthless weapons."

"But suppose there are works of art there, inestimable human creations?

We could have worked faster!"

Miyiko shrugged her shoulders and led the depressed Veda in the wake of their companions, out into the magnificence of a sunny day, to the joy of clean water and an electric shower to drown all pain.

As was his habit, Mven Mass strode bade and forth in the room that had been allotted him on the top floor of the History House in the Indian Section of the northern inhabited zone. He had arrived there but two days before after having finished work in the History House in the American Section.

The room, or verandah with an outer wall of polarizing glass, looked out on the blue distance of the hilly plateau. Mven Mass from time to time switched on the cross polarization shutters. The room was plunged into grey gloom and pieces of old cinema films, sculptures and buildings that he had selected appeared on the hemispherical screen. The African watched them and dictated notes for his future book to a robot secretary. The machine printed and numbered the sheets, folded and sorted them according to subject matter, descriptions or generalizations.

When he grew tired Mven Mass switched off the shutters and walked over to the window to stare into the distance with unseeing eyes as he stood for a long time thinking over what he had seen.

He could not help but feel amazed that much of mankind's recent culture had already passed into the limbo. Verbal finesse that had been so typical of the Era of World Unity, oral and written whimsicalities that had at one time been regarded as the hallmark of a good education, had completely disappeared. Writing for the sake of beauty, so widespread in the Era of Common Labour, had gone and with it the juggling with words that went by the name of witticism. Still earlier the necessity to hide one's thoughts, an important matter in the Era of Disunity, had ceased to exist. All talk had become simpler and terser and it seemed that the Great Circle Era would become the era of the third system of signals-comprehension without words.

From time to time Mven Mass- turned to the ever wakeful mechanical secretary with new recordings of his thoughts.

"The fluctuating psychology of art had its beginning in the second century of the Great Circle Era and was founded by Liuda Pheer. She first gave a scientific proof of the difference in the emotional perception of men and women and laid bare that sphere that had for centuries been regarded as the semi-mystic subconscious. The proofs she offered for the understanding of her contemporaries, however, constituted the lesser part of her work. Liuda Pheer did more-she indicated the main series of sensual perceptions that made it possible to achieve similarity in the perception of the two sexes."

A ringing signal and a green light suddenly called Mven Mass to the televisophone. A call that came during working hours meant something very urgent. The automatic secretary was switched off and Mven Mass hurried downstairs to the room where long-distance calls were received.

Veda Kong, with bruised and scratched cheeks and with deep shadows under her eyes, greeted him from the screen. Mven Mass was pleased to see her and held out his huge hands to her, causing Veda's worried face to break into a faint smile.

"Help me, Mven. I know you're working but Darr Veter isn't on Earth and Erg Noor is far away; besides them you're the only one I have to whom I can turn with any request. I've had a misfortune."

"What? Darr Veter "

"No, a cave collapsed during excavations."

Veda gave him a brief description of what had happened in the Hall of Culture.

"You're the only one of my friends who has free access to the Prophetic Brain."

"To which of the four?"

"The Brain of Lower Definition."

"I understand; you want me to calculate the possibility of reaching the door with a minimum expenditure of labour and material."

"You're right."

"Have you got the data?" "I have them before me." "All right. I'm listening."

Mven Mass wrote down some columns of figures very rapidly.

"Now you'll have to wait until the machine can accept my figures. If you wait I'll get in touch with the Prophetic Brain engineer on duty. The Brain of Lower Definition is in the Australian Section of the southern zone."

"Where is the Brain of Higher Definition?"

"That's in the Indian Section, where I am, now. I'm changing over. Wait for me."

As Veda stood before the empty screen she tried to imagine the Prophetic Brain. Her imagination pictured a gigantic human brain with its furrows and convolutions, alive and pulsating, although the young woman knew that they were electronic research machines of the highest class capable of solving any problem that could be solved by the known branches of mathematics. There were only four such machines on the planet and they all had special uses.

Veda did not have long to wait. The screen lit up and Mven Mass asked her to call him again in six days' time. later in the evening.

"Mven, your help is invaluable!"

"Just because I know something of the rules of mathematics, is that it? And your work is invaluable because you know the ancient languages and cultures. Veda, you're overdoing it with the Era of Disunity!"

The historian frowned but Mven Mass laughed with such good nature and so infectiously that Veda also laughed, waved him good-bye and disappeared.

At the appointed time Mven Mass again saw the young woman in the televisophone.

"You needn't speak, I see by your face that the answer is unfavourable."

"Yes, stability is below the safety limit. If you go straight to it you will have to remove almost a million cubic metres of rock."

"It will only be possible for us to tunnel to the second cave and remove the safes," said Veda, sadly.

"Is it a matter of such distress?"

"Excuse me, Mven, but you have also stood before a door that hid an unfathomed secret. Yours are great, universal secrets and mine are tiny little ones. Emotionally, however, my failure is the equal of yours!"

"We're companions in misfortune. I can tell you that we'll be knocking our heads against closed doors many times, yet. The stronger and more courageous our efforts the more often we shall come up against doors."

"One of them will open!" "Naturally."

"You haven't given up altogether, have you?"

"Of course not, we're collecting fresh facts and the indicants of more correct methods."

"And suppose you have to wait all your life?"

"What is my individual life compared with such a step forward in knowledge!"

"Mven, what has happened to your impassioned impatience?"

"It hasn't disappeared, it's been curbed-by suffering." "How's Renn Bose?"

"He's better. He's looking for ways to make his abstractions more precise."

"I see. Wait a minute, Mven, there's something important for me!"

Veda disappeared from the screen and when the light flashed on again, she was another, younger and more carefree woman.

"Darr Veter is returning to Earth. Satellite 57 is being completed ahead of time."

"As quickly as that? Is it finished?"

"No, it's not finished, they've only put on the outer walls of the hull and mounted the engines. The work inside is easier. He is being called back to rest and to analyse Junius Antus' report on a new form of communication around the Great Circle."

"Thanks, Veda. I'll be glad to see Darr Veter."

"You'll see him all right. I didn't finish. Supplies of anameson for the new spaceship *Lebed* have been prepared by the efforts of the whole planet. The crew invite you to see them off on the journey from which there will be no return. Will you come?"

"I'll be there. The planet will show *Lebed's* crew everything that is beautiful and lovable in the world. They also wanted to see Chara's dance at the Fete of the Flaming Bowls. She is going to repeat her performance at the central cosmoport in El Homra. We'll meet there!"

"Good, Mven Mass, my friend."

CHAPTER FIFTEEN

THE ANDROMEDA NEBULA

The huge plain of El Homra stretches away to the south of the Gulf of Sirt in North Africa. Up to the time the trade winds and doldrums were eliminated it had been known as Hammada, the Red Desert, a waste of sand and stone, especially the triangular red stones that had given it its name. In summer it had been an ocean of scorching sunlight and during the autumn and winter nights it became an ocean of cold winds. Only the wind now remained of the old Hammada and that sent wave after wave across the tall silvery-blue grass that covered the firm soil of the plain; the grass had been transplanted from the South African veldt. The whistling of the wind and the bowed grass awakened in man's memory an uncertain feeling of sorrow and, at the same time, a feeling that the great grassy plains are somehow close to his heart, something that he had met with before in his life-not just once before, but many times and under different circumstances, in sorrow and in joy, in good times and bad.

Every take-off or landing of a spaceship left behind a circle, about a kilometre in diameter, of scorched and poisoned earth. These circles were surrounded by red metal screens and were out of bounds for a period of ten years, twice as long as the harmful fall-out from the spaceship's exhaust would be active. After each landing or take-off the cosmoport was transferred to another place which gave its buildings the imprint of temporariness and made its staff kin to the ancient nomads of the Sahara who for thousands of years traversed the desert on a special kind of animal with a humped back, a long curved neck and big corns on its paws, an animal called the camel.

The planetship *Barion* on its thirteenth journey between the satellite under construction and Earth brought Darr Veter to the Arizona Plain that, on account of the accumulated radioactivity there, still remained a desert even after the climate had changed. At the very dawn of the application of nuclear energy in the Era of Disunity, many experiments and tests of this new technique had been carried out there. The radioactive fall-out has remained to this day-it is now too weak to harm man but is sufficient to check the growth of trees and bushes.

Darr Veter took pleasure not only in the great charm of Earth-its blue sky in a bridal gown of white clouds-but also in the dusty soil, the scanty, tough grass....

How wonderful it was to walk with a firm tread on solid earth, under the golden rays of the Sun and with his face turned to meet the fresh dry breeze. After he had been on the threshold of Cosmic space he could better appreciate the full beauty of our planet that our ancestors had once called "the vale of tears and sorrow."

Grom Orme did not detain the builder for he himself wanted to be present when *Lebed* took off. They arrived at El Homra together on the day the expedition was to leave.

While still air-borne Darr Veter n*oticed huge* patches on the dull steel-grey plain-the one on the right was almost circular and the other was more elongated, an oval with the narrow end turned away from the other. These patches had been made by the spaceships of the 38th Cosmic Expedition that had recently left.

The circle came from the spaceship Tintagelle that had gone to the terrible star T and was loaded with all sorts of apparatus for the siege of the disc ship from distant worlds. The oval was made by

Aella whose ascent was less steep; this ship was taking a large group of scientists to investigate the changes in matter that took place on the white dwarf of the triple star Omicron 2 Eridani. The ash that remained where the ships' exhausts had burnt up the stony ground was about five feet thick and was covered with a binding material to prevent its being wind-carried. All that remained was to move the red fences from the old take-off ground, and this would be done as soon as *Lebed* left.

And there stood *Lebed,* iron-grey in her heat armour that would burn off during her passage through the atmosphere. After that the ship would continue its flight with gleaming walls capable of reflecting any known radiations. Nobody, however, would see it in this magnificence except the robot astronomers that tracked the flight: these machines would provide the people with nothing more than photographs of a flashing dot in the sky. When a ship came back to Earth it was always covered with dross and scored with furrows and hollows made by the explosions of tiny meteoric bodies. Darr Veter remembered how *Tantra* had returned-greyish-green and rust-red with parts of her outer walling in a state of collapse. None of the people standing around *Lebed* would ever see her again since none of them could live the hundred and seventy-two years that must elapse before she returned -a hundred and sixty-eight independent years of travel and four years to explore the planets....

Darr Veter's work was such that he would probably not live long enough even for the ship to arrive at the planet of the green star. Just as in those days of doubt, Darr Veter once again felt great admiration for the bold ideas of Renn Bose and Mven Mass. What did it matter that their experiment had failed-what did it matter that the problem, one which affected the very foundations of the Cosmos, was still far from solution-what did it matter, if it was all nothing more than a figment of the imagination.... These lunatics were giants of creative thought for even in the refutation of their theories and the failure of their experiments people would make tremendous progress in many fields of knowledge.

Lost in thought, Darr Veter almost stumbled over the signal indicating the safety zone, turned round and saw a well-known figure. Running his fingers through his unruly red hair and screwing up his sharp eyes, Renn Bose came running towards him. A network of thin. scarcely perceptible scars had changed the face of the physicist by wrinkling it into an expression of pained intensity.

"I'm glad to see you well again, Renn!"

"I want you urgently!" said Renn Bose, holding his tiny freckled hands out to Veter.

"What are you doing here, so long before the take-off?"

"I saw *Aella* off, I'm very interested in the gravitation of such a heavy star. I heard you would come and so I waited for you."

Darr Veter waited for an explanation.

"I hear you are returning to the observatory of the Outer Stations as Junius Antus has requested."

Darr Veter nodded.

"Antus has recently recorded several undeciphered messages received from a Great Circle transmission."

"Every month messages are received outside the usual transmission hours and each month the transmission time is advanced by two terrestrial hours. In the course of a year's testing this amounts to an earthly day and in eight years it makes a whole hundred-thousandth of a galactic second. That is how the gaps in the reception of the Cosmos are filled in. During the last six months of the eight-year cycle we have been receiving incomprehensible messages that undoubtedly come from a great distance."

"I'm very interested in them and would like you to take me as your assistant."

"It would be better for me to help you. We'll examine the records of the memory machines together."

"What about Mven Mass?"

"We'll take him, of course."

"Veter, that's just wonderful. I feel very awkward since that ill-fated experiment of mine, I've a feeling of guilt as far as the Council is concerned. But I can get along easily with you even if you are a member of the Council and a former Director and the one who advised me against the experiment."

"Mven Mass is also a member of the Council."

The physicist thought for a while, smiled at some memory of his own. "Mven Mass, he has a feeling for my ideas and tries to concretise them for me."

"Wasn't it in the concretisation that you made a mistake?"

Renn Bose frowned and changed the subject.

"Is Veda Kong coming here?"

"Yes, I'm waiting for her. Did you know that she almost lost her life during the investigation of a cave, some ancient technical storehouse where there was a closed steel door?"

"It's the first I've heard of it."

"I forgot that unlike Mven Mass you have no great interest in history. The whole planet is discussing the affair and wondering what might be behind the door. Millions of people have volunteered to dig it out. Veda has given the problem to the Academy of Stochastics and Prognostication. Is Evda Nahl coming here?"

"No, she can't come."

"A lot of people will be disappointed! Veda's very fond of Evda and Chara is simply devoted to her. D'you remember Chara?"

"That's the panther-like girl… either Gypsy or Indian in origin!"

Darr Veter spread his hands in mock horror.

"How well you appreciate feminine beauty! However, I'm always making the mistake that people made in the past when they did not know anything about the laws of psychophysiology and heredity. I always want to see my feelings and my perceptions in other people."

"Evda, like everybody else on the planet," said Renn Bose, ignoring Veter's confessions, "will be watching the take-off."

The physicist pointed to a row of high tripods carrying chambers for white, infrared and ultra-violet reception placed in a semi-circle around the spaceship. The different groups of spectral rays introduced into the coloured reproduction made the screen breathe with real warmth and life in the same way as the overtone diaphragms " destroyed the metallic resonance in the transmission of the human voice.

Darr Veter looked towards the north whence came the heavily laden automatic electrobuses, swaying across the earth. Veda Kong jumped out of the first bus to arrive and ran towards them, catching her feet in the grass. At a run she threw herself on Darr Veter's broad chest with such force that the long plaits that hung down from either side of her head were thrown over his shoulders and hung down his back.

Darr Veter held Veda off at some distance and looked into that infinitely dear face to which her unusual hair-do imparted new qualities.

"I was playing the Northern Queen of the Dark Ages for a children's film," she said, panting slightly. "I hardly had time to change and could not stop to do my hair."

Darr Veter could imagine her in a long, tight brocade dress and a golden crown with blue stones, her ash-blonde plaits reaching down below her knees, with fearless grey eyes-and he smiled with pleasure.

"Did you wear a crown?"

"Oh, yes, and such a crown!" Veda's finger drew in the air the outline of a wide circle with teeth round it in the shape of clover leaves.

"Shall I see it?"

"This very day. I'll ask them to show you the film."

Darr Veter was going to ask who the "they" were but Veda was already greeting the serious-looking physicist who was smiling naively but whole-heartedly.

"Where are the heroes of Achernar?" asked Renn Bose looking at the spaceship that stood in splendid isolation.

"Over there!" Veda pointed to a tent-shaped building of milk-coloured glass and outside girders of lattice-work -the main hall of the cosmoport.

"Let's go there, then."

"We're not wanted there," said Veda, firmly. "They are watching Earth's farewell to them. Let's go to *Lebed*."

The men followed her advice.

As she walked beside Darr Veter she asked softly:

"Do I look too absurd in this old-fashioned hair-do? I could…."

"You don't need to do anything. It makes a charming contrast to your modern dress, plaits longer than your skirt. Let it stay!"

"I obey you, my Veter!" Veda whispered the magic words that made his heart beat faster and brought colour to his pale cheeks.

Hundreds of people were making their way unhurriedly to the ship. Many of them smiled to Veda or greeted her with a raised hand, much more frequently than they did Darr Veter or Renn Bose.

"You're very popular, Veda," said Renn Bose, "is that due to your work as a historian or to your notorious beauty?"

"Neither one nor the other. I mix with a lot of people both in my work and in my social engagements. You and Veter, you either hide in the depths of a laboratory or go away alone for some terribly straining night work. You do more for mankind and much more important things than I do but it is all one-sided and not for the side that is nearer the heart. Chara Nandi and Evda Nahl are much more widely known than I am."

"Again a reproach to our technical civilization?" asked Darr Veter, jokingly.

"Not to ours but to the leftovers of former fatal mistakes. Twenty thousand years ago our troglodyte ancestors knew that art and the development of sensations connected with it were no less important to society than science."

"In respect of relations between people?" asked the physicist, with interest.

"Exactly."

"There was an ancient sage who said that the most difficult thing on earth is to preserve joy!" Darr Veter put in. "Look, here comes another of Veda's loyal allies!"

Mven Mass, with a light, swinging tread, was coming straight towards them, his huge black figure attracting considerable attention.

"Chara's dance is over!" Veda guessed, "soon we'll see the crew of *Lebed*."

"If I were them I'd come over here on foot and as slowly as possible," said Darr Veter, suddenly.

"You're getting excited," said Veda taking him by the arm.

"Naturally. For me it's painful to think that they're going away for ever and that I'll never see that ship again. There's something inside me that protests against that inescapable doom, perhaps because there are people in the ship that are dear to me!"

"That's probably not the reason," said Mven Mass as he joined them. His sharp ears had caught Darr Veter's words. "It's the inevitable protest of man against implacable time."

"Autumn sorrow?" asked Renn Bose, with just a shade of irony as he smiled at his friend with his eyes.

"Have you noticed that it is the most energetic, vivacious people with the strongest feelings who mostly like the sad autumn of the temperate zones?" objected Mven Mass patting the physicist on the shoulder in a friendly way.

"That's true enough," exclaimed Veda.

"A very ancient observation."

"Darr Veter, are you there on the field? Darr Veter, are you there on the field? You are wanted on the televisophone of the central building by Junius Antus. Junius Antus is calling you on the TVP of the central building."

Renn Bose started and straightened up. "May I go with you, Veter?"

"Go along in my place. It doesn't matter much to you if you miss the take-off. Junius Antus likes showing things in the old way, the direct reception and not the recording; in that respect he is in complete agreement with Mven Mass."

The cosmoport possessed a powerful TVP receiver and a hemispherical screen. Renn Bose entered the quiet round room. The operator on duty pressed a button and pointed to a side screen where the excited Junius Antus appeared immediately. He looked closely at the physicist and, realizing why Darr Veter had not come, nodded to Bose.

"I also intended watching the take-off but at the moment there is an explorer-reception going on in the former direction in the 62/77 range. Take the directed ray funnel and focus it on the observatory. I'll send a vector ray across the Mediterranean to El Homra. Pick it up on the tubular fan and switch on the hemispherical screen." Junius Antus looked away for a moment and then added, "Hurry up!"

The scientist, experienced in Cosmic reception, did all that had been ordered within two minutes. In the depths of the hemispherical screen a gigantic galaxy appeared which both scientists recognized as the Andromeda Nebula, or M 31, long known to mankind.

In the outer turn of its spiral, the one nearest the onlookers, and almost in the very centre of the lentil-shaped disc of the enormous galaxy, a tiny light appeared. There a whole system of stars branched off, looking like a thin hair although it was probably a huge sleeve of the galaxy a hundred parsecs in length. The light began to grow and the hair became bigger, while the galaxy disappeared beyond the field of vision. A stream of red and yellow stars stretched across the screen. The light changed into a little circle that gleamed at the end of the star stream. On the edge of the stream there was a prominent orange star, spectral class K, and around it the barely perceptible dots of planets were revolving. A disc of light was placed over one of them, completely covering it. Suddenly it all began to whirl round in red curves with sparks flying out of them. Renn Bose closed his eyes.

"That's a rupture," said Junius Antus from the side screen. "I've shown you a memory machine recording of what we observed last month. Now I'm going to switch on to a direct reception."

Sparks and dark-red lines were still whirling round on the screen.

"What a peculiar phenomenon!" exclaimed the physicist. "How do you explain that 'rupture,' as you call it?"

"I'll tell you later. The transmission is beginning again. But what is it you think strange?"

"The red spectrum of the rupture. In the Andromeda spectrum there is a violet bias, in other words, it should be drawing closer to us."

"The rupture has nothing to do with Andromeda, it is a local phenomenon!"

"Do you think it accidental that their transmitting station is placed on the very edge of the galaxy, in a zone that is even farther removed from the centre than the zone of the Sun in our Galaxy?"

Junius Antus cast a sceptical glance at Renn Bose. "You're prepared to start a discussion at any moment, forgetting that you're talking with the Andromeda Nebula at a distance of 45 parsecs!"

"Yes, yes," muttered the embarrassed Renn Bose, "that is, at a distance of a million and a half light years. This communication was transmitted fifteen thousand centuries ago."

"What we're looking at now was sent out long before the Ice Age and the appearance of man on Earth!" Junius Antus had become more amicable.

The red lines slowed down their movements, the screen went dark and then lit up again. A dully lit plain could scarcely be discerned in the twilight with mushroom-shaped structures dotted here and there. Near the front a gigantic (judging by the extent of the plain) blue circle with an obviously metallic surface gleamed coldly. One above the other two huge discs, convex on both sides, hung directly over the centre of the blue circle. No ... they were not hanging but were slowly rising higher and higher. The plain vanished and only one of the discs remained on the screen; it was more convex below than above and there were crudely spiral ribs on both sides.

"Is it they ... is it they?" exclaimed both scientists, almost together, thinking of the perfect similarity of this image with the photographs and drawings of the spiral disc the 37th Cosmic Expedition had found on the planet of the iron star.

Another whirl of red lines and the screen went dead. Renn Bose waited, afraid to take his eyes off the screen for even a second. The first human eye to see something of the life and thoughts of another galaxy! The screen, however, did not show any further signs of life. Junius Antus spoke from the side-screen of the TVP.

"The transmission has broken off. We cannot wait any longer because we are using too much of Earth's power resources. The whole planet will be astounded. We must ask the Economic Council for reception hours outside the regular programme at intervals more frequent than at present, but that will only be possible in a year's time, after so much has been spent on the dispatch of *Lebed*. Now we know that the spaceship on the black planet is from there. If Erg Noor had not found it we should never have understood what we have seen."

"And that disc came from there? How long did it fly?" asked Renn Bose, as though talking to himself.

"It has been flying dead for about two million years through the space that divides our two galaxies," answered Junius Antus, sternly, from the screen. "It flew until it found refuge on the planet of star T. Those spaceships are apparently built to land automatically despite the fact that for thousands and thousands of years no living hand has touched their mechanism."

"Perhaps they live a long time?"

"But not millions of years, that would contradict the laws of thermodynamics," answered Junius Antus, coldly. "Even though it is of enormous size the spiral disc could not contain a whole planet of people… or intelligences. As yet our two galaxies cannot reach each other, cannot exchange messages "

"They will," declared Renn Bose, confidently, said good-bye to Junius Antus and returned to the cosmoport whence the spaceship *Lebed* had just flown off.

Darr Veter, Veda Kong, Chara and Mven Mass stood somewhat apart from the two long rows of people who had come to see the ship off. All heads were turned in the direction of the central building. Noiselessly a wide platform swept past them accompanied by waving hands and shouts of greeting, something that people only permitted themselves in public on very special occasions. The twenty-two members of *Lebed's* crew were on the platform.

The vehicle drew up against *Lebed*. At the tall retractable lift stood a number of people in white overalls, the twenty members of the ground crew, mostly engineers working at the cosmoport: all of them had tired, drawn faces. During the past twenty-four hours they had checked all the expedition's equipment once more and had tested the reliability of the ship with the tensor apparatus.

In accordance with a custom that had been introduced with the first Cosmic expeditions the Chairman of the Commission reported to Erg Noor who had again been appointed commander of the spaceship and of the expedition to Achernar. Other members of the commission placed their insignia on a bronze plate bearing their portraits which was handed to Erg Noor; after this they moved away to one side and those who had come to bid farewell to the crew surged round the ship. The people drew up in front of the travellers, permitting their relatives to reach the small platform of the lift that was still vacant. Cinema cameramen recorded every gesture of the parting crew, a last memory of them to be left on Earth.

Erg Noor noticed Veda Kong when she was still some distance away: he thrust the bronze certificate into his wide astronaut's belt and hurried to the young woman.

"It's good of you to have come, Veda!"

"How could I not come!"

"For me you are a symbol of Earth and my past youth!"

"Nisa's youth is with you for ever!"

"I won't say I'm not sorry about anything because it wouldn't be true. I'm sorry, first of all, for Nisa, my companions and myself.... The loss is too great. On this last time on the planet I've learned to love Earth in a new way, more strongly, simply and unconditionally."

"But you're going, nevertheless. Erg?"

"I must. If I were to refuse I should lose Earth as well as the Cosmos."

"The greater the love the greater the deed."

"You've always understood me perfectly, Veda. Here's Nisa. I've just been admitting nostalgia to Veda."

The girl with the shock of red curls lowered her eyelashes: she had grown thinner and looked like a boy.

"I never thought it would be so hard. You're all of you so good ... so pure ... so beautiful... to leave you, to tear one's body away from Mother Earth...." The astronavigator's voice trembled. Veda instinctively drew the girl towards her, whispering the mysterious words of feminine comfort.

"In nine minutes the hatches will be closed," said Erg in a soundless voice, his eyes fixed on Veda.

"It's a long time yet!" exclaimed Nisa simply and with tears in her voice.

Veda, Erg, Veter and Mven Mass like others present were surprised and grieved that they could find no words to say. There was nothing with which to express their feelings in face of a magnificent deed that was to be performed for the sake of those who did not yet exist and who would come many years later. Those who were leaving and those who were staying behind knew everything. What more could be said?

What wishes, jokes or promises could affect the hearts of people who were leaving Earth for ever to plunge into the void of the Cosmos?

Man's second system of signals proved to be imperfect and gave way to the third. Profound glances expressing passionate feelings that could not be transmitted verbally were met in tense silence or were engaged in making the most of El Homra's wretched landscape.

"Time!" came Erg Noor's metallic voice like the snap of a herdsman's whip-the people hurried to board their ship. Veda, sobbing quite openly, pressed Nisa tightly. For a few seconds the two women stood cheek to cheek, their eyes tightly closed while the men exchanged parting glances and handshakes. The lift had already taken eight of the astronauts into the black oval of the hatch. Erg Noor took Nisa by the hand and whispered something to her. The girl blushed, broke away and ran to the spaceship. She turned round before stepping into the lift and met the big eyes of an unusually pale Chara.

"May I give you a kiss, Chara?" she asked in a loud voice.

Chara did not answer but jumped on to the lift platform, trembling all over, put her arms round the girl astronaut, then, without a single word, jumped down again and ran away.

Erg Noor and Nisa went up together.

The crowd stood motionless as the lift stopped for a moment opposite the black hatch in the brightly illuminated hull of *Lebed* and two figures, a tall man and a graceful girl, stood side by side receiving Earth's last greetings.

Veda Kong clenched her fists and Darr Veter could hear her joints cracking.

Erg Noor and Nisa disappeared. An oval door of the same grey colour as the hull moved out of the black opening. A second later the most discerning eye could not have detected the place where there had been an opening in the steep flanks of the huge hull.

There was something human about the spaceship standing vertically on its landing struts. The impression was, perhaps, created by the round globe of the nose, surmounted by a pointed cap and gleaming with signal lights that looked like eyes. Or perhaps it was the ribbed bulkheads of the central, storage part of the ship that had the appearance of the pauldrons of a knight's armour. The spaceship stood on its struts as though it were a giant standing on straddled legs, contemptuously and arrogantly peering over the heads of the crowd.

The first take-off signals sounded ominously. As though by magic, wide self-propelled platforms appeared beside the ship to take away the people. The tripods of the TVP and the floodlights crawled away from the ship, too, but they kept their lenses and their rays fixed on it. The grey hull of *Lebed* seemed to fade away and diminish in size. Evil-looking red lights glowed in the ship's "head," the signal that the crew were ready to start. The vibration of its powerful motors made the earth tremble as the spaceship began to turn on its landing struts to get direction for the take-off. The platforms with the people seeing the ship off moved farther and farther away until they were to the leeward of the safety line that gleamed phosphorescent in the darkness. Here the people jumped down from the platforms and the latter went back for the others.

"They'll never see us again, or our sky, either, will they?" asked Chara, turning to Mven Mass, who bent low over her.

"No, unless it's in a stereotelescope."

Green lights flashed up under the ship's keel. The radio beacon turned furiously on the tower of the central building sending out warnings of the giant ship's take-off in all directions.

"The spaceship is being ordered away!" a metal voice of tremendous power shouted so suddenly that Chara shuddered and clung tight to Mven Mass. "Everybody inside the danger circle raise your hands above your heads. Raise your hands above your heads or you will be killed! Raise your hands above your heads, or ..." the automaton continued shouting while searchlights raked the field to make sure that nobody was left inside the danger line.

There was nobody there and the searchlights went out. The robot screamed again and, it seemed to Chara, more furiously than before.

"After the bell rings turn your backs to the ship and shut your eyes. Keep them shut until the second bell rings. Turn your backs to the ship and shut your eyes!" howled the automaton with alarm and menace.

"It's frightening!" whispered Veda Kong to her companion. Darr Veter calmly took from his belt half masks with dark glasses rolled up into a tube, put one mask on Veda and the other on his own head. He just had time to fasten the buckles when a huge, high-pitched bell rang out, swaying back and forth under the roof of the signal tower.

The ringing stopped and the grasshoppers, indifferent to everything, could be plainly heard.

Suddenly the spaceship gave a howl that penetrated right to the marrow of a man's bones and its lights went out. Once, twice, three times, four times the howl swept across that dark plain and the more impressionable people standing there felt that the ship itself was crying with sorrow at the departure.

The howl broke off as suddenly as it had started. A wall of indescribably bright light shot up round the ship. Everything else in the world ceased to exist for a moment except that Cosmic fire. The tower of fire changed to a column, stretched out longer and thinner until it became a dazzlingly bright line of fire. The bell rang for the second time and as the people turned round they saw an empty plain on which was a huge patch of red-hot soil. There was a big star high up in the sky-the spaceship *Lebed* was moving away from Earth.

The people wandered slowly back to the electrobuses, looking at the sky and then at the place where the ship had taken off, a place that had suddenly become as lifeless as if the Hammada El Homra had returned, the desert that had been the terror of travellers in days gone by.

Well-known stars gleamed on the southern horizon. All eyes were turned to the point where the bright blue star Achernar burned in the sky. *Lebed* would reach that star after a journey of eighty-four years at a speed of 800 million kilometres an hour. For us, on Earth, it would be eighty-four years but for *Lebed* it would be forty-seven. Perhaps they would find a new world, just as beautiful and joyous, in the green rays of the zirconium sun.

Darr Veter and Veda Kong overtook Chara Nandi and Mven Mass. The African was answering the girl's questions.

"No, it is not sorrow but a great and sad pride-such are my feelings today. Pride because we rise ever higher above our planet and merge with the Cosmos, sorrow because our beloved Earth is becoming so small. Long, long ago the Mayas, the red-skinned people of Central America, left behind them a proud and sad inscription. I gave it to Erg Noor and he'll have it written up in the library-laboratory of *Lebed*."

The African looked round and noticed that friends who had caught up with them were listening, too. He continued in a louder voice:

"Thou who will later show thy face here! If thy mind can think thou wilt ask, "Who were they?" Ask the dawn, ask the forest, ask the waves, ask the storm, ask love. Ask the earth, the earth of suffering and the earth beloved. Who are we? We are the Earth!' I too am Earth through and through!" added Mven Mass.

Renn Bose came running up to meet them, panting for breath. The friends surrounded the physicist who told them in a few words the unprecedented news-the first contact between two gigantic stellar islands.

"I hoped to get here before the take-off," said Renn Bose, sadly, "to tell Erg Noor about it. While he was still on the black planet he realized that the spiral disc had come from a far distant world, a completely alien world, and that the strange ship had been flying for a long time in the Cosmos."

"Will Erg Noor never know that the spiral disc has come from such tremendous depths of the Universe, that it has come from another galaxy, from the Andromeda Nebula?" asked Veda. "What a pity that he did not hear today's reception!"

"He'll hear about it!" said Darr Veter, with confidence. "We'll ask the Council to sanction power for a special transmission. I'll call the spaceship through Satellite 36. *Lebed* will be within range of our transmitters for another nineteen hours!"

GLOSSARY

1. Billion-is used in its European meaning of a million millions (10^{12}).
2. Parsec-the unit of measure of astronomical distance, equal to 3.26 light years or 32×10^{12} km.
3. Sporamin-a drug to maintain the organism active over long periods without sleep (imaginary).
4. Anameson-atomic fuel in which the meson bonds of the nucleus have been disrupted; it has an exhaust velocity equal to the speed of light (imaginary).
5. Bomb Beacons-automatic radio robots transmitting signals powerful enough to penetrate the atmosphere of a planet. They were dropped from the spaceships for reconnaissance purposes (imaginary).
6. Independent Year-a terrestrial year that is Independent of the speed of the spaceship.
7. Spectral Classes-are indicated by the letters 0, B, A, F, G, K, M. They range from hot blue stars with a surface temperature of 100,000° C. to red stars with a temperature of 3,000° C. Each class has ten descending degrees of magnitude shown by indices, as A_i. There are special classes N, P, R and S with an augmented content of carbon, cyanogen, titanium and zirconium in their spectra. N. B. In other systems of classification the spectral classes 0, B, A and F are all called „white stars" and not „blue stars" as here.
8. Quantum Limit-velocity close to that of light (subphotonic velocity) at which a solid body cannot exist: the point at which the mass is equal to infinity and time is equal to zero.

9. K-particles-particles formed inside the atomic nucleus from fragments of the circular meson cloud (imaginary).
10. Isograves-lines of equal intensity in a gravitational field (imaginary).
11. Atomized Solid Oxygen-oxygen that is not in its usual molecular form (02) but in the form of separate atoms. This form produces more intensive chemical reactions and permits of greater compression than the molecular state.
12. Optimal Radiant-the optimal radius of the orbit of the spaceship about a planet and outside its atmosphere; the radius that gives ship a constant, unchanging orbit; depends on the volume and mass of the planet (imaginary).
13. Kelvin Scale-a temperature scale beginning from absolute zero which is - 273° C, or - 459° F. The temperature 320° K is equal to 4- 47° C. or 116.6° F.
14. Silicolloid-made of silicon, a transparent material produced from fibrous silicon-organic compounds (imaginary).
15. Silicoborum-an amalgam of borum carbide and silicon to produce an extremely hard, transparent material (imaginary).
16. Chlorella-a seaweed with a considerable albumin content.
17. Chromokatoptric Colours-artist's colours with a strong reflection of light from the inner layers (imaginary).
18. Repagular Calculus-a calculus in bipolar mathematics that deals with moments of transition (repagulum) from one state or condition to another and from one mathematical sign to another (imaginary).
19. Bipolar Mathematics-mathematics based on dialectic logic, with opposite analyses and solutions (imaginary).
20. Cochlear Calculus-a division of bipolar mathematics dealing with progressive spiral movement (imaginary).
21. Tiratron-an electronic instrument (electron lamp) to stimulate and maintain the nervous processes in the human organism, in particular the beating of the heart (imaginary).
22. Neurosecretory Stimulators-drugs made from the nervous excretions of the organism (neurosecretory substances) acting specifically on certain nerves (imaginary).

23. Geological Bomb-a bomb of great explosive power dropped on to a planet under exploration to get samples of matter contained on the surface of the planet and hurled into the upper layers of the atmosphere by the explosion (imaginary).
24. Stochastics-a branch of mathematics studying the laws of large numbers.
25. Cytoarchitectonics-a detailed study of the structure of the brain according to the distribution and specialization of the nerve cells.
26. Third System of Signals-thought transmission without speech (imaginary).
27 Overtone Diaphragms-diaphragms that transmit the overtones of the human voice and so remove all difference between the living voice and the sounds of its reproduction (imaginary).

ABOUT THE AUTHOR

*Ivan Efremov (*born 1907), novelist, author of much science fic*tion, professor* of palaeontology, is a great favourite with Soviet readers. The Foreign Laguages Publishing House has issued two of his books in English, Stell*ar Ships, a*bout beings who came to us from the stars, and Land of Foam, an historical fantasy, the scene of which is laid in Greece, Egypt and Central Africa in the days of Early Antiquity.

Ivan Efremov's new story, Andromeda, deals with the future. This is scientific fantasy on a grand scale, it tells of a gigantic growth of science and engineering on Earth, of a new type of society, it shows life in all parts of the Universe in the Era of The Great Circle, and interstellar organization that keeps Earth in permanent contact with the entire Cosmos.

The time of the story is …

In respect of time Ivan Yefremov has the following to say:

"The first serial publication of *Andromeda* had not been completed when Soviet sputniks began their nights in orbit round the Earth. Confronted with this indisputable fact it was a pleasure to realize that the ideas on which the story had been based are correct.

"The fulfilment, with amazing speed, of one of the dreams of the story posed a question that I had to answer; to what extent do the historical prospects unfolded in *Andromeda* ring true? At first I had thought that the gigantic transformations of our planet and life on it described in the story could not be effected in less than three thousand years. I based this calculation on world history but did not take into consideration the rate of acceleration of technical progress and, more important still, the possibilities that communist society will offer mankind.

"In preparing the new edition I reduced my original time by a whole millennium, but the launching of the sputniks showed that the events related in the story could occur much sooner. All definite dates in *Andromeda* have been made indefinite so that the reader may fill them in according to his own concepts and feeling for time.

"The mass of scientific information and intricate terminology used in the story are the result of a deliberate plan. It seemed to me that this is the only way to show our distant descendants and give the necessary local (or temporal) colour to their dialogue since they are living in a period when science will have penetrated into all human conceptions and into language itself."

Made in the USA
Middletown, DE
08 December 2023

44981592R00213